Daughter
by Spirit

V. Anthony Rivers

A
SBI
PUBLICATION
A STREBOR BOOKS INTERNATIONAL LLC PUBLICATION
DISTRIBUTED BY SIMON & SCHUSTER, INC.

Published by

Strebor Books International LLC
P.O. Box 10127
Silver Spring, MD 20914
http://www.streborbooks.com

ISBN 0-9674601-4-X
LCCN 2001089635

Distributed by Simon & Schuster, Inc.
1230 Avenue of the Americas
New York, NY 10020
1-800-223-2336

Cover photographer: Keith Plummer
Cover models: Lisa and Karlin Fox

First Printing January 2003
Manufactured and Printed in the United States
10 9 8 7 6 5 4 3 2 1

Acknowledgments

As I sit back and take a mental trip from childhood to now, all I can say is damn, what a journey it's been thus far and thank God for the experience. I honor the past and look forward to the future.

A special thanks to those three angels that have blessed my life and opened the door to a dream in the making: Martina, Tanya, and especially to Zane for her guidance and inspiration.

Many warm hugs and thanks to Valerie, the Brownwoman Extraordinaire.

Thanks to Hope for bringing special meaning to the word. Your reflection is incredible and your jeans are nice, too. Thank you, Kim Roseberry. Make sure you stay strong and keep reaching. Diana Williams, you watched my growth and helped me endure those chickenhead experiences. I thank you for the love and friendship shared.

To the Yolanda Experience, a moment in time that impacted my life and ultimately guided me here, this place where creativity lingers deep within. This body and soul of a man deeply sensitive to love and the trials and tribulations of life. I'm grateful for my reflection, though it took a while to move on and I'm still learning.

A special mention to both Grandmas: Alzata and Senora. Strength and beauty, beauty and strength personified.

Special love and thanks to Mommy for the never-ending love, support, and more love and support. It's been a long road. The memories and how fast time has gone by amaze me.

I look to the sky and I can see much more than the Sun, the Clouds, or the Moon. Much Love to Dad and Grandpa. I hope to honor them always as I take each step. I've heard the words "I'm proud of you son" many times and with that said, I'm proud to be who I am and to continue the tradition of making a deep impression as I'm blessed with life.

I'm so grateful for this opportunity and with all that said, I hope you all enjoy *Daughter by Spirit*, one very special version of love. It's a reflection of the power of the human spirit and the beauty of true friendship. Never take your experience for granted because every moment has meaning.

Daughter by Spirit

November Friend

1.
Christian Erickson
Collision Course

"Dreams of being unconscious, lying next to me a past whose time I try to measure."

I wondered where it all came from and pondered the things going through my head as I sat there in bed next to someone I'd met recently. I couldn't believe how we'd ended up there so fast, but quite honestly it seemed like a natural progression at the end of our first date. The lady was so beautiful when I saw her that first time. I've come to the conclusion that the grocery store is definitely a great place to meet somebody. Talk about a meat market. A brotha can find top grade-A quality there.

When I saw Tanya trying to select a head of lettuce, my heart skipped a beat. The lady was looking just as fine as she wanted to be, dressed in a sleeveless black turtleneck, form-fitting jeans, and leather boots. Her golden glimmer hair was shining under the bright lights in the produce section and that honey brown complexion of hers had me mesmerized. I was just hoping that she wouldn't catch me staring at her, but I guess I didn't try hard enough. She saw me drop my yams all over the floor while I struggled to find the opening of the plastic bag. I hate those things. Sometimes it takes me two minutes just to discover that I'm playing with the wrong end of the bag. After I finished looking goofy, I kind of made my way over to her as inconspicuously as I could.

"Hey! I don't think you picked up all your yams," she said to me.

"Huh?" I responded naively.

"Look over there. You left two on the floor."

She pointed but I wasn't even paying attention to what I'd

dropped. I was checking her out and hoping she was doing the same of me.

"I don't believe those are mine," I responded.

"Well, you're the only one walking around here dropping yams!"

She couldn't help but smile at my plea of innocence but it was obvious that she wasn't buying what I was selling. Maybe it was my effort that was seemingly keeping her interested or perhaps it was the *I-wanna-get-to-know-you-in-the-worse-way* smile on my face. Whatever the case, anything from that point on would be all good to me.

From the start, she had me smiling and feeling warm inside. I love a woman that's not only beautiful, but also a challenge to speak to. As we stood in front of the vegetables debating about yams and how many I'd dropped, she managed to squeeze the more important questions into the conversation. You know, she cut to the chase before we lost ourselves in mindless words that revealed nothing.

"What's your name?" she asked.

"I'm Christian."

She had a smart look on her face and laughed softly, so I kind of knew what was coming next.

"I didn't ask for your religion. I just wanted to know your name."

"Ha, ha! I knew you were gonna say that!"

"Christian what?"

"Christian Erickson."

She smiled with an expression of enlightenment on her face. I think she was also checking me out, trying to keep her thoughts discreet.

"How about you?" I asked her, glancing at more than just her beautiful hazel eyes.

"How about me what?"

She continued to decide on her vegetables. She tried to pretend like her shopping was more important than the conversation we were having. I could tell she was digging me pretty good though. I stood before her dressed in a black Karl Kani turtleneck sweater, carpenter jeans, and some tan Timberland boots. I love feeling comfortable but I was a bit on edge in her presence. In fact, I was beginning to sweat.

"You're gonna make this tough, huh?" I asked her.

She grinned and chuckled to herself as I stood there with my arms folded. I watched her relish in the fact that she had me struggling to keep the conversation going.

"Okay, what's your name?" I asked quietly.

"Tanya Moore."

She was leaning over the vegetables at first, but when she said her name she appeared to be teasing me a little. Maybe it was just my imagination but she stood up slowly and raised her right eyebrow before speaking her name.

Maybe she could sense that her name sounded like music to my soul. I kept saying it over and over in my mind. Sometimes there are certain ladies names that just feel good to me and hers was one of them. Of course it helped that she was as fine as she could be. Tanya started to look at me funny after a while, like she had something else to do and I was impeding her progress. I took that as a hint that she wanted to continue shopping, *alone*. She was looking so good that I was just trying my best to think up something new to ask her. You know, those exceptional words that would make her laugh, smile, and say, "Come help me pick something out for dinner so I can cook for you tonight." That kind of thing. I don't know. Sometimes life just can't keep pace with wishful thinking, I suppose.

"Can I walk along with you, Tanya, or is your shopping a private affair?"

"You're funny. I like that!" She giggled. "You know how to pick squash?"

I directed my index finger to the nearest bin. "What? This right here?"

"Are you serious? You know you're pointing to a lemon, don't you?"

Well, at least I got her to laugh. She shook her head in a way that let me know she enjoyed the surprise meeting between the two of us.

"Listen, I need to do this faster so I'll just give you my number, okay?" she said.

"Are you in a hurry, Tanya?"

"Yeah, I need to pick up someone. My sister's baby. Plus, I have a lot of other errands to run."

I was almost seeing warning signs when she was talking about picking someone up. For a second, I thought she'd say that she had to pick up her baby. Not that I have anything against women with kids. I've just always hoped to find one without any. I'm speaking from past experience, but I'm always first to recognize that when love calls, you better answer regardless of who it is and what package they bring to the table with them.

"Thanks, Tanya," I said after she handed me a piece of scrap paper with her number scribbled on it. "How soon can I call you?"

"Actually, tonight would be good. I've really enjoyed talking with you. Your sense of humor is interesting."

"Hmm, only interesting huh?" I said in my sexiest tone.

Tanya touched me on the arm and sent a surge of electricity through my body before walking toward the registers, pushing her cart. "Yes, call me tonight."

Naturally, I watched her walk away and what an interesting sight it was.

That day was really cool. Such a beautiful moment in my life as a single man. As I focused in on the fact that I was sitting next to Tanya in bed a week later, I couldn't help but wonder where it was all gonna lead. I believed in love, but I wanted to make sure Tanya and I had a great friendship as well. We'd just had some incredible sex and I felt as though I should ask her if it was all right. I didn't want to jeopardize something potentially very special. Plus, I was wondering if I needed to get out of bed and make the woman some breakfast. I didn't want to risk scaring her away so I decided to wait and cook for her next time. She really looked good lying there with her gorgeous body half-buried underneath my cream-colored bed sheets and brown comforter. I couldn't help but quickly reminisce about the softness of her skin against mine. I could see her breasts peeking out from under the covers a little bit. She was moving around slightly, a bit restless, so it wouldn't be long before she woke up. I could barely wait to see that beautiful spirit shine once more.

Tanya Moore was definitely fine. She inspired me to reminisce practically all the time about the smallest things. I remember calling her the night after we'd met in the store. Tanya was running around her house like crazy. She informed me that she had a client coming over to check out some of her interior design ideas.

"How can you show somebody how to make their house beautiful if your house is a mess, girl?" I teased.

"Be quiet!" she responded.

I could hear her laughter in the background as she took the phone away from her mouth. I imagined her moving things out of the way so she could find a spot to sit down while she talked to me.

I must have been right because she said, "Let me sit down for a moment. Just for you, Christian."

"Thank you, Tanya."

"You're too much, but I like a man that keeps me on my toes."

"What are you doing after you take care of business?" I asked her.

"I'm just gonna curl up with a good, sexy romance novel or maybe this erotica anthology book that I picked up the other day since I'm not getting any."

She punctuated her voice to make sure I understood clearly what she was saying. Shoot, I had been going through a drought recently myself so she wasn't alone with what she was thinking.

"How about we go out this weekend, Christian, if you're not too busy?"

"Sounds cool to me. You plan on getting something?" I asked her to see how she'd respond.

"You got something to give?"

Her response didn't really surprise me. In fact, it was funny because we always seemed like we were challenging each other. Tanya always matched me line for line, word for word. I was curious to find out when I would hit a soft spot in her. I wondered constantly if her challenging spirit was a front for any kind of hurtful past. If it was, I couldn't see it at that point. Tanya seemed like a natural when it came to being happy and a smart-ass at the same time.

After sitting there watching Tanya sleeping for what felt like an hour, I noticed her finally waking up.

"Hey, sleepy head!" I said to her as she stretched her lovely body.

The sound she made was analogous to the sounds she made when we'd gotten busy the night before. Those sounds are what brought me out of my daydreams about our recent past and into appreciating once more her lying in my bed with her fine self.

"Hey! What you smiling at, boy?"

After examining every inch of her, I finally made eye contact with her. "Nothing. Just happy to see you again."

"You've probably been watching me sleep, huh? Is that why my breasts are exposed?"

She was trying to cover up but it was too late for that. I began to lick my lips in an effort to tease her and make her think I'd been doing more than just watching her sleep.

"Ooh, Chris, you are no good!"

Soon after we'd enjoyed another moment of joking around with each other, I laid back down with her. I was hoping we could get up and maybe go do something, but I didn't mind enjoying some more cuddling.

"We gonna do something today, Tanya?"

"No, I need to get started on this project I have going, but I'd love to see you next weekend."

"Okay, maybe we'll go somewhere then."

"Maybe, but for now I do have an hour to kill."

"Is that right?"

Tanya moved nearer to me and began kissing my chest very softly. She had this seductive gaze on her face that let me know she wanted to have power over me. I could feel the smoothness of her thigh sandwiched between my legs. I took a peek toward the foot of the bed and noticed her moving like a beautiful wave. Her body slowly unveiled as she removed the sheets from our bodies. Her skin was silky on all parts and her behind was faultless as I placed my hands on it to facilitate her continuous grinding against my thigh. It wasn't long before she began to moan passionately from the intense motions that our bodies were making. That was just the beginning for her because she immediately climbed on top of me. I could feel myself cross her threshold. Tanya whispered to me about her wetness as her warmth enveloped me. She rode me solid and rapid and didn't stop until she reached that incredible peak.

"Damn," I whispered.

Tanya was moving so smoothly and with incredible rhythm. When we kissed deeply once again, we found ourselves exploding very passionately. I don't know who screamed the loudest, though it was in all probability me. Afterwards we shared deep, concentrated kisses. Tanya continued to lay on top of me with her forehead pressed against mine and that's how we remained for the next hour.

After that hour elapsed, Tanya got up to get dressed and I watched her every move. She was pretty swift at getting her clothes on. She threw her hair up in a ponytail and squeezed inside her tight jeans. She also borrowed one of my shirts, which at first felt a little outlandish to me; especially with it being one of my favorite Fubu jerseys that I liked to wear on the weekends.

"Hey! What are you doing with my shirt?"

Tanya giggled. "I saw you wearing it and I couldn't wait to put it on. I love the material."

"Okay. Just let it be known that you're *borrowing* it."

I tried to let her know I wasn't kidding by emphasizing the word *borrowing* and I didn't stutter when I said it either.

"I know, sweetie pie. Thank you."

After getting dressed, Tanya sat down on the bed so we could talk a moment longer. She continued to fix her hair the best she could without a comb while I worried that I might not see my jersey again.

"You know what? I really enjoyed last night and I can't wait to see you again," she told me.

"Thanks, but I have to say you're really something, Tanya. One day I guess I'll learn more about you instead of sharing these love-ly moments where we hardly talk to each other about anything deep. Maybe you'll even let me ask some slightly probing questions instead of the usual news, weather, and sports stuff."

"Well, don't probe too much, sweetie," she said just before leaning over to give me one last kiss.

I wondered what she meant by that, but I wasn't gonna try to ask her at that point. She might've tried to run away from any hint of serious discussion that soon so I just sat with my hands on my head and watched her walk out the bedroom. I found myself smiling, even as I heard the front door close. I couldn't wait to see her again and that was a new kind of feeling for me.

2.
Maiya Christine Hightower
What could be next?

"Maiya Christine Hightower! Damn, gurl, you must be bad with a name like that!"

The fool was trying to get his mack on and I was hardly interested.

I had to endure the same kind of tired come-on lines earlier that day at the car wash. I decided to learn how to wash my own damn car or, better yet, find a real man to help me. I wasn't having any luck in that area. They kept showing up with fool written on their foreheads like the man that was trying to hit on me at the credit union.

"Thanks. My parents picked a good set of names for me, I guess," I replied ingenuously.

"Damn, they did everything right with you!"

The man had obviously lost his mind, talking like that to me, but I didn't want to go off on him. I was just too exhausted to be mean.

I tried to remain polite. "Can you take care of this for me so I can go? I'm late for work."

"Sure! Let me ask you something. You think you and I could ever do something together? Maybe go out?"

I couldn't believe he was trying to ask me out so I just simply smiled and pretended that I didn't hear him. He'd already heard me speak so it would've been tough to pretend that I didn't understand English. Just before I walked out the door, he was still trying to get at me. With the right outfit, decent breath, and some intelligence, he might've been okay. But the way he was coming at me, throwing the damn word around like candy, I didn't even think so.

"Hey, cutie pie! Ms. Hightower?" he shouted, drawing the attention of other customers.

I just strutted out the door without looking back. I'd heard enough of his silliness. I figured I'd better call the credit union later just to make sure he'd deposited my money properly. I knew that would be a hassle with all that automated shit and PIN numbers that they make you remember.

I'd been batting a thousand lately with men. All I yearned for was a man that was sweet, strong, gentle, and honest. Did he even exist? I liked to believe that he did so I resolved to put up with all the men pulling at my hair to see if it was real. I had a date that night with a guy named Reginald Winston. I used to joke around with him when we first met and he seemed extremely kind.

"You like to be called what?" I asked him during our first meeting.

"Reggie," he responded.

"Veggie? Like a burger?" I joked.

"No, Reggie. Short for Reginald?" he explained.

He didn't seem to catch my joke, but he was really sweet. He sounded so comical trying to explain himself. His voice was so proper and he made noticeable attempts at sounding as intellectual as he could. I almost accused him of attempting to sound white, but I hated it when my own friends said that about me. It took me a little while to get used to his voice but thinking about his nice body made it easier. He told me that he worked out at the spa every day after he got off work. I can appreciate a man that takes care of himself, but there was something misplaced about Reggie. After I found another turnoff, my favorite line was, "But he's really sweet." I probably said that a little too often. I was just too damn picky for my own good and spending too much time fantasizing about that brotha Damon on *Soul Food.* I could've just withered away waiting for someone like him to come along. Instead, I was spending my Blockbuster nights with a light-skinned, conservative, Ivy League graduate named Reginald Winston. When I asked him if he was a Republican, he just looked at me and asked, "Aren't you one, too?" Actually, I was just playing with him so his response took me off guard.

Another thing I had to get used to was Reggie's love for opera and classical music. I could be talking and all of a sudden he'd interrupt me and ask me to listen to something. I usually missed whatever it was he tried to point out. Music Appreciation back in school was one thing, but adults have a choice to decide what they want to spend their lives listening to and those styles don't appeal to me. Reginald was the first brother I'd met that knew so much about opera. It was a nice change, but I prefer a man who can be all things, have that hint of danger, and still be a sweetie pie all at the same time. Reggie tended to be too conservative and shunned away from doing fresh things.

I listened to my messages while I put on light makeup for the evening. Reggie didn't like for me to wear it in excess. He didn't want it to get on his shirts when he placed his arms around me for what he termed *display time*. Those were his exact words one night when he instructed me to brush my hair and prepare for *display time*. I couldn't believe his audacity, but that's what he said just before we entered the restaurant for dinner. Part of me almost stopped to let him walk in alone, but then I remembered how much I wanted to go to that particular restaurant.

"Good evening, Ms. Hightower!"

I instantly recognized Reggie's voice on my machine.

"I'm looking forward to taking you out tonight and I just wanted to make sure you were properly informed as to what type of affair we were attending. I want you to be ready for display time," he said.

"There he goes with that display time shit!"

"By the way, tonight we're doing something that's more in your league. I'm taking you to dinner and perhaps a movie so you can get away with wearing something very casual, if you'd prefer."

"Negro, please!"

I couldn't believe he was telling me how to dress. Even my "But he's really sweet" line didn't stop me from wanting to give Reggie a piece of my mind or just cancel the date altogether. I could hear my mother saying, "Maiya, remember your manners." Being able to close my eyes, envision her smile, and listen to the sound of her voice was a great source of comfort.

I could hear my pager going off someplace in my apartment. I needed one the size of a basketball so I wouldn't lose it all the time. Just like always, I found it buzzing around on the floor. Usually when I'd come home from work, the first thing I'd do was drop everything and plop down on my couch. My pager usually ended up in that routine place.

I glanced at the familiar number on my pager. It was my girl-friend, Stephanie. She usually called me before I had a date so I decided I'd better call her and then go downstairs to wait for Reggie. He never made the effort to come upstairs and knock on the door. Instead, he'd always blow the horn.

I punched in Stephanie's number right quick. "Hey, girlfriend! Why are you paging me?" I asked excitedly.

"You know why, girl! Is it Reggie tonight?" she asked like it was a surprise to her.

"Of course it is. Who else could it be? Sometimes I wonder if I'm wasting my time but at least I'm getting fed."

"I heard that, girl! So, when are you gonna sleep with this guy and see if he's proper in bed, too?" Stephanie asked in her thunderous voice.

"No you didn't just ask me that!"

"Yes, I did! You know he ain't really your type and it ain't gonna last so you might as well have some kind of memory other than the opera or whatever else he does for you!"

"You're crazy, girl. Don't make me have to pass him on to you so he can bore the hell out of you, too."

"Well, Maiya, why are you going out with him then?"

"He's a sweet guy and I like him because he's different, but this may be the last date tonight. I don't know. I'm not sure," I tried to explain to her unsuccessfully.

The more I tried to clarify why I was seeing Reggie, the more I was compelling myself not to go.

"Damn, girl. You're sounding desperate and I don't think you even believe what you're saying."

I did sound kind of pitiable, not at all like myself, but I thought everyone deserved a chance. Maybe Reggie would show me something different that time.

A car horn started blaring beneath my window.

"Hey, girl, I can hear the horn blowing outside and I know that's him."

Why I was willing to risk another boring evening was beyond me, but I was somewhat excited about the possibilities.

"He blows his horn for you?" Stephanie asked with skepticism.

"I'll call you later, Stephanie."

When I walked outside my building, there he was, sitting in his car already gazing at his watch. It had only been two minutes since he blew his horn. His pride and joy, his Cadillac Seville, was clean and buffed up as usual. Reggie loved talking about his car. You would've thought it was his child.

"Hey! What were you doing up there?" he asked as I opened the door.

He didn't even let me climb inside before trying to get the 411 on everything I was doing before he blew his precious horn.

"I was talking to my girlfriend."

"Girl talk, huh? I don't suppose that I was the topic of conversation?"

"You were mentioned, but nothing deep was said."

The conversation in the car on the way to the movie theater didn't get any more exciting. I found myself thinking about where else I could be on a Saturday night. Not only did I have to endure all of his questioning but I also had to put up with some loud ass, symbol-crashing music coming from his CD player. I noticed he had individual controls for the air conditioning. Why couldn't it have been the same for music listening? I craved to listen to something that would put me in an enhanced frame of mind. The stuff he was listening to made me want to open the car door and jump out while the car was in motion. When we pulled into the parking structure of the mall where the movie theater was located, Reggie was still trying to unearth what I was talking about on the phone with Stephanie.

"So, you still won't tell me what you two ladies said about me?" he asked with an unpredictably cute smile on his face.

"I don't remember now."

"Uh—huh, I get the hint, Maiya."

Once we got inside the mall, I kind of enjoyed walking with Reggie. He looked too adorable in his jeans and leather coat. I wished he was a little bit taller but being six feet exactly was good enough. I was hoping he would at least hold my hand as we walked, but that was one hint that seemed to escape his attention.

"Reggie, if you really must know, we just mentioned the customary girl stuff about how handsome you are. You know how it goes. It was really nothing exciting," I told him after noticing that my silence about his favorite subject was making him act indifferent.

I couldn't believe how I kissed up to him sometimes just to avoid hurting his little feelings. Plus, I didn't like us walking together in silence and he still hadn't held my hand.

Reggie led me toward the wall of the department store. "Hey, Maiya!"

It appeared that Reggie had something on his mind that needed to be said.

"Yes? What's this about?" I inquired.

"I would love for you to stay with me tonight and perhaps the rest of the weekend, if you're so inclined."

"If I'm so inclined? What brought this on all of a sudden, Reggie?"

"I'm not sure. Perhaps I'd like to take things to that next step."

"Excuse me? Next step?"

I was perfectly aware of what he meant and suddenly holding his hand lost its appeal.

"Maiya, I think you're a beautiful and strong woman. You're doing considerably well as a computer analyst and before we met, I never would've believed that a woman as beautiful as you could be equally intelligent."

Being an analyst, I started analyzing his statement and it didn't sit quite right with me. "I'm not so sure I like the sound of that, Reggie."

I could tell by his reaction that he sensed my irritation. "It's a compliment and you should really take it as such."

My infamous *wait-a-minute-Negro* side was about to rise. Trying to tell me what I should do just pushed yet another wrong button.

"Can you please explain what you just said to me?" I asked him evenly.

"We're both gifted people and I'm not entirely sure how often you get to speak with others on this level. I want you to realize that this is the level you should always aspire to be on in your personal life as well as your professional life," he tried to make clear to me.

"I'm doing just fine, Reggie. Where do you get off judging me like that? Nothing you've said has been a compliment to me. In some ways, it feels like a putdown, but the only difference is that you seem to be coming through the backdoor with your remarks."

I was infuriated with Reggie and wasn't about to display zilch for him anytime soon. He was proving that he wasn't the one for me. I didn't care to spend time with a man that made me feel the urge to always set him straight. If I wanted to be stressed out like that, I could've juggled three jobs and skipped over a social life altogether. I needed to be able to relax and escape when I was with that special someone in my life.

I wanted to scream, "This fool ain't the one!"

"Maiya, this isn't going well. Perhaps we need a time out or something. Maybe we can discuss this later."

"Time out? I think your ass should forfeit the game, Reggie."

"What? What kind of woman would say such a thing?"

He was acting like he was revolted by my behavior, but I couldn't have cared less. His reaction had no affect on me whatsoever.

"Goodbye, Reggie!" I said as I walked away.

As soon as I got around the corner from where we'd argued, I remembered the most important thing.

"Hello, Stephanie?"

I really didn't want to make the call, but I didn't feel like spending a wad of cash on a taxi to get back home either.

"Maiya? What's up, girl?"

I hoped she wouldn't start laughing at me when I said, "I need a ride."

Stephanie did just that, of course. After she picked me up from the mall, Stephanie ended up laughing the entire drive home.

I was elated when she pulled in front of my building. "Thanks for picking me up, girl."

I was tired and disappointed, but Stephanie was having a ball at my expense. I got out of her car.

"Call me later, Maiya. You're better off without him," Stephanie said, trying to keep a straight face.

"Okay, I will."

I watched Stephanie pull off, pausing to take in some fresh air. It felt good to be walking up to my building. Anything but being back at the movies with Reggie.

There was a gorgeous man standing out front. He was truly my breath of fresh air after what I'd been through that night. I decided to adjust my foul attitude long enough to see if he needed some help. After all, I'd wasted my efforts on Reggie so why not get my flirt on a little before the night was over.

He wasn't that tall but he looked like dessert to a lonely woman such as myself. He had short dreads and a milk chocolate complexion. He was mighty appealing to me.

I adjusted my burgundy wrap on my shoulders and cleared my throat before I said something to him.

"Excuse me. Are you trying to get in?"

"Yes, I am, but there's no answer so I was about to leave," he responded in the cutest accent.

"Where are you from? Where are you from?"

I had to ask that question twice because the first time it sounded like I was coming on to him sexually. Maybe I was but he didn't need to know that already.

"I'm originally from Barbados, but I grew up on different islands in the Caribbean. I love it out here in California, but I miss home, you know."

"Wow, Barbados. That's nice. I'm Maiya. I live in the building. Are you coming to see your girlfriend?" I asked, hoping that he would say no.

"Oh, no. I have no girlfriend. I'm just visiting a friend from school."

"School? What's your name?" I asked him anxiously.

"My name's Nicholas and I'm taking courses in real estate. I'm also what's known as a sanitation engineer. Perhaps I shouldn't tell you about that. Are you familiar with that description?" he asked in a shy but proud manner.

"You're talking about a trash man, right?"

"Yes, ma'am!" he responded.

At first I kind of looked at him funny when he told me what he did, but after a while I didn't care. He was attending school so at least he had ambitions. Then again, his gorgeous muscles weren't enticing me to think about his grade point average or his yearly salary anyway. I hoped he'd ask for my phone number but his apparent shyness let me know that I'd probably have to take the initiative.

"Forgive me, Maiya, but it's cold out here and I think you should go inside. My friend isn't home so I should get going, too," he said in such a sweet way. Now he'd shown me that he was also a gentleman.

"That's nice of you, Nicholas." I started digging through my purse for a pen and paper. I wasn't about to let him slide by me. "Listen, I want to give you my number. Maybe we could have lunch sometime."

He eagerly took the number from me. "Sounds good to me."

I looked forward to talking to him again. It was a pleasant ending to my disappointing evening.

"Goodnight, Nicholas."

"Goodnight, Maiya. Very nice to have met you."

3.
Still On Course

I can see my life as an ocean. In the water, I begin to drift in a completely new direction. The winds of change remind me of where I've been, but new direction begs for my attention.

Damn, the phone was ringing! I didn't want to be disturbed.
"Hello!"

"Hey! I'm ready to come over now. Are you ready for me?"

"Tanya?"

"Yes, it's me."

Tanya finally called after telling me we'd hook-up three hours earlier. I hate waiting on people, but I wasn't going anywhere that night anyway so that gave me time to huff and puff while I waited for Tanya to call me back. Besides, I was hoping to complete the article that I'd been writing for the magazine. While I'm always available to spend quality time with a lovely lady, Tanya had habitually kept me waiting.

"Sorry for taking so long, baby."

"It's cool, Tanya. Shall I pick you up?"

"No, I'm on my way to you now," she responded quickly.

"Yeah, I thought so."

"Excuse me?"

"That's okay. I'll see you soon?" I asked to make sure.

"I'm leaving now."

Tanya rarely allowed me into her world and, for someone who was as busy as she appeared to be, she should've given me a little something to hold on to. Shoot, send me an email, send me smoke signals, or something to let me know I was in her thoughts. I didn't even get to hear her talking about her work. I just knew it kept her busy. If I were only privy to a little information about her, how would I miss her when she was away? There had been a month of weekend visits to my place that never included detailed conversations about our lives before we'd met.

I guess I was having the same complaint that most women have about men. I would've given anything to be able to hang out with Tanya and enjoy a movie or engage in lively conversation at a café overlooking the city. I knew of places around the city that would've been incredible backgrounds for long, deep, and passionate kisses shared between two people working their way towards love. I guess I was just dreaming when it came to that kind of stuff. Maybe Tanya wasn't even thinking about the possibilities between us. We may have been intimate, but it didn't feel like we'd made love and were headed for something special.

Damn, I couldn't believe my phone was ringing again. I usually didn't get a lot of calls.

"Hello?"

"Greetings, homeboy!"

It was my good friend Nicholas on the phone. We'd met two years earlier at the park during a pick-up basketball game. He was on the court trying to do his best imitation of Allen Iverson but I was standing tall like Mutumbo, blocking all his shots. "Get that out of here!" I'd shout. That was a good day when we'd met and we'd kind of clicked ever since. Not only did we get along really well but we were also able to go girl watching without chasing the same ladies, which definitely helped. There was no competition between us unless we were on the court or shooting some pool. That's when we'd end up wanting to kill each other.

"Hey, Nicholas. What's up?"

"I met a stunning woman last night when I was outside of Pam's apartment."

"Damn, isn't that taking a chance? I hope you aren't trying to get with her, whoever she is. If they live in the same building, then that's going to be some trouble there!"

Pam was his girlfriend, but they'd been having problems lately because of her addiction to cocaine. That was my girl, though, so I tried to lend a hand of support whenever she needed one.

"This lady was beautiful, Christian. She was dressed in black with this burgundy thing around her shoulders. She's kind of tall. Man, she looked so fine! I'll have to be careful when I go there next time, but I know I'm gonna see her again. I have to see her again!"

Nicholas was pretty excited about his new found friend and I couldn't wait to see why she had him willing to take a risk like that. Actually, by the way he'd described her, I guess I could see why.

"Did you tell this lady that you were seeing somebody?" I asked him.

"I can't worry about that, but no, I didn't tell her yet."

"Alright, Nicholas, but if this lady is all that, then you need to be up front with her, don't you think?"

I was at the point where I was tired of both parties in the war of relationships deceiving one another. All the games people have to endure just to get to the promised land of love, honesty, respect, and sincerity. I hoped Nicholas didn't mess things up. I believed he should've figured out what he wanted from Pam before he committed to trying to get involved in something new. Pam was definitely a sista that you didn't want to play around with. She could get mad in a hurry and let you know about it, too.

"Christian, this lady looks like a model. Plus she seems so easy to talk to. You know how Pam can get a little bossy sometimes. Well, this lady seems laid back, man."

Before he could finish his thought about this mystery lady, I had to cut him off because I had another call coming in.

"Hold on, Nicholas." I clicked over. "Hello?"

"Hi, Christian. I'm sorry but it looks like I won't be able to make it after all," Tanya said softly.

"Yeah, why is that?" I asked, even though I'd kind of expected it.

"Work related stuff. One of my projects fell through and I need to make sure the other one is a go."

"Okay. I hope things work out, Tanya."

"Thanks. Don't be mad, okay?"

That was wishful thinking on her part.

"I'm not mad. Just a little disappointed. We were just gonna stay in for the night anyway, right?" I said, attempting to mask the sarcasm in my voice.

"See, you are mad. I knew this thing between us would be difficult because I'm trying to get this new business going. Then I can concentrate on being with someone and devoting special time to that person," she stated convincingly.

I had a feeling our little adventure was coming to an end. "I understand that, but you don't understand how I am. Once someone comes into my life and shows me that I have a chance, I always tend to focus only on them. I have this habit of being totally faithful to the pursuit of love."

"So, I'm the only one you've been seeing? You should see at least two. That way if one makes you mad, you can call the other."

I was hoping she was kidding, but had the feeling that she wasn't. Hearing that shit turned me off. I took a deep breath and thought for a moment. I'm sure Tanya could feel the power of my silence. I could sense her trying to listen closely.

"Hello? You still there?" she asked.

"I'm here, Tanya." I replied despondently.

"What are you thinking about?"

"Nothing really. I guess you should go and take care of that project, right?"

"Yeah, I really need to. Call me tomorrow so I can see what my schedule looks like, okay?"

Gee, thanks! I thought to myself, but I knew I wasn't gonna call her anytime soon.

"Hello? Call me, okay?" she asked again.

"Yeah, of course!" I lied with false enthusiasm.

During that disappointing moment with Tanya, I forgot all about Nicholas being on the other line. When I checked, he'd hung up already. To be honest, I was highly disappointed in both Nicholas and Tanya, but I guess I couldn't judge them too harshly. Tomorrow would be another day and time for me to start fresh. Life's filled with reasons to start over so I decided to learn from that chapter and turn the page to something brighter.

I've always hated moving from woman to woman, experience to adventure, and trying to act as though it doesn't bother me when it truly does. I usually end up turning the phone off and going to sleep with the hopes that when I awake, I can move on without the feeling of disenchantment resting on my shoulders.

Speaking of the phone ringing, right then it was jumping off the hook and not a single call had been about work.

"Hello!" I answered firmly.

"Greetings."

"Nicholas, what's up? Sorry about earlier."

"Hey, Chris, I'm at the hospital right now," he said in a near whisper.

"Something happen while we were on the phone?"

"Yeah, I got word that Pam had a bad reaction to something so I had to pick her up and bring her to the hospital."

"You need me to do something?"

"Yeah, that's why I called. I drove her here in her car so I need a ride, if you don't mind."

"Oh, okay! I'll be there soon."

I hoped everything was gonna be okay with Pam. I imagined something of a medical nature had to happen sooner or later. I was just glad it wasn't as bad as it could've been. She was a great lady without the drugs, but unfortunately they'd become her dearest friends. She escaped the world and soothed her disappointment whenever she needed to. I always told Pam to feel free to call me when she was feeling down but, apparently, I couldn't give her the same high as that cocaine. I don't know. Seems like folks don't recognize the high you can get from a beautiful, supportive friendship. Isn't laughter a reflection of feeling high? Pam kept me laughing with all the shit she'd been talking. I liked to tease her about looking like "Erykah Badu on steroids." I only said that cause she liked to wear head wraps all the time and cop a creative attitude when she didn't want to be bothered. Plus, she was a *thick sista*, too, and that's why I'd mentioned the steroids. I liked to bother her all the time. I even called her at the job just to tease her sometimes. She worked as a secretary for an entertainment company, but her passion was sculpting, which she was very skilled at. I wanted her to make a statute of me deep in thought.

In response to my request, she asked me, "You want to watch yourself deep in thought?"

"Yeah, that would be cool!" I told her.

"You're funny! But isn't that like a man to want to look at himself think? Y'all just think a little too much of yourselves!"

She laughed at me, but she looked forward to the challenge of my request. We'd made several attempts, but something always came up at the last minute. I'd come to believe that the drugs always stepped in the way and told her, "It's time for us." She'd give me those sad looks before apologizing about not showing up when we were supposed to meet.

When I finally made it to the hospital, the first thing I saw was Nicholas talking to this doctor who looked really nice from behind. She had dark brown hair hanging past her shoulders and looked to be about 5'6" in height. Since things didn't work out with Tanya, I was free to look at this doctor with all kinds of intentions running through my mind. When I got closer, Nicholas made eye contact with me and then the doctor turned around.

Damn! I thought to myself.

The doctor was beautiful. Her dark brown eyes were serious right then, but I was thinking that, with the right inspiration, they could light up the world. She was holding a chart against her chest and I couldn't see any rings around her fingers, but that may not have meant anything. Her long, white coat was parted in the front and I couldn't help but imagine parting it some more. I'd never seen a doctor look that good before. She had me hooked instantaneously.

When Nicholas started talking, I'd almost forgotten he was present. "Hey, Chris! The doctor says that Pam will be okay, but she needs to consider getting some kind of help."

I continuously gazed at the doctor while Nicholas was speaking. The more I looked, the less I could comprehend what he was saying.

"I'll be right back. I want to check on her again," the beautiful doctor said.

I wasn't able to peruse her badge to get her name, but her eyes had me going crazy. I watched her walk away before realizing that Nicholas was pulling on my jacket.

"Hey! Thanks for coming here, man."

"Coming where?" I responded, still watching the doctor walk away. My heart dropped when she turned the corner and was out of my sight.

"Hey!" Nicholas shouted, waving his hand in front of my face.

"Oops! Sorry about that. I'm glad I'm here for you, too."

"Yeah, I noticed."

"Pam's going to be okay. She's strong. That doctor's got it going on, though!" I told him.

"Yeah, she does look good. I think her last name is Oliver."

"Cool, but what's her first name?"

I kept checking to see if she was coming back rather than looking at Nicholas while he was talking.

"The same name as all of them," he responded.

"Shut up, man! Don't even tell me her first name is Doctor!"

Time went by quickly as we waited in the emergency department for another hour. After that, we went up with Pam after they'd admitted her for the night. I stood close by with Nicholas, hoping I could get a chance to speak with the doctor. I saw her at the counter speaking with a nurse so I decided to make my way over to her. I stood by patiently, waiting for my chance. I could hear her soft voice speaking with the clarity of a true professional. She definitely knew what she was doing and looked incredible doing it.

"Hi, you waiting for me?" the doctor asked, catching me off guard. I was pretending to be engrossed in the action of all the nurses and doctors running everywhere.

"Oh, yeah. I just wanted to make sure my friend is going to be okay."

"She'll be okay. We just need to keep her for the night," she responded with a smile.

"Thanks."

My admiration must've been a little too obvious as I stood there staring for a moment. I studied her as she turned the page of a chart that she was holding. Her gorgeous, well-manicured hands and the diamond bracelet that adorned her wrist had me locked in a serious daydreaming state of mind.

"Anything else?" she asked, still maintaining her smile.

She held the chart against her chest, almost in a hugging fashion, waiting for me to respond. I wished that I were in her arms at that moment. How come small objects always get the most fun?

"No, nothing else," I said as I turned around to walk back to Nicholas.

I stopped once again and turned to look at her. She had returned to writing something in the chart.

"You sure you don't want anything else?"

My mind and heart were racing, and I wasn't sure if I should say anything. I feared that if I spoke, she'd be able to hear my heart beating in my throat or I'd get tongue-tied and say the wrong thing. I was nervous with anticipation and I couldn't figure out how I could possibly ask her out on a date.

"Well, this is hard!" I said.

We both laughed, which made things a little easier from that point.

"I'd like to get together with you, doctor. Maybe we can talk and get to know each other."

"Oh really? You haven't even asked me my name yet."

She returned to writing something in the chart, awaiting my next comment.

"That's very true. I guess I was nervous about it."

"My name's Sabrina or you can call me Dr. Oliver," she told me in a wise cracking way.

She knew she had me in the palm of her hand and she took full advantage of it. I felt like a puppet with my strings being pulled.

"Man, she has you good!" I could hear Nicholas saying in the background.

Sabrina was laughing at the entire thing. I smiled at her but gave Nicholas a mean look because he wasn't helping at all.

"Why don't you tell me your name?"

"I'm Christian and I'm cool once you get to know me."

"What happens if I don't get to know you? How do you act then?"

I wondered if all women attempt to keep us men on our toes by issuing challenging remarks. Was I setting myself up for another potential duel with a female?

It was time for me to put my creativity to work so I could give the lady something to think about.

"Well, Dr. Oliver, I believe that no matter what, you will feel my sincerity and beg for the chance to be a part of my experience. You'll want to know me because I'm dying to know you."

She placed her pen seductively on her lips. "Is that right?"

"That's right, doctor."

"Nurse? Do we have a straight jacket?"

Everyone laughed.

"Damn!" I could hear Nicholas say behind me.

"Ouch!" I said. She looked and sounded so lovely but that comment had hurt.

Her eyebrow was raised, expressing a little interest. She kept pressing the pen against her lips and watched me attempt to brush off my embarrassment. Actually, I couldn't wait to show her just how interesting we could be together.

"We may have to do lunch, Christian. Maybe you can show me some sincerity then," she finally said, letting me off the hook.

"Well, I'll give you my number and you call me for a dose of it," I quickly responded as she handed me her pen and a sticky pad off the nurses' station.

Nicholas stepped forward to add in his two cents and whispered, "Yeah, he's full of it!"

"I can imagine," Sabrina responded in laughter.

I couldn't wait to get in the car and take Nicholas home. He was getting on my nerves with all the joking around at my expense.

"Hey, sorry about that in the hospital," he told me as we cruised through a string of flashing yellow lights in the middle of the night. "You have to admit it was funny and I couldn't resist having a little fun myself."

"I know, Nicholas. It's cool."

After dropping him off at his place, I took the fast route home. I was so happy to be back. I was gonna fix me something to eat, write a little bit more, and watch videos. As I walked up to the front entrance of my apartment, I noticed a figure step out quickly.

"Who's there?"

"Sorry, baby," Tanya responded, coming into view.

"Tanya? What are you doing here?"

To be honest, she'd almost scared me to death coming out of nowhere like that.

"Didn't mean to sneak up on you, but I wanted to make up for tonight if I could."

"How do you plan on doing that?"

"I'm gonna get in bed with you and screw your brains out!" she stated boldly.

I wasn't really shocked by her statement because she'd turned me off earlier. In fact, I'd expected a comment like that from her. She did look incredible in the darkness. She was gracing black stretch pants and a long flannel shirt. She smelled good, too, and when all of a man's senses are stimulated, it's hard not to become weak.

"Can I come up with you?" she asked.

I didn't ponder it two seconds before replying. "Well, it's kind of late and I can't see myself making you drive home at this hour, so I'll say okay."

"Okay, great!"

She must've assumed that all was forgiven, but I wasn't so sure I could. Though she stood there looking incredible, I just couldn't forget what had happened and exonerate her so quickly.

Once we got inside, there was an aura of tension in the living room. Tanya sat on the couch glancing at me with a heartrending expression on her face. She unbuttoned her flannel shirt and removed her shoes before stretching out on the couch. Once I stood over her and got a better view, Tanya did look extremely enticing. I was aroused but played it off by telling her I was going to take a shower. I planned on using only cold water, too.

"Okay, baby. I'll be here waiting for you when you get back," she said.

"Yeah, I know."

My lack of enthusiasm was definitely done on purpose and I hoped that she'd pick up on every little hint.

The phone starting ringing while I was in the shower and I prayed Tanya wouldn't answer it. One ring went by. Two rings went by. Two and a half rings. No third ring. I turned the water off quickly, even though I still had soap on my body. When I went into the living room, Tanya was on the couch glued to the television.

Maybe she didn't answer or maybe the person just hung up, I thought to myself.

She wasn't acting as though she'd answered the phone and I

wasn't sure I should ask. I checked my voicemail to see if anyone had left a message.

"Hi, this message is for Christian. This is Sabrina calling to say hello and to see if you might be interested in having lunch. We might have to do it here at the hospital, but let me know if you're interested."

I couldn't believe that the lovely doctor had called already and, at the same time, I wasn't sure if I should pursue something with her. I supposed I could just enjoy a friendship with her, but I was sure she could already tell that I was interested in more. Sometimes I just get into these moods where I don't want to go through the process of telling my story over to a new person entering into my life. I wish we could just hand out résumé's and life stories. "Here, read this and get back to me if you're still interested," I would say. Then I'd ask if everything was cool or if my qualifications matched.

As I stood there thinking about the possibilities of Dr. Oliver and myself getting together, I could feel Tanya approach me from behind.

I was dressed only in a towel and, before I knew it, the towel was removed and I could feel her naked body pressed against mine. The feeling was like getting a warm surprise, and I couldn't resist leaning back into her arms. She moved her hands upward and massaged my chest. I took a deep breath and closed my eyes as I reached back and squeezed her behind. I pushed her against me tighter. I noticed her breathing pattern begin to change. I could feel her face against my back. Her hands were massaging me tighter as she moved them down to my manhood. I was very aroused.

"There's no need for whoever that was, baby. I'm here now," she whispered to me. I pulled away after she made that comment.

"What's wrong?"

"I didn't like what you just said."

"Sounds like you must be seeing someone else. I told you I didn't mind because that's the way everyone does it these days." Tonya smirked like she thought she knew everything.

I wasn't crazy about being put into a category with everyone else. I've always believed in concentrating on one woman romantically at a time. I believe in developing something special without the distraction of trying to keep track of multiple women on the side.

"Tanya, I'm not seeing anyone right now and, as of recently, that includes you!" I lashed out at her.

She became quiet and stood with her arms folded. She was looking at me as though she couldn't figure out what she wanted to say next.

"Did you consider us really seeing each other?" I asked her quietly.

"Can't you give me time, Christian?" she softly asked.

"Why do you need time, Tanya?"

"I don't feel like I have it all together. I'm starting a new business, trying to keep my personal life together, and trying to start something with you. I know I'm not reliable when it comes to us getting together but..."

"That's true," I interrupted.

"Be patient with me, okay?"

"I suppose we can give it time, Tanya. But tonight let's not do anything, okay?"

She simply nodded her head.

I couldn't believe we'd had such a serious talk, albeit brief, standing in front of each other naked. We both smiled and then she returned to the couch. I went into the bedroom to put on some pajamas. After awhile, I returned to the living room where we talked and watched videos all night. Our time together felt really good and I began thinking that perhaps I was jumping the gun too soon. Hanging out with that beautiful doctor was becoming an afterthought. I wasn't sure I could go through with it now that there appeared to be some degree of understanding between Tanya and myself. I was beginning to see a difference in her. Perhaps something that would allow our relationship to grow. She seemed to finally be interested in developing something greater than just weekends of pure sex. I loved being with her intimately because her body was incredible. The softness of her skin kept me smiling for days, but I wanted and needed more. I wanted that kind of passion that comes from serious emotions. I wanted us to breathe in each other's spirit with the belief that when we awoke in each other's arms, we would begin a new level in our relationship. Love is very powerful and can provide fuel for anyone's determination to succeed in life. I desire that type of fuel and I pray that one day I won't have to keep turning it off and on again because of uncertainty in a relationship. Maybe now my worries could truly be over. I hoped Tanya was ready because I knew I was.

4.
A Night To Forget

I was feeling blessed. My article was accepted in the magazine that I work for, Urban Exclusive, and my time with Tanya had been pretty cool lately. We'd see each other at least two or three times a week and she was having great success with her business. To celebrate we'd decided to accept the invitation of Nicholas to meet him at this popular club in town called Chase the Apple. If you ask me, I think they should've substitute Onion for Apple but that's another story. We were supposed to meet Nicholas the following night and he'd promised to introduce us to Maiya, the new lady in his life. I was actually looking forward to that just to see what she was about. Nicholas hadn't stopped talking about her since they'd met. Personally, I missed talking to Pam, but she was going through treatment right then and could've been away for yet another week. Nicholas didn't talk about Pam that much, but I knew he cared for her. I figured he was mostly just fascinated with Maiya. Apparently, she was playing it cautious with him because the club would be their first time getting together at night. They usually met for an hour here and there, for lunch or just to talk. By the way he described their meetings, it didn't seem like a love connection to me. I could've been wrong, but the lady just seemed to be keeping Nicholas at a distance. Maybe I was working on blind assumption because of my closeness to Pam.

I'd met with the editor of the magazine that day and I'd been assigned to do a story on friendships between black men. I hoped to get pretty deep with the story. You know, throw in my personal touch. I realized I didn't have a lot of male friends, but I enjoyed the ones I had very much. I tended to encounter those situations where jealousy came into play and eventually the friendship had to end because of all the tension. I hated having to go through that kind of stuff with a man, just as I hated it when relationships with a woman came to an end. For me, it was kind of like building bridges only to destroy them the next day. You start to wonder what's the point. Sometimes you end up making an unconscious decision not to begin new friendships or relationships and that's not always a good thing for your personal growth.

Anyway, that meeting went really great and I knew I was chosen for the story because of my last assignment. I'd written from a very sensual as well as spiritual point of view on the potential of love. My favorite subject was love and since I was in the process of questioning my situation with Tanya, I couldn't help but relate it to the story I was writing. Tanya came to my mind quite often and I knew she'd be the inspiration for many of my thoughts in the near future. She called to see how my day was going and it felt incredible to have a lady think of me in such a sweet way. I could walk around with a new level of confidence because I had someone special in my life. I thanked her with such excitement. I believe we talked for an hour or more.

"Chris, honey, you made me miss my lunch," she told me over the phone.

"I did? You should be missing me more than your lunch."

"Yeah, I suppose I should."

After we hung up the phone, I found myself thinking "Yuck!" because we sounded mushy. We were starting to sound like one of those couples deeply in love with each other. I guess that was a good thing, but we were going to have to find new words to express the love that we felt so that we didn't sound so damn corny.

The next day came pretty quickly. I was anxious to see how the night turned out. It was time to scoop Tanya up before heading over to the club. I was dressed in my usual black ensemble and couldn't wait to see what Tanya had on. My mind was on meeting the woman Nicholas was always talking about, but first it was time for Tanya.

The drive was sweet. I was getting my groove on and not paying enough attention to the road. I was listening to a little old school. They were playing *Flashlight* on the radio and I was getting excited. I didn't know why, since I couldn't really dance but I knew how to groove. As I got closer to Tanya's condo, an uncontrollable smile appeared on my face. Suddenly I couldn't wait to see her. She'd probably think I was sweet for saying that, but life felt even sweeter when I arrived at her door. The weather outside was a misty rain and kind of cold. I loved breezy nights, but I wished it wasn't wet outside. I took time out to adjust the coat and check my face before I rang the doorbell. I looked pretty decent. Right then, I was feeling good as I started to recognize the time of the year. It was only October but I felt as though my Christmas would be good that year. Maybe I'd take Tanya somewhere special. I would've loved to take her up to the mountains so that we could have a white Christmas in front of a fireplace. I was thinking way too far ahead. I needed to get through the rest of that month and then tackle November.

"Hey, you!" Tanya said as she opened the door.

"Looks like you're going to be doing some dancing tonight!" I said teasingly.

She was wearing a tight-fitting outfit underneath her black leather coat. I couldn't take my eyes off her body without gritting my teeth and proclaiming how fine she was with one word: Damn!

"Let me get inside with you, girl!"

She smiled, opened her coat, and gestured for me to come closer. "Come on in," she whispered, issuing a dare.

"Tanya, I think we need to get going."

She pulled me in tighter and started to rub against me. She was really making things hard, but I guess that was her purpose. She was causing my legs to weaken with the beautiful sounds she made and the words she chose to whisper.

"You've got me so wet, baby. I thought I'd get this way while we danced, but I'm there already!" she said, edging me on.

I felt her breathe in deeply and she squeezed me tighter. She was driving me crazy and drowning me with her passion.

"Tanya?"

"Yes, Christian."

"I'm going to wait in the car for you!"

I stepped away with a big smile on my face. I had to close my coat because I was shy about my obvious excitement.

"You're silly!" Tanya said.

We finally arrived at the club after making a few stops. Tanya had to drop off some blueprints and I must admit to having my first jealous moment. Her client was a man of obvious wealth and when he saw Tanya dressed in her tight party outfit, he examined every inch of her with his eyes. I wasn't too thrilled by that, but I didn't want to fall prey to any jealous feelings. People should avoid those kinds of thoughts because they never get you anywhere.

The music sounded great as we walked into the club. I could feel the power beneath my feet when I strolled in with Tanya holding my hand. Folks were raising their hands in the air like they were trying to keep the roof from falling in. The whole scene was pretty hypnotic and I couldn't help but bob my head up and down like a hip hop star walking on stage to the beat of his own song. Tanya was getting excited seeing all the lights traveling around the room. The deeper we got into the club, the more excited she seemingly became. In the distance, I could see Nicholas waving in my direction. I pulled Tanya closer to me while she was bouncing up and down to the beat of the song playing. It sounded like some kind of Jill Scott groove pumping through the speakers.

"Hey! I see Nicholas over there!" I shouted.

I also saw him dancing with a very lovely woman dressed in red. Maybe that was the infamous Maiya that he worshiped so much. The dress she had on was pretty sharp. She was wearing what appeared to be a red bra that was connected to the lower part of her dress by a sheer, see-through material. The bottom half of her dress was long and she looked good. I don't know much about women's clothes but Maiya was working what she had on and I was feeling a little guilty about staring at her as long as I did.

"Hey now!" Tanya shouted when she saw Nicholas.

She raised her hands in the air, along with the rest of them, and began to get her groove on.

"Hey, what's up?" Nicholas shouted.

I merely glanced at Maiya and she gave me a quick smile. I put my sights on Tanya, twisting and shaking her body. Her moves had me thinking that I was in for a special night with her. When the music slowed down, Nicholas touched me on the shoulder.

"You want to meet Maiya now?" he asked me.

"I'll meet her after this."

I found myself getting lost in the arms of Tanya and I wanted to prolong the moment. She was singing along with the song and squeezing me tighter. She put her mouth near my ear and sang part of the song. "Until the end of time, I'll be there for you." Then, as she backed away to look into my eyes, she sang, "I truly adore you." This song was one of my favorites by Prince and now I had a very special memory to attach to it. After that slow jam break, the action picked up again. The DJ got the party started back up. He played a song by Ice Cube and I began to wonder what kind of memory I'd attach to what I was hearing. "You can do it. Get yo back into it." I thought I could find some inspiration in that song, too.

After Tanya and I finished dancing, I glanced over at Nicholas and it appeared he was still waiting for us. The man was really anxious to have us meet Maiya. More and more I could sense how important it was to him so I let Tanya know that we were wanted. I had reservations about meeting the lady because I was close to Pam. Deep down I felt that Nicholas should be with her. I realized that he shouldn't stop living or trying to have fun, but it seemed like he would leave Pam if Maiya simply asked him to.

"Hey, Chris! I want you to meet Maiya!" Nicholas shouted.

"Hey!" I responded as I reached out to shake her hand.

She started to say something, but I looked away. I felt Tanya elbow me so I'd pay attention, but I didn't feel as though I wanted to know Maiya. I realized I was acting mean, but I didn't really care. Tanya made conversation with Maiya so I just let her represent the both of us.

"Chris, what's wrong, man?" Nicholas whispered in my ear.

"Nothing, man. I just don't know what else to say besides hello."

"How do you think she looks?"

"She's alright. What, you want me to tell her she's fine?"

"Damn, I thought you were my boy!" Nicholas responded, backing away from me.

"What do you want from me, man?"

"Be cool with her, for me."

"Okay! If she's cool with me, I'll be cool with her."

Nicholas grabbed Tanya by the hand and led her to the dance floor. The DJ had the music moving and the crowd was hyped. After that Ice Cube jam, he segued into Erykah Badu and now he had everybody dancing to Jay-Z. Nicholas and Tanya were having a good time out on the dance floor. I knew he'd try to force the situation by leaving me alone with Maiya. I wasn't too thrilled with that.

"So, you want to dance or anything?" Maiya asked me.

"No, maybe we can grab this table over here."

"Okay, fine."

I was looking at her and wondering what could be going on inside her head. I'm sure she was doing the same thing with me.

"Have you two known each other for long?" she asked.

"Close to two years, I believe."

My attention wasn't really on the conversation. As I was talking, I kept looking around for a waiter. Maiya was probably thinking, *What's up with this guy?*

"Hey! Is there some kind of problem you want to tell me about?" Maiya inquired with a serious look on her face.

"Nah, just feeling a little tired, I suppose."

"Oh really? Is it emotional or physical?" she asked.

I couldn't tell if that was a serious question or if she was just messing with me because I wasn't really saying anything. Then again, maybe she was just trying to spark a conversation. I started thinking that maybe I should lighten up just a little bit so I made an attempt to respond.

"It's more emotional because I'm writing a story about friendships between black men. I'm trying to take a lot of it from personal experience as well as what I wish for in the future."

"Wow, that sounds very exciting! I'd love to read it someday!"

"Maybe so," I responded with no interest in my voice.

"Well, I'm gonna go and dance with Nicholas. It was nice meeting you, Christian."

I waved as she walked away. I also sneaked a little peek at her and I must say she did have style. I'm not blind when it comes to physical beauty but something about her turned me off, though I didn't really give her a chance. Perhaps I was just tripping and thinking about Pam. I didn't believe I had to worry too much because I doubted that Maiya and I would have much contact anyway.

"We should go, baby," Tanya whispered.

She'd snuck up behind me before I noticed. Tanya gave me a look that spoke louder to me than the music that was blasting inside the club.

"I'm right behind you," I told her.

"We can do it that way, too!" she said as she grabbed my hand and pulled me through the crowded dance floor.

As soon as we found the nearest exit, we were out of there and on our way to a place where we could play with each other for the rest of the night. I absolutely loved the way we bonded.

5.
How Long Must I Resist?

I had to fight off Nicholas with a broom when he brought me home from the club. My dress must've had him wanting more than just a dance all night. It had been a while for me, as far as intimacy was concerned, and I must admit that I would've loved to enjoy a night of passion. In fact, I'd been thinking about it a lot recently. I couldn't really imagine Nicholas as being passionate or romantic, but he was very attractive. I'd never been with a man from the Caribbean before. Getting busy while a man moans and groans with an accent was rather intriguing. Only thing, I didn't want to start laughing at him if he started sounding ridiculous.

I decided to call my girlfriend, Stephanie, to let her know that I'd had a good time on my date and planned on seeing Nicholas again. Maybe that was her already. The phone was ringing and I hadn't even taken my shoes off yet.

"Hello," I answered.

"Maiya, are you still mad at me?" the voice asked.

"Who is this?"

"This is Reggie. Can we talk for a moment?"

"We can talk for a moment on the phone, but I hope you're not trying to ask me out again."

"Yeah, I'm hoping we can get together. I know I may have said some wrong things and perhaps treated you badly, but don't you have any kind of forgiveness in your heart?"

"Please don't try to make me out as the villain in all this, Reginald. I truly believe that you're not right for me. The two of us would only be fighting constantly if we were together."

"So, you're not gonna give us any chance at all? I believe you *need* to see me, Maiya. You're just in denial as to how you really feel."

"You're out of your mind, Reggie!"

"No, I probably know you better than you know yourself."

He was beginning to sound like a major fool.

"I have another call coming in. Hold on, Reggie."

"Hello?" I answered.

"What's wrong?" the male voice asked right away.

"Nicholas?"

"Yeah. Why'd you pull away from me?" he asked, sounding like a confused little boy.

It must not have been my night because I had two grown men acting a fool on the phone.

"Nicholas, I had a great time with you tonight."

"Yeah, so what happened at the end?" he asked.

"Nicholas, I'm not about to sleep with you right away. You had your hand up my ass, trying to get you some. That wasn't romantic at all. Did you think you were turning me on?"

Nicholas was silent and I knew I had to deal with the fool on the other line as well. I didn't like the way I was feeling right then, after I'd enjoyed my experience at the club. Those two men were driving me crazy. Nicholas's friend seemed to have a problem with me and now I was juggling two fools on the telephone. I was starting to rethink my call waiting option.

"Nicholas, I really had a nice time but I never want to be pressured into having sex. I'd love to go out with you again. I'd love to see where this may lead, but if it's all about sex, then you might as well let me know so we can part ways."

"Sorry, Maiya. I definitely want to see you again."

"Okay, I'll call you tomorrow," I said as I clicked back over to Reggie.

"Hello?"

"Okay, Maiya, meet me for dinner tomorrow night at my place," Reggie demanded.

"No thank you, Reggie. Listen, there's no need to call me. I'm not interested and you should find someone else that you can control and who'll make you happy."

"You're still in denial, Maiya."

"I know you've heard this before, Reggie, but goodbye?"

That felt strange and I couldn't believe he'd had the nerve to say that I *needed* to see him like he was the answer to all my prayers.

He'd been eccentric from the start. I suddenly wished that I'd never met the fool.

I picked the phone back up and dialed Stephanie's number.

"Hey, Stephanie."

"Hey, girl."

"I just had two men on the phone acting like little boys."

"What are you talking about, Maiya?" Stephanie asked.

"Reggie called and said that I was in denial about my feelings for him and Nicholas called to ask why I backed away from him when he had his hand all in my ass."

"Ooh, I need to hook up with Nicholas. You go, boy!" Stephanie shouted.

"Shut up, girl! I'm not trying to go there right away."

"Well, when are you gonna go there? Don't you think your body needs a man's touch? Get you some!"

"I'd love it, but only at the right time. I feel if I just allow myself to indulge in sex, then something bad will happen."

"Girl, just have some fun! Then maybe the fun will lead to more fun and, after a while, you never know what might become of it."

It seemed like Stephanie was trying to say that sex was the answer to all of life's bullshit.

"What about that strange guy, Reggie?" she asked.

"I don't want to get with him!"

"No, girl, what was he talking about?"

"He seems like one of those fatal attractions or something. I don't want to talk about him anymore."

"Well talk about something, shit. I'm living through your adventures, Maiya!"

"Huh? You're always getting your freak on so don't even go there. I bet you had somebody last night."

"This is true, girlfriend. I did," she admitted hesitantly.

Stephanie and I talked for about four hours. She kept me laughing and, sometimes, she shocked me with her free-spirited attitude towards sharing her body with someone. In a way, she had me contemplating indulging with Nicholas. I wasn't even sure how to approach the idea of being intimate with a man anymore. I figured I could let it happen, but I wished Nicholas could be more gentle and romantic about it. I didn't like being grabbed like a rag doll. The one thing I could honestly say about his not so talkative friend was that he seemed like a gentleman and was truly into his lady. I didn't like the way he came off with me. I was still curious as to why he'd acted the way he did. I was going to find out what magazine he worked for so I could read some of his work. Stephanie tried to ask me questions about Christian, but I didn't know what to say.

"You think he's serious about that lady he was with?" she asked.

"Yeah, I think so."

"What if he came on to you? Would you go for it?"

"Why are you asking me that?"

"Cause I want to know! Why are you trying to act like you

don't be looking at the dick or checking a man's ass out, Maiya?"

"Stephanie, I'm still trying to figure out what I see in you!"

"Shut up, girlfriend! You know you love me!"

Stephanie had my curious nature on the rise but I definitely wasn't the type of woman to chase after somebody else's man. Besides, first things first. I wanted to see what Nicholas was about. Interestingly enough, I'd just found out that his last name was Brown. That blended perfectly with his chocolate complexion.

It was time for bed. I decided to invite Nicholas over for dinner the following weekend and possibly make it a night for him to remember. I was new to that sort of thing. Being forward with a man made me nervous. I hoped nothing bad came out of it.

The more you fear a situation, the faster it comes around to see how you'll respond to it. When I invited Nicholas over for dinner, he accepted before I could finish my sentence.

"Are you crazy? I'll be counting the days; the minutes; the hours!" I remember him saying.

The night arrived and it was time to see where it would take us. I knew he'd be over at any minute and I was sitting on pins and needles. I selected a loose-fitting, blue satin wrap dress. I loved the way it revealed my legs without showing too much unless I wanted it to. It made me feel extremely sexy. The dress was long enough to keep him from knowing that the possibility of sex was on the agenda. I cooked one of my best pasta dishes and I had some nice slow jams playing in the background. I couldn't believe that I baked a lemon meringue cake for dessert. I found the recipe in *Ebony* magazine. Nicholas would want to appreciate all the trouble I'd gone through.

Suddenly the phone rang. I knew it had to be Nicholas waiting to be buzzed inside the apartment. I took one last look around. Everything was ready.

I could tell he was excited because it didn't take him long to find my front door and knock.

I answered it. "Hi, Nicholas!"

"Wow, Maiya!"

By the way he was gazing at me, he seemed to be losing his mind. He was ogling me like a piece of steak broiled to perfection.

I wanted to tell him to stop staring at me, but I remembered that I was the one who'd invited him over. It was time for me to exercise patience and control over my habit of getting an attitude. Maybe that's why I was stuck in the lap of celibacy.

"Maiya, can I have a hug?"

"Of course you can. Come here," I responded.

He seemed really sweet as we hugged. He was smiling like a little boy, but then he started with those hands again. I didn't stop him this time because I wanted to at least give it a try. I could feel him getting excited. His manhood was pushed against me and I got aroused myself. We moved over to the couch and there I was worried about dinner. He was putting some serious wrinkles in my satin dress. The kissing became really heavy and before I knew it, he'd opened my dress up to reveal my thong panties. The sight of those made him almost burst out of his pants. I felt him lick the outside where it covered my hot spot. That alone made me arch my back. His tongue sent a shock wave inside my body. I was practically on fire and wondering what took me so long to indulge. While he was down there concentrating and moving his tongue around nicely, I began to feel him anxiously tug at my panties.

"Ooh, wait a minute!" I told him.

I don't know if he heard me but he did stop for a moment. After that, I let him reach up to fondle my breasts. His hands were rugged and strong. He stopped for a second so he could remove his shirt. Then he lay down on top of me and I could feel the strength of his upper body squeeze me tighter. His strong chest was against my warm breasts and it felt overpowering. So many things were going through my mind as the passion was building. I was somewhat confused by it all. Once again Nicholas reached for my panties but this time he succeeded in ripping them off. I could hear them tear and, for some reason, the sound was frightening to me. My mind was racing so much that I failed to recognize that he was entering me without a condom on. His thrusting motions became stronger and his moans louder. He gripped one of my wrists while my other arm was pinned inside the couch. I could feel the sweat from his forehead on the side of my face, dripping down my neck. It wasn't long before his body stopped moving and all I could hear were the sounds of his heavy breathing slowing down.

I was too shocked to move once I realized that Nicholas had just come inside of me. I stayed in that position, lying with his heavy body on top of me. I could feel his heartbeat as I watched him fall asleep. After a few hours went by, Nicholas woke up. We didn't talk much and I'm sure he could tell that I was feeling strange about what happened. I eventually asked him to leave. When Nicholas walked out the door, I locked it behind him. I didn't ever want him to come back. I'd never had such a repulsive feeling before and I never wanted him to touch me again.

What had happened between us wasn't my style. I'd drummed up the courage to invite Nicholas over after talking to Stephanie, but I couldn't blame her for my actions because I'm a grown woman. I'd given away something special and it was my own fault.

For some strange reason, I got the idea to read some of the stories that Christian contributed to a magazine. I was actually impressed with some of the things he wrote. I found comfort in his words as I listened to music by Yolanda Adams. I was in desperate need of inspiration coming from all angles. As I read Christian's thoughts on women and the power of love, I was snowed under by the spiritual level expressed through the words he chose. I wished I could call him right then. I needed a man in my life that I could communicate with. Not someone that was going to abuse the time we spent together. I harbored no interest in pursuing Christian, but his words really connected with what I was feeling.

"My Privilege to Love" was the name of an article in Urban Exclusive. Christian Erickson wrote it and I couldn't believe that this was the same guy that I'd met the weekend before at the night-club. The very same guy that refused to make conversation with me. It was unbelievable.

In the dead of winter, I find myself usually alone. As I settle back on my memories, I realize that once again I was in love. Not that love was a stranger before but, once again, it took me on a journey not known to this man. Unknown but respected, I'm so thankful that a woman has blessed my life. She

*brought with her a magical fuel that keeps me raging inside. I'm blessed with
the wisdom that takes me beyond the realm of being a normal guy. My path
illuminated with the privilege of truly understanding why.*

His thoughts moved me deeply on a night when I found my
heart screaming for the words of a sensitive man. Someone that
could be introspective, share his thoughts, and never close his
heart. Why did that seem like such an unrealistic dream? I had a
newfound revelation as I read more of Christian's work. Somehow
I'd figure out how I could talk to him again. I had to break through
the wall that was up when we'd met and let him see that we had a
lot in common. I knew he had a woman, but I hoped that she
wouldn't mind if I sought out a sincere friendship with Christian. I
needed to renew my faith in men. I needed a reason to believe
what my mother had once told me about loving a man and finding
my soul mate. Maybe that was asking too much of Christian, but
the least he could do was help to return my smile.

I'd called my mother the night before and I couldn't believe
how patient she was with me. I sat there motionless on the phone,
saying absolutely nothing.

"Baby, did you call me for a reason or did you just want me to
hear you breathing?"

My mother had the sweetest voice and, after listening to it, I
began to feel a little bit of life coming back inside of me. I could-
n't tell her what was troubling me, but I felt much better because I
had her near, even though it was just her voice.

"You're gonna eventually tell me what's wrong, aren't you,
Maiya?"

"Yes, but right now I just need rest, Mommy," I told her as I
wiped my tears and curled up on the couch.

"You need to get out the house, girl, and get away from those
computers. You sound terrible!"

"Mommy, I've been out and that's a part of the problem!"

I could tell she didn't understand my frustration. I just hoped
that it didn't sound like I was taking it out on her.

"Tell me something, Maiya," she said softly.

I waited patiently for my mother's question. I was thinking it was gonna be about a man, but she caught me off guard with this one.

"Maiya, sweetie, you're into computers right?"

"Yes?" I answered cautiously. "That's what I do for a living, Mommy."

"Maiya, I hear things, you know. Are you having computer sex?"

"What? Mommy, I don't believe you asked me that!" I shouted before finally doing something I hadn't done all night. I began to laugh.

"Well, you seem so troubled that I figured you were doing something strange like that, unless you're out there involved in some freaky deaky stuff out in Hollywood. I hear about those parties and I know all too well about your girlfriend Stephanie."

"You're crazy, Mommy. By the way, Stephanie said to give you her love."

"Is that heffa there with you?"

"No and I think you've been watching too much television, Mommy."

"I made you forget about your troubles, huh, baby?"

"Yes, I feel better now but I think I'm gonna start worrying about you though."

"Oh, I'm gonna be just find, young lady."

"Yes, ma'am."

6.
If I Ask Why, I'll Go Crazy

I was drinking tea and coffee like crazy. I was trying to stay up so I could finish my article. How could I write about friendship between men when it seemed as though mine was disappearing? There was a strange feeling in the air. I'd called Nicholas and, as soon as I brought up the subject of Maiya, I could feel the tension. I told him that I'd try to be cool around her. Welcome her into the circle, so to speak.

"I bet you will," he'd responded with anger.

I just ended the conversation because I didn't want to get deeper into whatever Nicholas was feeling at the time. To top everything off, I'd heard that Maiya was trying to contact me, leaving several messages at my job. I didn't know if Nicholas heard about that or what. Maybe that was what had him acting so strange. Maiya had left her pager number, fax number, home number, and even her email address. I was curious about what she had to say, but I wasn't in a hurry to know just then. All those attempts at trying to contact me could only spell one thing and that was drama.

Tanya was at my place and angry because I hadn't gone to bed with her. Maybe since everything had been going so good for me recently, it was high time to experience a little turmoil. So there I sat wired with the anticipation of what Maiya wanted to tell me and wondering when or if I'd finish my article. I could hear Tanya's footsteps in the bedroom. It was nearing four in the morning so I knew she was going to say something.

Tanya came out into the living room and walked right past me without saying a word.

I faked a smile "Hey, you."

Tanya still didn't utter a word. She just grabbed her coat and put it on over her pajamas. When she reached the front door, she turned around to leer at me. "I might as well be at home if I'm gonna sleep alone."

She walked out so fast that I didn't have a chance to respond. For some reason, Tanya seemed anxious to be together that night and, unlike other times, she had very little patience with my writing. It was definitely a strange night and I couldn't figure out why people were acting like they were. Maybe it was something in the air.

Taking a chance on Maiya didn't sound like a good idea at all. To put it mildly, we hadn't gotten along at the club, so I was a little hesitant to get in touch with her. I felt bad about Tanya leaving like she did but I had to black that out to somehow finish my writing. Hopefully she and I would be able to discuss whatever was troubling her and move past it. That particular time of the year was always tough for me with regards to friendships and relationships. Those around me just seemed to disappear. I hoped Tanya didn't choose that route because I felt like we were developing something truly special. My mind kept telling me to put my worries behind me and get back to writing. If only I could learn to listen to myself like I expected others to do.

After reliving and contemplating all the madness that I was about to experience under the guise of friendship, I felt like I was headed to the depths of enlightenment. I wondered sometimes, why does pain and frustration have to happen in order for you to speak directly from your soul? I knew that when I got into a mellow mood like I was right then, my writing flowed with ease. Words were escaping from the depths of my soul that I hoped would inspire thought and, eventually, uplift.

"I can see the formation of lies completing this circle of friendship. Not only is love fragile, but the bond of friendship can be broken just as easily. What's the best route to avoid pain and discomfort? Should we simply stop speaking and let the tension fade or will it always exist? Outside influences and a lack of communication cut very deeply into the bond. Even during good times, one action can derail the beauty of true friendship. I suppose we then must ask, was the friendship real? I don't claim to have any answers, but I do have a heart. I walk strong, but never do I wish to walk through another's existence. I want to be a part of others who wish to share and explore what we've all been blessed with …Life."

As I sat back and took a good look at what I'd written, I knew that it came from the inspiration of what I was going through with Nicholas. It was hard to explain. Somehow it all had to do with Maiya, Pam, and myself. Maybe something had happened between Nicholas and Maiya, but he refused to talk about her. He just repetitively stated that she was cool and wouldn't go any further than that. Pam had left a message saying that she could feel Nicholas pulling away from her and she had the feeling that he was seeing someone else. She didn't sound too thrilled about that. She kind of hinted at wanting to take action. I didn't want to be in between whatever was happening but I felt that I should probably speak with Pam.

The phone started ringing and I wondered if it might possibly be Pam calling me back.

"Hello?"

"I finally caught up to you. I hope you don't mind me calling you at home," a soft voice said.

"That depends on who this is," I responded.

"This is Maiya, Nicholas's friend."

"Maiya," I responded cautiously.

There seemed to be a nervous tension for quite a while as we both struggled to figure out what to say next.

"Christian?"

"Yes, I'm here."

"First let me say that I enjoyed your work. I read some the other day and that's kind of why I've tried to contact you."

"Thank you, but that doesn't really explain the urgency of your messages. Is this about Nicholas?"

"Well, mostly it's about me and just the desire that I have to speak with a man. You know, a voice of reasoning from the male point of view. I want a friend, Christian. Nothing romantic or sexual."

"I hear you, Maiya, but I think that we need to speak about your situation with Nicholas. It's probably what's causing his strange reaction towards me."

"There's nothing really between us. I know he likes me a lot, or he wants me, but I want something else and I don't think he can give that to me," she explained.

"What else do you want, Maiya?"

"Something real, Christian. I want that special connection that comes from developing something over time, and I want that natural spark that you find in two people that are meant to be together."

"From outside appearances, I'm sure you attract many."

"I get my share, but none take the time to become attracted to what's inside."

My attempts to compliment her on her looks seemed to fail. Maiya was a gorgeous lady and now I could see that there was definitely more to her. She was a lady that yearned for someone to communicate with. I felt myself gradually opening up to her the longer we talked. My guard relaxed a little bit.

"Let me ask you something, Christian."

"Okay," I responded.

"Why were you so mean to me when we first met?"

I began to laugh. I was expecting that question.

"It's hard to say, Maiya."

"Why?"

"Let me first ask you, is it definitely over between Nicholas and yourself?"

"Yes, we haven't talked about it but after our last moment together I think he knew. It wasn't good, what happened. I found him not to be the gentleman that I'd hoped he would be, but I also blamed myself for that night."

She started to really get deep into whatever happened between her and Nicholas until she apparently realized that she was giving up more information than she wanted to.

I continued with my thought. "Since I know it's over between you two, I can tell you that I was mean because I'm friends with the woman that Nicholas is seeing. She's a lady that's going through some hard times right now with an addiction, but I was hoping that Nicholas would really support her through it rather than hook up with someone new."

"I see your point and I accept your apology."

I could almost hear Maiya smiling through the phone.

"Apology?" I asked.

"Yes, because you were rude!"

We both started laughing, mentally reliving that night and the mean looks I'd given her inside the nightclub. I did let her know over the phone that I thought she looked beautiful.

"Don't try to get out of it with compliments, Christian!" She laughed. "First, before we talk further, Christian, let me tell you that what Nicholas and I had was just the beginning of a friendship. We weren't seeing each other. I thought he was nice when we first met and I was looking forward to knowing what might happen. I'm glad you told me about his girl but, regardless of that, I found out the hard way that he is not the man for me."

Maiya kept returning to that night with Nicholas many times

during our conversation. She had me feeling like a boy being led to a cliff but not being allowed to see what was down below. Through her words, she showed me that something might've happened that night and just before she revealed everything, she stopped talking. Still, I refused to push for more because I wasn't completely sure that I wanted to know. I was enjoying the conversation with Maiya and I'd never expected her to be the type of person that she turned out to be. She seemed like a really cool lady and I felt extremely comfortable about getting to know her.

"Christian, thank you for tonight," Maiya said softly.

"You leaving me already?" I asked jokingly.

"I'm feeling tired, but definitely not leaving you. Some of us do work regular jobs, you know."

"Oh well, I don't know what that feels like, but that's cool. I hope we can see each other soon, Maiya. I dig your spirit. It's really sweet."

"Okay, Mr. Don't-Have-To-Work-In-The-Morning!"

It seemed like I'd lifted her spirits somewhat. That was a good feeling.

"Goodnight, friend," I said in a warm tone of voice.

She was silent for a moment. It felt as though she was giving me a hug. I could feel her breathe in my words and I could hear her sigh before she whispered, "Thank you."

7.
Discover To Endure

I was seeing the doctor that day for a reason that I'd hoped wouldn't exist for at least another few years. I knew something would happen if I ever went against my feelings and listened to someone else. I couldn't blame Stephanie for convincing me to do what I'd done, but I definitely wasn't thinking straight. I'd allowed a lustful desire to convince me to invite Nicholas over that night and now I was suffering the consequences. What was I gonna do about it all?

My friendship with Christian was so important to me and I

wondered how he'd take the news. It had been a few weeks since we'd started hanging out and they had been the best weeks of my life. We were enjoying a friendship with no pressure. I felt like I was lost on an island of comfort whenever we talked or got together. He was like magic to me and gave me such inspiration. I knew that I had affected his situation with Tanya, but she should've understood that she was the one he wanted to be with. She seemed extremely selfish and blind, if you ask me. I kept wanting to scream in her ear, "Wake up, girl!"

I'd spoken to good old Reggie and he was still trying to get with me. I had to call him because I discovered a note that he'd placed under my door. That scared me, so I called and asked him not to ever do that again. If I had walked out or been around during that moment, I would've jumped out of my skin. I felt like he was stalking me, so I called him and asked him to stop. He apologized and I hoped that was the end of it. I needed to get my daily dose of Christian pretty soon and, unfortunately, I had to call Stephanie also. She'd implied that she had some interesting news for me about Nicholas. I didn't know if I wanted to hear anything about him. Knowing her, she was likely to admit that Nicholas was one of the many guys that she'd slept with. If she had, then I felt just as sorry for her as I did for myself.

I called Christian first. It was time for my special dose. "Hi, Chris!"

"Hey, what's going on?"

"I have a doctor's appointment, but I wanted to call you before I left."

"Cool, why are you going there, Nicholas?" Christian asked.

"Nicholas? What did you call me?" I asked him before I realized the reason for the name change. "Umm, is Tanya there?" I asked sarcastically.

"Yeah, that's right."

"Tell her I said hello and that I'm dying to meet her someday. Maybe we can have a threesome."

I couldn't help but play around with Christian. It was funny to hear him try to pretend like he wasn't talking to a female.

"Now, you know I can't do that, man," Christian responded nervously.

"I hope we can talk later, Christian. I could use a hug and a little cheering up."

"Oh, is it serious?" he whispered.

"No, I just need to talk."

It was gonna be a while before I could get up the courage to tell him what was really going on, but I could never get enough of spending time with him. Talk about a man that could relax you with his mere presence. Tanya needed to wake up soon.

"Why are you going to the doctor, Maiya?"

"Huh? You said my name?"

"Yeah, Tanya went to the bathroom. Why are you going to the doctor?"

"Just my yearly check up. You know, female stuff."

"Okay. We'll talk afterwards then, right?"

"Yeah, I'll call you when I get back."

When I hung up the phone, I stood up and took a very deep breath. I wasn't sure where the day was gonna take me but I'd be glad when it was over. I truly believed that the doctor was only gonna confirm what I already knew. I'd been late that month and it didn't take a genius to figure out why.

8.
Strange Attitude

It was always nice to hear Maiya's voice, but right then I was wondering why Tanya had come over that day. She'd just been sitting there the entire time, saying absolutely nothing. She looked good wearing a long, blue denim shirt over a really short black skirt and I just loved her legs. However, she was making me nervous with the silent treatment.

"Who was that, Chris?" Tanya asked.

"That was Nicholas. He was just seeing what I was up to."

"Oh, is she pretty?"

"Excuse me!" I responded with shock.

Tanya looked away. "Never mind. Just a thought I had."

"Seems like you just came over to think and not talk to me. What's going on, Tanya?"

"Nothing. Just wanted to spend some time with you."

"Okay, so why are you so quiet?"

Tanya simply shrugged her shoulders and moved closer towards me. She held me close and put her face against mine. That felt really good and as I positioned her body closer to mine, I felt as though I were a part of her spirit. I could sense something wrong and I could feel her desire to tell me.

"You okay, Tanya?"

"Just have a lot on my mind, sweetie." Her words were followed by a kiss.

She smothered me in a special way and I couldn't help but become aroused. I closed my eyes, began smiling, and started thinking that something good was about to jump off.

Damn, I get excited easy! I thought to myself.

Tanya suddenly pulled away. "I have to go, Chris."

"You have to go?"

"Yes, I just needed to know that you still desired me."

"I don't understand that kind of thinking but, if you must know, I feel like you're the most incredible woman on the planet. You confuse the hell out of me sometimes, but I love being with you."

My mind began to drift as she began kissing me again and whispering in my ear. I was wondering about Maiya. Whenever you connect with good friends, you can tell when they are hiding something. I guess a lot of times I pressured my friends to reveal their thoughts. I was all about detailed reflections because I definitely gave back exactly what I'd asked for. Nevertheless, I could only be there for Maiya when she decided it was time to tell me what was up.

"What are you thinking about?" Tanya asked.

"Nothing, just trying to take in this feeling I'm having of being so close to you right now."

After I said that, I looked at her to see if she could tell I was lying.

She said nothing in response so maybe it worked that time.

"I have to go now, baby," she whispered.

"So soon, Tanya?"

"Yes, I just came over to be with you for a moment. As they say, it's all about quality time, not quantity."

"Sounds good to me, but I'm thinking quantity would be my choice right about now."

"Thanks for saying that, Christian."

"Anytime."

An hour went by and I found myself watching videos while waiting for Maiya to call. I kept wondering what her visit to the doctor was all about, but I dismissed it in my mind as one of those female things. I knew that was what she told me but, at first, I didn't believe her. As for Tanya, she had me feeling weird and, at the same time, I wanted her badly. That lady was definitely blessed with a great body. Sometimes I wished she was a little less confusing and more able to express herself like Maiya, but I couldn't afford to be picky. But after a while, you get a little tired of playing all the guessing games. I felt like taking Tanya out for a special night on the town. It was almost the end of October and, despite the strange moments, our relationship still continued. Hopefully it would grow into something special. I needed to take it one day at a time, though, because I didn't know which Tanya would walk through the door next time.

Just as I pondered that thought, a knock came at my door and I wondered if Tanya had changed her tune yet again and ventured back. I was shocked when I saw Pam standing on my doorstep.

"Pam? What's up, girl?"

"Hey, Chris! How's my buddy doing?"

"Who me?"

"Shut up and come here!"

We embraced and it felt great. Pam looked like a new woman. She was dressed nice and stood tall for a short lady. She had on a funky afrocentric skirt, a Dada shirt covered by a sweater, and she was wearing a scarf around her head to match the outfit. It was one of those really nice scarves, too, with rhinestones in it.

"I'm doing good, Pam, but I'm more interested in how you're doing," I told her.

"I'm doing good, Chris. It's hard sometimes, but I'm trying."

"I'm glad. You got time to sit and talk? I've missed you, Pam."

I held her hand and led her to the couch. I felt like a little boy anxious to speak to his older sister.

"I've been hearing about you, Christian."

"Oh?"

"Yeah, the women. The nice articles, which I read. I'm very proud of you."

"Thank you, but what women are you talking about?"

"I heard about someone named Tanya and then I heard about you flirting with my doctor. Thanks for your concern about me!" Pam said sarcastically.

"Oops! You heard about that?"

"Yes, so I'm wondering who else you're seeing. I thought for sure that you would've found one lady for yourself by now."

"I'm seeing Tanya, but you know being with a woman is never easy and smooth for me."

"Shut up! Don't even start with that!" Pam shouted with her hand held up. I guess she was trying to tell me to talk to the hand because I wasn't making any sense to the rest of her.

"I'm glad you're okay, Pam."

"Thank you, Chris."

Our conversation went on for an hour before she finally brought up the subject of Nicholas. I was actually keeping time because I was surprised we hadn't talked about him sooner.

"When is the last time you spoke with Nicholas?" she asked.

"Umm, it's been about two weeks now, maybe more."

"Are you two still friends? What's going on?"

It was beginning to feel like she was probing for answers to indirect questions. I could see it in her face. Pam believed something was going on that no one was telling her. Actually, I wasn't really sure what to say to her.

"I still consider him my best friend, but I'm confused about the tension between us as well," I said.

"You must know where it comes from, Chris. I need to know what's going on."

"I'm sorry, Pam. You're gonna have to ask Nicholas. If I told you where I thought this tension came from, then you might run out of here angry and confront Nicholas without thinking clearly."

I had tried to keep my mouth shut but it wasn't working. I seemed to be confusing her more, making matters even worse.

"Something's going on, Chris. I thought you could be straight with me like good friends are supposed to be."

"I want to, Pam, but certain things shouldn't come from me."

"That's not right, Chris. Now I have to go see Nicholas just to ask him what's going on?"

"Yes, that seems like the best thing to do at this point."

"How about if I call him from here?"

"If that's what you wish to do, Pam, go ahead."

Pam didn't hesitate to go over to the phone. She dialed the number in record speed and I felt it necessary to leave the room. I could still hear her from the distance, no matter which room in my apartment I tried to hide in. The tone of her voice had me worried about answering more questions. She was obviously about to go off.

"Nicholas! I'm over Christian's place and I want to know what's going on between you two!" she demanded.

I wished I could hear his response but I imagined he was ducking her questions just like I was.

"Why the distance between you guys? You used to be good friends and hang out all the time."

Listening to the silence in between each time Pam spoke had me feeling like I could scratch the paint off the walls.

"That's bullshit. I haven't heard from you since I started my treatments. You've been staying away from me and now I'm noticing that your friendship with Chris has changed somehow. Can you explain that to me?"

Pam was loud and furious. She wasted no time letting Nicholas have it. She told him off about everything from the lack of spending time with me to the fact that he never called or visited her when she was away.

"Are you listening to me?" Pam shouted. "Hold on! The other line is ringing. Hello?"

I was about to have a heart attack because she was answering my phone when her temper was boiling hot. It drove me crazy that I could only hear one side of the conversation between Pam and whoever was calling me.

"Girl, I'm the one who should be asking you since you called, but this is Pam and you are?"

Well, at least I knew it was a female on the phone. If it was Tanya, that was immediate trouble because she jumped to conclusions as quickly as Pam did.

"Yeah, he's here, but you need to call back or I can tell him you called. I'm on the other line with my man, just in case you're wondering," Pam said.

That was a relief. I didn't have to worry about that person thinking that Pam and I had something going on.

"He's never mentioned you to me. How long have you two known each other?" Pam asked.

Her curiosity was starting to take over and so was mine. Pam knew about Tanya and she knew about the doctor so that left one person.

"Just friends, huh?" Pam said sarcastically.

Damn, that had to be Maiya.

"Take care, Maiya. I'll tell him you called."

Yep, that's exactly who it was.

Pam immediately clicked back over to Nicholas. I could tell she had to search her mind for a moment because of the interruption.

"Now, back to what I was saying."

Once again I had to listen in the distance. I started to walk a little bit closer to the living room where Pam was so that I could possibly hear the conversation a little clearer. Of course I could still only hear Pam.

"I'm not upset! Well, actually I am upset, but I just want to know what's going on between you two and why you seem to be shutting me out!"

I was standing there listening to Pam and wondering if the entire apartment building could hear her shouting.

"So, who is Miss Thang that I just spoke with?" Pam asked.

Now she really had me worried. Pam was about to start something by letting Nicholas know that Maiya had just called. Hopefully he had no idea who she was talking about.

"Some chick, Maiya, just called here!"

Oh shit, here we go! I thought to myself.

"Well, do you know anything about her?" Pam asked.

She seemed to be getting pretty annoyed with Nicholas. I figured he probably wasn't answering her, but I bet he was wondering why Maiya was calling me.

"Something's going on here and I don't understand it. I'll talk to you later, Nicholas, cause y'all making me tired!" Pam said.

Pam didn't sound like she waited for any response. She hung up the phone while I tried to re-enter the room as quietly as I could.

"I'm gonna go, Christian. Y'all gonna have to work this out somehow."

"Sorry, Pam. I just thought it would be better if you spoke with Nicholas, that's all."

Pam gave me a pretty mean look before heading towards the front door.

"Did he mention me?" I asked her.

"A little bit. By the way, someone named Maiya just called you."

Pam walked out the door and didn't look back. I had no chance to respond or ask her anything before she left. More than that, I wanted to know what Nicholas might've said to her. Once again my phone was ringing and it took me a moment to collect myself before I answered it.

"Hello," I answered with my mind not yet focused.

"Hey, man, what's up with Maiya calling you? You guys didn't even get along when you met her at the club. What's up with that?"

Nicholas fired questions at me one after the other. I had no chance to answer calmly.

"Are you trying to get with Maiya? You saw how fine she was and now you have to fuck with her, huh?" Nicholas continued.

"Say what?"

"Fuck you! Are we trading women now? Maybe you were messing with Pam just now, too! Do I get to fuck Tanya?" Nicholas shouted.

"Hold on, man! Why are you so angry?"

"I don't need this shit! You ain't right, Chris! Now I see why Maiya won't speak to me anymore. Because you're in the picture now!"

"Well explain it to me, Nicholas! I want to know what happened between you and Maiya. Why does she get quiet when I mention your name? Why are you always avoiding talking about her?"

I fired questions at him with the same intensity that he'd displayed to me.

"What did she tell you?" Nicholas asked.

"She told me nothing, so far, but I'm wondering if you did something like force yourself on her. You wouldn't do some shit like that, would you?"

"Fuck you, Chris! I had sex with her, but she was into it."

"Okay, Nicholas. I guess we have a new understanding then."

I was hurt by the anger he was showing towards me. I felt like I could no longer trust the person that I'd once considered my best friend ever.

"I think you two were putting up a front in the club. You probably fucked her before me, Chris, and to play it off, you acted like you didn't like her."

"I don't care what you believe, Nicholas. That was my first time meeting her. You're trippin now, man!"

"Yeah, we'll see then!" Nicholas shouted just before hanging up the phone.

I was feeling really down at that point. I couldn't believe I'd had such an angry conversation with a so-called good friend. I felt trapped in a circle of broken trust and angry emotions. Pam walked out with no desire to speak with me. That alone was a blow to my heart because I thought the world of Pam. Now I was convinced that my friendship with Nicholas was history; especially after that conversation. How could we possibly return to anything civil after what had just went down? The way he was talking to me and accusing me of sleeping with Maiya was crazy. But now I knew something did happen between those two. I definitely wasn't going to jump to conclusions where Maiya was concerned because I still wanted her to tell me what happened. I don't believe you can find truth when everyone speaks with emotion and says things with anger in their hearts. Nicholas and I were shouting at each other and not really talking to each other. I prayed I never experienced that kind of anger with a beautiful spirit like Maiya, or Tanya for that matter.

9.
Loss Of Time

I couldn't believe that I'd allowed personal turmoil to affect my job. I missed the deadline on my story about friendship. I didn't feel qualified to write it because of my failed friendship with Nicholas. I seriously doubted that we would ever speak again. It had been a week since the emotional exchange. I had nightmares, constantly wondering why it had to happen in the first place. When Maiya called me later that night, I found myself taking it out on her. Being human, I just needed to vent my emotions. I picked the wrong time to do that but, luckily, she took my call later that night. I apologized to the point that it almost seemed like a proposal and I even sent her flowers the next day. Recalling the initial conversation, I felt really bad because I'd accused her of everything that had gone wrong.

"Maiya, you've caused my friendship to end. Why couldn't you just tell me what was going on from the start?"

"Christian? What are you saying?" she responded frantically.

"I'm saying, you have to be honest! How can I trust you if you're not telling me things?"

"Why are you angry with me? I really need you right now!" she pleaded.

I couldn't believe I was so hard on her. After she hung up on me, I went for a long walk outside. I was beating myself up because I knew I was wrong. I took everything out on her when that anger should've only been directed at Nicholas. When I called Maiya later on, she was quiet the entire time. She answered the phone in tears so I knew that I'd hurt her pretty badly. She told me that she never stopped crying after we'd spoken that first time. When we were finished with the second conversation, it was like making up with a baby sister and I even promised to take her out.

"Where you going to take me?" she asked.

"I think I owe you that dance, remember?"

"What old romantic movie have you been watching, man?" she asked, brushing off my attempts to be suave.

I was happy to hear her laugh at that moment and it continuously brought a smile to my face. I couldn't believe that I'd gone off on her the way that I did and I couldn't thank her enough for allowing me to apologize. Losing a friend is like losing a special time in your life. I had memories of great times with Nicholas, but since we no longer associated with each other, we could never relive the good times. Never is a very long time and that didn't feel too good.

10.
Lunch Date

It was a new beginning for me as I waited for my lunch date to arrive. I'd heard very little from Tanya, but that was mostly my fault because I'd been playing the hermit role recently. I'd been taking things hard. Pam still wasn't speaking to me and I'd heard that she was considering relocating out of state. I prayed that she'd see the light and call me up soon. Pam had always been a dear friend, but her doubts and confusion were understandable. That was yet another reason why I couldn't see going through with the article on friendship. Without a doubt, I could write about the methods to ruin friendships. It all boiled down to communication and trust. I played all of my mistakes over and over in my mind and contemplated writing the thoughts down in case I needed them later for an article on self-pity.

"Hello, Christian?" a female voice said in the distance.

I heard her repeat it a couple of times before I focused on her.

"Sorry I'm a little late," she said, extending her hand out in front of me.

The hand was gorgeous with long fingers, natural-colored nail polish, and one diamond filled ring. I was tempted to kiss it, but that wasn't my style. Plus, with my recent luck, she might've taken her hand away, which would've been embarrassing.

"Did you have to wait long?" she asked.

"No, I kinda lost track of the time anyway," I responded.

"You do seem lost. I was watching you for a moment before I yelled out to you."

"I seem lost? Why do you say that?"

"Just an observation."

"Well, I was thinking about the past few days and all the nonsense that I've been through. I had a falling out with my friend and that seems beyond repair."

"Well, hopefully I can cure any sadness you might have today."

"I believe you've already given me reason to smile, Sabrina. You're a good doctor after all, huh?" I told her sarcastically.

"Oh, don't start with me! You remember what I did to you at the hospital."

"Yeah, you operate good!"

It was nice to experience a breath of fresh air in the form of a lovely woman. Sabrina Oliver had me leaning forward with my hands underneath my chin. I paid attention to everything she expressed to me. We sat in an outdoor café, enjoying a light lunch, and talking about her life during medical school. It was really nice to see such a beautiful woman so into her work. I was smiling so much that, at one point, she became embarrassed by the attention I was giving her. I couldn't help but smile in her presence. She was still as fine as ever. Perhaps even finer than when I saw her that night at the hospital.

"You're a good listener, Christian. Now it's your turn," she said.

"My turn for what?"

"Your turn to share what goes on in the mind of a man like you."

I had to take a minute to think about that. She'd turned the spotlight on me and I wasn't sure if I was ready to display myself to her. I was usually the first person to reveal his innermost thoughts, but I was struggling this time.

"Why are you so hesitant?"

"Not really sure," I responded.

"Is this part of the reason you were lost in thought earlier?"

"Not really, but I guess with all the recent turmoil and losing friends, I'm just feeling a little battle-fatigued."

"That's not good. Don't let yourself get stressed out."

"Thanks, I won't."

"Is that your beeper going off or is it mine?" she asked.

We both were interrupted by the sound.

"Hmm, I believe it's mine," I responded.

"You going to make a call? I'll wait for you."

"Yeah. Thanks, Sabrina. I'll be right back."

I made my way to the phone booth in a hurry. I recognized Tanya's number. I felt a sense of relief and excitement, hoping that she was calling to see if we could hook up later. I punched in her number as fast as I could. I'd been missing her a lot lately.

"Hello?" she answered.

"Tanya, I was hoping to hear from you. How have you been?"

"Excuse me, Christian, but what did you tell Nicholas?"

"What do you mean?"

"He called me this morning and he must've had some kind of problem. He told me that I was supposed to get with him because you'd hooked up with his lady?"

I was shocked by what Tanya was saying to me. I looked over towards Sabrina sitting at our table, and had a feeling that she could sense something was disturbing me. I had to turn around so that she couldn't see my facial expressions or possibly read my lips.

"Nicholas is very angry with me right now, Tanya. You don't need to involve yourself in our fight," I said calmly.

"I'm sorry, but I think I'm already involved. My name's been dragged into this and I want to know what you said to him. Are you sleeping with Maiya?"

"Not at all, Tanya. You're the only woman I've been intimate with this year. Nicholas is accusing me of all kinds of things involving Maiya, but he's just reacting to the fact that she no longer wishes to be involved with him."

"Well, I'm not liking this one bit, Chris! He told me that you two were exchanging women and that I needed to come to his place so he and I could have sex. I don't like being put in the middle of whatever it is you two have going on."

"I understand that completely, Tanya, but I can't control Nicholas. I'm trying to figure out why he's so upset with me. His girlfriend Pam no longer speaks with me, either, and now here you are confronting me about the entire situation."

Tanya became quiet for a moment. I could hear her breathing like she was boiling inside. I was preparing myself for her to begin screaming but she surprised me by doing the opposite.

"I don't like being a part of this, so I'd appreciate it if you'd tell your friend not to call me please," she said calmly and with no emotion.

"I'll see what I can do, Tanya."

"Bye, Chris."

Her goodbye seemed final. I stood there with the phone in my hand trying to pretend like the conversation didn't end so abruptly. The situation with Nicholas was getting ugly. I wondered what else might become of the fallout surrounding our defunct friendship.

"You okay?" Sabrina asked. I turned around to find her hand on my shoulder.

"Yeah, I'll be okay."

We walked back to the table together and that alone was very comforting. I wasn't sure if I was going to be good company for such a great lady. I really hated to trash her day with my drama. Maybe Sabrina expected to go someplace after lunch because she was dressed nicely in a three-quarter length beige coat over a two-piece black pantsuit. Yes, indeed, Dr. Oliver seriously had it going on.

"I guess I shouldn't ask about your phone conversation," she said.

"Well, just another person that I'll have to add to the overall body count."

I tried to make light of the situation but it was definitely nothing to laugh at.

"You must be involved in something serious, huh?"

"Kind of, but it mostly deals with my friend that I was with at the hospital."

I didn't want my situation scaring the beautiful doctor away. I couldn't imagine her going through any kind of relationship problems, but I guess we all go through drama at one point in our lives.

"I won't pry, but you know I'm curious," she said with a cute grin.

"It's such a long story, but I can tell you that my friend believes that I'm involved with a lady that he's interested in."

"Is that the woman who was my patient?"

"No, it's another lady that he met recently. I'm now friends with this lady, but not at all romantically involved."

"Oh really, and who are you romantically involved with?" she asked, stirring her drink slowly with a straw.

"Honestly? I'm involved with the woman that just paged me but, because of all the drama and turmoil, I believe that's come to an end as well."

"Sorry to hear that. Do you love her?"

"That's hard to say. I care for her, but we've only been seeing each other for a couple months now."

"So how do you feel about meeting or perhaps dating others?" Sabrina asked cautiously.

That question was interesting to me because it hinted at the possibility of us getting together. I liked every aspect of that possibility and began to wonder what would become of a friendship between us. Thoughts of Maiya also danced across my mind. I began to wonder about her availability to me, now that it seemed Tanya was walking out of my life. I was at a fork in the road of life waiting for a decision to be made. It wasn't like I had the kind of choice to make where I could snap my fingers and either one of the women would then be mine. It felt great bonding with Sabrina, but where would our interests lie after we got to know each other? I knew what it was like to be with Maiya. Our friendship was really becoming something special. I could be intimate with her on an emotional level and not have to worry about the consequences. How deep could I go with Sabrina?

"Are you deep in thought?" Sabrina asked.

"Huh?"

"I think I lost you again, Chris!"

"Sorry, I'm still here."

After our lunch together, we decided to walk down the boulevard and continue our conversation on foot. I loved the way she swayed when she walked. Occasionally she would brush against me and smile, bringing attention to the thoughts behind her lovely eyes.

"This is a beautiful day, don't you think?" she asked.

"Yes, it's pretty nice!" I responded.

"Wait until you see it during Christmas time. This area is really nice and romantic."

"I can tell you like this time of year, don't you?"

"Yeah, it's my favorite. Don't you like it, too?"

"Well, yes, I like it because of the weather and everything, but for some reason I tend to lose friends during this time of the year."

My words took away her smile. "Excuse me?"

"That's okay. I don't want to start talking serious again because I want you to have fun, Sabrina."

"Great, let's go in here!"

Sabrina grabbed my hand and took me into a store that sold miniature merry-go-rounds and porcelain dolls. She was so excited about being inside that she squeezed my hand tightly. I couldn't believe that such a serious doctor would become almost childlike at the mere sight of what we found in the store. She watched in amazement as the merry-go-round spun around and played sweet sounding music. When I pointed in the direction of a doll that stood out to me, she almost started to cry.

"Oh my God!" she said with her hands pressed against her face.

"You okay?"

"Yeah, that doll just brings back memories of something my father gave me."

She walked over to the doll slowly, as though it were pulling her strings and guiding her towards it. While she was looking at the doll, my pager went off. I looked at the number and it was Maiya. I couldn't help but smile and wonder what she wanted.

"I hope that's not another crisis," Sabrina said.

"I don't think it is, but I'll call later."

"Are you sure?"

"Yeah, I'll wait."

As we walked out the store, Sabrina kept looking at me in a funny way. I wasn't sure if she was trying to read my thoughts or if she wanted me to do something.

"You're thinking about calling that number, aren't you?"

"What do you mean?" I asked innocently.

"The person that paged you is on your mind and you want to call them, don't you?"

"Yeah, I do."

"I don't mind, Christian. I need to get back to work anyway, so maybe we can talk again later today or sometime during the week."

I could sense a slight disappointment in her voice and I really hated to see her joy come to an end.

"I'd like very much to call you later," I told her.

"Okay, you have my number so give me a call," she said as she walked the rest of the way to her car alone.

I stood there watching her walk away until she was out of sight. Sabrina had shown me two sides of her personality and she had me totally intrigued. I found her to be the ultimate professional doctor: strong and intelligent. But when I had her in that store with the dolls, she reminded me of an innocent little girl. She walked around in total amazement with her eyes filled to the point where I was waiting for a tear to drop. I felt guilty that my situation ruined her beautiful moment. I guess I took those things too personal, but I hoped I could apologize to her in some way.

11.
Casualty To The Game

Christian would be over soon and my heart was racing like crazy. We hadn't seen each other that much in the last three weeks. He'd been working hard with his writing and making sincere attempts to win back his friendships with Pam and Nicholas. I wasn't sure if he'd given up on Tanya, but I knew he missed her very much. He'd made no attempts at romance with me and, even though part of me wished that he would, I was glad that he hadn't thus far. I had to tell him that I was pregnant by Nicholas. I'd kept it a secret up until then, but if I waited until I started showing, I was sure Christian wouldn't be too happy. I felt bad enough about hiding something from him all that time. That was something I couldn't do because he gave so much without expecting anything in return.

My phone was ringing and I assumed it was Christian waiting to be buzzed in.

"Hello," I answered.

"Hey, girl!"

"Stephanie?"

"Yeah, it's me. How are you holding up?"

"I'm okay. Nobody knows yet except you, so I haven't experienced any drama yet."

"That's good, but I'm sorry for convincing you to get with that fool at all."

"Well, it's done now, Stephanie, so don't even feel bad about it."

"Nah, girl. I ran into that fool at the store and he was getting all up in my face and talking about you. He told me about you two having sex and how he was about to hook up with Tanya next. Who in the hell is Tanya? I thought he was losing his mind."

"Tanya is someone that Christian was dating, but they fell out and it was because of the things that Nicholas said. You shouldn't even pay attention to him, girl. He's a trifling man and he's just trying to make things hard for everybody right now."

"Damn, girl, he scared me and you know I usually don't pay attention to these fools when they start acting up."

In the five years that I'd known Stephanie, I'd never heard her sound so concerned. She had me fearing what Nicholas might do next. Telling him about my pregnancy would be the hardest thing I'd ever have to do because I wanted nothing to do with him.

"I'm telling Christian today," I said to Stephanie.

"Oh yeah? He better not flip out like I imagine his ex-friend will."

She had a point, but I believed with all my heart and soul that Christian would stick by me no matter what.

12.
Flight To Chicago

I wondered how Maiya would respond once I cancelled our date that day. Unfortunately, I had to leave town for a funeral. Maiya would understand. Why was I even second-guessing that? I hesitated about calling her, but I couldn't possibly leave town without her knowing.

"Hello?" Maiya answered.

"Hey, Maiya!"

"Christian! What time are you coming over?" she asked excitedly.

"I can't make it after all."

"Why, you okay?"

"Yeah, but I have to go out of town for a funeral."

"Oh, I'm sorry. Is it someone you were close to?"

"A friend. What did you want to talk to me about, anyway?"

"I'd rather tell you in person, Christian. It can wait. Just have a safe trip, okay?"

Maiya almost seemed relieved that I wasn't coming over.

Maybe she was truly wrestling with whatever she had to tell me. I was kind of nervous about going to see her, anyway. The funeral was going to be sad and it came at a time when the loss was truly great. I was curious to see who showed up and who didn't.

I was on my way to Chicago for the funeral less than two hours after I'd spoken with Maiya. I was traveling light because I'd get there just in time and I planned on hopping in the nearest taxi to get to the funeral home. It was my understanding that the cemetery was in the same place where the service would be held. I'd also heard the grounds were really beautiful so I hoped it would be good place to say goodbye. Death is so final when it sneaks up unexpectedly. I was just grateful to be able to attend and pay my last respects.

I decided to look on the brighter side of things for a moment and thought about Tanya's call the night before. It was like a beautiful reunion. We caught up on old times and she told me that she realized that I could never do the things that Nicholas accused me of doing. Apparently, she'd had some sort of revelation.

"I wish you'd spoken to me more about it, Tanya," I whispered into the phone.

"I know."

"I would've even gone so far as to give you Maiya's phone number and let you speak with her."

I was sounding cocky but I meant every word of it. Tanya continued to apologize for the harsh way that she'd spoken with me. Once we got past all that nonsense, everything was back to normal.

"So, when are we gonna fuck?" I asked her, borrowing that line from the movie *Boomerang*. Grace Jones said that to Eddie Murphy and now it was my turn to use the same corny line.

"Oh my goodness!" Tanya responded.

I caught her off guard and we started laughing all night long over the phone. All the tension had disappeared between us. She wanted to come with me to the funeral, but it was something that I wanted to do alone. She was really worried about me going, but sometimes you have to put a closure on things in order to move on gracefully. I was just thankful to know that she wanted to try again and continue the beauty of where we were headed.

"I miss your hugs, Christian," she said to me.

"I miss getting my moan and groan on!"

"Oh my goodness! What has gotten into you?"

I shocked her completely but she still seemed elated to be talking again.

"Just playing, Tanya. I want us to get back to love. Know what I'm saying?"

"Is that right? Are you trying to romance me?"

"If you can feel it, then you know I speak with sincerity. I tried to be macho and think I could get over you without a struggle, but I was dying inside because there was no reason for us to end what we'd started. When we're together, it feels like magic. Things have been tough in the beginning and I even remember times when I thought you were a selfish…"

She cut me off. "You don't have to go there, Christian. I get your point."

She knew that I was about to use the B word and, for once, it was appropriate.

"We've done too much making up, Christian, in such a short time."

"I know, Tanya. I love passionate relationships, but we shouldn't have these struggles over small things created by others."

"You've made your point, baby. So we gonna fuck when you come back?" she asked in her sexiest Grace Jones imitation.

"Damn!"

"I got you that time, huh?"

"Yes to both questions." I told her eagerly.

I was feeling good after that conversation but then reality sunk in after I realized that I'd be headed to Chicago the next day for a sad occasion. As we began our descent, I hoped for a smooth landing. I was nervous because I hadn't flown in years.

I'd been working on a special essay about friendship. I missed the other deadline, but this time I felt as though I'd have something to say because of what had happened between my friends and me. I decided to call it "Circle of friends and emotions."

I loved the fact that Tanya had returned. I had beautiful Maiya constantly wishing me well and being there for me as a friend. I had a distant friendship with Sabrina and before Pam left town, she'd promised to keep in touch. All in all, I still felt the circle had been destroyed and would never truly be repaired because of Nicholas. His anger was motivated by jealousy and a refusal to give up on a false belief that Maiya belonged to him. She told me of some guy named Reggie who felt like he owned her, too, and that made me ask her, "What are you doing to these men?"

"I have no idea!" she responded.

Shoot, I was about to write it off as some sort of "pussy control" but I didn't want to sound too sexist in front of my educated friend.

It would take some major soul-searching and a lot of humility for Nicholas and I to become friends again. I believed in my heart that I could do that. I would've given anything to make the circle complete, but the destruction had in many ways become final. When anger and jealousy come into play, friendships shatter like glass. I cared about everyone in the circle, but right then I was constantly bending over to pick up glass. The pieces were sharp and cut me with memories that hurt but taught me so much about the value of life and the finality of death.

Sometimes I wondered if I was giving up too fast? The answer could've only been no because I was willing to make amends. The problem was that Nicholas was hell bent on destroying the circle even more. All energies had been placed in the direction of negativity with no chance for a change in direction. I didn't want to be a part of that energy so I simply went where I could remain in the direction of love. Right then, I needed Tanya in my life. I also needed Maiya and anyone else that was willing to be a positive influence. I'd bought Sabrina that porcelain doll that she liked so much and sent it to her. She was thrilled to death. We talked for a long time and she was left with the impression that I felt strongly about another woman, that woman being Tanya. She told me that she enjoyed herself with me and would love it if I'd keep a star next to her name so that I'd immediately recognize her as a good friend. I was in heaven after that conversation because she was a great lady.

Chicago was dreary that day and I was glad I'd come equipped with a long coat. It was freezing out there and I didn't come all that way to freeze to death. The cabdriver was pretty cool. At least, he didn't take the long route. Maybe he was being respectful since he was taking me to the cemetery. I wanted to get the ordeal over with and return to Tanya in Los Angeles. I truly missed my lady, even though one moment she'd make me angry and the next she'd have me fall head over heels in love with her again.

All the funeral stuff had me thinking deeply about my own future and why it seemed like people had to endure so much to find happiness. Why couldn't I just connect with one woman and live happily ever after? Then again, that might have been boring. Maybe I was where I was supposed to be. I was wading through the drama and picking up wisdom at every corner. All I knew was that I had to make things count. As they always say, life is short and sometimes it takes death to make us appreciate it. Death is like the proverbial ton of bricks falling on our heads. My trip to Chicago was an eye opener and, hopefully, it would make me a better man. That kind of shit would be boring so I guess I was where I was supposed to be.

Winter seemed to have hit Chicago early. It was the first week of November and there was already snow on the ground. It was nice to see snow, but I had no time to enjoy it. The road we traveled was rather slick and we were on the last stretch leading up to the cemetery. I could see the beautiful green trees standing tall in the distance, strategically placed among the well-kept grass. The flowers appeared damp but still hadn't lost their beauty.

I felt I would need to make a return visit because I knew I'd never forget my friend. I had no idea what I would say to the family and found myself struggling to swallow as the car got closer. I tried desperately to fight back tears. I'd been strong up until then and I assumed that a little longer shouldn't be too hard. As the tall trees appeared to be parting in front of us on the narrow road, I could see just ahead and to the right, a small crowd of people dressed in warm black clothing standing over the burial site. I'd missed the first part of the service, but managed to make it to the actual burial.

As I approached the area on foot, I noticed no familiar faces. I felt kind of out of place until I saw my friend's casket. While I could not see her, I imagined her looking peaceful, unlike the last time I'd seen her. The closer I got, the more my feet struggled to take the next step. My legs felt heavy and my heart weighed a ton. Now that I was there, I wished there were someone beside me to hold me up.

I decided to keep my memories focused on the good times we'd spent together. The time I dropped one of her huge sculptures or the time we snuck in an X-rated movie theater only to be bored at the action on screen. We ended up falling asleep until a guy masturbating in the next aisle scared us because he came so loud. I couldn't help but smile at those moments.

Why are you leaving me, Pam? I thought to myself.

A couple of tears finally fell from my eyes. I was angry with her for a moment because she was such a beautiful and creative soul. She'd found so much happiness within herself when she sculpted. The only thing that equaled the love she had for sculpting was the false since of security that she'd found with drugs. She was convinced that they added to her creativity, when all the while they were destroying her desire to continue developing her God given talent. She had no more time for creating because she was so busy getting high and escaping the world. Another thing that made her happy was her love for Nicholas and seeing that he wasn't there to be with her made me lose even more respect for him. She would've done anything for him and, in her last days, it seemed as though she had no idea whether he loved her or not.

I was thankful that I'd gotten a chance to speak with her before she passed away and we'd promised to get together. I was hoping to make the trip to Chicago so that she could take me to a Bulls game and finally do a statue of me deep in thought. I could always hear her laughter whenever I thought of the request that I made a while back. Pam was at peace and I only wished I could say the same about myself. I wasn't at peace, but I was on a special journey headed that way. Through friendship and love, I believed I could find it. And through life, I believed I could demonstrate what it took to get there. While standing over Pam's casket, a few more tears fell.

"I'm gonna miss you so much, Pam, but I'll be okay. I'll keep my eye on the sky every once in a while to see if you're giving me a thumbs up. When I see a star, I'll know it's you smiling down on me. I love you," I said as I kneeled before the casket to pray and say goodbye. My thoughts weighed a ton as I left my friend behind, resting in peace. Life goes on, but it was going to take a moment for me to get over the loss that I felt. I could no longer hold Pam's hand. Instead, I can only revisit memories to see her smile again.

13.
In My Dreams I've Told You

A week elapsed before I finally contacted Maiya. I needed to know what she wanted to tell me and anxiety was about to drive me crazy. Once I pushed her into a corner, so to speak, I figured it out by myself by putting two and two together.

"Are you pregnant, Maiya?" I asked her cautiously.

"Yep," she responded.

I remembered how she'd been hesitant to discuss her night with Nicholas a while back. I always thought something had happened, but I didn't want to accept it. She hadn't seen him since that night, which made me believe that it was a bad experience. Nicholas told me that they had sex, but I'd been waiting for Maiya to tell me about it, or at least let me know that it was the reason for so much tension going around. Nicholas had so much anger in his heart that I tried to avoid any kind of confrontation with him.

"Did he force himself on you, Maiya?" I asked her.

"No," she responded quietly.

"It's hard to explain, Christian. It was the way it happened. It wasn't like I'd hoped for. He was able to put himself inside of me. I guess I have to take responsibility as well, but I just thought he'd be more of a gentleman about it and make the night special. Instead it was quick and he just took what he wanted. It didn't seem to matter who I was." Her tears made it harder for her to continue speaking.

After Maiya had composed herself, we continued to talk further about that night with Nicholas and how it made her feel. She told me that, for a long time, she'd been rehearsing breaking the news to me in her mind. I was blessed to have someone value my friendship the way that she did, but it was hard to believe that my opinion mattered so much to her. I guess that was an insult to myself to even think that way.

"You're one of a kind, Christian. Your friendship has taught me so much. I know you've probably heard this from other women, but you have a way of teaching without making it obvious. You're a beautiful man with a passionate soul and I hope that Tanya recognizes it soon. I can't believe she let you out of her arms for so long."

"Damn, girl, are you trying to make my head big or something?"

"I could go on for days, sweetie."

She asked me if I'd received a letter in the mail that she'd written to me. I let her know that I did and that I was very touched by her words. I believe she was making sure that I knew how much she cared about me before letting me know about the pregnancy. Guess she wanted to ease the shock or, perhaps, soften the blow.

"I'd been walking around with that letter in my purse for a week before I sent it." She sighed.

"I enjoyed the letter, Maiya, and I'll hold on to it forever. It's hard to believe that the things I've said and done have touched you so deeply. I'm blessed by your friendship and thankful that you didn't let my early attitude keep you away," I said, referring to our first meeting in the nightclub.

"It did keep me away!" She laughed.

I repeated to her some of the words she'd written in her letter. Words of praise and kindness, words that reflected the beauty of friendship, and words that imagined the fulfillment of love. She'd touched me with her own wisdom and by the way she questioned her journey, her experience.

"Can a soul become wise without dealing with pain?" she'd

written as an opening statement in her letter about friendship and life.

In her letter, she'd shown me the power of caring for another and how we all affect each other's lives. I can only imagine what effect Nicholas must've been having on those around him. When we touch lives, I always wonder what the effect will be over the long run. Like most people, I wondered if I had done things differently, could I have saved the life of a friend. I doubted that I could've changed the outcome of what happened with Pam, but I believed I'd contributed in a positive way to her journey. That belief kept me going most of the time, especially those days when I thought about her a lot.

Going back to Maiya's letter, I could feel the strength of her desire to move on with her life. I was proud that she wasn't allowing this to destroy her but, at the same time, I'd noticed that she kept to herself a lot more. Her spirit was so alive before and she was always out in the world "doing her thang!" There was one part of her letter that really made me smile and I suppose it was kind of an ego boost, too. I sat there laughing at myself because I'd actually highlighted that portion of the letter. I really felt good about being there for her as a friend. The letter read:

There are many men in pursuit of me, that's the God's honest truth, but never have I run across a man like you in my life. Your words and emotions are powerful. Your kindness and sweetness are delightful. Your friendship is priceless. Your words hit like a fist. You don't make waves, as they say. You make indentations on a person's life. If no one else ever really sees that about you, I have. I believe you have to be dead not to see that about you.

Words like that made me wonder what I'd been saying to such an incredible woman. Was my reflection the same with others? I wondered what my affect on Tanya was and if she would've described me in the same manner? I read that part of the letter to Maiya and she laughed at me for recognizing that section.

"Oh you love that, don't you, Christian?"

"Yeah, I think I want to have it framed and put next to a poster-size picture of myself deep in thought, just like I used to say to Pam."

"Oh don't even start getting a big head!"

"I won't. Don't worry," I reassured her.

"How are you holding up after the funeral?" Maiya asked.

"I'm cool. It was sad seeing Pam in the casket. I was in tears most of the time and couldn't find any strength to meet and talk with her family. They were probably wondering, who is this stranger? I was just focused on saying some last words to Pam and somehow letting her know that I loved her and appreciated her friendship."

As I described the day of the funeral in detail to Maiya, she began to cry. She could feel my loss and prayed that things would be less stressful from that moment on. We talked further about her plans on keeping the baby and her desire to keep Nicholas out of it completely. I understood her decision but I believed that he should at least be told about her pregnancy.

"Please don't tell him, Chris!" she begged.

"No, it has to come from you, Maiya."

"I will soon," she responded.

That was the end of that conversation and now my attention was focused on getting together with Tanya. She and I had plans to see a movie and have dinner. I wanted to take her to a restaurant but she insisted on cooking for me instead. I think she just wanted to rip my clothes off and I was always happy to oblige that request. It had been a while since I'd seen her and just the thought made me want to stand at attention in more ways than one. She was incredible and I always fit just right in her arms. If she was ready to lose that fear of love, then I was hoping to connect with her in a way that was both emotional and spiritual. I wanted the opportunity to love her on a level that would take us beyond friendship and into a bond that allowed me to communicate in ways that very few seemed to understand. I needed her inspiration in order to touch the world when I spoke about love. I needed to become a part of her soul so that I could continue to grow as a man.

Right then, I could hear Pam's voice in my head as I looked to the sky.

"You need to stop trippin, man! Stop talking so much and do your thang!"

"I hear you, friend," I said, blowing a kiss to the heavens where I knew she was resting.

14.
Introduce Your Life To Me

Tanya was waiting for me in her living room. She made herself comfortable after we returned from enjoying a movie. I had an absolutely good time eating some Junior Mints and occasionally reaching over to spill some popcorn on her lap. I was trying to grab as much as I could, but you know how you always end up dropping most of what you pick up anyway. Tanya had a stomachache from all that fake butter I poured over her large popcorn. I made her drink a lot of water afterwards so I thought she would make it okay. When we arrived at her condo, she slipped away to the back to put on something more comfortable. When Tanya rejoined me in the living room, she instantly lit up my smile. She was wearing only my flannel shirt that she'd taken and never returned. I hadn't forgotten about that Fubu jersey either. I still hadn't gotten that back. Nevertheless, I found myself putting those issues on hold because, as Tanya stood before me, I could tell she wasn't wearing anything underneath my flannel shirt. That had a brotha excited about his immediate future.

Now it was my turn to freshen up as I checked myself out in her bathroom mirror. She told me that she was ready to talk seriously about our relationship. She wanted me to express myself in the same manner that I used when writing about life. She said she wanted an introduction into my soul. Shoot, I thought I had been doing that all along anyway but, if not, then I planned on communicating with her like never before. My steps from that moment would be more than physical. They'd be spiritual and they'd push the emotional envelope constantly.

"Come on, Christian. Introduce your life to me," she spoke softly when I entered the room.

I moved closer and she took my hand. I leaned forward. My lips touched her cheek as softly as a feather until I reached her ear.

"Why didn't you believe in me before, Tanya?" I whispered.

"What do you mean?"

"Nicholas told you something and, without question, you believed him. You accepted jealousy over love."

"I'm sorry," she said as my hand made its way inside the flannel shirt.

"Your heart's beating fast, Tanya. What's wrong?"

"Nothing," she responded nervously.

I could feel her body temperature changing as little sweat beads formed at the top of her head. We kissed very passionately. Tanya was taken by surprise. Apparently, she'd never realized the depth of my desire for her. We stopped kissing for a moment and gazed deeply into each other's eyes.

"No more questions after tonight, Tanya. I already know what I want and I'm hoping you'll meet me where I stand, willing and ready."

"Ready?"

"Yes. Ready to believe that everything is possible. That you and I are possible."

We sat on the couch looking into each other's eyes but it wasn't long before Tanya forced me to lean back against the armrest. She slowly began moving her body against mine. The closer she was to me, the more I felt her breath against my chest. My words began to stir her emotions into an animal-like response. She was like a cat gripping its claws into the ground and making its way up a steep incline. She held on tightly and slowly grinded in a circular motion against me. She sunk her teeth into my shoulder before letting out a big sigh. I could feel her reaching her peak as she continued with more intensity than before.

"You like that?" she whispered.

Before I could answer, Tanya lay back and pulled me on top of her. We faced the other direction on the couch and it was my turn to grind against her body.

I didn't answer her question. I wanted her to figure out the answer based on how much she desired me to continue. Each time we began our lustful moments, it didn't take long before we climaxed in each other's arms. We were all over that couch for the first half of the night and when the opportunity presented itself, I wasted no time in carrying Tanya into her bedroom. Her bed was very inviting because it was neatly made up and had lots of pillows lying on top. As I placed her heavenly body on top of the sheets, her ass sank into the bed like soft butter. I couldn't resist going down on her. She arched her back and accepted every inch of my tongue. She tasted so good and her scent had me aching to be inside of her once more.

"Can I be inside of you?" I asked seductively.

"Now?" she responded.

"Yes, now."

Each thrust from that moment on felt like I was making my way to a new destiny. The importance of the night was about more than just sex or any other lustful intentions. We were on the verge of creating a bond that could last a lifetime. Tanya made my thrusts even more intense by pulling me harder into her. I could feel her grip around me inside as though she would never let me go. That night forever wasn't long enough for me. The sound of eternity made more sense to the emotions I was feeling. I didn't want any substitutes that made love appear to be any less than what I was imagining it could be. It was very real and Tanya had to be prepared to abandon all doubts and fears.

Tanya and I made love the entire night. It felt as though we were both trying to find out who could last longer. Tanya had always shown me that she had a competitive spirit and whenever I was blessed with intimacy, I noticed her spirit would come alive. As the lovemaking became aggressive during the night, I could see Tanya gritting her teeth and grunting as though we were in a wrestling match. During sex, she was like an animal but when I introduced my soul to her that night, I was able to change the arena. When she found herself in the middle of our passion, she realized that I was more about connecting with her rather than satisfying or pleasing myself. I wasn't there to fuck. I wanted to make love to her.

"What's gonna happen next, Christian? Where do we go from here?" she asked.

"It's not about where, Tanya. It's about having a chance to get there."

I was tired of the guessing game that men and women put themselves through. I wanted to know the potential of our relationship. If the destiny was friendship, then I wanted to know so that I would be available to someone else that wished to knock on the door to my soul. The dating scene was not really for me and waiting for a woman to overcome her fears created by past relationships just wouldn't do anymore.

"What are you thinking about?" Tanya asked.

My mind was a million miles away. I was reliving my own life as though it were flashing before me. I questioned my next step and whether or not I could back up what I'd expressed to Tanya. My emotions were surrounding me and preparing for a strong attack.

"Christian?" she asked with concern.

I could barely hear a word she said to me. All I knew was that I was falling, but not in a negative direction. I was ready to tell her how I felt and I didn't want to hold back any longer. A few tears met my intentions and before I could speak, I cried in her arms.

"I love you. I know that now more than ever before," Tanya said.

Tanya cried along side of me and pulled me closer to her. Tears grew into passion as once again I found myself deep inside of her. We wasted no time in finding heaven. We climaxed in each other's arms. Now out of breath and wanting to fall asleep, I made my promise before sinking into total bliss.

"I want you in my life forever, Tanya. Love can never happen without you so I believe you know what I'm asking."

Tanya nodded her head yes and we fell asleep in each other's arms. I knew where I stood now, no longer having doubts about us.

15.
What's Keeping Me Here?

I heard a knock on my door at 2 a.m. and it almost sent me into a state of panic. Sleeping didn't come too easy but once I did fall asleep, I began having nightmares about the men I'd been meeting lately. It took four or five hard knocks on my door before I realized it wasn't my imagination.

Who the hell could be at my door at this hour? I asked myself.

I was afraid to answer and I couldn't believe that anyone could get in without me buzzing them into the building. I thought it was a secured building.

I looked through the peephole and found another nightmare standing on the other side of the door. I believed he could hear me from his side and knew I had approached the door. After that, I called on the only one who could help me at the moment.

"God, please!"

"Maiya! Open the door!"

"Go away, Nicholas! What are you doing here?" I screamed. "How did you get in?"

"Open the door, Maiya! We have to talk!"

I didn't care if the neighbors heard because I was feeling like I needed help desperately. I thought about calling Christian, but I didn't want him involved in the mess.

"Why are you here?" I cried out.

Nicholas began to calm down for a moment, which put me slightly at ease. It gave me a chance to catch my breath for a second.

"Please let me in, Maiya, so we can talk," he said calmly.

At that point, I didn't think I had much choice. I knew he would stay outside my door until I came out so I opened it and let him in. After he walked in, I shut the door but stood near it as he walked further inside of my living room. It was dark so he could only see a shadow of my face. I was angry and scared at the same time.

"What's going on, Maiya? How come you won't return my calls or see me anymore?" he asked in the darkness.

"Why should I? You've been acting like a jerk and causing trouble for Christian. You didn't even go to Pam's funeral so what's up with that?"

"Fuck Christian! How do you know about the funeral, anyway?"

"I just know! What do you want, Nicholas?"

I wanted him to hurry up with whatever he wanted to say to me so that he could leave. I was feeling more and more concerned about what he might do because it really looked like he was getting very agitated.

"I'm turning on these fucking lights first!" he shouted as he leaned over to turn on the light near the couch.

He looked at me like I was a different person. I knew I hadn't been taking care of myself the way I should've and all the worrying I'd been doing lately had caused me to have circles under my eyes.

"What the hell is wrong with you?" he shouted.

"Leave me alone!" I screamed back.

"What's going on, Maiya?" he continued as he reached out to touch me.

I backed away immediately and, without thinking clearly, I blurted out the words that I had hoped to say to him calmly and over the phone. "I'm pregnant!"

Nicholas backed away, looked at me, and started acting even more agitated.

"Okay! Now I know I was right about you and Christian. I don't fucking believe you two! Putting up that front in the club like you did? You fuck him before you did me?"

Nicholas began to really frighten me. I thought for sure he was gonna do some physical harm to me by the way he continued looking at me as he waited for an answer to his questions. I moved towards the phone and grabbed it.

"Go ahead and call him!" Nicholas shouted.

"What do you want from me? Why can't you stop?" I asked as I pleaded for him to stay away from me.

"Don't worry, I'll stop. You lied to me, Maiya. I stopped seeing Pam because I thought I had a chance with you. Pam's gone now but you're still here?" he said as his voice went from loud and aggressive to cold and without emotion.

After he spoke, a cold chill swept across my body. I began to feel like I was in danger. I was in complete shock and even though I had the phone in my hand, my eyes were focused on the angry man standing before me. He began to come towards me, but his only action was the force of his words.

"Fuck you, Maiya!" he said as he walked out the door.

For the rest of the night I sat on my couch, still holding the phone and shaking nervously. I had no idea what to do and I knew I wasn't gonna go to sleep until it was daylight. I felt so helpless and I'd never been that way in my life. How did I get there? What happened to the woman that I was proud to look at in the mirror every day? Nicholas took something away from me and I didn't know how to get it back. Never had I wanted to run away but right then it was my only option. I felt too ashamed to even call my mother and using Christian to help me learn to love myself again wasn't the answer.

"Baby, where are you?"

That was the sound of my mother on my voicemail two days earlier.

I wanted to return her call but I didn't think I could hide the lack of respect that I had for myself. I had to get away in order to have a healthy baby. Christian was breathing new life into a dream that he'd had for years. He wanted to do more than pursue Tanya. He wanted to love her for the rest of his life. He knew what he wanted and I could've never been selfish enough to ask him to help with my problems. I knew he could make me smile and give me reasons to move forward, but the joy I received from my dear friend was merely temporary at best. The solution to my problem was my own strength and I had to find it or I'd lose my baby and possibly my life. Right then, I was terrified of leaving the apartment. I just wanted to jump inside my mother's arms and stay there forever. I wanted to release my fears and uncover the real Maiya. As I sat there trembling, the only arms that held me were my own.

Five in the morning and I was still awake on the couch holding the phone. For some reason, I felt secure with it in my hands. The only person I thought about calling was Christian. I had really been spoiled by his beautiful soul. He was the only one that I thought about reaching out to. I realized that he wouldn't always be available as things continuously progressed between him and Tanya. I hoped she would finally see the light and love him the way that he deserved. I craved to talk to her and ask why she'd taken so long to come around, but it wasn't my place. If she would only wake up, she'd realize how lucky she was.

The phone rang and I almost jumped out of my skin. I hesitated but decided that I should see who it was.

"Hello."

"Maiya! You okay?"

"Oh my goodness! Christian!" I shouted and then I cried.

I had been on the couch all night, holding everything inside of me, and staring at the door fearing that Nicholas would come back.

"Were you asleep, Maiya? I'm sorry if I woke you," Christian said calmly, having no clue about what had gone down between Nicholas and myself mere hours earlier.

"I've been wanting to call you. I'm scared, Christian."

"Why are you scared?"

"I had a really bad scene with Nicholas."

"So you finally let him know about the pregnancy?"

"Well, he came over without calling. I've never been this scared in my life. I just kind of blurted out that I was pregnant and now he believes that you're the father. I don't know, it just all happened so fast."

"Why would he think that? No, don't answer that. I know he's really angry with me. He has this sick jealousy over the friendship I share with you, but…"

"Nicholas is sick with anger *period* and he frightens me now!" I interrupted.

Christian and I talked for another hour before he finally shared his good news with me. It almost made me feel bad about going on and on about the drama that kept happening around me.

"Hey, I think Tanya and I are finally getting serious now. I think we can take this all the way, Maiya!" Christian said with the excitement of a little boy.

"It's about time she woke up!"

"Thanks, Maiya. Yeah, she finally woke up, but now we have to get you straight. I hate the way all this negativity has changed your life. I'm not speaking to the girl that put that strange guy in his place! What was that fool's name?"

"Oh, that was Reggie!"

Christian made me laugh by bringing up that idiot again.

"Exactly! Don't you remember how you took care of him with no problem? That's because you had strength!"

Christian was really laying into me this time. I could tell he was fed up with the way I was acting. He loved me as a friend, but he also believed in what they call *tough love*. He was giving it to me then and I had no choice but to listen.

"I need to go away!"

"You'd just be running away! Is that what you want to do?" Christian asked.

"What other choice do I have?"

"Stay and have the baby. I'll help you when I can."

"No, I think I'm gonna leave in the middle of December. Christian, I can't take it here anymore and if I see Nicholas again, I'll just die. He scared me so badly that I haven't moved from this position all night."

"You want me to come over?"

"No, Tanya may not like that."

Just talking to Christian made me feel safe. I relied so much on the comfort of his spirit that I would be lost if he weren't around.

Even in his presence over the phone, my tears dried up. My smile had me thinking that last night didn't really happen. I was forgetting all the drama that nearly gave me a nervous breakdown. After another hour of talking with Christian, I could hear Tanya in the background.

"You better go now," I told him.

I took a few deep breaths before hanging up the phone. I felt like I'd gotten a few extra doses of his positive spirit, which I really needed so I could get myself back on track. I didn't even know if I still had a job, but I was definitely serious about going away soon to have my baby. I had to make a complete change so that I could find a new me. My toughest decision was the prospect of having to break away from Christian for a while and, when I did that, I would be going through withdrawal. I was elated that Tanya was prepared to return the love he gave her and be there for him. How could I be a good friend to him if I was afraid of my own shadow? I didn't love me anymore but I loved and cherished my friend with all my heart.

16.
Unlikely Time For Tears

I felt close to Tanya in so many ways. I had confidence in myself as a man and a sense of direction now that Tanya had blessed my life. Tanya was always the highlight of my day. I was surprised by her reaction when I told her that I had been speaking to Maiya.

"Who was that, baby?" she asked.

"Maiya," I responded carefully.

"Oh, you coming back to bed and can you still get it up?"

Tanya started laughing and I was looking around wondering if I was in the right apartment.

"Damn!" I responded.

She never thought twice about me talking to Maiya and I felt like either she was hiding her feelings or she truly was comfortable in our relationship. Perhaps I could finally enjoy what we had without hesitation. I could do things for Tanya without wondering if I was going too far. No more guessing games. I could love her with the knowledge that neither of us feared the outcome of our time spent together.

"Well, you coming back to bed, baby?" Tanya asked again.

I went back to bed and it was funny because after an hour of kissing and cuddling, we fell asleep in each other's embrace. That made the night truly special.

The next day came and my first meeting was hell. The editor of my magazine explained the details of a story he wanted me to do on abuse. That was a subject I couldn't relate to, but I knew I'd learn a lot from just investigating and doing research on it. As I sat there listening to the editor, I found myself watching the minute hand on the clock ticking away. Everything he said sounded like meaningless chitchat to me. I was trying to use mental telepathy to move the hands of time faster. I was going to have to read more books on the subject because my attempts failed to work. After that, I had one more meeting before it was time for my lunch date at Rome Café with Tanya. She promised we could share a lobster together and sit close enough to feed each other without using our hands. Now that had a brotha excited but, then again, everything excited me.

"Hello, Christian. Are you with us today?" the editor asked.

"I'm here, sir. I'll get on the research today after lunch," I responded.

"That would be perfect. Looks like you have a lot on your mind today, Christian," the editor said with forced concern.

"Just writing in my mind, I suppose. Abuse is not my favorite subject, but it's definitely an important one. I'll get on it for sure."

"Okay, that's good! Well, now, I believe we can end the meeting on that note, everyone!"

I was so happy that the editor was finished with us. I ran my ass to the bathroom after that meeting because I had been drinking water every two seconds just to keep my hands busy. Then I packed my notepad and headed across town for another meeting that I had with a counselor. He wanted to speak with me about Pam and to also give me some belongings that she'd left behind when she'd been discharged from their treatment center. I didn't mind the meeting because I really missed her a lot. I loved any opportunity to talk about the Pam that I knew. That's the greatest thing about being proud of a friend. You'll waste no time in shedding light on the positive side of their spirit. She was so talented and the world would never know. Maybe I could somehow change that in a small way.

Mr. Riley, Pam's personal counselor, was waiting for me in his office once I finally arrived at the treatment center.

"Good morning!" he said enthusiastically.

"Hey, how are you?" I responded, shaking his hand.

"I heard about you quite a lot while Pam was here. I was so saddened to learn about what happened with her. I don't wish to keep you long, but I have something to show you that Pam left behind."

Mr. Riley was a slightly chubby man wearing a nice, wrinkled dark gray suit. He looked like one of those psychiatrists with just as many problems as his patients. He left the room and before I knew it he was coming back through the door carrying an unfinished statue. If I wasn't mistaken, it looked like me.

"What the hell?" I said in shock.

"I believe this is you, huh?" Mr. Riley asked.

"It looks like me!"

Pam, what did you do? I said to myself.

After taking a closer look at the statue, it appeared to be me sitting down with a pen and pad. The pad was on the top of my legs, the pen was in my right hand, and my left hand looked like I was picking my nose. I started to laugh because I felt like Pam had managed to get in one last joke at my expense.

"She has me picking my nose! Can you believe that?"

Mr. Riley noticed the same thing.

"I wasn't sure myself. I thought that perhaps she wasn't finished with that part of the sculpture," he said.

"Oh, she's finished alright!" I responded.

At that moment I wished that Pam were there so that I could not only call her a few names, but also give her a hug because I missed her so much. The statue gave me new inspiration for the other article that I was writing on friendship.

"Do I get to have this?"

"Most definitely! That's why I called you!" Riley responded.

I was under the impression that I was coming there for a serious meeting, but what a surprise to be given something created by a friend whom I loved so dearly. I couldn't wait to show Tanya what Pam had done. Pam got me good with that one. I couldn't believe she actually had me sitting there picking my nose. I'd told her that I wanted to be deep in thought and she'd put me with my finger deep inside my nose.

"Rome Café!" I yelled. I was so happy to see the outside of this small but very comfortable restaurant. I knew that Tanya was already waiting inside for me with a beautiful smile. When I walked in, I got a couple of smiles and snickers because of the statue that I was carrying, but I didn't mind too much.

Pam, if I ever make it to heaven I'm gonna tell you about this one! I thought to myself.

I felt like I was moving in slow motion as I walked to the outdoor patio in the rear of the café. The sunlight hit my face, forcing my eyes to appear like Clint Eastwood's in his old Western movies. I was looking pretty cool, dressed casually in a dark brown sweater, brown slacks, and loafers. I found Tanya sitting underneath an umbrella looking too fine. She stood up when I approached the table with her arms opened wide. I couldn't get there fast enough.

"Wait a minute!" she said before I could get my hug.

Uh-oh, here we go! I thought.

"I know you're not giving me a statue of somebody picking his nose! What are you trying to tell me?" she said accusingly, folding her arms across her chest.

I held it up higher so she could get a better look. "This is me. Can't you tell?"

"Well, I can watch you pick your nose in person! You don't need to remind me of your favorite thing to do by giving me a statue of it!"

"Oh, sit down woman!"

The jokes came one after the other. Tanya wouldn't let me live that one down at all. She had all kinds of jokes up her sleeve.

"That's really nice, Christian. She got you good! I wish I could give her a high five for that one."

Tanya enjoyed teasing me a little too much so I tried to turn the tables on her.

"Take your panties off and give them to me, Tanya."

"Say what! Where did that come from?" she asked in total shock.

"You afraid?"

"Yes, and you're tripping, Christian! I don't mind in the car, but here in the restaurant?"

"No, I just wanted to get you off the subject of this statue."

"Oh, you're silly and being too sensitive about it."

"No, you're right. Pam got me and I miss her."

"I know."

We got past our opening moments of fun and then we had a very special lunch together. The waiter smiled in awe of us every time he came over because he knew that something special existed at our table. We made every moment count and we never hesitated to move closer for a kiss. Our lunch lasted a little over an hour, but for me it felt like it was only ten minutes. I didn't want to leave Tanya, but I knew that it wouldn't be long before we were together again.

"Thanks for lunch, baby," she said, leaning against her car.

"You're more than welcome."

"Are we on for tonight? I want to cook dinner for you."

"Yeah! I'll stop and get some wine or something."

"Sounds good to me."

Tanya wrapped her arms around my neck and pulled me in close.

Every kiss we'd shared lately had so much more meaning behind them. That was where I'd wanted to be all along and she was finally on the same page.

Tanya just captured my heart all over again each time I was with her. That sounds kind of mushy stuff coming from a man that tended to scare women away, but I was blessed to know that Tanya had retired her running shoes. Work was going at its usual slow pace. It was the typical time of the day when I'd sit at my desk searching for things to say in my next story. I would often call Pam during that time of day for some encouragement, but I could only lean back and close my eyes with the hope that she would inspire me as I relived the amazing times we'd spent together.

My story on friendship was supposed to concentrate on black men, but it ended up taking the direction of a small group: both males and females who find themselves no longer friends due to a lack of communication. I felt compelled to write about it, especially since I was currently living it. It was scheduled to go to print in the next month's issue and I hoped that Nicholas would find it within his heart to read it. I couldn't believe that he'd become so out of control. It amazed me that so much had changed in such a short period of time. Unfortunately, things had changed for the worse and I could hardly recognize two of my friends. Nicholas could no longer be trusted and Maiya had lost all of her self-confidence.

I prayed that Maiya would come out of her stupor on a positive note and return to being the amazing woman that I had grown to love and admire. As much as I hated to admit it, I did think leaving town was the right thing for her to do. It would've been unfair for me to dissuade her from going to a place where she would feel more comfortable. I wanted her to have peace of mind so that her baby could come out healthy, beautiful, and happy. No woman should have to endure a tumultuous pregnancy. That is a time to count blessings. Hopefully, her move would only be temporary. If not, long distance phone calls were likely to break me. I needed Maiya's wisdom as I embarked on my journey of love with Tanya. I needed advice when I hit those tough times in a relationship and I believed that Maiya would never hesitate to tell me to stop acting stupid. I loved using her as my outlet for venting thoughts. When I wasn't calling her on the phone, I usually ended up writing her letters. I couldn't imagine how many I'd written to her, but surely there were enough of them to fill up two novels and then some. I thought the rest of the day away and the time began to pass quickly. I decided to leave a bit early because, as they say, "I had it like that!"

17.
Two Meetings Of Chance

"Excuse me, miss!" I could hear this voice repeatedly shouting in my direction as I grabbed my keys and walked faster. I wanted to leave because the owner of that voice was someone I really didn't need to see right then.

"Maiya, slow down!" the voice continued.

God, help me! I thought.

I walked as fast as I could and tried to hide around the corner. I thought I'd gotten away from him after I ducked into a store inside the mall. Much to my dismay, he found me.

"There you are! Why are you running away from me?"

"Not now, Reggie!" I told him with as much force as my tired spirit would allow.

"Not now? What do you mean by that?"

I was about to tell him off but he interrupted me before I could start.

"Why do you look so tired?"

"Can you leave me alone, please?" I asked.

"Is it that time of the month? Is that the story?"

My frustration caused me to lose my patience and almost my sanity. "Maybe if I tell you, then you'll leave me alone!"

"Tell me what?"

"I'm pregnant."

A huge smirk came across Reggie's face. "Oh really? And does *Miss Wonderful* know who the father is? Looks like you should've stuck with me, lady, so you could at least be with a man that can take care of you in your condition."

He spoke to me in such a condescending manner. I just rolled my eyes at him. Reggie stood there looking at me and acting like I needed to explain myself to him.

"What do you have to say now, Maiya?"

"Nothing, Reggie."

I tried to just leave it alone and walk away.

"Wait, Maiya," he called after me. "Maybe we can talk about us again."

"There is no us, Reggie. Why don't you see that?"

"Nothing to see, Maiya, except that you need a man now more than ever before. I'm willing to help you through this if you become my lady. You can stay with me, we'll have this baby, and then maybe have a few more together."

"Why... What do you... Why are you..." I was so shocked by this man standing before me that I couldn't finish any of the questions that I wanted to ask him. I was losing my mind. I felt the need to either push him out the way or stand there and curse him out. I ended up doing neither and simply walked away.

"Maiya, I'm not giving up. You have my number so call me anytime of the night or day, sweetie," he said.

All I could do was shiver at any thought of him and me together. When he said sweetie, implying we'd had something going on before, I felt like I tasted something bitter.

Me and that fool? Oh, no! I thought as I walked out of the mall.

I took the deepest breath in the world when I sat inside my car. I went to the mall for the special purpose of buying something nice for Christian and yet another fool causing trouble for me ruined my whole moment. Somehow, I had to stop allowing men to pull my strings and change my attitude so easily.

18.
Familiar Grounds

I finally made it to the grocery store. I wanted to get a little wine and some dessert. I had a serious sweet tooth and I planned on eating more than just Tanya later on tonight. I couldn't believe I'd just said that to myself but it was so true. It had ended up being a pretty good day. All my meetings went great and I was able to leave work early.

"Yuck! What are you doing here?" a voice said in the distance.

I didn't think it was directed at me so I kept walking to see if there was anything else that might interest me in the store.

"Are you ignoring me, mister?" the voice continued.

It sounded like the person was disguising his or her voice, but I didn't want to turn around and deal with someone who was going to be ignorant.

"Alright now! I'm getting tired of your shit!"

"Say what?" I said as I turned around to find Tanya laughing hysterically at me.

"Yeah, have your fun, miss lady!" I told her.

I felt a little embarrassed for not recognizing her voice.

"We meet again, huh?" Tanya asked.

"Yeah, you gonna make this one hard, too?"

"No, what do you have in mind?"

"I want some heated romance tonight. I want to talk, I want good food, and I want some love making to jump off also!"

"That's a mighty long list of things, young man."

We had a good time in the store going back and forth with each other. I don't know if anyone else had twenty-minute conversations standing in an aisle of a grocery store, but we always got a kick out of our moments.

"I might as well follow you home, huh?" I asked Tanya.

"No, I don't think so!"

"Why?"

"Because dinner isn't ready yet and you should go home and freshen up for tonight. I'm making a special dinner with candlelight and a few other things, so you better call me before you come over!" she instructed me. There was no chance of changing her mind either.

I felt pretty good knowing that the night meant more to her than just a simple get together for dinner.

"Okay, Tanya. I'll call you."

After walking Tanya to her car and watching her get inside, I felt so thankful. I wanted Tanya to always know my feelings about her. I needed her to recognize that no part of the love that I gave to her was temporary. My vision of Tanya and myself was forever and, by the grace of God, I felt like she finally recognized the importance of our relationship. I could remember all the conversations I'd had with Maiya where she'd told me not to give up on Tanya. I'd come close a few times, really close, but Maiya was so right and now I felt it was extremely important to follow up on every desire that I had. If it was truly in my heart to see this thing all the way through, then I couldn't leave any doubts between us or try to move forward with any degree of uncertainty.

"Hey, baby!" Tanya said as she drove up behind my car.

"Hey!" I responded with a smile.

"I love you."

When she said those words, I felt the earth moving in slow motion. I froze for a moment as I noticed her facial expressions change.

"Well?" she asked.

"Huh?" I responded.

"What are you gonna say back to me?"

"I'll call you tonight to see if it's safe to come over?"

"Now you know that ain't what you're supposed to say!" she screamed out the window.

"I love you too, Tanya."

She sat in her car for a moment, smiling and making eye contact with me. I felt almost like a little child. I couldn't keep my eyes focused on her without feeling a little shy about it. Before I knew it, she was getting out of her car and coming towards me.

"I need one more, baby."

I couldn't refuse so we immediately began hugging. We shared a warm embrace that felt strong enough to change the world. So many things raced through my mind all at once. The kind of love I felt for that woman made a man want to change all his priorities. I needed to do things for us rather than just myself. My desires to further my professional career were no longer for personal reasons. I needed to do it for us.

Tanya exhaled before letting go of me. "Okay, I have to go now."

"I love you very much," I whispered.

She blew me a kiss.

"Ooh, nice ass!" I shouted as Tanya returned to her car.

"Stop it!" she responded bashfully.

19.
Heavy Drama

Whenever I walked through my front door, I found bills and more bills. One day soon, I hoped to come home to Tanya and the same kind of warm embrace we'd just shared in the parking lot. After that, I could imagine her handing me a stack of bills and saying, "Here you go, dear."

I noticed the light blinking on my answering machine and hoped it was filled with messages of good news. I didn't want anything to ruin my day. I clicked the play button.

"Christian, I think I'm gonna have Nicholas thrown in jail."

Maiya's voice was the first message I heard and I was almost hesitant in listening further.

What now? I wondered.

"Your old friend just threw a brick in my car window. He's totally out of control and I'd hate to think what he'd do if he saw one of us in person."

I asked myself, "Do I really want to deal with this tonight?" Before I could come up with a definite answer, my phone started ringing.

"Hello!"

"Christian? Did you get my message?"

Obviously, I had no choice but to deal with the drama because it was Maiya calling back to see if I'd made it home.

"Yeah, I got it. How do you know it was him?"

"I saw him standing beside my car when I looked out my apartment window."

"Are you really going to call the police?"

"I'm not sure. I want to but I don't want all the hassle. I don't want anything to do with Nicholas."

"I wish there was some way to get through to him. All this isn't necessary. He still doesn't believe that you're carrying his baby, huh?"

"No, Christian. He doesn't, which is so foolish of him. In a way I'm glad that he doesn't believe it's his, but I know that his disbelief is making him act like a fool right now. To me, he just gave me some sperm but he isn't the father!" Maiya responded in anger.

"Damn, Maiya!"

"I know that's a crazy thing to say, but I knew something like this might happen!"

"You can't start second guessing things now. You have to get past all this turmoil in your life."

"Can you come over right now?"

"I'm expected for dinner tonight with Tanya."

"Fine," Maiya responded quietly.

"Why'd you say it like that, Maiya? You're going to make this hard, aren't you?"

"No, I don't want to cause more trouble. Can you call me tomorrow or late tonight if you come home?"

"I will and, tomorrow, let's get together for lunch or something." I felt guilty about not going over there but I couldn't let Tanya down. "Maiya?"

"Yes?"

"Call your mother and let her know what's going on."

"I was thinking I should, too. I definitely need to talk with her right now because I'm losing control."

"Just do it for me, Maiya. Call your mother and I'll see you tomorrow."

"Okay, Christian. Sorry for making you feel pressured."

"That's okay."

My mind was so heavy after that conversation. I ended up running a stop sign on my way to Tanya's place and getting pulled over. Thoughts were racing through my mind and a sincere concern for the future of a friend was at the forefront.

"A moving violation! Yet another reason to hate the world," I hissed to myself after receiving a ticket from a less than friendly motorcycle officer.

As I continued driving, I felt a lonely cloud over my head. My spirit felt like it was being bounced around from one extreme to the other. I had so much to look forward to with Tanya and I couldn't wait to take many steps with her. On the other hand, I was worried about Maiya and all the things she had to suffer through after her experience with Nicholas. I almost felt guilty about the possibility of seeing all my dreams happen while Maiya was slowly falling into the depths of her own depression.

For a moment, I started to drive over to see her, but then a vision of Tanya being disappointed in me changed my direction. I'd been strongly considering confronting Nicholas about all the drama, but I wasn't sure it would be the wise thing to do just then. I wasn't ashamed to admit that I was a little fearful about what might go down if I did confront him. I didn't want to be involved in a brawl with a former dear friend. Nicholas was the man I'd planned to have by my side when I got married one day. I'd wanted him to be the godfather of my future kids. I'd wanted him in every step of my life and now I felt myself wishing he would disappear so that all of us could get back to a life of good friends and good times. Life used to be fun within my small circle of friends, but it had turned into the most trying time I'd ever experienced. With Pam no longer there and friendships destroyed forever, I felt as though I was beginning a completely new life. I thanked God every minute because my new beginning was accompanied by the dream of a lifetime. I had a woman that was not only beautiful, but kept me wanting more of what she held so deeply inside her soul. I wanted her to be the first thing I saw when I awoke in the morning and the last vision that I had before I died.

Damn, that's marriage material. I needed to break out the kneepads!

I was waiting for the right moment, but I would soon ask her and when she said yes, I would be the richest man in the world. I would be blessed with love to the most extreme. I had to laugh when I thought about Tanya possibly answering me with a negative response. Something like, "No, I'm not ready!"

Nah, that ain't gonna happen! I told myself convincingly.

20.
Good Times Living Without Me

I spoke with my mother and it felt like I broke her heart and let her down completely. Her trust in me was very sacred and I believed I had lost that as well. When I first called her up, she was so happy. In fact, she said that she was smiling so hard because of my call that her cheeks were actually hurting. That was the kind of pride she'd always had in me.

"Maiya, I talk about you every day, baby!" she told me.

Just hearing her speak those few words made me want to give up the very idea of telling her about my pregnancy and the rest of the turmoil in my life. There I was about to ruin her happiness, but I couldn't keep it from her any longer.

Tears were streaming down my face as I uttered, "Mommy, I'm pregnant."

She didn't respond.

"Mommy, I'm pregnant! Did you hear me?" I repeated.

At that point, I was crying almost hysterically. The only response I was getting from my mother was silence. I knew she was disappointed but I just couldn't bare it if she hated me. I'd pleased her in so many ways. We talked constantly about accomplishing things in my career; making sure I found a good man before getting married and having a baby. We always talked about doing things the *right way* and there I was pregnant by someone I didn't care for or even know that well.

"Mommy, please talk to me!" I pleaded.

I couldn't believe my mother's silence. Over and over I begged for her to speak to me. She was tearing my heart apart and there was nothing I could do about it. I knew I'd destroyed her trust in me so no matter how much pain I was feeling, hers probably felt twice as strong. I was her daughter but, as I held the phone, it was like talking to a complete stranger. My mother pulled away like she felt nothing for me any longer.

"Mommy, I love you," I said one last time before hanging up the phone.

It had been one traumatic experience after the other and, just like the other times, all I could do was stay inside my apartment. Once again I found myself sitting on the couch staring into space. I was alone with a life growing inside of my stomach. How could I bring a baby into the world when I couldn't stand looking at myself in the mirror?

Christian called to leave a message on my voicemail and, somehow, I knew he would have to cancel getting together the next day.

"Maiya, I can't make it tomorrow after all. Tanya and I are having a special get together and I'm really thinking about asking her to marry me!" he'd said.

I could tell that Christian was very happy and excited, even though he was trying hard to mask it from me. He was trying to downplay his happiness in the face of my sadness and I adored him for that. I believed my troubles probably just brought him down.

I hadn't talked to Stephanie in a while and I was in desperate need of her crazy sense of humor, so I dialed her number.

"Stephanie!" I shouted as soon as I heard her voice.

"Hey, girlfriend. Where have you been?" she asked.

"I've been here! Where else am I gonna go?"

"I called your job and they didn't sound too happy when I mentioned your name. You haven't been answering your phone at home and you know how I hate answering machines. Why haven't we gotten together lately?"

Stephanie seemed concerned about me and it was a nice change in her personality. I was used to her laughing at my problems, but she was a very supportive and sensitive friend, despite being a *hoochie mama*.

"You worried about me, girl?"

"Just a little bit!"

Five minutes later, Stephanie and I began crying and we didn't stop until we were interrupted by a call on my other line.

"Hello?" I answered.

"Baby, come home so we can make everything alright."

When I heard those words coming from my mother, I almost fainted. I thought I had lost her when we'd spoken earlier so her call came as a total shock.

"I will, Mommy! I'm scheduled to leave on December 1st and I can't wait to come home! I would love for you to meet my friend Christian one day. He's the kind of man that we used to talk about me finding someday."

"Is he the one who made you pregnant?" she asked carefully.

"No, but I'll tell you all about it soon. I didn't want this to happen, Mommy, and I promise I'll make you proud of me again."

"You just come home and get away from whatever's making you hate yourself. I can hear it in your voice, baby."

My mother can always read the truth behind anything I say to her. She doesn't have to see me with her eyes in order to know how I'm feeling. The only thing she needs to do was listen.

After talking to my mother, I switched back over to Stephanie.

"That was my mother."

"How is she?"

"She's disappointed, but she loves me and wants me to come home. I'm so happy now."

"Are you gonna go?"

"Yes, but at the first of the month."

"You need to go now, girl!"

I didn't blame Stephanie for saying that. Because of all the tension that Nicholas was creating, I felt like I was racing against time.

"I have to wait for one very special reason," I said to Stephanie.

"What's that?"

"Christian. I have to do it for Christian," I said, even though I knew she wouldn't understand.

Christian had given me so much through our friendship that I felt I had to do something special for him. I had to be there for him. I knew that when he saw me, it never failed to bring a smile to his heart. We were able to look at each other and recognize the true meaning of the moment without saying a word. I wouldn't miss out on that opportunity for anything in the world.

"If I was you, girl, I'd get my ass out of here!" Stephanie said in her own special way.

"I can't. Not now."

I had one more week before I was scheduled to leave Los Angeles. I hadn't decided if the move would be forever but I knew it would be a long time before I returned. I couldn't take any more moments with Nicholas and I didn't know if it was right or wrong, but I didn't ever want the baby to know about the man. My baby would have no father. We would just have each other's love and support.

I would also miss my phone calls to Stephanie. Even though I definitely didn't intend to stop calling altogether, I just felt like I wouldn't have much to say to her any longer. She was always expecting to hear about adventure or drama after my dates. My dating future was dismal and I didn't think I would venture into getting to know another man anytime soon. I'd be raising my baby and had little motivation about bringing a man into the mix. Maybe as things improved and I went out more, I'd have something for Stephanie to tease me about. She always did know how to turn my experiences into a laugh fest. Usually for her own enjoyment, not mine. There was this one time when I couldn't wait to tell her about a special date with Christian. I wasn't able to call her on the night of the date and it kind of slipped my mind after that. Well, actually, I didn't want her reading too much into something that was purely innocent and sweet.

"You went out with Christian?" she asked in disbelief when I finally told her.

"Yeah, what's wrong with that?" I responded.

"Christian, your writer friend?"

"Yes, that's the one. Girl, you know who I'm talking about!"

"What about Tanya? I thought you and Christian were just buddies."

"Yes, we are buddies. This wasn't a real date. Just two friends hanging out together."

"Then why are you sounding like you all in love, Maiya?"

"Do I sound like that?"

"Yeah, girl!"

Stephanie had me blushing. While I could secretly admit that Christian was extremely easy to develop feelings for, I had no intentions of ever crossing that boundary. What he and I shared was very special and I never wanted to complicate matters by trying to get closer to him romantically.

"So, tell me what happened, Ms. Thing?" Stephanie asked.

"Why did you say it like that?"

"I don't know, girl. I'm almost tempted to ask you if you had sex with him, by the way you're sounding."

"You're crazy, Stephanie! I told you, Christian and I are just friends."

"Uh-huh. He's probably just one of those poetry brothas trying to get at your heart through words. A writer is like the worse kind of mack daddy, girl!"

"What?"

"You heard me, Maiya! I guess I'm gonna have to school you on another type of brotha, huh? You know I've got experience with all kinds!"

"Did I mention you were crazy, Stephanie?"

"You want me to shut up, Maiya, so you can tell me what happened?"

"Umm, yes. That would help!"

"Okay, girl. Go ahead."

"Thank you, Stephanie!"

Stephanie had me laughing so much that I almost forgot what I wanted to say about Christian. There really wasn't much to tell about the date we had and I probably shouldn't even have used that word to describe our moment. I was confused. It was one of those times when a woman feels so comfortable and so special in the presence of man that you just want it to go on forever, if possible. We had such great chemistry talking over dinner. I laughed and smiled so much while listening to him. Of course we'd had conversations about Tanya, as well as the dreams he had about starting a family, but that only added to the evening. I found his thoughts to be so endearing and I got an extra kick out of seeing a grown man blush as he spoke about love.

"Girl, when did all of this happen?" Stephanie asked.

"Not too long ago. Actually it happened about two weeks before his friend Pam passed away. He was trying to apologize for going off on me about Nicholas. Around that time, things weren't going so well with Tanya but he still had dreams about the two of them being together. I think he also had a date with some doctor friend of his around that time."

"Oh, see, there you go!" Stephanie interrupted.

"What?"

"A mack daddy, girl! His true colors came out during that time!"

"Oh stop! I'll admit that he was at a crossroads, but his heart was and always will be with Tanya."

"At a crossroads? People sound stupid when they say that!"

"You're so mean, Stephanie! But, no, Christian admitted to me that romantic thoughts went through his head and it touched me. I'm not going to lie. But, I never want what we have to be ruined."

"Uh-huh, like I said, girl."

"What?"

"Mack Daddy!"

"Whatever, girl!"

21.
A Hint Of Good Things To Come

My visions still kept me hoping for a return to friendship. I had a dream one night that everything was okay. I wanted so much for a return to what I had with Nicholas not too long ago. I wished we could go back to the time when everything was right. I loved Maiya as a friend but before she came into our circle, everything was perfect. However, she was definitely not to blame for what happened and I realized an apology was in order. Nicholas was the one to blame and it scared me to think what all his anger would result in. I called him for yet another attempt at reasoning. All his anger and contempt should be put away before it did more than just hurt the feelings of others.

"Did Maiya tell you about her car window?" Nicholas asked.

"Yeah, she told me and I couldn't believe you're this angry!" I responded.

I was trying so hard to figure out why he was wasting all his energy hating and wanting to destroy everything around him. Before I could question or reason with him, his emotions grew like a snowball rolling down a mountain.

"I still don't believe that bitch is carrying my baby. I know it's yours. We used to be friends!" Nicholas shouted.

"As crazy as it sounds, I believe we still can be. I always think to myself that there's hope, you know," I said calmly.

I could feel him relaxing a little as though I was getting through. I thought that maybe this was my chance to speak to him while he was thinking rationally.

"Are you willing to meet in person? You gonna put away all that anger for a moment so that we can get together and talk?" I asked.

"Yeah, okay. I'm willing," Nicholas answered.

We both agreed to get together for lunch next week. Neither one of us was reluctant about it. The month of November was almost over and I felt as though good things were about to happen. Maybe I stood a real chance at making things better between all of us. I was getting excited because if all went well, the circle of friends could come together and be complete again.

22.
Can't Believe It's December

Maiya came over to congratulate me. She brought me flowers and a new pair of underwear.

"This is for your honeymoon, boy," she said sarcastically.

"My honeymoon?"

"Yes, this will get her in the mood as soon as she sees your skinny legs!"

I'd called her the previous night to let her know that, after four attempts and seven glasses of wine, I finally asked Tanya to marry me.

"I need you in my life forever and even that's not long enough," I'd told Tanya.

"What are you saying, Christian?" she'd asked nervously.

"Umm, you know. Damn!"

I'd finally gotten it out and Tanya had accepted after about two glasses of wine herself. Maybe I should've asked her again just to make sure, but right then I was on top of the world. Everything was falling into place and my future felt like a dream in the making.

I spoke to Maiya about a meeting I'd planned with Nicholas and she seemed both pleased and nervous about it. She told me that Nicholas was not the same person that I knew before and couldn't be fully trusted.

"I heard something different in his voice."

"What sounded different?" Maiya questioned.

"I just heard a possibility that he'd be willing to listen to reason. Then we can all get on with our lives."

I told Maiya that, deep down, I wished for Nicholas to still be the best man at my wedding, but from what had happened, I knew that couldn't be a reality. Maiya's concern grew with each moment that we talked about the meeting with Nicholas.

"When are you meeting with him again?" she asked.

"Tomorrow."

"Where?"

"We haven't decided yet."

Maiya came up with the idea that Nicholas and I should meet in front of her apartment.

"Why would you want us to meet there?" I asked her.

"After you two talk and straighten things out, then maybe all three of us can clear the air somehow."

I wasn't sure about her idea but, at the same time, I couldn't see anything wrong with it.

"I'll call Nicholas later tonight and tell him to meet me in front of your place," I said.

She was happy that I agreed and seemed somewhat relieved, too. After a few silent moments and more concern, Maiya took a deep breath before changing the subject.

"So! Tomorrow will be December first and look at you!"

"What about me?" I responded.

"You're on the verge of getting married and I'm still here for you as a very dear friend."

Maiya knew how important it was for me to make it to the month of December with friendships and romance still intact. My smile lit up the room as I thought about how I wished someone very dear to me were still there to see all of it.

"Are you excited?" Maiya asked.

"Kind of nervous!"

I was feeling nervous because something I'd been anxious to make a reality was now just that. Tanya and I were very serious and we were even talking about where we would live after we walked down the aisle. I could see her excitement as she spoke about possible wedding gowns and where we'd spend our honeymoon. I made myself nervous with thoughts about what our kids would look like and what type of husband I'd be after a few years passed by.

"After you get married, Christian, do me a favor," Maiya said.

"What now?"

"Don't get an attitude with me, boy!" she shouted.

"Okay, what can I do for you, Ms. Thang?" I asked jokingly.

"Make sure you don't start letting yourself go! I don't want to see any fat potbelly hanging over your belt when I come visit you!"

She practically bowled over with laughter and that was music to my soul.

"I won't! You watch me and see me get even sexier than I am now!"

I was beaming with confidence and I guess you could say the reason was because my heart was full. I could stick my chest out for once and it wouldn't be for macho reasons.

"Oh, excuse me!" she responded.

Time flew by so fast while talking with Maiya. The day was pretty much over and when I glanced at my watch, I noticed that it was almost time for Tanya to come over. It was great to see Maiya. She seemed kind of happy and I could tell she was more relaxed now. I could feel her spirit lifting because she knew that, in a few days, she would be away from this town. Nicholas would be out of her life, too, and I guess that was a comforting thought. I figured I'd be spending money on plane tickets to Oklahoma. That's where she was headed. *Damn, that was far!*

"Are you sure about tomorrow and our meeting with Nicholas?" I asked her, just to make sure.

"Yes, I want to straighten things out. I believe that after we talk, I'll know whether or not I'll keep in touch with him. I have to see that he's really going to change before I allow him into my baby's life."

"I can understand that. I have a feeling everything will go well tomorrow, so I'm looking forward to it," I reassured her.

As Maiya continued to talk, I found myself going blank on her. My thoughts were changing directions. I began floating on a mental cloud known as Tanya. I couldn't wait until she got there so we could hug and feel the closeness that we shared. I experienced an aching inside my heart when she was away from me for too long. I lived for each second, just knowing that it wouldn't be long before her smile returned to my vision.

"Christian? I need to go because I have my girlfriend waiting on me, okay?" Maiya said, interrupting my thoughts.

"Okay. I guess I'll see you tomorrow, then?" I asked, walking her to the door.

"Yes. Goodnight, sweetie."

Maiya gave me a kiss on the cheek and then left. We'd spent almost three hours talking, but now it was time to get ready for Tanya.

Tanya always dressed like nobody's business when she was dealing with her clients, so I knew she'd look good coming straight from work. I was truly blessed and by the sound of my doorknob turning, I could hear love on the way. I realize that it was strange to look at a doorknob and feel excited about it. I'd given Tanya her own key a few days before and we both sensed a certain importance in that decision. She'd held the key in her hand so tightly that day and I never saw when or if she'd ever put it down. We'd exchanged kisses and so much more. One thing was for sure, we wouldn't be complaining about a lack of sex anytime soon.

"Hey, baby, I'm home!" she announced with the biggest smile on her face.

"How long have you been preparing to say that?" I asked her.

"How long have you been wanting to hear it said to you?"

"Ever since I met you."

"I can't believe how you look at me. Is it gonna be like this all the time?" Tanya asked.

"I believe so. I'm very serious about the vows that I'll share with you, Tanya. I want you to know, without a doubt, what I'm feeling."

It often felt like I was repeating myself, but until they came up with stronger words, I had to keep saying what was in my heart. My feelings grew stronger every day, if that was at all possible. I wanted to be on my own personal discovery mission for the rest of my life. I wanted to discover new ways to express my love for Tanya.

"So, what did you cook for me?" Tanya asked.

She caught me by total surprise because I knew that there was something I was supposed to do that day. Cooking had never once entered my mind.

"Oops!"

"Uh-oh, is it time for our first argument?" she asked, pretending to be serious.

"No, I can throw something together really fast."

"No, you can't! We'll just go to a restaurant, baby."

As we walked out the door, I kept thinking to myself how fun it was going to be to always have her near. I was going to be with this woman for the rest of my life and I couldn't wait to get it started. It was so cold outside. I felt like shouting to the world because, instead of zipping up her coat, Tanya simply moved closer to me.

Thank you, God, I thought to myself.

I'd been doing a lot of looking up and a lot of kneeling down. I wanted to show how thankful I was and I wanted to forever keep Pam's memory alive. I was imagining that I would one day tell my kids about Pam. I could show them the sculpture and describe her strong personality. That was a woman who wouldn't take anything from anybody but, at the same time, she would melt like ice cream if you complimented her on how she looked. I missed her so much and I knew that she would be inside that church when I was standing with Tanya before God, expressing my love.

"How do you like this place?" Tanya asked me as we waited for our food.

"The décor is always pleasing to the eye in here!" I responded.

"Yeah, I love coming to Jack in the Box, too, baby!"

Tanya and I laughed so hard that we had tears in our eyes before they called our number to pick up the food. I could do anything with her and feel like I was a kid at Disneyland. When we went grocery shopping, I enjoyed watching her freeze to death in the frozen food section. I promised her that I would bring an extra coat when we went to the grocery store the next time. I didn't want her shivering like she had been.

After we fed each other fries and ate those wonderful sandwiches, we decided to go to the beach and walk around. I told her we could walk under the moonlight and feel our souls illuminate.

"Let's just listen to the ocean instead, baby," she responded sarcastically. "You just get too deep sometimes!"

I loved to express myself on matters of the heart and soul. Tanya was like no other to me and if being with her had been God's plan all along, then I was so thankful that I'd never given up. Sometimes I thought about what would've happened if I'd brushed her away or didn't accept those early apologies. I wondered if I would be as happy as I was right then. I wasn't sure what would've happened. Just thinking about it at that moment took away from the smile I was sharing with her. The smile reflected what I was truly feeling inside.

"How long do I have to wait for us to get married?" I asked anxiously.

"What?"

"How long, Tanya?"

"It takes some planning, baby, so don't make me hit you by asking me to go to Vegas and get married."

She held a clinched fist in the air and displayed her intentions.

"Oops!" I exclaimed.

"Yeah, I got your oops right here!"

She was right about one thing. The ocean did sound wonderful as we walked in the sand that night. I could imagine doing that very thing one day, holding hands with our kids.

"You feeling any regrets?" Tanya asked me as we walked in the deepest part of the sand.

It was starting to get really cold so she moved closer inside my arms. We were walking barefoot and the sand was pretty cold.

"What's there to regret?" I asked her.

"I don't know. A lot of men have second thoughts or wish they had hooked up with someone else before the woman that they're marrying came along."

"Oh."

"Oh?" she asked.

"No regrets or second thoughts, Tanya. I love you from the deepest part of my soul."

We kissed under the moonlight with passion and urgency. Tanya felt it so strong that she pushed me down on the hard, cold sand. My body was shivering at first, but once she began kissing me deeper and pressing her body against mine, I had no perception of where I was or how cold it might be. I pulled up her dress slowly to reveal her legs and, before I knew it, Tanya pinched me.

"Ouch, girl!"

"It's too cold to be out here screwing in the sand!"

"Well, you just killed that erection!"

"I think you can get it up a few more times!"

We had so much fun together. When we got home, the only strength we had was to shower together and lay in each other's arms. We didn't talk at all. We remained silent and simply gazed into each other's eyes before falling asleep. I knew what I'd be dreaming about and I was destined to wake up in a very erect situation. I hoped Tanya didn't mind being poked in the stomach.

23.
My Window To The Future

I was nervous with anticipation that day. In an hour or so, I'd look out my window and find Christian and Nicholas standing there. I couldn't wait to see Christian and give him a sweater that I'd bought him. I'd neglected to give it to him the day before, but I really wanted him to have it. I couldn't possibly thank him enough for his friendship and for his help during the crazy times. It felt like we were saying goodbye, in a way. I knew that we could talk on the phone, but just always knowing that he was physically near had been comforting. I was going to get on with my life and he definitely had to prepare for major changes in his own, getting married and all.

"Hey Maiya, who's gonna give me those sisterly hugs that I so desperately need all the time?" Christian had asked me.

"You won't need those anymore, sweetie, because Tanya will nurture you and love you."

Sometimes, he amazed me with his wisdom about love. Other times, I found him to be childlike and innocent. I adored the contrast in him. I wished a little bit of him had rubbed off on Nicholas, but I guess I couldn't ask for everything. Crazy Reggie could've used a personality change, too. A few nights earlier, I'd gotten up the nerve to call and tease Reggie. My excitement about leaving had gotten the best of me and I just wanted to rub it in his face.

"Maiya? Oh, damn, you came to your senses!" he'd shouted into the phone.

"Yeah, I'm getting as far away from you as I can!"

"Excuse me?"

"I'm moving away from this town so life will be worry-free!"

Half of me felt guilty about calling him up to gloat.

"I ain't worried, girl, because I know you'll call me and ask me to fly you back here. You're going to always wonder what your life would've been like with me in it, Maiya. I'm the best man you never had!"

After that comment, I no longer felt guilty.

"Reggie?"

"Yes, sweetheart," he answered.

"Why are you the way you are?" I asked, truly wondering why.

"Meaning what?"

"Meaning so arrogant, bordering on asshole."

"I beg your pardon, Maiya! You should feel proud that I even talk to you after the way you've always been rude with me. You left me in the mall that time but I've still remained a gentleman. I'm not at all like what you're used to and I guess that's why you're pregnant right now, isn't it?"

"Anyway! Just wanted to say goodbye so that I can really celebrate my departure from this city!"

"Maiya? How about I come over right now so that we can say our good-byes in a proper fashion."

The only thing I could do was shake my head and laugh. The man had turned out to be a highlight for me.

"Take care, Reggie. I'll definitely never forget you."

"So, I have a chance after all, huh?"

"Goodbye," I said in disbelief.

That conversation had gotten me absolutely nowhere and, as I thought about it, I had no idea why I'd even called him. Then again, it was rather funny and it was a good way to get rid of my worries, which never seemed to stay away for very long.

Unfortunately, those same nervous feelings were kicking my butt that day. I'd just spotted Christian pulling up in his Navigator. He seemed to be sitting inside so I assumed he was going to wait there instead of coming up to my place first. I waved a couple of times but I couldn't get his attention. I hoped that we were not making a mistake by having Nicholas come over there. The nervous tension I was experiencing was so profound that I decided to call Stephanie. She was just as nervous as I was about the day's events.

"Call me as soon as they leave your apartment, girl!" she'd instructed me the day before.

I decided not to wait until they left. I needed to talk to her while it was all going down. I wasn't about to go through the ordeal alone, so I dialed her number.

"Stephanie!" I shouted as soon as she picked up the phone.

"What, you guys finished already?"

"No, Christian is outside waiting for Nicholas."

"Oh, no! I've been pacing the floor wondering what's going on, Maiya, and now you're telling me nothing's happened yet?"

"Wait! Christian is getting out of his car now and looking down the street!"

"Girl, you gonna give me a heart attack!" Stephanie screamed.

"Hold on, Stephanie. No, he just got out to lean against his car."

Since he was now standing beside his car, Christian was able to make eye contact with me in the window. He looked up, smiled, and I returned his smile with excitement. I waved to him like I was a schoolgirl in love.

"He can see me now, girl!" I told Stephanie.

"That's good. Maybe Nicholas isn't gonna show up."

"I hope not, but those two need to clear the air since there's always the chance that they'll bump into each other. I'm leaving, so I don't have to worry about Nicholas after tomorrow."

Moments later, my heart completely sank because Nicholas pulled up and parked a few cars ahead of Christian. I couldn't stand to look at Nicholas. I swallowed hard because seeing him made me so uncomfortable. I was feeling like I should change my mind about letting him come up there.

"Maiya, what's going on now?" Stephanie asked.

"They're talking. Both of them are standing away from each other with their arms folded."

While I watched the two of them talk, I could only imagine what they were saying to each other. I knew I was the main topic but, from that distance, I could only hear whispers as I focused on

Christian's body language. He seemed a little agitated and nervous while Nicholas appeared angry.

"Maiya, would you say something?" Stephanie shouted in my ear.

I tried harder to listen to what they were saying outside.

"Shh! Wait, girl!" I told her.

"Man, you're stupid! Why you gotta be like that?" I could hear Christian shouting.

Nicholas just turned his back and wiped his face. He seemed nervous, like he was trying to relax his hands, but I couldn't tell if he responded to what Christian said.

"Do they look like they're gonna fight?" Stephanie asked.

"Oh my God!" I shouted.

"Maiya?"

Stephanie's voice faded away from my conscious mind. All I could hear were the echoes of my screams.

"Christian! Christian!" I screamed at the top of my lungs.

I became hysterical, to the point of almost falling out of my apartment window. I didn't know what to do, but I realized that I was still holding the phone in my hand.

"Christian!" I screamed again, hoping that he would hear me.

I was so hysterical that I couldn't get my legs to move. I suddenly remembered that Stephanie was on the phone.

"He shot Christian! He shot him!" I cried hysterically.

I could barely hear Stephanie's own cries to get help but, somehow, I found the strength to lean over the windowsill and look outside. I saw Christian's lifeless body lying beside his car. In the distance I could see Nicholas crying, still holding the gun in his hand.

"Get away from him!" I screamed out the window.

Seeing Nicholas in the street gave me the strength to run outside and protect Christian's body. I dropped the phone on the floor and ran outside without any shoes on. I paid no attention to Nicholas standing nearby with the gun still in his hand. I had to be with Christian.

"What did he do to you?" I gathered him into my arms and rocked him back and forth.

Christian struggled for air. He coughed a few times and I thought that maybe there was a chance for him to make it.

"Don't die, okay?" I pleaded.

"I'm okay, Maiya. I'm okay," he whispered.

I could hear sirens in the distance and I prayed hard that they were coming our way.

"Maiya, I have to catch my breath," Christian whispered.

"Just be still for me," I told him.

"I'm okay," he said one more time.

As the sirens got closer there was a deafening silence between Christian and me. We looked into each other's eyes for a while; reliving every moment we'd spent together in a quick instance. I sensed him telling me how much he loved me and I told him the same in return. It felt like we were connecting in a way that let me know he would always be there for me. If I'd closed my eyes and clutched my heart, I could've seen his smile and heard his voice. As I held him in my arms, his eyes sparkled one last time and the formation of a smile began to appear. Suddenly I could feel something leave his body.

Christian died in my arms and I barely spoke a word to anyone until a month after arriving at my mother's house in Oklahoma. I was thousands of miles away from the body of the most beautiful man I had ever known. He was my best friend, my brother, and a sweetheart whose spirit had become a part of me. Losing him devastated me and took away my voice. How could I speak with Christian no longer around breathing life into words and gestures that the rest of us take for granted? In such a short time, he'd brought so much out of me and inspired so much in me. I found out that I was having a daughter and I was going to do my best to be a great mother like my own. I planned on naming my daughter Angelina Christiana. I believed Christian was an angel and he was somewhere in heaven telling me, "Stay positive and be beautiful."

His life ended at a point in time when he felt like the richest man in the world. Tanya took things as hard as I did and I heard that she went away for a while. I didn't know what had become of her, but I smiled and cried at the same time when I saw her bending over the casket at the funeral. She was so nice to me when she held my hand and we approached Christian's body together. When she leaned over the open casket, I could hear her whispering as tears fell from her eyes.

"They delivered the wedding dress to me, baby, and I put it on for you last night," she'd said.

I still had no voice to speak with then, but I did have enough strength to help Tanya walk from the casket. Time was a blur after that. I could only remember crying as the minister read some of Christian's words about life and the pursuit of love to all the people mourning this special loss.

God placed me on a path of consciousness recently that united sincerity with determination and focus. When I opened my eyes, I witnessed a very special gift. I found friendship and I found love. I found something that could transform my soul into a spirit that will continue to embrace those that I love, long after I'm gone.

I had never seen so many saddened people before but I could truly feel Christian's spirit inside that room. He'd touched lives in a special way and losing him so soon felt like the greatest tragedy ever. In one instance, God turned my voice back on for a moment. Somehow I felt the strength to say something I only communicated in silence with Christian. "I love you."

Ten Years After Love Went Away

23.
It's So Hard To Say Goodbye

Dear Maiya,

When I opened my eyes today, I felt an overwhelming desire to shout. I'm surrounded by so much love. I'm so thankful for you believing in me the way you do. Instead of shouting, I'd much rather reflect upon what I'm feeling right now. You know my never-ending quest to find friendship and love that last beyond the usual short time frame? Finding you was indeed a blessing and I can't believe that, even for one minute, I didn't like you at first. That makes me laugh now, but hopefully you know the reason behind that moment of stupidity. I pray that when you receive this letter, it'll simply be an extension of the love we've shared in so many wonderful conversations. Right now, it's time for me to return to my writing. Try to smile when you read this, Maiya, because I truly believe that somehow I will know.

Love,
Christian

I couldn't believe it had been ten years since I'd stood over a spirit that embodied so much love. My best friend, Christian Erickson, was a man so full of life, love, and wisdom. He was taken away by jealousy but he remained with me at all times in spirit. I'd placed him inside my heart and I would never let go. I often thought about him and all the times we used to talk for hours upon hours. Though he wasn't my lover, I still felt a very intimate connection with him. I could remember so much life and happiness in his presence. It wasn't until I thought about that fateful day that I relived the devastation of losing him. A lot of times I blamed myself, but then I thought about the way Christian led his life and realized that nothing he did was in vain. He died knowing that he was loved and that alone made his passing a peaceful journey. I missed him dearly and I thanked God that I'd held on to all the beautiful letters that he would send me. I remembered complaining about the flow of paper coming to me and how he would only laugh.

"Christian?"

"Yes, Maiya."

"Don't you believe in using a telephone? You write me just about everyday, it seems like."

"Yeah. What's your point, home girl?"

"My point?"

"Yeah. I fail to see one, Miss Lady."

"Never mind!"

He had a way of making me forget why I was complaining. Now I would read his letters all the time for strength. Sometimes I would read them for guidance. My friend was very wise for such a beautiful, young soul. Even his questions had me in awe. I wondered constantly where he came up with the inspiration to communicate in the way that he did.

"Why does beauty have to be taken away?" he asked me during one of our conversations about life.

"What do you mean?"

"It's rare that I can see something beautiful grow into more beauty. It seems as though if it's a flower, it dies. If it's a woman, then gradually over time her beauty is taken away by negative experiences."

I wasn't sure how to respond to Christian at the time. I simply sat there and listened as he worked things out in his own mind. He saw something wrong and he wanted to put himself on a personal journey to correct the error.

"I know we all have moments where we say the wrong things to people. We find ourselves in situations where we just don't click with an individual," Christian began to explain.

"What are you getting at?" I asked.

"Well, I can't remember calling a woman a bitch, but I know I've thought about it."

"Say what, boy? You're losing me!"

"Sometimes I feel lost myself, Maiya, but I just wonder why we find ourselves motivated by certain things."

"Things like what?"

"Things like abuse and showering someone with negativity, which in the end takes away so much beauty. Take a look at you, Maiya!"

"I'm okay!"

"Not really!" Christian responded.

"Huh?"

At that time, I was feeling the affects of a bad decision that I'd made. It was a moment that made me hate myself. If it weren't for Christian, I don't know how my life would've turned out by then. I often pondered how one decision could affect so many others. I knew that by allowing Christian's friend, Nicholas, to enter me on that terrible night ten years earlier, it affected all of our lives. Christian was no longer calling me up every night or writing beautiful letters. He'd lost his life at the hands of someone he'd once considered to be his best friend. In reality I only knew Christian for such a short time, but his impact on my life would be forever.

Why indeed does beauty have to be taken away?

All I could do was look to the sky and pray that Christian could hear me somehow. I could definitely relate to what he'd once asked me. Because of my mistake, I'd lost so much and yet I'd gained one of the greatest responsibilities that can be bestowed upon a woman. I'd become a mother who was determined to never let her daughter feel like a mistake. I loved my baby and now that she was ten years old, I was proud of the foundation of love that I'd given to her over the years. She knew nothing about Nicholas, but already she had memories of Christian that she could hold inside of her precious heart.

I often wondered if I'd done wrong by allowing my baby to believe that Christian was her father. I imagined how hurt she would feel if she found out the truth. I was determined to keep that from her. I always wanted her to grow up with a healthy attitude towards men and never accept those that disrespected her. When she was a little baby, I would sit, read letters, and watch her marvel at the way I felt moved by what I was sharing with her. I wasn't sure if she understood what I was reading, but she recognized the love coming from the pages. Since she was ten, I got so excited because I didn't have to read to her any longer. Now that she was able to read for herself, she would simply go to the closet, grab a few letters, and read them. I believed that each time she read a letter; she placed that memory into her own heart. Angelina discovered life through Christian's words. I liked to believe that I'd paid the ultimate tribute to Christian by naming my daughter after him. I named her Angelina Christiana. I even gave her his last name, Erickson. I knew he was smiling up in heaven because she was turning out to be such a beautiful spirit herself. She was intelligent beyond belief and despite the secret that I'd kept from her, I tried to share all my life's experiences so that she could grow into a stronger lady than I had ever imagined.

Raising Angelina had been the greatest gift ever and, at the same time, it had been very challenging. My mother had helped tremendously, even though she didn't agree with my decision to expose Angelina to the memory of Christian the way that I had. My mother and I had endured major battles about it, but my intentions were to have a positive male figure in my daughter's life. When she began her life out on her own one day, I wanted her to have something strong within her heart to hold onto. She needed to be able to recognize true sincerity when spoken by a man. I wanted her to one day find her own Christian and, unlike me, I wanted her to grab that man and be truly embraced by love.

"That's not healthy, Maiya!" my mother would say to me.

"Why is it not healthy?"

"Because Christian is not her father. In fact, he belonged to another woman."

"I know this and I supported Christian every step of the way in his pursuit. But, as a friend, I loved him dearly and I will not let him go. I don't want Angelina to ever experience a man like

Nicholas. It would kill me if she found out that her father was sitting in jail because he killed the man that she truly adores and carries with pride in her heart."

"I love you, Maiya, and God knows I love little Angelina, but how can I answer her when she asks me questions about her father?"

I wasn't sure how to respond to my mother's question, but I found myself pleading with her to never tell Angelina about Nicholas.

"I won't tell her. That's your responsibility, but it pains me to keep quiet when she desperately asks me something that I don't feel comfortable answering."

"I know, Mommy."

One of my greatest memories in the years gone by was when Angelina had come home crying. Tears were streaming down her face and it took her hours before she told me what was wrong. In my first attempt to speak with her, she turned away. She ran to her room and closed the door. I began pacing back and forth as I cried out to her to tell me what was wrong.

"Angelina! Honey, what's wrong?"

Eventually, I left her to herself so that she could deal with her troubles.

An hour went by and then I saw the door to her bedroom open. She came out with a very sad look. She had dried tears all over her face. She walked from her bedroom to my room down the hall. She was there for ten minutes before I began to wonder what she was doing. I walked to my room, only to find her reading some more of Christian's letters.

"What are you doing, sweetheart?"

At first, Angelina didn't respond and it wasn't until I sat on the floor beside her that I realized what she was doing. She was reading a letter that Christian wrote to me not long before he was killed. The letter spoke of love and friendship. It talked about illuminating kindness in an effort to bring people closer.

"Do you understand what he's saying in the letter, honey?"

"I think he's talking about love, Mommy."

This letter touched me back then so deeply but now it only made me feel sad. I remember how I was feeling so down at that particular time. All my actions towards everything and everyone were negative. Whenever I walked out of the house, I was angry and when I went home, I escaped into my loneliness. The one thing, the only thing that I was excited about was Christian's happiness.

"Can you read it for me, Mommy?" Angelina asked.

"Just a little bit, sweetheart, and then you're gonna tell me what's wrong. Okay?"

"Okay." Angelina nodded.

"If I may share my light with you," Christian wrote.

He was so excited about his life at this time. He wrote this letter to me just before a special date that he had with Tanya. She had to be the luckiest woman in town to have such a beautiful man in love with her. In the letter, Christian talked about standing close so that I could absorb his spirit.

"Maiya, where's the strength that you carried once before? Did I stand too close to you and take it away?" Christian asked in the letter. "No one deserves more happiness than others. No one means more to me than you do and if I can share this light with you, please allow me to pass it on."

"Were you sad, Mommy?"

"Yes I was, Angelina. Mommy was going through tough times and Christian just wanted me to be happy."

"Didn't he make you happy?"

"All the time, but it's more important that you make yourself happy so that when you love someone, you can both bring happiness to each other. When one person is sad and can't be cheered up, it makes the other person feel frustrated and worried," I tried to explain.

"I'm sorry, Mommy."

Angelina was beginning to sound a lot like me. I was always apologizing to my mother for one reason or another. I didn't want Angelina to ever feel sorry. I guess I expected a lot out of her, but I truly wanted her to be strong when she grew up. I didn't want her to ever let a negative man change the direction of her life. I'd given Nicholas too much power in my life in such a brief amount of time. He'd changed how I felt about myself. Christian had me believing that love was possible but Nicholas had managed to convince me that I had no self-worth, or perhaps I'd allowed him to.

"Why you believe in the negative so easily astounds me, Maiya. Do you believe in our friendship?" I remember Christian asking.

When he asked me that question, it was during one of the very few arguments that we had. He was the only man I'd ever known that I rarely disagreed with on something.

"Yes, I believe in our friendship!" I responded.

"Well, I believe in it with a passion and that's why I get angry when you start walking around like you don't care about yourself."

He was speaking louder than I had ever heard him before. I thought he was going to give up on me because most of my responses to him were shoulder shrugs, sighs, and gestures of doubt.

"So what are you saying?" I asked him.

"Your disbelief in yourself is turning me off. How can anyone want to stick around if you refuse all help and put down every positive comment thrown your way?"

Once again, I simply shrugged. I could see anger boiling inside of him and that alone brought tears to my eyes. As I returned to reading the letter to Angelina, I felt overwhelmed with the memory of Christian. His letters were always so powerful to me and his memory only kept the bond tight. Angelina watched my every expression as she looked at the words on the page and then looked up at me.

"Can I read the rest, Mommy?"

"Yes," I whispered, trying to hold back my tears.

Angelina began to read and I was very impressed by the sound of her voice. She read as though she understood everything on the page. She spoke with emotion and she expressed every thought. I believed that was a tribute in itself to the beauty of Christian's spirit.

"Maiya, as always I feel as though I must bring you with me. As my closest friend, I want you to feel the same happiness that I'm feeling. All that I'm about to accomplish, I want you to see. The madness that we've been through, I want it all to cease. I know you're going to be leaving soon, but today I am going to see you and make you happy. If you don't smile, I'm gonna kick your…"

I reached for the letter. "Let me see that now, sweetie."

I interrupted Angelina from reading because I remembered that part of the letter contained several curse words. No matter what, I was a mother and I wanted to keep my daughter from using foul language as long as possible.

"I've heard that word before, Mommy!"

"I guess you have, but I don't want you getting used to hearing it. Okay?"

"Okay, but I've heard worse, you know!" She sounded like a little Miss Smarty-pants.

"Oh have you now? We may have to have a little discussion about that, young lady!"

I was smiling from ear to ear as I sat with my Angelina on the floor. We had papers spread out everywhere, but right then our focus was on each other. I truly believed that my daughter would end up being my very best friend as she grew and began to grasp the challenges in life.

"So, are you going to tell me why you came home looking so ugly today?" I asked her.

"I was being teased today at school and it made me feel sad."

"What could anyone possibly tease you about, baby?"

"About not having a father," she said despondently.

I could feel Angelina's sadness when she said that to me. It seemed to really affect her and it made me wonder once again about my exposing Christian's letters to her.

"What did you tell them, Angelina?"

"I told them that my father was gone and they told me that he must not have wanted to be with me."

"I know you don't believe that, do you?"

"I don't know."

"Please don't believe that, okay? You weren't born yet when your father passed away."

It hurt me to say that because of the secret that I keep but, as I said before, I felt I had to. Angelina had found so much strength from the love behind Christian's words. I wanted her to grow up as a lady of beauty and respect. I didn't want her to be a weak and jealous person like Nicholas. I refused to even acknowledge him as her real father.

"Angelina?"

"Yes, Mommy?"

"If you want to make me happy, then I want you to never feel like you need what others have. I want you to love who you are and know that everything you'll ever need and want is always inside of you."

"Okay, Mommy. I'll try."

As I looked at my daughter, I could hear the words of my sweet friend, Christian.

"The beauty of your heart and the influence of those that love you unselfishly will always keep you grounded. Even when you stray occasionally, you'll never be unreachable to where you can't return with even more strength from your experience," he'd once written in a beautiful article about growing up.

I hoped that I explained things to Angelina in a way that she could truly understand. I didn't want her to ever jump on that journey of destruction that had taken the life of Christian and changed all our lives forever. I wasn't even sure if Angelina was listening as closely as I would have liked her to.

"Bless her little heart," my mother always said.

I could hear those words so clearly and, with any luck, maybe one day Angelina would remember what I'd told her and truly hear what I'd said.

I absolutely loved that day. Angelina and I continued to sit on the floor and talk. I felt as though Christian were watching us and lending his spirit to the love that I was sharing with my daughter. I'd had many talks with her before but when she brought home a problem that affected her badly, I felt extra proud when I knew we'd solved it with a positive understanding. Angelina was growing up so fast. I was going to see to it that she was able to enjoy her childhood and, at the same time, mature into a beautiful young lady. I couldn't be with her at all times, but my influence would forever exist whenever she needed love and guidance. My mother laid a foundation of self-respect and, for the most part, I think I kept her proud. There were only two things that I'd done in my life that she'd frowned upon. One was the mistake I made resulting in my pregnancy and the other was our disagreement about making Christian's memory a strong part of Angelina's childhood.

Virginia Ellen Hightower, my mother, had always been a pillar of strength in my life. At first, I used to always feel that I was very much like her. I used to walk strong and give everyone a piece of my mind. I still couldn't figure out why I'd allowed my situation to destroy that part of my personality, but somehow it had happened. So many of my friends had noticed the changes. The three most important people in my life had even pointed it out to me when they felt it necessary.

Christian had once asked me, "Damn, home girl, where's the Maiya that slapped me in the back of the head when I failed to hold the door open?" Then, another time, there was Stephanie asking me about this guy I was seeing at the time. "Hey, girl! Why are you putting up with his trifling shit like that?" At different times, she and Christian had both noticed a certain weakness in me that had never been displayed before. However, their comments weren't as powerful as what my mother had said concerning the change in my behavior.

"Maiya, I did not teach you to be stupid. I did not show you how to let men control and take advantage of you. I'm not to blame for you losing your courage, but I love you and I will help you find the daughter that I raised to become a woman," she'd said to me.

I was in complete silence when she'd let me have it that day. I didn't want to cry and I didn't want to show her any emotion because I feared she would only continue with her lecturing. I knew I'd disappointed her recently because I hated what I saw in the mirror myself. I'd felt that way for the past ten years, but I could escape when I was with Angelina. Through her, I could start all over again.

"Before you decide to just live your life through Angelina, I want you to at least give your own life another try!" my mother had pleaded.

I knew exactly what she meant but it was going to take a while before I could walk out of the house thinking that the day would begin a new chapter in my life. My life had been the same for the past ten years. My purpose had only been to make sure that my daughter's life was ever changing and constantly happy.

24.
Time Rings Impatiently

I had an alarm clock going off inside my mind and it was ringing because of a certain realization. It had been ten years since I'd had a man. I was beginning to wonder if I was simply punishing myself or if I had a real phobia about getting out and finding someone again.

"Ten years without getting you some? Girl, are you sure we're best friends?" Stephanie shouted in disbelief over the phone.

"You're still crazy, Stephanie, but I've missed you!"

"Well, what you need to do is come out here so we can go clubbin' again. Do something exciting for a change."

Her invitation sounded so good to me, but the thought of returning to LA gave me the chills. I could only imagine the obvious when thinking about it. I would experience a lot of memories of losing Christian and I would be closer to Nicholas, which didn't sit too well with me at all. I would've loved to see Stephanie and it was only fair that I visited her since she had come to Oklahoma to visit me three times in the last five years. As my mother always said, I'd have to sit and pray on that one because my plans were to never return to LA again. I'd said my good-byes to Christian and that was one of the most traumatic days of my life.

I often thought about what kind of life Tanya had led for the last ten years. Christian loved her so much and it wasn't until I stood next to her at the funeral that I could finally witness the love she had for him. I recalled seeing her in the club when we'd first met.

She seemed to be a person who enjoyed life and she had a really sweet closeness with Christian. But when we stood together in front of his lifeless body, I could really see the reason why he'd loved her so much. I listened to her speak and I watched as her tears fell into the casket. She'd held my hand when we stood there but, after the funeral, we'd never seen each other again. I had no real way of finding out what happened to her, but I hoped she would manage to get on with her life. To lose such a beautiful soul in such a tragic way was something that was very hard to get over. I could only imagine it to be twice as hard for her since she was his fiancée. They were both at a point in their lives where they realized that they wanted to be committed to each other. I wished her well, wherever she is.

Right then I was going to take a long hot bath and think about the fact that it was time to start turning my life around. I'd been walking in a daze, looking sad, and trying my best to raise my daughter. I was still a beautiful woman and the least I could do was see who was out there for me. I could never lower my expectations, but I had to stop comparing others to a man that was truly one of a kind. I could remember how elated I became one time when Christian sent me a letter that spoke of our future in the next lifetime.

"Meet me next lifetime because in this one you're my most treasured friend. The next one, maybe more?"

I got so excited, just from reading that one line, that I couldn't finish reading the rest of the letter. I guess you could say that I had certain desires for him, but I truly respected his love for Tanya. He could've definitely had his way with me on that day but I knew that if I'd tried anything, he would've only looked at me as if I were being silly. One time, when I came into the living room half-naked, the only thing he did was ask me if I had a bruise on my leg. I just laughed and thought it was so cute.

"Why are you laughing? Doesn't that shit hurt?" he'd asked me.

"No reason. I'll be back, okay?" I'd responded with a smile.

The combination of good memories and a hot bath felt fantastic. My thoughts of the future were what keep me tensed and that was what I needed to change.

Angelina was asleep in her room and all was quiet in the home.

I decided to call Stephanie and talk to her. I needed her warped sense of humor at the moment. The next day, I would take a look around and experience something or someone new. I was always walking around in sort of a tunnel vision kind of way. I didn't speak with anyone and I rarely said hello. I went to work and then I got my baby from school. That was the only time when I lit up or showed any signs of happiness. The next day, I wanted to try to be happy the moment I stepped out of the house.

"Stephanie, where are you?" I shouted as the phone continued to ring.

"Hello?" she answered, seemingly out of breath.

"Finally, girl!"

"Who is this?" Stephanie demanded to know.

"It's me, Maiya!"

"Oh, sorry girl!"

"What are you doing, Stephanie?"

"I'm getting my freak on, girl. What do you think?"

I had a feeling something was going on because she never allowed the phone to ring more than three times. Hearing her say what she was doing made me burst out laughing. I hadn't done that in a long time. Of course, I was speaking of the laughter.

"I'm sorry, girl! I guess I'll call you tomorrow then?"

"Okay, just make sure you call in the evening because this brother looks like he may last longer than most."

"You're a trip, Stephanie."

"Whatever, girl."

"Bye, Stephanie."

It was nice to laugh really good for once. I needed to call my friends more often. I had another friend at work, Lisa. She'd invited me out with her several times but I'd always refused. I decided to take her up on her offer, *finally*. Maybe she could introduce me to a nice guy or simply give me a reason to smile. I didn't think she could compare to Stephanie but, from the few conversations we'd had, she seemed like a genuinely sweet person. I needed to talk with someone and, next to Stephanie, there was only one other living person that I could truly open up to.

Looks like no one knows how to answer their phone right away these days, I thought to myself as the phone continued to ring.

"Yes?"

"Mommy, you better not be doing something freaky over there!" I squealed jokingly into the phone.

"Excuse me, young lady?"

"Oops, sorry Mommy. I just got off the phone with Stephanie."

She giggled. "Oh, and what is that loose woman up to these days?"

"She's still the same and still makes me laugh all the time."

"I'm glad, baby, because Lord knows it's been a while now! You just mope around the house like you've had your heart broken or something."

"More than my heart's been broken, Mommy. My life was devastated. My life was changed."

I had so much anger in my voice when I said that.

"I know, baby, but I just get tired of seeing you so down all the time. It's been ten years now and it's time for you to be happy again. One thing I'll say about your hoochie-momma friend is that she keeps you happy, baby."

"What?" I responded with laughter. "Listen at you, Mommy!"

"Well, Maiya, after you talk to her, you always seem happier."

"Yes and I miss her, too."

"You need to make some friends out here, sweetie."

"I know. That's kind of why I called you."

I told my mother of my plans to change my life from that point on. I wanted to share with her my desire to truly be happy again.

"It's good to finally hear you talking like that," she told me.

It was great to talk with my mother. She seemed happy and it had been a very long time since I'd heard her look forward to something that I was about to do. Our entire conversation was positive and we only talked about me. I was kind of surprised that there was no mention of Angelina. I guess she recognized that Angelina was the strong one. She was going to be happy, no matter what. I loved my daughter immensely and I prayed that she would always love and respect me, her mother. I wanted to make sure of her happiness by showing her my joy in being her mother. She shared in my happiness when I read to her, but I wanted her to see that I was happy within myself; not just when I was reading a letter from Christian.

"I miss you, Christian," I whispered.

As I shut my eyes and thought about my friend, I could hear tiny footsteps walking in my direction.

"Mommy, are you okay?" Angelina asked.

"Hey! What are you doing up?"

Angelina was adorable in her blue snow-flaked pajamas with the little footies attached. She looked so much like me, except that I'd allowed her hair to grow like crazy. It was so long and thick.

"I couldn't sleep, Mommy."

"Well, good! Maybe I can cut your hair because it's much too long, sweetie."

"Oh noooo! I'm really sleepy now!"

"You are?"

"Yes, Mommy!"

"Goodnight, Angelina."

Watching her run into her room was such a funny sight. I got so much of my joy from Angelina.

When the sun shined through my window the next day, I felt an awakening. It was going to be the day when I finally said yes to moving on. It may not sound like much to most people, but just accepting the invitation of going out with a friend of mine was a big step for me.

"Mommy, when are you gonna wake up?" Angelina shouted from the opposite side of my bedroom door.

Hearing her voice gave me an even stronger awakening as I realized I had overslept.

"I'm sorry, baby! Here I come!" I yelled out.

"Oh, Mommy!"

I could hear her walk away. When I got up, my face was swollen but nothing could get in the way of the day. Driving Angelina to school was fun. She sat there quietly; poking her lips out and giving me mean looks. I just smiled at her and blew kisses.

"Stop being so mean, sweetie!"

Angelina just shrugged her shoulders and looked the other way. She looked so cute sitting there trying to be angry. I could tell she's going to be one headstrong lady.

"I wouldn't be late if daddy was here," she mumbled.

"Watch your mouth. You're cute, but I'm still your mother!"

I'd heard that line many times in my life so I thought I'd try it out. Just like with me, it didn't work and I simply got the usual shrug of the shoulders.

I finally got Angelina to school and before I let her get out of the car, I gave her a piece of my mind. I reminded her of her place in this world and explained the meaning behind the word respect. After that, I kissed her, fixed her hair one last time, and reminded her of something important.

"Angelina?"

She turned to look at me. Her lips were no longer poked out and I thought she understood my lecture.

"I don't want you to ever walk away from me angry."

Angelina remained silent.

"I want us to always talk about things, okay?"

Angelina nodded with some degree of understanding.

I reached out to her. "I love you, baby."

"I love you too, Mommy."

We enjoyed a very sweet hug. I watched her run up the stairs and into her school. I had a few tears in my eyes as I sat in the car until she was completely out of sight.

Now it was my turn to get my day started. I was ready to walk into my office with nothing but attitude. Even though I'd been in darkness with regards to my personal life, I was still very good at what I did. My work habits and intelligence have always impressed my friends throughout my life. When it comes to that stuff, I don't think I disappointed anyone, including my mother. My struggles only occur in my personal life.

"Maiya, you're such a beautiful woman. You could probably have any man you want," I remember Lisa saying to me.

I also remember my response and how confused she'd looked after I spoke.

"Can you bring Christian back to me?" I'd asked her.

Lisa could only look around the room and wonder who I was talking about. All she could suggest was that I join her for lunch. She seemed to have this thing about doing lunch or dinner. I think she felt it was a good way to put problems on the table and talk about them. She was really nice and I felt she'd be a friend that would always want the best for me. I didn't think Lisa would supply me with any kind of burst out laughter like Stephanie, but I was ready to have some fun.

Actually, there was a man at work that had caught my eye a couple of weeks earlier. But soon after he'd opened his mouth, my eyes closed completely. Right away, he'd reminded me of that egomaniac that I'd dated years earlier. My once in a lifetime adventure by the name of Reginald Winston. Well, at least I thought it was a once in a lifetime thing. This guy, Ron, came in a close second to Reggie.

"I know work isn't the place for romance, but I think you and I need to break the rules!" he'd once told me.

"Is that right?" I'd responded.

"Either that or you should put in your resignation!" he'd continued.

As I thought about it, I couldn't help but laugh. Back then, I was still very much the anti-social person so my only response was a blank stare. I looked through him and then I walked away. After that, I noticed he was cautious every time he saw me. I found myself smiling a bit because I'd kind of stopped him in his tracks. He seemed timid and shy about approaching me. He probably didn't know what to expect.

I hoped that in my desire to move on, I didn't hurt others in the process. I wanted to be strong and display confidence, but I didn't want to seem unapproachable.

"Damn, Maiya! I've noticed a new kind of smile in you today. I think it's time you got to know me better!" I could hear a voice say in the distance.

Uh-oh! I thought to myself.

"Aren't you Ron?" I asked.

"Don't pretend like you don't know me!"

"I must not since I had to ask."

I guess he wasn't as timid as I thought he was after all. I walked away without looking back. I wondered if I was being mean and, in all honesty, I hoped that I was. I couldn't wait until I made it to my office. Relaxing behind my desk always felt good, especially when I had a moment to myself. When things were quiet, I thought about Angelina. She was growing so fast and time wasn't about to slow down or allow me to keep track of every possible mistake that I might make. I didn't believe I'd made a mistake by having Angelina think of Christian as her father, but my mother did make me feel guilty about it. At times, I wanted to grab letters from Angelina's hands, but it was too late for that. She was fantasizing about seeing him. I wished I could make that a reality for her. She wanted stories and I wished the memories could be my reality right then, too.

"Maiya?" A female voice called out from the doorway.

I glanced up to find Lisa standing there.

"Hey!" I responded.

She was looking cute in a dark lime top and knit skirt. She always talked about me being so attractive but I thought she was the one who could've had her pick of the crowd. Apparently, she was just a little shy when it came to men. I loved her curly, shoulder length haircut.

"You okay? I came to see if you wanted to do lunch today?"

"I'm okay and yes, let's have lunch today."

I noticed Lisa instantly light up with a smile on her face. She seemed totally surprised that I finally said yes to her offer. I couldn't keep saying no to someone who was totally sincere in her effort to be a friend. As Christian would tell me constantly, "Greeting a positive gesture with constant negativity only makes you feel like a fool. Eventually your looks aren't too far behind." Christian was deep in that way and all those years of feeling angry at the world had created this intense shell that surrounded my heart. What I must've looked like on the outside to others must've really been unkind. Lisa seemed intrigued with me all the time. We'd never held a conversation that lasted more than fifteen minutes so I was sure she wondered what went through my mind.

"I've always wanted to ask you about this picture and the quote beneath it," Lisa said as she pointed to a picture on the wall.

It was a picture of Christian, smiling, and underneath was a beautiful quote that he'd written: "Raise love to a new level and make it your life."

I was silent for a moment as Lisa continued to ask me about it.

"Is this someone that's close to you?"

"Very close, but he passed away years ago."

"Oh, I'm sorry to hear that. Do you miss him?"

"I miss him probably more than humanly possible."

"Maybe I shouldn't ask about him, but it's a beautiful quote. He must've been really sweet."

"He was unlike any man I've ever known or will ever know. But, that's the past and now I want to look forward," I said with a deep sigh.

I tried to convince Lisa that I no longer felt the loss of Christian, but I could tell she wasn't buying any of that. She looked at me with concern and seemed to be waiting for the tears to fall. I was determined to remain strong and I definitely didn't want to start crying in the office.

"Well, I sure didn't mean to bring back any sad memories. I was just really curious about the picture."

"It's okay, girl!" I responded with a reassuring smile.

Even though I was feeling the pain of the memory, I liked for my memories to give me strength. I wanted to smile each time instead of cry.

"Well, I'll see you in an hour, Maiya. Lunch is on me since I made you sad."

"I'm okay, Lisa. Really!"

Maybe I would look sad more often if I would be able to get a free lunch out of it.

"See you later!"

"Okay, Lisa."

The day seemed perfect for an outdoor lunch. Since Lisa was paying, I took advantage of the moment and suggested this cafe that was known for good food and nice looking guys.

"I heard about that place before," she told me.

"Oh and what did you hear?" I asked her with a coy smile.

"Just that they had good sandwiches. Why?"

"Nothing, just wondered," I responded, still smiling.

When we finally walked into the restaurant, I had so much life in my walk. I was smiling from ear to ear and moving like I was at a nightclub. I felt like I'd been away for a long time and it was great to get back to civilization. Lisa was more than likely wondering what was up with her new friend. I was beaming and the weather was great. Everything was just right for my first day at trying to move forward and away from being lost in the past.

"This is nice!" Lisa said.

"Very nice. What do you have a taste for?"

"I just want a really good sandwich," Lisa responded excitedly.

I found her to be really nice. I couldn't help but think about how Stephanie would be if she had been with me. Food would've been the last thing on her mind because she would've been looking around the room for men. I found myself doing just that and it wasn't too long before I made eye contact with a handsome man. I guess with me looking his way, he immediately found the courage to come over. Lisa was busy looking at the menu and I was preparing myself for the man's approach. I wondered what he would say or whether he would try to come up with something clever.

"Hey, what's up!" he said in a deep voice.

Hmm, this man sounded delicious! He isn't clever, but his voice is really nice, I thought to myself.

I was embarrassed by all the thoughts that were running through my mind. I was thinking that Stephanie had been way too much of an influence on me or maybe I'd just kept other sides of myself very well hidden. Nobody had better call me a hoochie, though.

"Hi, how are you?" I said.

Lisa was caught totally off guard and almost spilled her drink when she heard him speak.

"Hello," Lisa said softly.

"Hello to both of you!"

I could see his eyes attempting to examine other areas that

were below my chin, but I didn't believe he was that daring; especially with him standing so close to our table.

"My name's Tracy," he said.

Tracy? I thought to myself.

A man with a woman's name but at least he didn't sound like a woman. The man sounded good and he was nice and tall, too.

"I'm Maiya and this is my friend, Lisa."

"What's up, Lisa?"

Not a strong vocabulary, but that's okay for now, I thought.

"You mind if I pull up a chair?" he asked.

Lisa shook her head no, still in a state of shock that a man had approached our table.

"I mind because I'm having lunch with my friend," I told him.

I stunned him and Lisa both with my response, but I also put them at ease by smiling. I meant what I said but I did let him know that we could talk another time.

"So, you wouldn't object to having lunch with me sometime then, right?" he asked, handing me his business card.

"No, we can do that," I responded.

"Cool. That means I'll get the same kind of attention that your friend is getting now, huh?"

"You might, but don't get too happy, okay?"

"I won't. Nice to meet you, Lisa. Maiya, I guess you'll call me soon, right?"

"Yes, I will. Nice meeting you, Tracy."

The old Maiya Christine Hightower was back. I missed talking smart to men and it felt good to have that fiery spirit running through me again.

"You're something else, Maiya! I never would've expected you to respond like that!" Lisa said.

"Yeah, I used to really be bold a long time ago. Girl, I would've told him off and never even thought about calling him."

"Are you gonna call him?"

"Yes. I think it's about time I had a date!"

"Has it been a long time?"

"It's been years, girl!"

Lisa and I enjoyed a very long lunch together and went back to work an hour late. No one seemed to miss us, but we felt a little guilty about having such a good time and enjoying the beautiful weather outside.

"Lunch tomorrow?" Lisa asked.

"I don't know. That depends on what happens with Tracy," I responded with a devilish smile.

25.
I Knew You Before We Met

Time was flying by so fast. I had no idea that six months later I would still be dating Tracy. I'd made sure to take things very slow with him, although we had been intimate a few times. I could honestly say that the sex had been great, but something was missing. I love a man that has a smooth and gentle quality to him, but I also like for him to be passionate. I want to feel his passion when we make love, when he talks about his work, and when he talks about his future. Tracy was cute, very sweet, but I was still attempting to find his passionate side. Our first nighttime date had a beautiful beginning, but a quiet ending. I stood on my doorstep waiting for a kiss. He'd told me all night long how much of a flirt he was and how he was such a *go-getter* in the game of love and romance.

Maybe I'm expecting too much, I constantly said to myself.

Sometimes, my head started hurting because I was thinking that I could be comparing him to Christian. I wanted that kind of passion in a man. I didn't want him to be crazy, but I did want him to be excited about life.

When our second date happened, I was so wound up because I thought that things would be different. Things were different in that Tracy showed up at my door with exotic flowers and a framed picture of me that he'd taken when we went to lunch one day. He loved to take pictures. He was a frustrated photographer, along with being a college instructor. He was very handsome, well-groomed, with a liquid smooth voice; not to mention a gorgeous russet complexion.

"What am I worried about?" I shouted to the sky.

I was trying, with all my heart, to be patient and allow things to blossom into something extraordinary. I wasn't quite sure how Angelina felt about him. She was sweet when he helped her with her homework one particular day, but she never asked about him. I would think that, if a young girl looks up to a man, she would asked questions about him. To that day, Angelina still questioned me about Christian. Anyway, on the night of our second date, Mr. Liquid Smooth decided to use the magic in his voice to romance and beguile me. He asked me questions about my past, my future, how I did my hair, what I used on my skin, my favorite actors, and whether or not I wanted any more kids. I sat across from him with my hands on my chin and my eyebrows rose. I couldn't believe all the questions he asked me. I felt like giving him one of my smart answers because I wasn't about to run through every question that he asked me.

"My past is a trip and my future could be exactly the same!" I told him.

Tracy sat up straight after I said that. He nodded his head and began to smile. I toasted my glass to him because he was looking extra fine that night. I really appreciated the picture that he'd given me but, instead of keeping it, I gave it to my mother. To my surprise, not only did she love the picture but she also really liked Tracy.

"A teacher and so handsome, too!" she told me.

"Yeah, and he tries to be a mind reader. He's practicing to be a psychic as well as a photographer!" I responded sarcastically.

When I said that, I was making reference to a time when Tracy went on a little mind expedition. He was trying to focus on what he thought I was feeling. He also let me know that I was no stranger to him and that when he saw me, he knew exactly what my personality would be like.

"I knew you before we met!" he told me.

"Is that right?"

"Yeah. I even knew what your voice sounded like before you opened your mouth. That's why I was mesmerized when we first met. I don't even remember what your friend looked like."

Hmm, I thought to myself.

"Right now you're wanting me to go on. Tell you more, right?"

"You read minds too, huh?" I asked.

"Only when I feel connected to someone."

I had to quietly admit to myself that Tracy was making me swoon, even though I didn't believe a word he was saying. My best way to prevent sighing like a fool was by saying something smart.

"So, what am I thinking now?" I asked.

"Looking deeply, I can see that I could be in trouble if I continued."

"I don't know about trouble, but I may read off a few choice words to you if you don't watch out!"

We both laughed and that night ended up being very special. The kisses were sweet and, after I invited myself over his house, we shared a night of intimacy. I wish I could say it was passionate and wild, but it was simply sweet and tame.

Just before daybreak, I awoke to his gorgeous body lying next to me. I wanted to climb on top of him and ride him while he was asleep. In order to do that, he had to cooperate slightly. All I could do was smile as I looked at him. I peeked under the sheets and then I kissed his forehead. He was still sound asleep and so I turned on the television and watched the morning programs. As I stared into space, reliving the previous six months, I couldn't help but wonder how things would be in another six months. Angelina hadn't complained about me not spending time with her yet. That had been a major concern of mine. One day, Tracy offered to take us both to an amusement park and then to dinner. I was so excited and secretly I had these dreams of us being like a family, but my headstrong daughter soon brought me back to reality.

"Mommy, I don't want to go out with you guys!"

My first inclination was to tell her off and then force her to go, but I was more patient by then.

Am I getting soft? Am I in love? I asked myself. *God, I hope not!*

I couldn't stay mad at Angelina because I wasn't about to force the man into her life. I was still trying to get to know him myself and if she had any desire to find out more about him, then she would ask me.

I got a call from Stephanie one day and she told me about a conversation that she had with Angelina. I had gone to the store with Tracy and my mother was keeping her granddaughter company while I was away. Stephanie told me how excited Angelina had become when she suggested a visit to LA.

"Why did you talk to her about coming out there?" I asked.

"I think it would be nice if she came out here!"

I didn't know how to react because, not only did it frighten me to have her in Los Angeles, but also I was angry at the suggestion.

"How can you just totally disregard the life you had out here, Maiya?" Stephanie asked. "What are you still afraid of?"

"Everything! My baby doesn't need to be out there!"

"I think it would be nice. She can stay with me and I can feel like a real auntie or big sister."

"She does miss you, Stephanie, but it's really hard for me to let her come out there. She's so curious about Christian, even to this day. She wants to visit his grave, she wants to see where he lived, and she even wants to meet his family."

"What do you tell her?"

"I just say that his parents passed away. I actually never met them before and don't know much about his family. I guess I'm finally starting to regret letting her think that Christian is her father, but now it's too late."

"Too late?"

"Yeah, she worships him. She's taken most of my letters and keeps them in her closet."

"Get out!"

I explained to her that, on one hand, I didn't mind her affection for Christian, but I feared what would happen if she found out he wasn't her father. Letting her go to LA alone could only result in some sort of discovery that might not be too kind.

Seven months and counting. I found myself juggling everything in my life as I tried hard to avoid walking such a tightrope. I received a promotion at work that gave me more responsibilities, I had a potential relationship developing, and I had a young lady at home that was growing extremely fast.

"Mommy, what would you say if I brought a boy home?" Angelina asked bashfully one day.

"Excuse me, young lady?" I responded.

She giggled. "I want to bring a boy home."

"And what do you plan on doing with this boy?" I questioned her as I stood with my hands on my hips.

"Nothing, just homework. What do you think we're gonna do, Mommy?"

"I guess I'm sounding old, but I don't know!"

So many things were running through my mind. It wasn't that long ago when I'd asked my mother the same thing. Time had flown by and I needed to wake up because I was now the parent. Sometimes, she had me wondering about who was more adult, but I was older and that made me right.

"What's this young man's name, anyway?"

"His name's Dante!" she responded in a shy manner.

"Who?"

"Dante!"

"Dante!" I said in the same tone of voice that Angelina spoke in.

She sounded so cute and it was apparent that she had a crush on the young man. Unless he wanted to get run over by a station wagon, he'd better treat my baby right.

"I'm going to let him come over Angelina, but I want all the doors left wide open."

"Okay, Mommy."

"If you need to show him where the towels are in the bathroom, make sure the door is open."

"Okay, Mommy."

"If you take him to the bedroom, I want the door open."

"Yes, Mommy."

"If you take that boy out into the backyard, I want that back door open."

"Okay, Mommy! Okay!" Angelina shouted.

"I may think up some more things so don't go too far!" I teased her.

"Yes, Mommy! I'm gonna call Dante and let him know, okay?"

"Well, you can practice now, Angelina, by making sure that door is open even when you talk to him on the phone."

Angelina walked away with her lips poked out and her hands on her hips. She was adorable, but I'd meant everything I'd said. My little baby was growing up beautifully and smooth talkers come in all ages.

"I'm better off if I just go over his house," Angelina mumbled.

"What did you say, young lady?"

"Nothing!"

"Whenever you think you need to see this Dante person, you bring him over here!" I shouted.

I'm extremely protective of Angelina and I don't plan on ever changing that habit. I told her that I wanted to meet Dante as soon as possible. It was two days later and Dante was supposed to come by after school. She told me that he was two years older, which was so comforting to know. I thought that sarcastically just so I could keep my sense of humor throughout all of it. I checked for gray hairs that morning and found three that weren't there before Angelina announced the new phase in her growing up process. My Angelina was showing interest in boys and pretty soon she'd be a teenager. That was when I would have to buy a lock and a cage to put her in while I was away.

I better call my mommy! I thought to myself.

Another drawback to having a young lady growing up was that, sometimes, I heard giggling when I picked up the phone.

"Angelina? If you don't get off this phone!" I shouted.

"Okay, Mommy. I was just talking to Dante."

"You'll see him soon, young lady. Say goodbye!"

"Okay, but I'm gonna go outside and wait for him!"

"You do that. Now tell him goodbye."

My attitude was on the rise and there was nothing I could do. Somehow I had to get used to the new change in my daughter.

There was no telling what I'd be dealing with in the near future. Now it was time to do what I'd started to do: call my mother.

"Yes?" she answered.

"Mommy, why do you always answer the phone like that? Can't you say hello?"

"Is this my daughter? What do you want?"

We both started laughing.

"I'm sorry, Mommy, but I'm feeling kind of strange because your granddaughter has a boy coming over!" She laughed harder. "Why are you laughing so much?"

"That's good! You're not getting any sympathy from me, Maiya, with all the hell you put me through."

I couldn't believe how much my mother was teasing me. She even had me feeling guilty about how much trouble I had put her through when I was a kid. I guess Angelina was doling out the payback for it.

"Sweetie, you still cause me trouble, so I guess you have a lot of years to worry ahead of you with Angelina."

"Thank you so much, Mommy."

"Anytime, baby!" my mother said, laughing continuously throughout our conversation.

"You're enjoying this too much, Mommy! Wait. Someone is at my door. Hold on."

As I walked to the door, I could see the silhouette of someone standing near the window. I could tell it was a man, which could only mean one thing.

"Surprise!" Tracy shouted when I opened the door.

"Hey!" He was holding a bouquet of carnations. "More flowers, huh?"

"Yeah," he replied, handing them to me. "You deserve flowers all the time, Maiya!"

"Is that right! What are you doing here?" I asked him.

"Can't a man surprise his lady?"

"Hold on. My mother's on the phone, okay! Come in and close the door!" I ran back to the phone. "Hello, Mommy?"

"Yes?"

"That's Tracy, so I have to go now."

"Ooh, Mr. College Professor, huh? Have fun, baby!"

"I've noticed you like him, Mommy. We'll have to talk about that next time."

"Bye, baby!"

I took a deep breath before going back into the living room area. I couldn't decide whether or not I considered Tracy to be my man. When he'd made that statement moments earlier, I had a weird feeling about it. Now that I'd been alone with my daughter all those years, it was difficult having a man constantly craving my attention as well. Tracy was sweet but now that he was falling in love, he made too many requests for my attention. I wasn't sure what I wanted but, if I were to follow my heart, I could've honestly said that I was a long ways from being in love with the man. Something was missing and he just didn't excite me like I felt a man could. Maybe I was beyond getting excited.

"Hey, Maiya. Get over here, woman," he said in his deepest voice.

I started to turn around and go back into the other room. Maybe I was just in a bad mood that day and simply needed to relax a bit.

"Okay. One second," I told him.

I found myself doing other things and I knew it was rude, but I wasn't interested in cuddling up with him right then.

"Why are you cleaning up now that I'm here?" Tracy asked.

I shrugged my shoulders and simply leaned over to pick up some of Angelina's clothes. After that, I started straightening up magazines. I was about to put them in alphabetical order because I wasn't in a loving mood. Maybe the thought of Tracy coming over unexpectedly had me behaving like that. I was confused. Nevertheless, I didn't wish to cuddle on the couch.

"Is there a problem, Maiya?"

"No, I'll be there in a second."

"I think something's wrong and I wish you would tell me. Why are you being so distant?"

I could only shrug my shoulders at first. Somehow I had to think of something to say so that I wouldn't hurt his feelings too badly. It was probably too late because I could sense him getting restless.

"Maiya, this is strange because everything has been great between us. I came over today to see you and talk about things getting more serious."

"More serious?"

"Yes and I didn't think you'd have a problem with that, until now. Maybe there's something you want to tell me, Maiya?"

I had more thinking to do as Tracy paced back and forth in my living room. He stood there looking at me with a serious stare. I felt like I'd eventually say something that would incite an argument and I didn't want that to happen.

"What the hell is going on?" Tracy shouted.

I looked at Tracy like he'd lost his mind. The door opened wide and it was Angelina walking in with her little friend. She looked at Tracy and then looked at me. The room was very tense and I felt a little embarrassed that she'd walked in on an argument.

"Hi, baby, is this your friend?" I asked Angelina.

Angelina nodded her head yes as the little boy walked into the room. He just looked at us with wide-eyed curiosity and an innocent smile; probably wondering what was going on.

"Excuse me, I'm going to go now," Tracy said.

I just leered at him and waved because I wasn't sure what was going to come from my mouth. I let him get in the last word and that alone had me stressed out for a moment.

"I'm going to call you later so we can finish this discussion," Tracy told me.

Once again, I simply waved goodbye.

Now it was time to entertain two cute little kids. My smile came back pretty fast when I saw Angelina grab Dante's hand. I could see what she liked in him because he was a little gentleman.

"Hi, Ms. Hightower!"

Dante greeted me with a nice handshake, maintaining a curious look on his face. I could tell that he was schooled in the fine art of good manners. When we all sat down, Dante actually waited for me to sit first.

"You seem very respectful, Dante."

"Thank you, Ms. Hightower."

"You're making me feel old saying that!"

"Sorry!"

"Mommy! What else is he gonna call you?"

Angelina just had to throw in her two cents, with her smart butt.

I taught her everything she knows, I thought to myself.

"Mommy, can we go in my room?"

"You don't want to talk to me?" I asked.

"Not really!" Angelina responded.

"I don't mind!" Dante said.

"He's just saying that to be nice!"

"I don't think so, Angelina. Dante is a sweetheart. You could learn something from him, but I love you, sweetheart," I said, blowing a kiss to Angelina.

"Now can we go to my room?"

"Okay, but remember what I said about the doors around here!"

Angelina wasted no time grabbing Dante's hand and pulling him in the direction of her room. Dante gave me one last look before leaving and I could already tell he liked Angelina very much. Either he was very sweet and shy or a very good actor. He was probably a little of both, but still he was very well-mannered.

I found myself walking quietly around the house. I kept an ear to the wall and jumped at every unfamiliar sound. Dante might have been a gentleman, but that was my baby he was with in the room.

"You two alright in there?" I shouted from the living room.

"Yes, Mommy!"

I assumed I could trust them. Angelina was just as strong as I was. I couldn't imagine anyone talking her into doing something she didn't want to do.

"Baby? Are you sure you don't need anything?"

Well, I had to ask at least one more time.

"No, Mommy!"

Moments later, Dante walked into the living room with a wonderful smile on his face.

"What are you smiling at?"

"Nothing, but I can tell you're worried about us, huh?"

"Yeah, I am. But you seem like a sweet young man, Dante. Where did you learn such good manners anyway?"

"Mostly from my mother."

"Dante! Where are you?" Angelina shouted from her room.

"You might be in trouble now, Dante!" I teased him.

Angelina was running around with her hands on her hips. She reminded me of someone who constantly had an attitude. Of course, I was like that myself and I believed it wouldn't be long before Angelina became a young woman of strength. She had always impressed me and I never thought I would have so much admiration for my little baby. I just prayed that she didn't have to go through the same nonsense that I'd been through. I believed she already had a head start on me because she'd made a great choice in Dante. They were too young to be considered boyfriend and girl-friend, but I imagined if they continued in that direction, they might ended up being very close.

"God please protect my baby and, Christian, if you're listening, watch over her, too," I whispered to myself.

Dante attempted to have a conversation with me, but Angelina took him away before he could get settled on the couch. I hoped he remained sweet because that was the only way he'd con-tinue to set foot in my house. As I watched Angelina do everything but handcuff the young man, I received a familiar phone call.

"Hello?"

"Hey, girl!"

It was none other than Stephanie on the phone. That immedi-ately brought a smile to my face. She seemed happy but I could also sense a lonely feeling in her voice. She was thirty-something, just like me, and she still hadn't experienced a real relationship with a man. She was more to blame than anyone else because of her lifestyle. She was the sweetest hoochie-mama I knew.

"What you doing, Maiya?"

"Not much. Just keeping an eye out on Angelina and her boyfriend."

"Her boyfriend? You know she's too young to have a man!" Stephanie shouted.

"What man? Don't say it like that or you'll make me go in there and throw him out the house!"

Stephanie started laughing because she knew she was only instigating trouble and trying to get me worried.

"Dante's really sweet, anyway. I'm more worried about him than I am Angelina!"

"Dante?"

"Yeah, Dante."

"That's a cute name. Maybe he's the one."

"What?"

"Just kidding, Maiya. Anyway, I called you because they're running some of Christian's poetry and thoughts in that magazine he worked for."

"Really?"

"Yeah, a friend of mine told me about it and I immediately thought I should call and tell you."

"Why did you have to bring up Christian?" I asked her.

I was feeling like I'd done very well with keeping things in perspective and not thinking too much about him. I was hoping to get to the point where I could put him to rest deeper inside my heart. I couldn't continue holding onto his memory so strongly.

"What's wrong, Maiya? I thought that would excite you."

"It's okay, Stephanie. I've just been trying not to think of him so much so that I can move on. I've been wondering if his memory is preventing me from finding someone else."

"Why would it do that? You and Christian weren't in a relationship or anything."

"No, he was my heart. He was my very special friend on an emotional level as well as a spiritual level."

I was beginning to get a lump in my throat. I felt myself returning to memories that always brought tears to my eyes.

"Maybe I shouldn't have told you this, Maiya."

"No, I'm glad you did, Stephanie. Can you get me a copy of the magazine?"

"You sure, girl?"

I quietly said yes to Stephanie as I fought back tears. Time usually heals wounds but it never takes away the memories of a beautiful person. Christian was so beautiful to me, but I was thinking that I better stop with those thoughts before I really started crying and turning all red.

"Hey, Maiya!"

"Yes?"

"Why haven't you called me to tell me about Tracy? You know the routine, girlfriend! You're supposed to call me before you go out on dates!"

"Yeah. You're right, Stephanie."

"Well?"

"Well, as of today that chapter is closed!"

"Get out of here! What did he do?"

I started laughing. Little did Stephanie know, but I was to blame for the abrupt ending of my relationship with Tracy. Although I hadn't had that final conversation with him, I fully intended to end things between us.

"Mommy! I'm gonna walk Dante home now," Angelina said as she came into the room.

"No, you're not!" I shouted. "Hold on, Stephanie, girl. Angelina's losing her mind and about to see me get angry in a second. It's dark outside, Angelina! Plus, girls don't walk boys home!"

"Mommy, why not?"

"I'll drive you guys, but you're not walking him home!"

"You tell it, girlfriend! You sound like my damn mother!" I could hear Stephanie shout into the phone.

"You're not helping, Stephanie!" I said as Angelina stood with her arms folded and rolling her eyes at me.

"It's okay, Angelina. I'll walk home by myself," Dante said.

"Thank you, Dante," I said, keeping a watchful eye on Angelina.

She had the same look that I usually had before I was about to say something that was dying to get off my chest. It was usually something mean so I stood ready to spank Miss Thang if I had to.

"Maiya?" Stephanie said.

"Hold on, girl," I glared at Angelina. "I'm sorry, sweetie, but walking him home is just not a good idea for a young lady at night."

"Don't you trust me, Mommy?"

"I trust you very much, Angelina, but I trust my own judgment about life even more. If you can't respect that I know what's best, then you'll have to go somewhere else and live. I don't want that at all because if Mommy ever lost her baby, she'd be heart broken completely."

"I'm sorry, Mommy."

Angelina and I started smiling and crying at the same time. I guess watery eyes ran in the family. We could get pretty emotional sometimes and being headstrong was definitely something that I passed down to her, too. She had learned so much from me in such a short time.

"Why you guys gotta cry?" Dante asked, walking towards the front door.

"Thank you, sweetie, for walking home by yourself. I can give you a ride if you want me to," I offered.

He simply shook his head no. I walked over to him and gave him a hug for being so sweet.

"Stephanie, you still there?"

"Yeah, girl, I'm here!"

"I need to spend some time with my baby, okay? Talk to you later and thanks for telling me about Christian."

"Okay, Maiya! Say hello to my little girlfriend, Angelina."

"She ain't so little any more, but I'll give her your love."

26.
Lost Years

Six years later and Dante was still coming over to the house. He'd turned out to be quite a young man; so tall and handsome. He had really been good for Angelina. He was very respectful and sincere about their friendship. If I didn't know better, I could've sworn that he planned on being a part of Angelina's life forever. I wasn't so sure where she stood on the subject, but she constantly talked about him. We were both very proud of his impending graduation from high school and his plans to attend medical school. It appeared that we might end up with a doctor in the family. Dr. Dante Young. That would be a good thing for all the future headaches Angelina would surely dole out to me. That young lady surely worried me.

In a few days, we'd be having a very special celebration. We were celebrating Angelina's sixteenth birthday. I couldn't believe how time had flown by so fast. Angelina was already taller than I was, and she had aspirations of getting into fashion design. I wanted to say that she got her creativity from Christian, but that wouldn't have been right. I knew he'd never stopped smiling from heaven ever since she was born and neither had I. She was my treasure and it was going to be hard to one day see her become someone else's gift. The way things were going, it would likely be Dante. Six years of always being together showed me a strong indication that something special was ahead of those two. I wasn't sure what I was going to get Angelina for her birthday, but I'd taken Dante to the mall and he'd bought several things for her. I was so touched to see him putting so much effort into pleasing her.

"How much are you gonna spend on her, Dante?" I asked.

"I have some money saved up, Ms. Hightower. I've been preparing for this for the last few months!"

I could only smile and help Dante whenever he needed it. We went to the ladies section and I watched as he picked out a very lovely aqua teal colored dress.

"You have great taste! You need to buy something for me!" I told him.

"No way!" he responded.

"Why not?"

"I'm running out of money!"

"I told you to be careful. Are you spending your school money?"

"No, not yet!" he said with a devilish grin.

Dante was so cute and innocent looking as he held up the dress and asked if it was the right size. After he bought the dress, he bought some shoes to match. I had to help him with that because he was about to buy the girl some leather combat boots. *Why do men love us in boots so much?*

"You go, boy. Where did you come from?" I asked him.

"Why you say that?"

"Because men never realize that a woman needs shoes to match her outfit so they only buy the dress and that's it."

"Oh, well, I want her to like what I give her."

"You must really like my baby, huh?"

"What do you mean?"

"Nothing."

Bless Dante's heart because he really tried hard to downplay his feelings for Angelina. When you love someone, it's pretty hard to hide the way it affects you and I could see it so clearly on his face. He had no trouble picking out the dress and I could tell that he'd been paying close attention to what Angelina liked and didn't like. I was so impressed by his effort and his shopping skills. I wouldn't have minded having him as a son in law; especially if he shopped for me.

"Why are you smiling, Ms. Hightower?"

"It's nothing, really. I just had a funny thought."

On the way back to the car, he showed me another special gift that he wanted to give to Angelina. I was getting jealous because I hadn't even started buying anything for her birthday yet and here he had three gifts for her already.

"What do you think, Ms. Hightower?" Dante asked.

He showed me something that I hadn't seen in years and never had a chance to buy for myself. It was a book that was out of print. The book was written by Christian years earlier.

"Oh my God," I responded.

I couldn't believe what I was seeing and soon after the shock wore off, I started having feelings of regret.

What did I do? I thought to myself.

Now I realized that Dante knew about Christian. That was something that I had hoped Angelina would keep between us. At that point, there was nothing I could do to roll back the hands of time. I'd made my decision years before and the affect had been positive where Angelina was concerned, but I still feared any damage that might occur later. I believed that as long as the true iden-

tity of her father remained hidden, she would continue to experience that positive affect. All I ever wanted was for her to grow up
believing that a man can be good. Of course, she recognized that
there were some fools out there, too. However, through Christian's
words, she recognized a beautiful heart. Dante remained her close
friend because of his heart. He was so kind and seemed to have a
good head on his shoulders. Hopefully, time would provide him
with a sincere knowledge about life because he was learning and it
showed a lot.

"I'm really amazed at you!" I told him.

"Why?"

"Because you love my daughter so much."

"What do you mean?"

"Nothing."

Yeah, he has a lot to learn still, I thought to myself.

I drove Dante home after that and then went to my mother's
house. She also had me feeling guilty because she'd bought
Angelina's birthday present already.

"I thought we were gonna go shopping together?" I asked her.

"You take forever, sweetie, and I wanted to get it done!"

"Aren't you something?"

"Well, you need to stop procrastinating all the time!"

"So now I have to go by myself?"

"It looks that way, dear."

"What did you get her, Mommy?"

For the life of me, I just couldn't think of anything to get my
daughter. She'd soon have a beautiful dress, a new pair of shoes,
and a beautifully restored book written by Christian, all of which
would be given to her by Dante. As my mother came back into the
room, she was holding yet another very lovely dress.

"You guys are gonna spoil Angelina!"

"Did someone else buy her a dress, too?"

"Dante did!"

"Oh, really?"

"He bought her shoes, too! Did you buy shoes?"

"No, grandma can't be spending money like crazy, you know!"

"Well, Dante bought her shoes to match!"

"Get out of here!"

"He sure did!"

I also told her about Dante's surprise. She gave me a look of shock and one of being slightly disappointed.

"You know my feelings on that subject, Maiya," she said.

"Yes. I know, Mommy, but it's my decision and I'll deal with things as they come."

"If she ever finds out."

"I know, Mommy!"

"Okay, sweetie."

We both stopped talking after that. I sat there for ten minutes trying to figure out how to break the ice and relieve the tension in the room.

"So, you gonna come with me, Mommy?"

"Come with you where?"

She still sounded as though she were disappointed. I felt like I should get up and leave but I didn't want to make matters worse. I hated it when there was a subject between two people that made them mad or disappointed with each other.

"I was thinking you might go with me to get Angelina's birthday gift."

"Have you decided what to get her?"

"Yes."

"What, pray tell, is that?"

"Why do you have such an attitude with me now, Mommy?"

"I just asked what you're getting for her, Maiya. Plus, I'm the mother and I can get an attitude anytime I want!"

"You certainly have one now!"

My mother just rolled her eyes at me after I said that. I didn't know how we started this little argument and it definitely wasn't getting us anywhere. The only thing I was getting was a headache because we'd been down that identical road a million times over the years. What was done had been done and it was too late to change things.

"I wish we wouldn't argue, Mommy. Do you want to go with me?"

"I'm not arguing, baby."

"Okay, but are you coming?" I asked.

"No, I have some things to take care of."

"Okay, then I'll talk with you later."

"That's fine, sweetie."

I decided to buy Angelina a very special diamond heart necklace. I wanted her to have something that would remind her of my love. If and when she was ever away from me, I wanted her to be able to hold the heart in her hand and think of me. I believed in love where the bond was spiritual and could be felt when the other person was not physically around. That was something that I'd always believed in. Through my friendship with Christian, I learned that it could definitely exist. As always, when I thought of him, I had to look up and let Christian know how I felt.

"I miss you."

It wasn't hard picking out the heart that I wanted. It had a beautiful shape to it and several diamonds in the middle. I bought a beautiful silver chain to go along with it.

"I'm so proud of myself," I told the salesman.

"Yes, you picked quite a combination there, ma'am."

"Thank you."

"You're very welcome, ma'am."

After having the diamond heart gift-wrapped, I decided to treat myself to something. I could never go into the mall, look around, and leave with nothing for myself. On the way to the jewelry department, I spotted a beautiful coat and a gorgeous, apricot colored dress. I decided to buy the dress since springtime was approaching. The coat can wait!

After buying the dress and looking at the sales receipt, I began to feel guilty and had foolish thoughts of returning it before actually wearing it. As I glided down the escalator with a smile on my face and my eyes focused on the fabric of the dress inside the bag, I felt like myself once again. Spending money is the best way to forget about trouble, until the bill comes.

I couldn't wait to get home. It had been a very long day and I felt like I'd been gone for a long time. I always tried to spend time with Angelina, no matter how old she thought she was. We'd

always found time to talk and I didn't ever want to change that tradition. I could talk to her about anything, even though there were
certain subjects that I purposely tried to avoid. When she spoke
about Dante, I tried not to probe too deeply. I really liked him and
I was slightly afraid that I'd one day hear about him making some
unkind advances towards her. Another subject that I tried to avoid
was the memory of Christian. Her questions about him were more
direct and detailed by then, which made me afraid to say too much
because she might've been able to pick up on the things I wasn't
telling her. She loved a man she had never seen before. Not only
did she love him, she also truly believed that he was her father. I
couldn't complain because that was exactly what I wanted her to
believe.

"Angelina!" I shouted as I walked in the door.

"Where have you been, Mommy?"

"Can't you just say hello?"

"Hello, Mommy! Where were you?"

"Excuse me, Angelina?"

"I want to make sure that everything's ready for my birthday
party!"

"Everything's ready, honey. Don't you worry about it!"

Angelina had that attitude that runs so strong in our family. I
wanted to have our usual chat when I got home, but I wasn't hardly
interested in hearing any sassy talk coming from a teenager.

"Am I gonna be able to get my hair done tomorrow?" Angelina
asked with a little more attitude than she really needed to show.

"Do you have your drivers license yet?" I asked her.

"No."

"Then how do you expect to get your hair done?"

"You're gonna take me!"

"Is that right?" I asked with a look of shock on my face.

"Mommy, come on!"

"You need to lose this attitude you have all of a sudden,
Angelina. I've been doing a lot for this party and making sure that
it'll be special for you. Don't make me get an attitude. I'll end up
canceling the whole thing!"

She gave me her full attention after I said that. Her attitude disappeared as she sat her young butt on the couch.

"You have to be careful how you present yourself sometimes, Angelina. I know you're a strong-minded young lady and I love that. But you also have to know how to control yourself and be more respectful, too. You have to know when to back off just a little."

Angelina became really quiet and stared at the floor.

"Tomorrow is your day, baby. I'm going to see to it that it's very special. I'd like to give you my present now because I want this moment to be private between us. I love you, Angelina."

I gave her the present that I'd bought and as she slowly opened the box, her expression changed from sadness to excitement.

"Mommy, this is beautiful!" she shouted.

After I helped Angelina put on the diamond heart necklace, I immediately received confirmation that I had picked the perfect gift.

"I'm so proud of you, Angelina, and I wanted you to have something that will always remind you of my love, no matter how hard headed you can be!"

"Thanks, Mommy."

After all of that was over, we both seemed to relax ourselves. Deep breaths soon followed as we sat on the couch lost in our own separate thoughts. Angelina was holding the heart in her hand and smiling. I felt really proud but wondered what she was thinking. I can never say enough times how beautiful my daughter is. I worry about her, but most of the time I feel like she will do much better than I've ever done with my life. She's so strong and, hopefully, nothing would ever diminish that strength. That's why I'd chosen to show her the beautiful side of a man. I wanted her to know what type of man she should accept into her life. A man like Christian was her only alternative and, so far, I thought Dante was on his way.

"Angelina?"

"Mommy?" she said at the same time I spoke.

It seemed as though we were both ready to ask the question that was on our minds during our mutual silence.

"You first," I told her.

"I was just wondering why you never married again and why you haven't had more dates these past few years?"

"Why do you want to know that?"

"Just wondering."

"Hmm…"

"Well, Mommy, you're beautiful and you look like you could've been a model when you were younger."

"Am I too old now? Is that what you're saying?"

"No, Mother!"

I reached over and grabbed Angelina in a playful way. I adored her curious mind, but I wasn't really sure how to answer her questions since I didn't know the answers myself. Time had just flown by so fast and, at the same time, I'd convinced myself to accept my fate of being a single woman for the rest of my life.

"What happened to Tracy?" Angelina asked.

"He's around somewhere, but he just wasn't for me."

"Oh. Has there been anyone else?"

"Not really."

"Mommy, that means you haven't been doing anything?"

"What you trying to ask me, girl?"

"You know?"

"You're starting to sound like Stephanie!"

I backed away so that I could look at my daughter as she attempted to ask me if I'd had sex recently. Angelina tried desperately to act innocent, but it wasn't working. I could recognize her question. It was so obvious, so Stephanie-like.

"Let me ask you about the men in your life, young lady!"

"What men, Mommy?"

"Your grandmother and I love Dante, but we also wonder if others have caught your eye."

"Oh."

"Oh?" I responded.

"I like Dante a lot, but he's always been with me. I don't know, Mommy. Sometimes I wonder if I should at least talk to some other guys, just to see what happens."

"What do you want to happen?"

"What do you mean?"

"You've been asking me about my life and I think you wanted to know how long it's been since I had sex."

"No way!"

"Uh-huh, whatever!"

I looked at Angelina as she struggled next to me. I could understand her dilemma concerning Dante, but I didn't want her out there chasing young men and getting caught up in a lot of nonsense.

"So, tell me more, sweetie," I said.

"I don't know. I just think I'm too young to already know who I may end up marrying one day," she said with confusion.

"I understand, baby. I do."

"I hope Dante understands. I know he likes me a lot and I feel the same way about him, but I just want to see what else is out there."

"The only thing that you should look for, Angelina, is whatever keeps you concentrating on your goals in life. Continue your education and live your life being honest and sincere about what you want and what you expect."

Angelina remained silent and focused on what I was saying to her.

"I believe I've instilled a good foundation of love and self-respect in you so I have no doubt that you'll succeed on many levels. But, I'll always keep repeating to you how much I love you and how I want you to never fall into the trap of being guided by jealousy or someone negative."

"Have you been heartbroken, Mommy?"

"If I answered that right now, I think I'd cry, baby. I don't want to cry tonight because I want you to know how important it is to be strong and be ready for life's changes. I wish I could protect you and prevent you from ever having a broken heart but I imagine that's just not possible."

"You think it'll happen to me?"

"I don't know, baby."

Tomorrow seemed to come as soon as I put my head on the pillow. Nighttime always seems to go by so fast after you've reached a certain age. I'd have to ponder that thought another time. I could hear the sounds of laughter coming from the living room. I had a bunch of young people out there, along with my mother and my friend Lisa. I was playing the proud mother role by helping Angelina get into her special, sweet sixteen dress. After slaving over the oven all night and day, I believed that it would indeed be a great day for her, thanks to all my efforts. I had the food ready, the cake was huge, and there were gifts everywhere. Dante was out there looking handsome in his suit and acting like he had something heavy on his mind. My mother was walking around with a box of tissue so that she could wipe her tears of joy.

"You think this will look nice?" Angelina asked.

"You're already beautiful, sweetie. This dress will only bring attention to that fact, but I hope not *too much!*"

Angelina managed a smile as she nervously fixed and adjusted her dress. I'd allowed her go to the hair salon and they'd done a great job. Just looking at her in the beautiful pale pink dress made me want to cry. I'd once had a sweet sixteen party myself but, somehow, Angelina's felt more special.

I could hear the noise starting to build in the living room. It sounded like more people had come over during the time I was helping Angelina get ready. She'd already introduced me to her friends: Monique, Justin, Tracy, Angela, and a few others that escape my mind. After a while, all the names began to sound the same. That young man, Justin, seemed to like Angelina, which made me nervous. The look he gave her scared me a lot. My mother never warned me about that time in my life. It was difficult to accept the fact that Angelina was turning heads and causing young men to look at her in a sexual manner. I cringed at the thought of that, but realized it was a sign of her maturity.

Dante was so sweet, but I worried about him also. Over the years, he had put so much into being with Angelina. He hadn't made any time for other friends, so it seemed like she was the only one he knew. I believed he considered Justin a friend and that only presented a potential for trouble that I'd seen before. I certainly didn't want to see those young people destroyed by jealousy because it ruined a great part of my life.

I could see Dante talking to my mother. I decided to go in and join the party because I'd done all I could do for Angelina. That young lady was making me tired with all the adjustments. I informed her that she needed to just get her butt out there. Whenever she was in the room, Dante seemed to really open up. It was great that she'd found such a sweet young man that early in her life. Yet and still, I wondered how he fit into her future. Our previous night's talk was very interesting and I hoped that Dante would be patient because Angelina seemed determined to go her own way. She was a strong-willed person with a healthy sense of curiosity. After she asked questions, she still wanted to know what it felt like. She wanted more than answers. That young lady wanted experience. I encouraged every bit of her curiosity, but I feared the day when it took her away from me. I knew that day was coming soon.

"Hello everyone!" Angelina shouted as she came in the room.

We all applauded the moment we focused in on how beautiful she looked in her dress.

"She looks gorgeous, Maiya!" Lisa whispered to me.

"It's about time you came out to greet your guests, honey!" my mother shouted.

"It's okay, baby. You look beautiful!" I told Angelina from across the room.

I noticed Dante applauding and smiling very hard. I wished I were near him so that I could've pushed him in Angelina's direction. For some reason, he was acting shy and bashful, which presented a problem. There was no shyness where Justin was concerned. I clearly recognized the dog in him as he made his way towards my daughter.

Wake up, Dante! I wanted to shout.

"Hey, Angelina! You look *too* good," I overheard Justin saying.

Angelina looked as though she was falling for everything the youngster was saying to her. He was smooth. I wanted to say something but this is one time when Angelina would have to discover the bullshit on her own.

"Why are you watching them so closely?" my mother asked.

"I just see trouble when I look at this Justin person."

"Is that right?"

"Yeah, but I want Angelina to recognize it for herself. It's not up to me anymore."

"Well, let me go talk to her then!"

I grabbed my mother's arm. "No, Mommy. Let her figure it out."

"Dante! Where are your gifts? It's time to open them up!" my mother shouted.

"Now, why did you do that?" I asked her.

My mother just shrugged her shoulders, but her little move worked because Angelina's attention was taken off Justin and redirected on Dante.

"Hey, girl. I'm gonna get going now," Lisa said.

"You're leaving already?"

"Yeah, I need to get up early in the morning, but thank you so much for inviting me to the party. Your daughter's so beautiful now! I'll see you tomorrow at work, Maiya."

"Okay, Lisa. Be careful driving home."

I could see Dante pulling Angelina to the side. I wanted to go over and eavesdrop but that wouldn't have been very nice of me.

"Angelina, sweetie! Open Dante's gifts first!" my mother shouted.

Mommy was really bold that day. We could all see that she wanted Angelina to concentrate on Dante.

"Dante wants me to open his gifts later!" Angelina shouted.

Dante quickly corrected her. "No. You can open these two now, but this one I want you to open later."

He must've desired a private moment with Angelina when she opened the gift that contained the restored book.

"Wow! This is beautiful!" Angelina screamed, holding up the dress that Dante bought her.

She held it against her body and I absolutely loved seeing Justin with a jealous look on his face.

"What you doin' buying dresses, man?" Justin inquired sarcastically.

"Be quiet! This is so beautiful," Angelina said.

"It's alright," Justin responded with disappointment.

I glanced at my mother. We both smiled because Justin was

mad. It was so sweet to see Angelina thanking Dante and giving him a big hug. Dante was bashful about it all. I wondered if he reacted that way when they were alone.

Hmm…

The party was going pretty smoothly. My mother did a great job preventing Justin from getting too close to Angelina. After a while, I could see Justin getting frustrated. Then he finally gave up. He settled for a big piece of cake and a lonely spot on the couch. For once I didn't mind seeing Dante and Angelina retreat to another room. I had a feeling that he wanted to give her the special gift that he didn't reveal in front of everyone else.

I heard a knock on the front door and yelled across the room. "Mother, I think someone is at the door!"

"I guess you want me to get it?"

"You're right there!"

Mommy just rolled her eyes and opened the door. Once our visitor stepped inside, my mother had yet another reason to roll her eyes.

"Hey, girlfriend! Where's Angelina?"

I rushed towards the door and threw my arms around her. "Stephanie! Why didn't you tell me, girl?"

"I don't know, but I didn't come all this way for you, Maiya!"

"Is that right?"

"Just kidding, girl!"

It was truly good to see Stephanie. When she walked through the door, I forgot about everyone in the room. She was my best friend and she was like family to me. I could see my mother still rolling her eyes at seeing Stephanie.

"Well, do I have to go look for Angelina?" Stephanie asked.

"Oh yeah! She's with Dante right now!" I said proudly.

"Ooh! You go, girl!" Stephanie shouted.

"Only you would have those thoughts," I told her.

"Hey, you two, there are other people at this party!" my mother stated nastily.

Stephanie strutted over to the table. "These look like kids to me!"

Once again, my mother rolled her eyes and headed for the nearest door.

"What's up with your mom, Maiya?" Stephanie asked.

"Who knows?"

"Well, I'm gonna get some of this cake over here and get my party on, even though there are no grown men up in here!" Stephanie obviously dreaded not being the center of attention at a party.

In a way, she did grab all the attention with her crazy ways. She took over as the guest of honor since Angelina was nowhere to be seen.

I was thinking positive thoughts to myself in order to take my mind off of what could be happening in that bedroom.

"Do you think they're getting their freak on?" Stephanie whispered.

"You are not helping, girlfriend!" I responded.

Stephanie laughed and continued eating her cake, teasing all the kids between each bite. The young men in the room seemed to be sneaking a few glances at her body, but none of them had enough nerve to say anything. Stephanie had a way of making everyone speechless, especially men or, in this case, boys.

The party was beginning to go nowhere since Angelina wasn't around. I kept thinking that I should go in there and tell her to get herself back out to her party. She had all those guests and they were there to celebrate her birthday. But then I thought about the dog sitting on my couch, Justin, and I was glad that she'd left the room with Dante. At least I was convincing myself that I was glad. To keep my mind off things, I started cleaning up empty plates and cups. Twice I had to knock Justin's feet off my coffee table.

"We don't do that here," I told him.

I felt pretty good about that. I didn't like that young man in the first place and wondered how he'd ever become my daughter's friend.

After watching Stephanie get her non-alcoholic drink on and tease the young kids some more, I walked near Angelina's room. I tried my best to eavesdrop, but couldn't hear a word. That had me wanting to kick the door open. I respected my daughter's privacy but, being the mother, I had a right to enforce my authority whenever I elected to. Still, I tried to settle myself down and not get too anxious. When I glanced down the hallway, I could see my mother giggling. She knew what I was up to and she's always a big fan of my struggles as a young mother. I guess she always knew that one day I'd go through and experience the same headaches that I'd put her through. Well, enough of waiting for Angelina to come out. I decided to do what I should've done ten minutes earlier.

"Angelina, why is the door closed?" I shouted.

I didn't hear a response so I immediately opened the door. Angelina was on her toes and appeared to be finishing a kiss with Dante. I began to wonder just how deep that kiss was and what else they had been doing in the room behind a closed door. Dante stood there bashfully trying to wipe his lips. I inspected both of them with a suspicious eye.

"Come in, Mommy. Dante was just giving me his gift."

My baby was just a little too good at playing things off. I figured the less I knew, the better off my nerves would be, so I didn't question anything.

"Oh, can I see what it is also?" I asked.

"You've already seen it, Ms. Hightower," Dante responded.

"Yeah, but open it, Angelina!"

"Okay!"

Angelina opened the gift slowly and, as soon as the top half was revealed, she instantly recognized what was inside.

"My privilege to love," she said softly. "Where did you find this, Dante?"

"I found it in an old bookstore. It was collecting dust but, as soon as I saw it, I had to get it for you!" he responded excitedly.

"You're so sweet!"

I just stood in the doorway with a smile on my face as I watched Angelina kiss Dante. She held the book so close to her heart and I sensed Christian once again smiling in heaven.

"Okay, Angelina, you thanked him enough already!"

"Mommy, why'd you have to come in here anyway?"

"This is why right here, sweetie!"

Angelina had me laughing. I could see quite clearly that she was the daring one of the two. I'd have to worry about her more than Dante. I shouldn't have had to worry at all because she was the one that would ultimately have to deal with the consequences. I was probably jumping the gun, anyway, so I elected to shut up for the time being.

"Angelina, you have people wanting to see you. Get yourself out there!"

"Okay," she responded.

"Okay?"

"Yes, okay!"

"Wow, I can't believe you actually listened to me the first time!" I told her jokingly.

"I do sometimes, Mommy!"

"Sometimes is right! That's my baby!"

Angelina Christiana Erickson
My turn to take on life

27.
Father's Day

Baby this and baby that is all I'd been hearing the entire week. I realized that everyone was proud of me, but I wanted to feel grown up. In a few days, I'd finally be graduating from high school. It had taken such a long time for the day to arrive, but it was finally approaching. They'd kept telling me that I was going to miss those days, but I didn't think so. There was no way that I was going to miss the jealous girls that I knew or the childish boys that tried to get with me. I'd had a few teachers that were great, but most of my real lessons came from my mom. Sometimes I got some great advice from Stephanie. She'd been like a close auntie to me. I would need her as I took my next step in life. I found myself wondering what I would miss about high school. I still had Dante by my side and I was grateful that he'd stayed with me after I revealed how stupid my judgment had been one day. I'd put us both in a bad situation and I'd given Justin something to brag about. I think Mommy knew I was headed towards the mistake that I made, but she didn't try to prevent it. I didn't know if I should thank her, but I did understand her decision to stay out of it and let me learn on my own.

My sweet sixteen had been a year filled with every kind of experience. I wasn't exempt from stupidity and definitely wasn't excluded from tragedy or tough times. I knew my mom and the people around me constantly said how beautiful I was, but that didn't give me a first class ticket to easy times. Mommy did often remind me of my place whenever she was around and, despite the headaches she gave me, I knew she was right.

I realized that I'd given her quite a few headaches, too. I held on tight to the necklace she'd given me. It enabled me to feel her presence when she was not physically around. Because of my intense love for my mom, the necklace kept me grounded at times when I wanted to soar. I'd tested her love and patience quite a bit. I didn't usually do things with the intent of doing harm, but sometimes I couldn't believe the things I did. Even though I always meant well, I was simply too young to know certain things. One glance from my mom and I knew exactly what I'd done wrong.

I'd seriously tested my mother's patience three months earlier. After spending the majority of my free time with Dante, I felt like I needed a change. Either that or I was just searching for a different variety of excitement.

"You were just foolish," Mommy had told me.

Grandma was in shock but didn't say much because she'd been sick recently. However, what she did say did slightly hurt.

"I don't know you when you act like that, baby," she told me on a day when I'd visited her in the hospital.

She'd heard about my joyride with Justin and about my coming home late after things had gotten out of hand with him. The expression on my mother's face that night made me feel so low. I wasn't able to reveal everything that happened until the next morning. My first mistake was lying to her earlier that night.

"You on your way to see Dante?" she'd asked.

"Yeah, he's gonna help me prepare for my finals."

"I don't know about your finals, but try not to have too much fun over there!" Mommy said sarcastically.

As I was running out the door, she told me to say hello to Dante. I ran around the corner with the most devilish smile on my face. I thought I was getting away with murder. Justin was sitting in a car waiting for me and seemingly had the same smile that I did. That alone should've been a warning of the trouble that was to come.

"Hey, Angelina!" he shouted as I opened the door.

I smiled nervously and got in the car. Maybe I was feeling guilty because I do remember thinking of Dante a few times as I rode with Justin.

My second warning came when we stopped at a nearby liquor store. Justin had one thing in his hand and five or six stuffed under his jacket.

"What are you doing?" I whispered excitedly.

He noticed the nervous smile on my face, which just added more energy to his already inflated ego. He began putting a few things in my pocket, too.

"Don't do that!" I told him.

"Just take this and walk out the door."

I could've sworn the guy behind the counter saw us. I thought it was over for me. When Justin came out and got into the car, I felt relieved and excited at the same time. He drove off laughing hysterically because of what he had just done. He seemed to really enjoy doing things like that, but came off as someone foolish to me. He tried to act like someone who lived his life on the edge, but I didn't see that at all. I began to loosen up as we got farther away from the store.

I'm never going back there! I thought to myself. *I'm gonna be too through if I go home tonight and see my stupid self on television as an accomplice to a robbery.*

After about a thirty-minute drive, Justin pulled into an area known for kids doing things that they shouldn't be doing.

"Why did you bring me here?" I asked.

"Are you scared?"

"No!"

"What's the story with you and Dante?"

"No story. We grew up together."

"That's cool, I guess," he said as though he didn't really care.

I could tell he was testing the waters with all his questions and wondered if he was truly being sincere. After a few futile attempts at kissing me, he continued with his questions. He seemed to get stuck after trying to ask me about my party plans for graduation night. The silence was beginning to get to both of us so he asked me to get out the car and follow him. We walked down to an old shack at the bottom of the hill, which was also a place where kids got into trouble.

What the hell am I doing going down here? I thought.

That was a question I couldn't answer for myself. Justin held my hand on the way down and I kept getting images of Dante. I'd always imagined that my first time would be with him. The closer we got to the shack, the more nervous I became. When we walked through the door of the shack, my heart started beating frantically.

What am I getting myself into? I pondered.

My mother hated Justin. That was starting to make me feel even guiltier. It began to feel so wrong. I glanced at Justin one time and even saw Dante's face. After I'd managed to erase his image from my thoughts, my mother's face appeared. I was on a serious guilt trip.

"Show me how bold you are!" Justin said.

"Bold?"

"Yeah, you act like you got it going on, so show me something!"

"What does that mean? Show you what?"

He stood there with his arms folded, looking at me, and more than likely plotting his next move.

He issued a challenge. "Tell you what. I'm gonna take all my clothes off and I dare you to do the same."

"What?"

"Come on!" he shouted.

"Are you serious?"

"We don't have to do anything. Just show me a little something."

Justin removed his clothes quickly. Somehow, I figured it wouldn't be such a big deal so I took mine off also. He got himself an eye full and I was feeling disappointed by what I saw. I started to feel cheap in a way, too.

Is that it? I said to myself.

After checking me out from head to toe, Justin moved close to me really fast and attempted to kiss me. He was struggling with his own excitement and I was feeling turned off.

"Can I hold you from behind?" he asked.

"Okay." We turned and faced a broken mirror on the wall of the small, dimly lit room.

There were spider webs everywhere, which freaked me out. The floor was cold underneath and there was nothing good about being in Justin's arms. I could feel him getting hard and rubbing himself against me. He put his nose against the back of my head and smelled my hair. As I stood there being held by someone I was beginning to dislike, my face reflected no emotion at all. I could see myself in the mirror and I cringed when Justin touched my stomach. As his hand brushed against my breasts and then toyed with the necklace that my mom had given me, I was in total shock.

"Oh my God!" I said out loud.

Justin didn't seem to hear my cry.

"Can you stop?" I shouted even louder.

"What?"

"Stop it, please!" I shouted as I pulled away.

The combination of my pulling away and him being startled slightly caused him to push me to the ground.

"What's wrong with you, Angelina?"

"I don't want to be with you like that!"

"What are you here for?" he shouted.

I thought he was gonna jump me but, instead, he picked up my clothes and threw them at me.

"What's up with you, Angelina?"

Justin had so much anger in his eyes that I was really worried. I remained on the cold floor while he put his clothes on.

"Can you just take me home?" I asked softly.

"Yeah, alright."

As he walked outside, I could hear him call me a bitch under his breath. He seemed pretty angry, holding up his baggy jeans while walking out the door. I had a feeling that the ride home wouldn't be very pleasant at all. After I finally got myself together, took a few deep breaths, and went outside, I could see that I meant nothing to him after all. When I got to the top of the hill, Justin and his car were gone.

"Oh no!" I screamed. "Damn it!"

I was losing my mind because I was scared to death. I knew I had no alternative but to walk back home. I could've called Dante but he would've asked me why I was out so late and so far away from home.

It was cold outside. I walked slowly with my arms folded. I was startled by every little sound that I heard and leery of every car that passed me by. One important thing that I forgot to do when I left home was bring some money. So there I was walking, scared, and a little bit hungry. When I got home, Mommy was walking into the kitchen. When she spotted me, she kept walking and I began to think that she knew something already.

"How was your evening with Dante?" she asked when she walked back into the living room.

I stood there, not knowing what to say. She was giving me a look without expression or emotion.

"Your clothes look very dirty. Did you fall somewhere?"

I shook my head no and continued to wonder what she was thinking or what she already knew.

"I happened to call and speak with Dante tonight. I wanted to ask you to stop by the store for me when you came home, but you weren't there."

"No," I said softly.

"You lied to me?"

"Yes."

"I'll talk to you tomorrow, Angelina. You can have some time to think about what you did," she told me as she disappeared into her bedroom.

When Mommy turned her back on me, I immediately started crying. I didn't know what to think or do because I'd never seen my mother look at me like I was a stranger before. I felt like there was no connection between us. When the next day came, I told her the entire story and explained what I'd done. For some crazy reason, I assumed all would be well after I'd had a chance to tell her everything.

"You still lied to me, Angelina," she said disappointedly.

"Yes."

"That's really hard for me to take, baby. I'll get over it eventually, but trust is very precious and very valuable. If you destroy it, sometimes you can never get it back."

"I'm sorry, Mommy," I whispered.

She continued to let me have it that morning and I never left the house that day. I found myself sitting around like a wounded puppy hoping to be loved. I thought I could give her the kind of looks that would make her feel pity, but she acted like she wanted me to get out of her face.

That day turned from bad to worse once Dante stopped over for a visit. We sat on the couch and all was good for a moment until Mommy walked into the living room.

"Tell Dante what happened last night."

"Mommy!" I pleaded.

"What's wrong?" Dante asked innocently.

"My daughter lied to me."

"Mommy, please!"

She walked out the room and left me alone with a very shocked friend at my side. Dante looked at me with so much concern and, at the same time, was completely bewildered. He wiped the tears that left trails down my face and continued to ask what was wrong. I struggled with telling him, but realized I had to. I feared the worse before letting him know anything, so I took a deep breath and held his hand tightly.

"Let's go outside," I said with a forced smile.

"Okay."

As we went outside and I told him everything that happened, his expressions of concern lessened. I could feel his hand losing its grip and his desire to pull away. As I described what happened, Dante kept his focus on the ground beneath him. He was in total silence and I could feel myself losing his trust and friendship. Mommy was so right about trust being so precious and I was scared to death that I had destroyed it completely. Dante didn't say a word and our connection at that point in time was gone. He stood there with his hands in his pockets as he listened to me struggle through my explanation.

"I'm sorry, Dante."

"I have to go now," he whispered.

"I didn't do anything because of you!" I shouted as he walked away. "Dante, nothing happened!"

He never looked back. I sat down on the steps trying to convince myself that he'd come back. On that day, he never did.

As the sun went down and the stars came out, I remained on

the steps. I could smell some enchiladas cooking and I could hear the floor squeaking inside as Mommy walked around.

"Angelina," Mommy said softly. "It's time to brush off that experience and move on, baby. I'm sorry I was hard on you, but you know you deserved it. Taking advantage of the trust of others always gets you in trouble."

My mother sat down on the stairs beside me and held me close. My eyes were closed and I was holding onto my necklace.

"You know, I didn't think you'd like that necklace when I gave it to you."

"Mommy, this is why I didn't go through with last night."

At that moment, I think I made my Mommy proud of me again. Her eyes lit up and we hugged on the stairs as the night air grew colder. After talking all night outside and smelling the enchiladas burning in the kitchen, we made peace with each other. She eased some of my pain and fear and I promised to never lie again. Keeping that promise would serve as a test for me, but I prayed that she would always know that I'd only lied so that I could prevent her disappointment.

"Dante will be back, baby."

"I don't think so, Mommy. I hurt him really bad."

"He will because you're in his heart so deeply. All that he's done for you is not something that a man would give up so easily. He'll be back so that he can give you more. I know he loves you, sweetheart."

"You think so?"

Mommy nodded and I could tell she loved the fact that Dante was still in my life.

Dante didn't come back the next day or the day after that, but he did come back. We had to endure the joking and the laughter of Justin every time he saw me walking. There were several occasions when Justin and Dante almost got into a fight but, thus far, I'd always been around to prevent it.

"Nothing happened, Dante. You do believe me, right?" I asked him one evening.

"Yeah. Don't worry about it, Angelina."

A couple of days passed and, with each day, Dante and I became closer. I'd spent a lot of time with him just so he'd know how much he meant to me.

"You know, I thought I lost you for a second," I told him.

"Almost, but I couldn't leave."

"I'm glad."

"So, I guess we'll remain friends for a while then, Angelina."

"That depends on if you'll help me with another problem."

"Excuse me?"

I informed him of my latest decision to go to Los Angeles and visit the grave of my father. I was about to graduate and move on to another chapter in my life and I didn't think it would be right if I moved on without having visited his grave.

"You're crazy, Angelina!"

"Why you say that, Dante?"

"You're gonna go to LA by yourself?"

"Yes!"

"Have you told your mom?"

"No."

"Then I know you're crazy!"

I knew what he was getting at, but I wasn't afraid of my mother's reaction. But, for the time being, I preferred her to find out about my plans after I returned from LA. I tried not to even think about the consequences.

"You're afraid to tell her!" Dante said sarcastically.

Maybe he was right, but I really felt like I was making the best decision for myself. I'd never feel right if I didn't visit Dad's gravesite. I wanted him to somehow know the affect he'd had on my life. Not only had my mother raised me but the wisdom and life of my father had also guided me. I'd never seen him. Yet, I felt like I could close my eyes and envision his proud smile. I wanted to sit next to his grave and tell him about my life. I still read the letters he sent to my mom and now that I had the book that he wrote, I could get a sense as to how he'd lived his life.

"So why the trip to LA?" Dante asked.

"It's a way of putting it all together!"

"Meaning what?"

"I can feel complete and kind of move on, too. I can stop wondering about how he lived and where he lived because I finally had a chance to be near him," I attempted to explain.

"He's always with you, Angelina."

"I know, but it's different if I'm out there."

"I guess I understand. Sounds like you want to say a last goodbye to him."

Dante was right. I did want to finally say goodbye to my father. I'd held onto the feeling of wanting to be near him for so long and now it was time to finally let go. I felt I could do that best if I visited his gravesite.

"Well, Angelina, I'm not sure what I can do but I'll help somehow."

"Thanks, Dante," I said with a kiss attached.

The older Dante got, the better his kisses became and I almost lost my focus. I really wanted to get things straight about my trip to LA and everything else in my life. I could sense he had some fears about me going, but he continued being very supportive. At times, I could feel an incredible amount of confidence coming from him and then there were times when he seemed very shy about his feelings. He took on a boyish quality that was really sweet.

"What are you thinking?" I asked him.

"Nothing. Just listening to you."

"Why do you seem so worried about my trip?"

"I'm always worried about you, Angelina."

"Maybe you're more worried about us. That's what I sense."

Dante was quiet for a while and just shrugged his shoulders as if to say everything was cool. I knew it wasn't and that was beginning to make me feel worried.

"Does this have to do with Justin?" I asked.

"No."

"Are you sure? I don't want us to ever have secrets."

"What if something did happen between you and Justin? Wouldn't you have a secret then?"

"I guess you're right, but nothing happened!"

"I know."

"But you haven't totally forgiven me for what did happen, huh?" I asked softly.

"It's not that, Angelina."

"What is it then?"

"I guess I fear that something will happen in LA. Who knows who you'll meet out there!"

"Something like that can happen anywhere, Dante. Are you asking me not to go because of that?"

"No, I'm not asking that."

Our conversation was really starting to heat up. Each time we opened our mouths, I feared what would come out. I hated feeling like each word had the potential to ruin a friendship. Arguing was the worst feeling in the world and I felt as though Dante and I were headed for a really big one.

"Dante, you know I'd never think about hurting you."

"I know, Angelina."

"Then why are we talking like this?"

"I don't know. I'm just telling you what goes through my mind sometimes."

"I guess my crazy moment with Justin really messed things up!"

"I can't really say, but it does make me fear losing you to the next person that might excite you."

"Don't say that, Dante."

"Well, we've been together for a long time. I don't think we've ever come out and said that we were seeing each other as boyfriend and girlfriend. It's more like we've just grown up together and we have feelings for each other."

"I don't know what to say, Dante. You're just gonna have to find some way to trust me. I've always thought about you being my first lover and never have I gone past those thoughts. I don't think about or fantasize about someone else coming along."

Dante sat next to me quietly as he listened to every word. I could feel his heart pouring out to me and, at the same time, I could sense so much fear. I wasn't sure if I liked that, but I did understand.

"I guess I should admit that I was curious about Justin."

"That's what I'm talking about!" Dante interrupted.

"Yeah, but I still can think things through and I know right from wrong, *eventually!*"

"I guess so."

"What do you mean by that?"

"Nothing."

The silence between us from that point only added to the tension that we were sharing. Dante kept his arms folded and I was trying to relax myself because my little temper was trying to come out. I didn't like where the situation was headed, but I couldn't figure out what to say in order to ease the tension.

"Dante, I just want to visit my father's grave. This trip is not like a vacation or anything."

Dante was still silent.

"I just hope that you'll back me up somehow, just in case my mother gets suspicious. I'm telling her that I'm visiting schools in Atlanta and D.C. That way I can have at least a week or two for finding out about my father."

"Two weeks?"

"I'm not sure, but it could be that long."

Dante became quiet again and I was starting to get annoyed.

"Maybe we should talk later because you're really acting funny-style, Dante! I'm just hoping that you'll be here for me. Never mind. Let's talk some other time!"

"It's okay. I'm listening," he responded.

"No, this ain't going too good so I'll talk to you later."

"Alright."

It took a couple days before Dante and I realized that we missed each other. I wanted to tell him that he was being silly but I didn't want to start the argument all over again. Besides, Dante gave great hugs and when I was in his arms, he seemed to really take his time in making me feel good. Justin seemed to have recently disappeared. I'd heard that he wouldn't be around for graduation because the car we were riding in that day was stolen. I guess that was a kind of payback for how he'd treated me. I could've laughed at him, but then I would've just been setting myself up for a future payback. I hadn't exactly been a saint. I'd lied to my mother and to Dante and my sentence for a while was extreme guilt. Soon, I would have to deal with that again because I'd already put the wheels in motion on my next lie. I couldn't wait to get to LA and I'd already contacted Stephanie about it. She agreed that she wouldn't tell my mom. She was reluctant and extremely quiet about the whole idea. She struggled about telling me things like she was hiding something.

"Don't you want me to come visit you, Aunt Stephanie?"

"Aunt Stephanie?" she asked with surprise.

"Yeah. Why do you sound shocked?"

"I don't know, but I've never heard you call me that before!"

Stephanie questioned my reasons for coming. She said the same thing over and over again. "Are you sure you want to do this?"

I was more than sure about going to LA and Stephanie finally agreed to support me throughout the adventure.

"Come on, girl. I'm here for you," she told me.

Now everything was in place and it was just a matter of getting my ticket. Dante promised to help and I already had some good money saved up. I'd been waiting for the chance to go to LA for a long time. Not only would I soon graduate from high school, but I would also take a step into adulthood during my trip. I guess that also made Dante fearful. It was kind of like he feared that we would grow apart but I didn't believe we would. I was very proud of him and he was doing well in school. I knew that one-day he would be such a caring and passionate doctor. He was already so sweet and loving. He called me the next evening and apologized for letting his fears get the best of him. I told him that I was the one that should be worried.

"Why you say that?" he asked me innocently.

"You're good looking, Dante, and you're gonna be a doctor someday."

"Yeah, so?"

"So, you're gonna be a great catch."

"I don't know about that!"

"Trust me, knucklehead!"

"Knucklehead?"

"Yeah, stop being so innocent and wake up!"

"I guess I feel like I've already found what I want as far as a woman is concerned."

"Oh really?"

"Yeah."

Dante became silent after that. I couldn't tell if he was being shy or just waiting for my reaction. Probably a little of both. I realized he loved me and I felt very close to him, too. It was difficult for me to say that I loved him because, once I made that commitment, I wouldn't be able to focus on the things that I wished to do right then. If I started being in love with him, I wouldn't have wanted to go to LA and do what I felt I had to do. Maybe I was being weird, but it was my choice.

The conversation eventually ended but, thankfully, it ended on a good note that time. I wanted us to surpass all the fear and confusion so that I'd know I had his support completely.

"Angelina, can I tell you something?" he asked before we hung up.

"Yeah, what's up?"

"I really care for you and I hope that the things I say to you don't turn you off in anyway."

"What do you mean?"

"You know, the way I express my feelings for you."

"I don't mind too much, just as long as you remain patient with me. I'm very thankful that you're in my life, Dante."

"Oh, good!"

"You're funny!"

"What do you mean?"

"Nothing. See you tomorrow."

"Okay."

Time flies when you keep yourself busy and don't sleep at night. I was worried about my trip to LA and a little bit about my graduation. Of course the plane trip made me nervous because it would be my first flight and, to top it off, I was headed into unknown territory. I was glad I had Stephanie to rely on because it would've really been scary if I didn't have anyone. My graduation was the next day and my mother was making me nervous about that. She was so excited and teary-eyed because I was growing up so fast. She'd bought me a beautiful new dress and she was all over me when I was getting fitted for my cap and gown.

"Give her something comfortable because she has a big head!" she'd told the lady.

"Mommy!"

"Sorry, baby! Here, put this on!"

She was making sure that the cap and gown fit perfectly. I couldn't have cared less. I just wanted to walk down the aisle and get my diploma. The following day, I'd be getting on the plane. Thinking about that just gave me a cold chill. I couldn't believe I was gonna go through with it. I told my mother several times that day that I loved her. I hoped I didn't overdo it because she might've gotten suspicious. I thought about how angry she would be if, somehow, she found out that I was in LA. I'd seen anger in her eyes before and that wasn't a pretty sight or a good feeling. I thought about telling her the truth before I left, but I was afraid to. I felt as though she would try to stop me. Grandma wasn't doing too well, but she was at home. She didn't rest comfortably, but she got so happy when we'd go over to visit. I knew that if I tried to confide in her about my trip, it would only worry her. I didn't want her to get nervous about me going away to LA. Besides, it was probably too late to change my story. I'd told them both about my trip to Atlanta and D.C. and they were excited about it already. Mommy bought me a new suitcase, which made me feel guilty. She was all excited, buying me things, and had no idea what I was really about to do.

"I know I don't have to worry about you getting hooked up with some crazy fraternity boys during this trip, right?" she asked.

"No, I don't think so," I mumbled.

I hated answering questions about the trip because I had to keep lying each time. I was hoping I could just tell one lie and then that would be it. It's definitely easier to be honest because you don't have to remember everything you've said.

I was tossing and turning all night. I woke up every hour just before finally getting up at eight. I wanted to get ready and have plenty of time to sit and relax before graduation started. I had to be to school at noon and the program would start around 1:30 p.m. Mommy fixed me a really big breakfast and talked constantly. Apparently, she was more nervous than I was.

"Why you so nervous, Mommy?"

"I don't know! I hope I'm not this nervous when you get married!"

"Married?"

"Yeah, how's Dante anyway?"

"Let's not go there, Mommy!" I said with my hand raised.

"You must've been talking to Stephanie recently because you sound like her now."

"She tells me that I sound like you."

"With that attitude?"

"Yes."

"I don't think so, Angelina!" she said with her hand raised.

We both started laughing, noticing the similarities in our hand gestures. It pleased me to have so much in common with my mom. Being so beautiful, I wished she would've found someone like my dad. However, I'd come to realize that he couldn't be replaced. His spirit was too strong and there was so much to measure up to.

"What are you thinking about, Angelina?"

"Nothing. I just want to get this day over with."

"Yeah, but I can tell that there's something else on your mind."

"I just wonder if my dad's looking down on me. I want this to be like a special father's day for him. When I march down the aisle, I want to have two things that I hold dear to my heart."

"What's that, sweetie?"

"I'm gonna have the necklace you bought me in one hand and the book that my daddy wrote in the other."

Mommy was silent and I could see her feeling my every word. I wondered what was going through her mind, but I could see that her heart was melting. I guess it was silent pride or maybe I had her missing Dad even more by reminding her of his spirit.

"I'm happy that you've kept Christian in your heart, baby. He's very important to me and always will be. After all these many years, I still miss him with a passion. I can imagine someone else might think I'm nuts, but that man was and still is amazing to me. That's the power of love and the beauty of real friendship, Angelina."

"I know, Mommy. I'm learning that myself."

"I hope so because you have the potential of having not only a great friendship but also a very beautiful man in your life for a long time to come. I pray that you both hold onto each other."

Mommy was so right about friendship. Maybe I was too young to understand the level that she spoke on but I did appreciate Dante. Sometimes he gave me a headache when he got too emotional, but I knew he cared for me a lot. Breakfast with Mommy was so great, even though she fed me a little bit too much. I wanted to go to school feeling light on my feet. Instead, I was feeling like I was pregnant and everyone knew. After arriving at school, I walked nervously through the corridors leading to the area where graduation was being held. I kept taking deep breaths because I was hoping that the breakfast I ate would hurry up and digest itself. I shouldn't have eaten that last pancake or put so much butter on my grits.

"Hey, friend!"

"Dante, you scared me!"

"Sorry, Angelina!"

"Aren't you excited? Why are you walking so slowly?" Dante asked.

He sounded like he'd swallowed a bucket of sugar because he was talking a mile a minute.

"What's wrong with you, Dante. You on drugs?"

"Huh?"

"Nothing."

"Well, why are you dragging, Angelina?"

"I just ate too much!" I said kind of forcefully.

"Excuse me!"

"I'm sorry, Dante, but I did eat too much and plus I'm kind of nervous. Let's talk later, okay?"

"Okay."

"Hey!" he shouted.

"Yes."

"I'm glad to see you have the book with you! I know your father is watching you right now!"

"Thank you, Dante!"

Dante smiled beautifully at me. I wanted embrace him after he'd said that about my father.

"Hey!" I shouted.

"Yeah, what's up?"

"Nothing. Just wanted to see your smile."

"Okay."

I could've sworn Dante was skipping through the hallways after we waved goodbye. That boy was in love with me and I was pretty crazy about him, too.

It was time to line up for the ceremonies. I'd never realized how many people I went to school with. It looked like it was going to be a long graduation. I was elated that my last name didn't begin with the last letter of the alphabet. Unfortunately, I was standing in front of a guy who loved to talk and kept kicking my heels as we walked. There was still no sign of Justin so he must've been truly tied up somewhere.

"Oops. Excuse me, okay?" the guy behind me said.

Please let this day end, I thought to myself.

Actually, my graduation day was extremely special. My dad was heavy on my mind and I wanted him to see what I'd accomplished so far. His spirit had guided me and I always felt near him. I yearned to have a very long talk with him and that was part of the reasoning behind my trip to LA. I knew that if he were there, I would've been in his arms, hanging on his every word like it was his last breath. His words alone told me that he was such a passionate and sweet man. He probably would've been light with his touch, but strong when he expressed himself. I often wondered how much I looked like him and how much of my personality was similar to his.

"Hey! What's that book you're holding?" the guy behind me inquired.

"It's something my father wrote."

"Cool, can I see it?"

"Not right now, okay?"

"Okay."

The guy was getting on my nerves. The worst part was knowing that I had to sit next to him throughout the long, drawn out speeches. I should've been up there giving a speech myself.

I began to daydream. I could imagine myself talking about how I'd grown up with such a beautiful mother and grandmother. I would've mentioned how I wished my grandmother would get better and how thankful I was that she was there watching me graduate. Grandma had caught pneumonia recently and had been getting weaker ever since. We attempted to make her stay home and rest, but she always wanted to get out of the house. She was always very active and I could see her influence in my mother and in myself, too. If I were giving a speech, I would've definitely talked about my mom. She'd raised me with a very strong belief in myself and made sure that I saw the benefit of having a good and kind heart. She punished me without hesitation if I showed any signs of disrespect and celebrated anything positive that I may have said or done. I learned to see individuals for who they were rather than placing them in categories. She made that lesson clear by always exposing me to the positive words and thoughts of my dad. We'd read his letters together and experienced everything that was emotionally beautiful. We'd cried, laughed, and felt in awe of a beautiful man that once walked this earth. Now we simply had to keep him in our hearts so that we might find our way through the world feeling loved for who we were and who we would become.

"Daddy, I wish you were here," I whispered to myself.

"I'm sorry. Did you say something?" the pest next to me asked.

"No."

"What are you thinking about?"

"Nothing."

"Well, you seem to be visibly moved by something."

"It's personal."

"Oh, okay."

I felt myself wanting to cry as I imagined standing in front of everyone giving a speech about my dad. I knew I could move everyone to follow me in shedding a tear for him because I felt like he had guided my every step in such a powerful way. I garnered so much strength through reading his words.

"You've guided my steps, Daddy, but soon I may have to try to walk alone," I'd probably say.

I believed I'd have so much to say when I visited his gravesite. Hopefully, he could hear me right then and when I got there, we would simply be continuing the conversation. His influence made me think in ways that I probably wouldn't have if I'd never known the power of his spirit and the way he lived his life.

"This is really boring, huh?" the pest asked.

"What's your name anyway?" I asked him.

"Peter Griffin!"

"Oh."

"What do you mean, oh?"

"Just wondering. That's all."

"So what's your name, if I may ask?"

"Angelina."

"Cool name! Too bad we never met before!"

"I suppose," I said, wondering what he meant by that.

"Have you chosen what college you're going to?"

"No, not yet."

"You're holding on to that book so tightly. Is it really that special?"

"Very special."

"Oh yeah, I remember you said that your father wrote it. When I first noticed it, I thought it was a Bible."

"Oh, well. As I said, it is very special."

"Cool. Is he here now?"

"Who?"

"Your father?"

"He's always with me."

"Oh, would you like me to leave you alone?"

"Kind of, yes" I said gently.

"I thought so. We're about to walk and get our diplomas anyway so it was nice meeting you, Anita!"

"Say what!"

"Oops! I'm not good with names."

I just turned my back to Peter the Pest when we all stood up. It was time to get our diplomas since all the boring speeches were finally over. I didn't listen anyway because I was paying tribute to the important people in my life. Unfortunately the pest interrupted me so I couldn't imagine myself thanking Dante for being my best friend throughout my life growing up. He was destined to become a very special man.

I could see Mommy and Grandma getting their cameras ready to take my picture. I hoped Mommy hadn't run out of film already because she was taking a lot of pictures earlier. I could almost see the podium. There were only about ten people ahead of me. I shouldn't have been so nervous about all this, after all. I prayed that I didn't trip as I was walking because I'd never hear the end of that. I couldn't see where Dante was in the crowd, so I hoped he'd gotten a good seat somewhere.

"We're almost there, Anita!"

Oh, I want to hit this guy behind me! I thought to myself and took a very deep breath.

I could feel my heart beating faster. The principal of the school was looking my way and smiling. I didn't think I would feel that way about getting my diploma but I was really excited by that time. It was a big deal after all, but I felt it was even more special because of the presence of my family and my father's spirit from above. I could see my mother checking her camera.

"This is the wrong time to check it, Mommy!"

I knew she was probably gonna miss her chance but, hopefully, Grandma would manage to get the picture. I found myself taking one last look to see if Dante was around, but still didn't see him. He must've been lost in the crowd somewhere.

"Angelina Christiana Erickson!"

My name was announced over the loud speaker and, as soon as

I heard it, I began to smile really big. I almost tripped when I took my first step but found myself excited as I shook the principal's hand and accepted the diploma. They had a professional photographer in front of the stage so I no longer had to worry about my mother fumbling around with her camera.

"Yo, baby!" a voice said from the side of the stage. "You were strutting across there, weren't you?"

It was Dante, waiting for me as I walked down the stairs. He had a bouquet of flowers in his hand and a huge grin on his face.

"Hey!" I shouted. "I was looking for you, Dante!"

"Really?"

"Yes, really!"

"Why?"

"Be quiet!" I shouted as I hugged him tightly.

"You looked too good up there on the stage, Angelina! Damn!"

"You think so, huh?"

"Yeah!"

"I want to get out of here, Dante! This thing was so boring but I feel very proud."

"You should feel proud!"

It didn't take long for Mommy and Grandma to come over to me. I think they could tell I was about to leave. There were still a lot of names to be called and probably another speech or two afterwards.

"Angelina, I know you're not leaving without coming over to us, are you?"

"No, Mommy!"

Actually, I was gonna leave but I would've at least waved to them before I left. Mommy told me just what I had expected to hear from her.

"Can you believe I ran out of film before you got your diploma?"

"Yes, I believe it!"

"Why did you let me do that then?"

"That's not my fault, Mommy!"

"Your grandmother was too busy crying to take any picture so we both missed that one, sweetie."

"That's okay."

Grandma pulled me into her arms. "You two need to hush for a second and let me hug my grandbaby!"

"Thanks, Grandma."

We were all one big circle of love. We exchanged hugs all around and even Dante got into the action because he'd always been like family. He looked so fine that day, too. He was wearing a light gray sweater over some black cargo pants. The black mountain gear boots on his feet made him stand even taller and that was nice to see. Dante had grown up so nice. He was already over six feet tall as it was. He was making me think of him in other ways besides being in the family. I pinched his butt while he hugged my grandmother. I could see the surprised shock on his face and I couldn't help but stick my tongue out at him and tease him with hints about what I might be thinking.

"Are you two leaving now?" Mommy asked.

"Yeah."

"Okay. I won't ask where you're going, but I just want you to know that I love you, Angelina. You did it, baby, and I'm very proud of you!"

"Thank you, Mommy!"

"I love you too, baby!" Grandma said.

"I won't be out too late, Mommy. Tomorrow I'll be getting on the plane, so I definitely want to be well-rested."

"Okay, Angelina."

Dante and I walked through the crowd holding hands and smil-ing. Our slow steps turned into a gentle run as we made our way through the crowd and out into the parking lot. We hugged and kissed as I dropped a few flowers on the way. I was feeling so close to Dante and felt like I could finally tell him what he always wanted to hear.

"I love you, Dante."

"Huh?"

"Nothing."

"No. You said it, Angelina!"

Dante let go of my hand and started running in circles. He was so happy that I thought he was gonna hurt himself.

"Will you stop that?" I told him.

I was feeling embarrassed, I was blushing, but I did appreciate him very much. I knew that I would miss him while I was away, but it was also comforting to know that I have him in my corner.

"Where we going, Angelina?"

"I don't know. I just want us to be together before I leave tomorrow."

"What do you mean?"

"Nothing in particular. I just want to spend time with you."

"Oh, I thought you were coming on to me!"

"I may do that, too!"

"Cool!"

Dante and I drove up to the same hideaway spot that Justin took me to. I thought I could settle down into a warm conversation without any memories of my recent experience, but I couldn't. I suggested to Dante that we go somewhere else that had fewer memories and no cars with fogged up windows parked next to us.

"You jealous of them?" Dante joked.

"No, I could always get busy with you if I wanted to."

"Oh."

"Just drive silly."

We couldn't find a quiet place to park. We did find a lonely looking hotdog stand with a guy behind the counter reading a newspaper and probably waiting for customers to come in. His apron was stained but it didn't appear as though he's done much cooking that day. There was no one inside. That meant that we had the place all to ourselves.

"You want something, Angelina?"

"Just water, thanks."

"Water?"

"Yeah, water."

"Well, I'm getting me something to eat. I might even get a large shake, too." Dante said proudly.

"You go right ahead!"

Dante had me feeling really great. Watching him order was a treat and just being near him was very special. He always wondered about me finding someone who would spark my curiosity. He failed to realize that he did that himself. I'd yet to discover all that was Dante and, at the same time, I felt totally connected to him.

Dante sat back down at the table with his tray of food. "Angelina, you talk and I'll eat! That water sure looks delicious!"

"Be quiet, Dante!"

As I sat on the other side of the table and watched him swallow his hot dogs, I couldn't help but remember some of our special moments together. Growing up knowing that he would always be there had meant a lot to me. I wondered what our future was. Sometimes, I worried about him because he put so much into being with me. If it weren't for me, he would've gone away to school instead of going to the local university.

"Dante, why didn't you go away to school?"

"You know the reason, Angelina."

"Me?"

"Yes."

"Did you at least consider it?"

"My parents asked me to, but all I had to do was look in my pocket and my decision was made."

"Your pocket?"

"Yes."

"What's in your pocket?"

"A picture of you!"

"Oh."

Dante smiled at my reaction. He knew that I was touched by what he'd said. I was good at hiding my moments when I was blushing, but he always knew when my heart had been touched.

"Why you asking that question anyway, Angelina?"

"I don't know. Just curious."

"What else are you curious about?"

"What do you mean?"

"You were deep in thought while I was eating."

"I was just remembering our times together."

"Oh yeah?"

"Yeah, first kisses, growing up together, fighting."

"I remember those fights!"

Dante laughed as hard as I did when we both remembered some of the fights we had as kids. We fought over ice cream one time, which is why he still had a scar under his chin.

"That gift from you has never gone away, Angelina," he told me with a smile just before covering it with a napkin to wipe the mustard from the side of his mouth.

I accidentally closed the door on his face that day when we had that fight and, somehow, he scratched his chin. After Mommy had separated us, we made up about an hour later. She made Dante and I sit quietly until we realized how stupid we were acting.

"I remember kissing you that day, Dante."

"Yeah. You did, huh?"

The kiss was very awkward yet still very sweet. We were little kids so we didn't know about all the tongue business that we engaged in as we got older.

"I think I like those kisses better, Angelina."

"Huh?"

"Nowadays you get too freaky for me, girl!"

"Forget you, Dante!"

Time was flying by as we continued to explore the past together. Dante ordered another chocolate shake and listened to me talk about my trip. I looked at him and wondered if his stomach could take all that junk.

"I can't wait to get there, Dante!"

"Aren't you scared about it?"

"No."

"You'll be going to a cemetery and you'll be faraway from home."

"I guess if you look at it like that. I try not to think about it."

Dante had a point about being so far from home but I didn't plan on going to visit my father at night. I was going during the daytime because I was gonna feel nervous enough already.

"Why do you need two weeks just to visit his grave?"

"I probably don't. I just said that to be safe. I do want to spend a couple of days with Stephanie. She promised to show me some of the places where Daddy hung out."

"Oh."

"Don't get quiet on me, Dante. You know I'm coming back."

"I know."

"I'll call you every chance I get!"

"I know."

"You know everything, huh?"

"Yep!"

"Be quiet, Dante!"

Dante finally finished his chocolate shake. I was exhausted from the day's events, so he took me home. I was glad that I could finally rest and contemplate getting on the plane the following day. My future was less than twenty-four hours away and it was more uncertain than ever before. My actions could cause so much anger in my mother and, possibly, sadness in my grandmother. For me this would be a major step in putting my father to rest inside of my heart. He died before I was born and no one had ever given me the details on how it all happened. I believed that Stephanie knew so I was gonna ask her during my visit. Grandma knew but, for some reason, I got the feeling she didn't like to discuss my father. The subject seemed to bring tension when she and Mommy happened to talk about him. I had no doubt that he was a good man. I just wanted to be near him somehow. I wanted to find his footsteps and walk inside of them so that I can truly feel his spirit. Then I'd tell him how much I loved him so that I could move on with my life knowing that I'd paid my last respects.

After being smothered by Dante's kisses and promising to call him as soon as I arrived, I finally made it home. The way he was practically in tears, I thought I better make sure I called him from the airport in LA. It felt good to have someone care so deeply about me other than my mom and grandma.

"Angelina?"

"Yes, Mommy!"

"You're home kind of early!"

"Yeah, I'm ready to get on the plane and go!"

"Oh really?"

"Yes, Mommy!"

"You seem to really be excited about this trip, huh? You know, I spoke to Stephanie and told her about your trip."

"When did you talk to Stephanie?" I asked nervously.

"Today. A few hours ago in fact."

My heartbeat switched directions from anxiously excited to stressed out and worried about what Stephanie may have said. Mommy didn't show any signs of being angry so I assumed I was in the clear.

"She's excited about your trip to the different colleges, Angelina."

"Who is?"

"Stephanie is! Aren't you paying attention?"

"Oh, yeah."

The more we talked, I could tell that Stephanie hadn't given away our secret so my trip was still on. I was walking a tightrope that was attached to destruction if anything should go wrong. Only Dante and Stephanie were privy to my real destination and both assured me that they would keep my secret. Somehow I'd figure out a way to tell my mother, but I felt I was doing the right thing by not telling her. Maybe I was being selfish because I was doing things for me at the expense of my mother's trust, but that was the decision that I'd made. I was gonna be close to my father and find a little something out about my history if I was lucky. I'd read his words constantly and memorized his thoughts. Now I wanted to see how and where he lived.

28.
My Destination Worries Me

I woke up feeling strange Saturday morning. I usually felt good because I could sleep late without Mommy beating on the door as she walked out the house. She was usually going to the store, to the Laundromat, or to the beauty shop. That allowed me a lot of time to be lazy and sleep in before she came back.

"See you later, sweetie!" she would tell me.

Now I was about to go into her room and make sure she was up. In a couple of hours, I would be boarding an airplane for the first time. Then three hours later I'd be in Los Angeles, probably wondering if I'd made the right decision.

"Angelina, you up?"

"Yes!" I responded so happy.

I guess I didn't have to wake up my mother after all.

"I thought you were still asleep, Mommy!"

"No. What time do I need to take you?"

"I want to leave in an hour!"

"You want breakfast?" she asked.

"No. I'm gonna start getting ready now."

"Okay, baby."

The entire situation had me excited and nervous. I was glad that I'd packed a couple of days before because I didn't think I could even organize my thoughts right then. Mommy seemed so proud because she thought I was going to interview with some colleges. She was definitely all about getting an education and learning how to use your mind to be able to think for yourself. She was a strong lady and everything I was stemmed directly from her. Hopefully, I'd always be strong also. I couldn't help but wonder how the trip would affect me after it was all said and done. I felt like I'd probably cry when I was standing over my father's grave and, at the same time, I'd feel lost in my surroundings. I could already imagine myself there and I felt scared about it. Last night, as I stood in front of the mirror, I'd actually found myself rehearsing what I might say when I arrived at the cemetery. I'd tell him about Mommy because he'd want to know how she was doing. And, I'd tell him about Dante. I'd tell him about my life growing up and I'd show him the book that he wrote. I carried his book everywhere with me and I knew he was feeling very proud, even though he wasn't alive to see it published.

"Angelina, are you almost ready yet?" Mommy shouted from a distance.

"Yes, just about!"

I was going like a casual bum in some jeans and a sweat-shirt because I wanted to feel totally relaxed on the plane. I didn't plan to take too much because I didn't plan on doing any kind of partying or socializing. My trip was a special history lesson and discovery for me.

As I walked into the living room, I could see Mommy standing with her arms folded like she wanted to say something. Because of the whole trip, I was overly sensitive to every expression. That's what happens when every step you're taking is a lie. I was trying so hard to make sure that she didn't find out about my plans and it was making me worry about everything.

"Are you going to meet with the colleges looking like that?" she asked.

"No. I'll dress up when I have my interviews."

"You don't have to dress up too much, but I hope you don't go in baggy clothing looking like a bum!"

"What's wrong with the way I'm dressed?"

"Never mind, Angelina. Who's picking you up anyway?"

"Nobody," I said softly.

"Excuse me?"

"I'll be okay, Mommy! All the arrangements are taken care of."

"Oh, really? Through the school?"

"Sort of."

"What do you mean sort of?"

She was asking questions about details I hadn't considered and driving me crazy. I didn't realize it would be so difficult. When all of it was over, my lying days would be finished forever.

"I have to make all arrangements, Mommy. They just told me they could assist if I found it necessary."

"Well, don't you think it's necessary since you'll be going alone?"

"No."

"Why not?"

"There's gonna be some other people that I know from school going there, too."

"Okay."

"So, am I okay now, Mommy? Can I go?"

"I guess so."

"Any more questions?"

"No more for now, Angelina, but you're gonna call me, right?"

"Yes. I'll call you as soon as I get there!"

Mommy told me it was okay to call her collect and I jumped for a second as I told her that I would just call her and pay for it myself. I didn't want any phone number showing up on her bill and getting me into even more trouble.

"I guess you just want me to drop you off when we get to the airport, huh?"

"Yes, Mommy. I don't want any goodbye tears."

"You're just a grown lady now, huh?"

"A little bit," I said bashfully.

"Okay. I'll just drop you off, sweetie."

Soon thereafter, we left the house and it didn't take long before I could see the airport in the distance. I had my hand over my heart because I was finally about to do what I'd been planning to do for months. I was glad that Mommy was dropping me off so there wouldn't be any long good-byes. She looked at me with so much pride, but I wondered what would be in her eyes when I returned? Even the prospect of my first flight didn't make me as nervous as what I might possibly discover once I landed.

"Who's this fool driving so close behind us?" Mommy asked.

"Huh?" I responded as I turned my head to see who she was talking about.

"Somebody's trying to get our attention. Is he crazy?"

As I turned around to look at the car behind us, I immediately began to smile. I could see it was Dante and he was waving frantically for us to pull to one side.

"Why is he flashing his lights?" Mommy asked.

"That's Dante!"

"Is it?"

"Yes."

"What does he want? He should've rode with us if he wanted to say goodbye."

"I don't know! Pull over, Mommy!"

She wouldn't pull over completely, but she did allow Dante to pull along side of us. He came so close to us that I thought he was gonna scrape against the car. Mommy would've surely cursed him out if he did and probably would've banned him for life from the house. I could see so much love in Dante's eyes and he seemed like he wanted to really reach out to me. He was trying so hard to position his car close enough to be able to say something to me.

"Boy, what are you doing?" Mommy shouted.

Dante smiled bashfully.

"Where are you going, Dante?" I asked.

"I just want to give you this," he said as he handed me a card attached to a rose.

"You two are gonna make me have an accident!"

"No we won't, Mommy!"

"Angelina?" Dante shouted.

"Yes?"

"Read it when you get on the plane!"

"Okay!"

"Call me!"

"Okay, Dante!"

As he slowed down and drifted behind us, we said goodbye and whispered I love you to each other. Now I felt like I was truly on my way and I could hear the planes as we entered the airport traffic. I felt a little bit of relief knowing that Dante was aware of what I was doing. I knew I'd be calling him everyday to tell him what was going on in LA. I wasn't gonna act like everyone else and wonder if I'd run into any stars. My schedule was full on what I'd be doing and I was sure Stephanie would come up with things to do, too. She was so cool and kind of crazy at the same time. I hoped I wasn't gonna find any men coming over while I was there. That might've been uncomfortable.

"It's a good thing that I'm dropping you off! It doesn't look like I'll find a parking space today anyway!"

"That's okay, Mommy."

It took a while but we finally found the right airline terminal. I felt a certain rush come over me as we came to a stop.

"This is it, baby. I know you're gonna be careful and call me anytime, day or night."

"Yes, Mommy."

"You're gonna stay away from those sorority boys and all those other people looking to take advantage of young women!"

"Yes, Mommy."

"You're gonna be sweet and kind and show how strong you are as a student. You've grown into some kind of lady, but you also have that side of you that gets you into trouble."

"I'll be okay, Mommy."

"Yeah, you remind me of myself. I know you say you'll be okay, but I can't help but be worried now that you're getting old enough to do things on your own."

It was beginning to feel like Mommy had so much to say to me. I felt like I was being lectured and, at the same time, she was recognizing that I was growing up. I could feel her struggling with the idea of trusting me to be away from home all by myself.

"Mommy?"

"Yes?"

"I need to go."

"Well, get your luggage because I'm not carrying that too, sweetie!"

"Yes, Mommy."

After I put my luggage on the ground, we stood there looking at each other. Most of the time, I looked away. I couldn't maintain eye contact without feeling bad about the lies that I'd told.

"Be careful, baby."

"I love you, Mommy," I said with the hopes that it wouldn't be the last time I could say it to her.

"Love you, too. Call me soon."

"I will."

Walking through the airport, I could feel so many eyes on me. Maybe I was just nervous but having those different people ask me for donations didn't help. It was such a new experience for me. I felt a little less weight after I checked my bags in, but seeing everyone in such a hurry had me on edge. I thought I was gonna jump to the ceiling when someone asked me for the time. I looked up my flight and I would be going to Los Angeles on flight 175. They said it would be on time so, in about three hours from then, I would be in LA. After my nerves settled down on the plane, I was gonna read Dante's card. He was so sweet to say goodbye in that way. I knew he hated getting up in the morning. I was holding onto my father's book pretty tightly, too, and that gave me some comfort. I felt like so many questions would be answered on the trip and when I returned, I would have a new sense of self and a very strong focus. I couldn't wait until we got on the ground in LA. I hoped the world would be ready for my smile because I would be beaming like never before.

"Bring me back some autographs, Angelina!" Dante had instructed me the day before.

"This ain't no vacation, boy!" I responded.

I sounded just like Mommy when I gave him some attitude. One thing I regretted not doing was spending more time with Grandma. I couldn't believe I'd let time go by without talking to her or telling her that I would be okay. I guess I feared that I would only tell the same lies that I'd been telling Mommy. Ever since I'd started planning the trip, I'd kind of shied away from speaking to Grandma. I hoped she didn't think that I'd put distance between us because she'd been ill lately. Hopefully I could make it up to her when I got back. I remembered how she'd compared me to her favorite flower and how she'd said that she wanted me to always grow inside.

"I can plant roses and watch them grow every year, but watching you grow is my greatest joy, baby. Your mother has planted a lot of love deep inside of you and I know you'll never disappoint her," she'd once told me.

If she only knew what I was up to, she would've never said any of that to me. But, in my mind, the trip would allow me to grow as a person. Dante was great at reminding me how pretty I was, but my grandma showed me how beautiful I could become. Mommy just kept me strong and brought out the attitude in me. She was so strong and intelligent that I could imagine it taking a very confident man like my father to be able to keep her attention. He also had the blessing of being so warm and sensitive. When I was little, she used to constantly tell me how beautiful he was. I wanted to make sure that beauty continued to run in the family. I wanted to do my best to make Mommy proud of me when I became an adult. She loved me, despite the mistakes I'd made in the past, and now I hoped that remained true as I deceived in order to learn my history.

I was on my way to the unknown and I could see that nothing changed, even if you're minutes away from going above and beyond the clouds. I'd already been flirted with and it was kind of scary. I guess that was why Dante was worried about me, but I didn't feel intrigued by it at all. Those men were older and looked like they had money, but I was much too young to worry about that stuff. Mommy had always talked to me openly about men, so that's why I wasn't falling for the deep voices and pretty watches. I may have looked naïve but this package came with a warning sign.

"Hey, what's your name?" one man asked as I boarded the plane.

"Hey, you wanna ride first class with me?" another man whispered.

One of them had the prettiest silver watch on and I was wishing that I could give it to Dante. Holding his hand with a watch on like that would've really made me smile. I missed Dante already and I bet he was thinking about me right then, too. He had really been there for me in so many ways. I realized I could be headstrong most of the time but, occasionally, I needed others to help me through it all. I couldn't do that trip without someone in my corner providing that safety net should anything bad happen. Mommy called me "Lady know it all" and, at the same time, she saw a lot of herself in me. That quality in me would serve as my protection in the outside world. It was protecting me then as I brushed off all the flirtatious comments and smiles thrown my way. They gave me a great seat on the plane right next to the window. When I wasn't looking outside, I just planned to bury my thoughts into the book that my father had written. I guessed I should also read Dante's letter sometime soon. I was hoping that it would be a beautiful letter and not something that was filled with worries and doubt. He seemed pretty confident just before I'd left, but it wasn't too long ago when he'd expressed all his fears.

"Excuse me, miss. Is someone sitting here?" a male voice asked.

"Yes, she'll be back in a second," I responded.

I guess I was being mean but that man had playa written all over him. I didn't need that.

"Let me know if you need anything. I found a seat close by," the man whispered from behind my chair.

"That's alright. I can manage."

I could see a woman coming down the aisle and she looked like the perfect person to sit next to. I didn't want to go through my first plane flight trying to defend myself or worry about who I was sitting next to. I wanted to be able to relax a little bit on the plane, just in case I was bold enough to go to sleep.

"Hello? Would you like to sit here?" I said as she approached my row.

"No one is sitting there?"

"No and it's kind of my first flight."

"Oh, you say that so sweet."

"Thanks. My name's Angelina."

"Oh, that's pretty! My name's Diana Jenkins."

"Nice to meet you. Do you live in LA?"

Diana seemed really nice. She was older than I was but still she seemed kind of young. She had a sweet voice and was kind of on the short side. She was about the same height as my grandmother. I think I got my height from my mother because we were both the same height and much taller than Grandma. Mommy said that I was taller than she was but it didn't seem like it.

"Actually, I'm from Chicago. I'm going to visit a friend," she told me excitedly.

"That's nice."

"How about you, Angelina?"

"I'm actually going to visit my father's grave."

"Really? You mean he passed away?"

"Yeah, before I was born so I never got a chance to meet him."

"Oh, that's so sad!"

"Yeah and, to top it off, this is my first trip to LA, too!"

"I wish you could be going for other reasons, but I commend you on not forgetting your father."

"Thanks for saying that because this has been extremely important to me for a very long time."

I explained my reasons for going to LA and Diana was so sweet in telling me stories about her own family. She'd lived quite a life herself and seemed like she would've made a great big sister. I was hoping that I could keep in contact with her, but I was almost afraid to ask. Besides, I didn't want to bring anyone else into the adventure that I was on. I didn't tell her about the lies I'd told in order to get on the plane that day.

"This is flight 175 to Los Angeles. We will be taking off shortly so we ask that you all fasten your seatbelts and place all seats in the upright position," the flight attendant announced.

My heart was beginning to beat faster. As I looked out the window and saw the airport terminal, I couldn't help but think about Mommy driving back home alone to an empty house. I wondered what was going through her mind right then.

"You okay, Angelina?"

"Yeah, just thinking about my mother."

"Oh, is she okay?"

"Yeah, this is the first time we'll be so far apart and I just realized that."

"That's so sweet but she must be proud that you're flying such a distance to pay your respects to your father."

All I could do was shrug my shoulders and get a little misty-eyed. I was even having thoughts of wishing I had never done it.

"We're now taxiing out to the runway. We remind you to fasten all seatbelts."

I guess it was too late to stop the plane.

"I bet your father's smiling in heaven to have such a beautiful daughter," Diana said.

"I don't know if I like this," I whispered to her.

"I don't like taking off either, but it'll be over soon."

We held each other's hand and took deep breaths. Once we got in the air and the plane finally straightened out, we were all smiles.

"There. That wasn't too bad," she told me.

"What was that?" I asked anxiously.

"Just a little turbulence, Angelina. I can tell you're not as comfortable flying as you wanted to believe, huh?"

"No, not at all."

"Strangely enough, I enjoyed my first time. It was the anticipation of the flight before I got on the plane that was keeping me up all night!" Diana said.

"I slept good last night, Diana. Today is what worries me!"

Diana laughed at me and, for the most part, she really kept me at ease. I was so thankful that she was on the plane. I wondered if she was going back to Oklahoma when I went back. I could use her kindness because she was very easy to talk to.

"I hope you know someone out in LA, Angelina."

"Yeah, I'm gonna stay with my aunt."

"Oh?"

"Yeah, she's not really my aunt, but she's a close friend to my mother. I've known her all my life so I consider her my aunt. She knew my father, too."

"That's great!"

"Yeah."

I found myself taking deep breaths and clutching my father's book. I was feeling slightly down because I was so far from home. I was definitely feeling homesick.

"You look like you're about to cry, Angelina."

"I feel like crying. I've never been away from home and this feels weird. I guess I'm still young, after all."

"Yes, you are young, but I really hope this turns out to be a good trip for you. I know I plan on having a lot of fun and just spending time with a good friend. You should try to have fun also."

"I don't know about fun. I just want to tell my father about my life and be able to move on from always wondering how he lived."

"Well, I hope you're not going to forget him."

"No, but I've always wondered how he lived and I think I've held on too tightly to his memory. This visit will make me feel complete and then I can move on and concentrate on school and my life ahead of me."

"I think I understand."

"I believe that Mommy was able to move on slightly because she was at his funeral, but she's never let go of him because she wanted me to know what kind of man he was. After that, I kept his memory alive within my own heart."

I explained to Diana how my father had written many letters to Mommy and about the book that he wrote.

"So his letters show you what kind of person he was, huh?"

"Yeah, I guess you can say that I've been raised by his spirit. Through his letters and the things that my mother told me, I was shown the type of man that I should only accept in my life if I ever fall in love."

"That's so sweet. I guess I can see why your mother would expose you to your father's words."

"Yeah, it's really helped me so much in my life."

"I have a feeling that you have a boyfriend, Angelina?"

"Yeah, kind of."

"I think you do."

"Yeah."

After spending the next thirty minutes talking about Dante and comparing his sweet ways to the words and thoughts of my father, Diana settled into a magazine. I went into some more deep thinking and stared out into the clouds. Now was a good time to read Dante's letter. I was curious to see what was on his mind before I left. They were about to serve lunch in a few seconds but I didn't think I could eat anything right then. My stomach was tied up in knots and I only got a slight relief when Diana was making me laugh or smile. As soon as I opened the letter and saw my name written by Dante, I began to smile. I got a nice feeling knowing that he cared so much for me.

Angelina,

I miss you already, just as I always do when we're apart from each other. I hope things work out for the best on your trip and I want you to know that I'm here for you. I wish you didn't have to lie to your mother in order to do this trip, but still I support your every decision. It's hard for me to believe that I feel so strongly about you. I have so much that I want to share and talk with you about. I pray that I'm a big part of your future just as I've been in your past. Of course, I'm hoping for things to happen on a greater level, but then you already know there's no secret as to how I feel about you. Angelina, I love you very much so please make sure that you come back safely. We have a lot of talking and a lot of fun ahead of us.

Love,
Dante

"You sure are smiling. What are you reading, Angelina?" Diana asked.

"This is a letter that Dante gave me before I left."

"See, you do have a boyfriend!"

"Yeah, I do."

I just kept smiling away with a feeling of content. I was finally able to settle back in my chair and close my eyes. For the first time, I felt like I was in love and, though it was a different kind of feeling, it felt great.

29.
What Have Your Eyes Seen?

They announced that we would begin our descent into Los Angeles in about thirty minutes. I couldn't believe I was almost there. My mind was racing with questions about everything from what it was like to how did it smell in LA. I never imagined I would get that excited. The plane ride had been an emotional roller coaster ride because I'd been scared one moment and excited the next. I could never thank Diana enough for all her words of encouragement and just for being so sweet to me. I imagined that whoever she was spending time with would truly enjoy a good friend. I hoped she didn't forget me. Surely, I would never forget her. I found myself preparing my face and hair like I was meeting a boyfriend or something. I was only gonna see Stephanie, so I don't know why I was doing all that.

"You don't look nervous anymore, Angelina."

"I know, but I'm starting to get a little excited now, Diana!"

"Oh, yeah? That's a good thing then."

"Yeah, I guess it won't be so bad after all."

"Good, then we won't have to hold hands for the landing?" Diana asked to see if I truly was over all my fears.

"No, we can still hold hands. Diana, please!"

Diana was so cool on the trip. I knew I wouldn't find anyone that nice on the way back. I felt so excited since the plane ride was just the beginning. I thought I would meet a lot of interesting people out here.

"You're gonna call your mother when we land, aren't you?" Diana asked.

"I will *eventually*."

"You better call her because I'm sure she's worried!"

"I will. I promise."

"Okay."

I began to wonder how I would react once I heard Mommy's voice. I'd be standing in LA when she thought I was in Atlanta. Lying was gonna drive me crazy. I could see the wings of the plane open up. I was clutching onto Diana's hand even stronger than when we'd taken off back home. She was more than likely wondering what had gotten into me. I hoped I wasn't hurting her, but this was finally it. The plane was beginning to slow and we were going down through the few clouds in the sky. It really looked beautiful out here and the pilot had already announced that it was seventy degrees in LA.

"I'm looking forward to this, Diana."

"I can tell. You seem so much more at ease."

"Yeah, I am slightly, but I'm also very excited!"

I was smiling so hard and looking outside as the plane flew over a freeway, seconds away from landing at the airport. I was feeling like I had come such a long ways, not only physically but also in my life. I couldn't believe I'd actually gone through with the trip.

"What are you thinking, Angelina?" Diana asked me with such a big smile on her face.

"Just thinking about what it took to get here and all that I'm gonna do now that I've arrived."

"Oh really? Of course first on your list is calling your mother, right?"

"Yes, Sister Diana!"

Diana laughed at my response and I knew she was really concerned about me out there alone. She could see at the beginning of the flight how homesick I was and now all that had faded away. Now I was like a kid in a candy store: excited, and ready to run off the damn plane.

"Well, Angelina, I have to admit that I'm gonna miss you, girl."

"Thanks, Diana!"

"Let me give you my number back home. If you want you can call me some time, I'd really love to know how things went with your trip out here. I don't know why, but I feel kind of worried about you."

"Thanks. I think I'll be okay."

Diana gave me her number and she was really sweet to do that. By the time we settled down for a moment, the plane had pulled up to the ramp. It was time to get off. I peeked through the window to see if I could find Stephanie. There was no way I could see her from there. All I could see were a lot of people standing around and they all looked identical from that distance.

"I guess this is it. You be careful, Angelina."

"Thanks, I will. You enjoy yourself, too, Diana."

Diana and I hugged for a moment. I felt like I was saying good-bye to my sister. Within three hours time, we'd grown so close and I didn't mind sharing my thoughts with her. I didn't tell her every-thing about the trip because I knew she might not have agreed with my decision to deceive my mother in order to come out there. I would have to put the flight behind me and get ready for the next part of my adventure.

I couldn't wait to get off the airplane so I cut through aisles in order to get closer to the front. I even left Diana behind since there was no sense in prolonging that goodbye. I couldn't stand the fact that it was taking so long so I used my pretty smile to nudge my way up a few spots.

"Thanks," I said to a man that let me cut in front of him.

"You're welcome, but I wish you'd sat next to me during the flight!"

I didn't realize that was one of the jerks that had tried to hit on me. I cut in front of yet another person looking the wrong way as we moved closer to the exit. When I saw the red carpet leading out to the waiting area, I got so excited. I hoped that Diana wasn't mad at me right then, but I just had to get off the plane as fast as I could. As I looked forward in the distance, I could see people standing on their toes trying to find their loved ones. I still couldn't find Stephanie, which made me think that maybe she'd forgot about me. I was look-ing in the opposite direction when I heard a sassy voice cry out.

"Hey, Angelina, girl!"

"Stephanie!"

"You made it, *finally*!"

Stephanie was so happy to see me and it was really good to see her, too. When I saw all those unfamiliar faces, I was starting to get scared. I was terrified at the thought of being out there alone. I must've paid too much attention to all the stories that I'd heard about LA. I couldn't wait to get to Stephanie's place so that I could relax.

"Do you live in a nice place, Stephanie?" I asked.

I probably sounded like a little naïve schoolgirl when I asked that question.

"Well, it ain't a house like you guys have, but I've got a nice little bachelor girl place."

Stephanie said that with so much pride and, once again, I hoped that I wouldn't walk in and find some naked guy lying around munching on Doritos and watching television. I was tempted to ask if there was a man at her place now, but I didn't want to offend her. I needed to have a place to stay while I was here so there was no need to start any kind of feud between us. First thing in the morning, I was going to the cemetery. I didn't want to waste time in visiting my father so tomorrow would be the day.

"Are you hungry, Angelina?"

"No, I just need to calm down a little bit."

"Oh, are you that excited?"

"Yes, very much!"

"Actually I am, too, baby girl! I hope you know I'm gonna support you through this trip, but I want you to be careful."

"Be careful? Why do you say it like that?"

"No particular reason, Angelina. I just want you to be sure about what you're doing and know that I'm here for you."

The way Stephanie was talking gave me an eerie feeling. It was like she was thinking that something might happen or perhaps she knew something that she wasn't telling me. In any case, she had me feeling strange. It's always what people don't say that makes you nervous and worried. I was already beyond being worried anyway.

On the ride to Stephanie's condo, we passed through many interesting areas. She drove along the beach and I saw all kinds of fine men and people who definitely had a screw or two loose. I was in the right place but I would wait until my next visit before I tried to join in on all that fun.

"You wanna stop, Angelina?"

"No, that's okay."

"No? You sound like your mother! Don't you want to get your flirt on and take advantage of being out here without a man?"

"No. I'll pass, Stephanie."

"You sound too old for someone so young, Angelina!"

All I could do was shrug my shoulders and be committed to my decision. Stephanie was the type to talk your head off until you gave in to what she wanted to do. My mother had warned me with so many stories about Aunt Stephanie. I recognized all the warning signs and definitely knew when to say no to her.

"So, what else will you do besides visit the cemetery?"

"I don't know. I guess we can hangout some time. I just want to spend the next few days visiting my father so that I can really feel his presence. I was hoping that you could show me where he lived and where Mommy lived."

"You sure you want to do that?"

"Yes, why?"

"I went by that street a few months ago and it just brought back too many memories!"

"Memories?"

"Yes, bad memories of when Christian died."

"He was killed, right?"

"Yes, hasn't your mother told you about it?"

"She never told me how it happened exactly or who killed him, but she told me that he died in her arms. That must've been heart-breaking for Mommy."

Stephanie seemed to get really quiet as I questioned her in detail about that fateful day. I guess it was traumatic for her in some way, too. I noticed that she wasn't able to look me in the eyes when she spoke about what happened. She probably didn't want me to see her eyes filling up with tears.

"Were you there that day?" I asked.

"No, sweetie. I was on the phone with your mother when it all happened," Stephanie answered quietly.

"So he died in her apartment?"

"No, he died on the street."

"How was my mother able to hold him in her arms before he died if she was on the phone with you?"

"Sweetie, can we talk about this another time? I feel funny telling you about all this right now."

"I guess so, but I just wanted to know."

"Let's talk about it later, okay?"

"Okay."

I didn't understand Stephanie's hesitation to answer my questions but I imagined that, in time, she'd feel comfortable and tell me more about what had happened. That was the first time I'd ever seen her all choked up and feeling uncomfortable about talking. She could talk forever but, right then, she was too quiet. I felt like I wanted to run to the nearest phone and tell my mother that I got Stephanie to be quiet. Speaking of Mommy, I knew that soon I would have to call her and let her know I was all right. I hoped I didn't sound too nervous myself while I was talking to her. Let's face it. I was supposed to be in Atlanta visiting a college out there, but there I was, on the West Coast, searching for answers about my father.

"You wanna go see the club where your mom met Christian?" Stephanie asked in a sly manner.

"You trying to get me to go party somewhere, huh?"

Stephanie just smiled and I knew what she was up to when she said that. I also knew that the club where my parents met was long gone. Just from watching the entertainment news shows on television, I could tell that clubs in LA didn't last too long.

"Is that club really still there, Stephanie?" I asked to make sure.

"No. I'm just kidding, girl!"

"I thought so."

"Did your mother tell you about that club?"

"Yeah, she told me about it and she told me about the night she met my dad. She said that they didn't really get along at first."

"No, they didn't. Plus, your mom was really seeing someone else that night anyway."

"Who was that?"

"I really shouldn't be telling you this stuff, Angelina."

"Come on!"

"I thought Maiya told you already. I didn't expect you to come with all these questions."

"Sorry, Stephanie. I'm just curious that's all."

"It's okay. I'll just tell you that his name was Nicholas and at the time he was Christian's best friend."

"Oh."

"Yeah, so since we're almost to my place can we please change the subject?" Stephanie pleaded.

"Okay already!"

When we entered the condo, it was my turn to show some hesitation. I was afraid of what I might find or who might jump out from behind a door somewhere. I guess I'd been left with a bad impression of Stephanie but, then again, she hadn't done much to change that. To my surprise, her condo turned out to be really nice and very neat also. She had some African-American art on her walls, a gorgeous fireplace, and beautiful plum-colored lace curtains covering her window. I was impressed. I was witnessing another side of Stephanie that I never knew existed. I wondered if Mommy knew that side of her best friend. Maybe it was a recent change.

"Did you clean up before I got here?" I asked jokingly.

"No. I keep my place looking good, honey!"

"It's very nice, Stephanie. I'm surprised!"

"Yeah, I know what you and your mother think about me but I still take good care of things. I don't want anybody leaving here with something to talk about or use against me."

"Well, I promise not to say anything bad."

"I know you won't because you've missed your Auntie Stephanie!"

"I'll miss you more if you tell me about my dad," I said teasingly.

"Maybe I'll tell you a little bit more, but you have to be patient with me, Angelina. That was one of the saddest days of my life."

I could tell that remembering how my father died was very painful for Stephanie. I'd never tried to get Mommy to talk about it for fear that I would get the same kind of reaction that I was finding with Stephanie. I felt as though Stephanie was trying to pick and choose just how much she would reveal to me and I didn't really understand that. I was thinking that I had to be bold with my questions but maybe, if I continued with the sly approach, she'd tell me things by accident.

"Stephanie, did my mom leave Nicholas for Christian?"

"I guess you can say that."

"Well, how would you say it?"

"Damn, sista girl. You be coming hard with your questions, huh?"

"I'm only curious."

"Well, she left Nicholas because of a bad moment. But with Christian, she found something that she always looked for. Someone that she could communicate with in a special way. Your mother is just like you in that it ain't important to get her flirt on. That girl just wants to talk, which I just don't get!"

"Well, there's more to life than just flirting or messing around."

"See, you're exactly like your mother!"

I was smiling at the comparison but I felt like Stephanie was trying to get me off the subject. One moment she was about to reveal everything and the next moment she found a way out of telling me something important.

"Now, tell me what the bad moment was between Nicholas and Mommy!" I asked excitedly.

I was ready for all the dirt as though we were two schoolgirls gossiping and telling secrets. Stephanie was really struggling.

"Well, your mother invited Nicholas over for dinner but things got out of hand. I blamed myself for a long time because I convinced your mother to take a chance on him and see what kind of fun she could have. I regret that even today."

"What happened? Did he rape her or something?"

"No, it wasn't like that."

"Then what was it?"

"Angelina, this is where I have to stop because it was a very personal and painful moment for your mother. I can't tell you any more than what I've told you."

"Then what can you tell me, Stephanie?"

"Let me just say that Christian was killed out of jealousy for what he shared with Maiya. He was a good man and he ultimately lost his life while trying to always be there for your mom."

Stephanie walked away after her last words on the subject of my mom and dad. I guess she also noticed my own sadness and how quiet I'd become. There was so much more to my father that I was dying to know because nothing seemed to change except that I found him to be more and more special. He seemed like a man who was so beautiful inside. After Stephanie left the room, I went into the bedroom that she was letting me stay in while I visited. As I was lying on the bed and thinking about everything that had been said, I couldn't resist opening my father's book and reading it. I read through a series of thoughts that he had on the subject of trying to uncover love. He called this chapter "Steps."

"I imagine myself reaching up to something I've searched for all my life. I had visions of grasping such a find and placing it near the spot that triggers my happiness," he wrote.

I was in complete awe when I read my father's words and, at the same time, I felt so much comfort. The older I got, the more I wished I could spend some time just sitting in his lap and listening to him speak about his life. He had such an understanding about love and reading his book allowed me to feel the strength of his emotions. As I read this chapter about taking steps, I could see that it was about coming closer to love. I wondered if he was writing it to Mommy because he talked about coming closer to a place where steps have already been made. Maybe he was talking about Nicholas finding my mom before he did. I didn't know. Maybe I wouldn't fully understand until I struggled to find love myself. Luckily, that might never happen because I had Dante.

"Angelina, did you call your mom?" Stephanie shouted from the other room.

I was glad she reminded me because it was getting late and I was on the verge of falling asleep. Mommy might've been wondering what was taking me so long to call her anyway. I wasn't looking forward to making the phone call and, hopefully, she wouldn't ask too many questions.

When daylight came, I woke up with a sign of good things to come. Whenever I woke up without a struggle, I always seemed to have a good day. I remembered Mommy telling me that my father always knew he was gonna have a great day if he either dreamt of a woman or had a good shave in the morning. I always smiled when I thought about that. I was so excited about that day. I thought I was gonna be nervous and afraid to go to the cemetery, but I couldn't wait to get there. I felt more at ease that morning because I'd finally made that call to my mom the night before. She was so happy to hear my voice.

"You made it okay! Wonderful!" she said excitedly. "Have you been to the school yet?" she asked.

"No, Mommy. I'm just relaxing right now."

"Relaxing?"

"Yeah. That was my first flight and I feel tired."

"Oh, poor baby!" she said sarcastically.

The great thing about our conversation was that it didn't last that long and I wasn't put in the position of telling more lies.

"Well, sweetie, I'm just glad you made it safely. Now we both can relax and get some rest."

"Were you worried, Mommy?"

"I'm always worried about you, baby!"

"I know, but I'll be okay."

"Okay, baby. Just call me if you need me and don't rest too much or you'll miss out on finding out about those schools."

"I won't."

"Okay. I love you, Angelina."

"Love you too, Mommy."

When I hung up the phone, I took a huge deep breath. I felt like I was in the clear and could now begin my journey. I was there now and there was no turning back.

"Now is the time to move forward," Mommy always told me.

She was usually right and now I was ready. But, as I looked around the condo, I noticed that Stephanie was gone. I was under the impression that she would take me to the cemetery and drop me off. I guess she had to do something that morning, but I wished that she had told me. Nothing was gonna ruin the special day for me, so I'd just take a taxicab. I was sure that person would know how to get to the Holy Cross Cemetery and, hopefully, I could buy flowers there, too. I'd have to talk to Stephanie later and see what happened. Hopefully she didn't leave because of all the questioning that I'd put her through.

It seemed like the longer I waited on the taxi to come, the better the day started to look. Despite my cheery attitude, the weather was looking gloomy but now the sun was coming out and the sky was clearing. Maybe that was a sign of my day to come or maybe it was just a typical day in LA. I was gonna look on the bright side and pretend that I was responsible for bringing out the sun. I felt like I was ready to take on the world because I had so much to say to my father. I must've spoken too soon because now the sun was no longer out. Maybe that was a sign of uncertainty or maybe I should stop looking for signs and get on with the day. Thinking about the outcome was really making me crazy. I found myself pacing back and forth and walking in circles all through the condo. I wished Stephanie were around to talk to me. I was tempted to give Dante a call, but I knew he'd ask me questions that I didn't want to answer right then. I just hoped he wasn't back home thinking that I might've been out there flirting and finding somebody new.

"Finally!" I shouted as I made yet another circle around Stephanie's slightly worn couch.

The taxi had arrived outside. I grabbed the big bag that I'd prepared. It was stuffed with my camera, some extra film, something to write with, a notepad, some suntan lotion, and anything else I could think of. You would've thought, from my appearance and everything that I was bringing, that I was going on a picnic or to the beach.

"Good day!" the cabdriver said as I approached.

"Hello."

I told him excitedly where I wanted him to take me and he kind of looked at me strange. I guess he'd never seen someone excited about going to a cemetery. I was just hoping he didn't take the long route to get there.

Now that I was finally on my way, I found myself reflecting on everything. I was thinking about how I'd feel and what I would say. I remembered a few weeks ago when I'd asked Mommy about my father. She had a really beautiful smile.

"Mommy, what would you say to Daddy if he were here right now?"

She had to think for a while. I could tell that she would have a lot to say. But, just like me, I thought she'd get really quiet because of her emotions becoming so overwhelming.

"I'm not sure, baby. I know I'd hug him really tightly and I'd be smiling from ear to ear, but I'm not sure what I'd say."

"What do you think he'd say?"

"He'd probably tell me to say something!"

Mommy and I started laughing and found ourselves sharing a very special hug. I'd really caught her off guard with my question and it only made her sit down and reflect on the past. We sat together for at least thirty minutes, holding hands and saying nothing. I felt so close to her and, when I closed my eyes, I imagined Daddy smiling over us. I could feel his presence with me as I sat in the cab and looked out the window. The traffic was pretty bad and we'd passed through areas where there were crowds of people walking along the sidewalks. It was around lunchtime and I guess that would've explained why there were so many people out and about. The windows were rolled up so I didn't hear too much noise coming from the outside. I was just sitting there like I was oblivious to the world. My thoughts were so strong that I felt like I was in a glass jar and ready to suffocate. The cab was moving in slow motion and I was beginning to get anxious.

"How much farther is it?" I asked.

"About ten more minutes."

"Can I roll down the window slightly?"

"Sure!"

The cabdriver could probably tell that I was no longer as excited as before. I was in a state of anxiety and worry. I was shaking my knee, taking deep breaths, and moving around in my seat constantly. The best thing for me to do at that point was to try to relax somehow. I didn't want someone to find a young woman, fresh out of high school, having a heart attack in the back seat of a cab.

I had my father's book with me, as I always did, and I held it tightly against my chest. Somehow, I always found comfort from it and that moment was no exception. I could always escape any type of worry whenever I thought about him or read his thoughts. I hoped when I had kids one day, they would read his book and share in the beauty of his spirit. I wouldn't expose them too much to him, but I would share a few stories from time to time. It is good to have stories to pass down from generation to generation. That way we can truly live forever. I probably picked that up from my grandmother because she wanted me to keep her memory alive. I planned on keeping everyone's memory alive, but I hoped and prayed that she didn't plan on leaving me anytime soon. I'd have to check on Grandma as soon as I got back home. Mommy said for me not to worry too much. That we all go through moments where we get sick. I think she was just trying to comfort me and think positive about Grandma's illness.

"We're almost there, Miss!" the cabdriver shouted.

I had to catch my breath because I could actually see the cemetery in the distance. It looked absolutely beautiful from there. It sat high atop a hill and was surrounded by beautiful flowers everywhere. As we got closer, I could also see a very grand entrance to the place. It was like we were in the driveway of some huge Hollywood mansion.

"Would you like me to drive you inside?" the cabdriver asked.

"Yes, just a little bit inside."

"Okay."

My mind was going crazy and my heart was beating so fast. My excitement returned when I sat up in my seat looking around like a little kid at Disneyland. As the cab approached the offices inside, I wanted to open the car door before he came to a stop.

"You want to get out here or should I drive you further up? This is a pretty big place, you know?"

The cabdriver seemed to be feeding off my excitement. I could see him smiling and getting anxious, too.

"It's very big! I didn't realize how big it would be!"

"I can take you up further, if you like."

"No, I should find out exactly where I need to go. I'm sure I can find out in this office over here."

"Yes, they should be able to tell you."

"Thank you. Bye!"

After I paid the fare and got out the cab, I didn't waste any time going to the office. I ran because I was so anxious. I knew you were supposed to be quiet and reserved when you were around places like that, but I was excited.

"Excuse me," I said softly.

"Yes, how may I help you?" the woman responded.

"Would you be able to tell me where someone is buried?"

"Yes, can you tell me the name?"

"Christian Erickson," I said with a huge smile.

The lady had to look at me twice because I was smiling. I guess I'd forgotten that people didn't smile much around there, but it was hard to hold in my enthusiasm.

"Let me see. Oh, yes," the lady said as she typed in the name.

She found the location of his grave and wrote down all the information for me.

"There's a map on the back of this brochure and I wrote down the directions to where he's located. It's actually not that far from here," she told me.

"Thank you. Is there a place where I can buy flowers around here?"

"Yes, right around the corner in the gift shop."

"Thank you!"

I guess that lady had never seen such an animated person going to visit a gravesite. She kept her eyes on me as I was leaving the office. She'd probably talk about me to her co-workers but I didn't care because I was very happy to be there.

I found the perfect arrangement of flowers for my father. I had heard from Mommy that he didn't care for roses. He preferred exotic flowers and that's just what I got for him. It was nothing too crazy, just some very beautiful orchids. Now I was all set and ready to walk up the hill. I passed by many headstones and graves with beautiful flowers lying on top.

I saw a headstone that read, "I wish you could've seen the world. Now we'll never know how you could've change it."

That one made me sad because it was for a little girl. The words kind of fit my father and now I wondered what words were written on his headstone. I also couldn't help but notice how beautiful and huge the cemetery was. I didn't remember any that size back home.

It felt more like a park than a place to visit loved ones that passed away. As I read the directions written down on the brochure, I could see that I was coming close. I just needed to walk over this one last hill and I would be in the right area.

As I approached the top of the hill, I stood next to a really tall tree. I found myself leaning against it as I took a deep breath. A silence fell over me because, in the very short distance, I could see my father's headstone. I could see his name written at the top and a lot of flowers placed in front of it. I guess he got visitors all the time or maybe the cemetery placed flowers on all the gravesites. I wasn't sure, but I had a feeling that he'd had visitors. I walked slowly, with my arms folded and my bag swung around my shoulders. My legs felt heavy and my heart was in my throat. I could feel my eyes getting watery. I immediately wiped them so I could clear my vision. I wanted to be able to focus on what was ahead of me, not only visually but also everything that I would say. As I got closer, I could finally read the words on his headstone. Beneath his name, it read, "Beloved friend, inspired soul." I expected to find more on there but I completely understood what it said.

"Hi, Daddy," I struggled to say.

I leaned over and hugged his headstone. I started crying and couldn't control my emotions. I completely crushed all the flowers that were at the bottom of the headstone but I didn't care because the feeling was so overwhelming to me. After about fifteen minutes of sobbing, I finally was able to talk.

"I made it, Daddy! I'm here with you and now you can see how much I've grown. I know you've never saw me before physically, but I guess you've watched every moment of my life from heaven. I love you so much and I hope I've made you proud. I can't believe I'm actually here!"

I was speaking at such a rapid pace that I began wondering if he could hear or even understand what I was saying. I knew he could feel my emotions and my need to tell him everything, but this was all too much for me. I knew it would be something amazing, but I didn't think it would be like that.

"Daddy, I hope you can understand why I had to lie to Mommy.

She would never allow this to happen. I don't think she ever wants to return to LA. I hope you know how much she loves you, too. She raised me with a lot of love and she always made sure that I knew about you. I feel as though you raised me also and I know I'm a good person because of your influence. You're such a beautiful man, Daddy. I wish you were alive. I know you're always with me, but I just yearn for you to be here. It's not the same. Just being able to think about you or read your thoughts isn't enough. I need you here!"

I was beginning to sound like a very selfish little girl, but once again my emotions were becoming overwhelming as I broke down and cried against his headstone.

"I'm sorry, Daddy. I guess I'm being selfish. I remember your words about selfishness. I know how you always said to love yourself is great, but always try to at least care about those around you. I care, Daddy, but I feel as though I was cheated by not being able to see what Mommy saw when she was with you. I can tell even today how much she loved you. Mommy still loves you the same way today."

After finally catching my breath and slowing down my rapid-fire conversation style, I enjoyed some quiet time. I sat near the headstone with my arms folded as I imagined being held by my father. I felt so at ease and I kept nodding off to sleep for short moments at a time.

"Daddy, I want to promise you something," I whispered. "Before I leave to go back home, I'm gonna write something to you. I'll read it and then I'll leave it here so that you can take it with you."

I couldn't believe I was talking that way but, at the same time, it felt natural. I had to say what was on my mind and in my heart. It didn't matter if someone was walking by and heard me having the conversation. As I sat near the grave, I no longer wondered if I'd made the right decision in coming out to LA. I no longer feared what might happen as a result of all that. I'd totally made peace with my father and that was the most important thing to me. Not to mention, I'd made peace with myself and now I could get on with my life. That night, I wanted to call Dante and tell him all about what happened that day. But the next day, I was gonna come back   there   and visit with Daddy. I also had a bone to pick with Stephanie about not driving me to the cemetery but, right then, I just wanted to rest.

The day had been both the greatest day and the most exhausting day of my life. I believed that everything would go smoothly the next day because I was over any type of anxiety and surprise. I could come back there and not feel so nervous next time. I was so happy that I'd come to LA, but I knew that when I spoke to Mommy again, I would feel just as guilty as before. Lying had shown me just how valuable the truth could be. I couldn't wait to get back home so that I could never have to tell another lie. All of it could be swept under the rug and I could get on with my life.

It didn't take long for me to get back to Stephanie's place. Maybe I'd lost track of time because I was in a total daze. I didn't even remember how much money I'd paid the cabdriver. I kept reliving the incredible day over and over in my mind. It had been so emotional and I still couldn't believe I was there experiencing it all. When I walked through the door, Stephanie acted as though nothing had happened.

"Hey, girl," she said as she walked towards the bathroom.

I couldn't believe she was acting so nonchalant. After putting my bag in the room, I sat down on the couch and waited for Miss Stephanie to return to the living room. I could tell she was avoiding an encounter with me because she was taking her time doing everything else.

"You want me to make you some dinner, Angelina?" she asked from the other room.

"No, thanks."

"Okay, I'm gonna make me something so let me know when you get hungry!"

"Stephanie?" I yelled out.

"Yes?"

"Could you come in here for a second?"

"Let me get this started first, okay?"

"Since when did you all of a sudden take up cooking?" I shouted.

Stephanie didn't respond, but she realized that she couldn't avoid my questions any longer. She walked into the living room, wiping her hands with a dishrag.

"I guess you're gonna ask me about this morning, huh?" she asked.

"Yeah, what happened?"

"I don't know, girl. I just felt really uncomfortable about going with you. Last night was hard, when you kept asking me about Christian and your mother, so it would've really been hard to go to the cemetery with you today."

"You should've just told me, Stephanie."

"I know, but I thought I could go through with it. I've put most of those memories out of my mind and, now that I see you, they're all coming back to me. You have such a beautiful look on your face when you speak about Christian and wanting to be near him. You remind me so much of Maiya and how she always looked forward to hanging out with him. She derived so much joy out of just talking to him and I could never understand why until it was too late."

Stephanie explained, in detail, the beautiful relationship that Mommy had with my father. I'd never seen Stephanie express herself that way. She had me smiling with every word, even though a few tears fell from my eyes. She spoke about the connection between the two of them that continued to that day, despite Daddy not being with us physically.

"Did you ever get to talk to him?" I asked.

"No, I never was able to and that's funny because I feel as though I knew everything about him. Maiya would tell me so much and, of course, I always joked around because she never mentioned sex. She always told me about their conversations and how they lasted forever. They uplifted her and made her realize the things she needed to know in order to move on from whatever problem she was having at the time."

"Really? She still does that today!"

I told Stephanie about how Mommy always remembered something that my father had told her in order to relieve the tension of her day. Somehow, he could say something to her and make her feel like her problem was not worth her time and worry.

"Yeah, that's how he always was with her. I kept joking with her by asking how good he was in bed, but she always said it was more than that," Stephanie said as she looked downward.

I could tell that, deep down, maybe she'd learned a thing or two from what Mommy had shared with her about my father. Maybe, despite her bachelor girl experiences, she really understood.

"Mommy told me that he took her to a level that kept her soul from ever wanting or needing for anything."

"Yeah, he was a sweetie."

Stephanie and I sat motionless on the couch. Remembering and thinking about my father's influence brought us closer together somehow. I had a feeling that even Stephanie had found a certain awareness about herself just from thinking about the past. I knew I had a nice awakening myself from this moment.

Stephanie's not an airhead after all! I thought.

After a few deep breaths and some nervous laughter, we both decided to call it a night. It was getting late and I needed to call Dante before I went to sleep. Tomorrow would be there before I knew it and I felt like I had a few more things to share with my father.

"Hey, are you going back tomorrow?" Stephanie asked.

"Yes."

"You want me to drop you off? I promise I won't leave you stranded this time."

"Okay, thanks!"

I was planning to ask Stephanie to take me anyway, but it was good to know that she had a conscience. Maybe because we'd reached a certain understanding, she was able to deal with her fear of taking me to the cemetery. I wasn't asking that she go inside with me. I just needed the ride.

"Goodnight!" Stephanie said as she walked passed my room.

"Goodnight."

Now, there better not be a female answering Dante's phone! I thought as I picked up the telephone.

I found myself dialing with a little attitude. I guess I'd heard too many stories about girls stepping in when you're away, but I didn't think Dante would mess around. Either way, I was experiencing my first moments of jealousy.

"Yello?" Dante answered.

"Yello? Is somebody there with you?" I asked suspiciously.

"Angelina?"

"Yes."

"Alright!" he shouted. "How are you? How did things go?"

Dante's excitement made me forget about my slight bout with jealousy. I didn't need to go that route anyway; especially after learning more about what happened to my father and his dealings with a jealous person.

"I'm okay. I just had a busy day."

"Did you do it?"

"Do what?"

"You know, go to the cemetery?"

"Yeah, I went."

"And?"

"And what?"

"Angelina! Why are you doing this to me?" Dante shouted in frustration.

I loved it when I pissed him off because, no matter what, he was always so sweet.

"It was so emotional, Dante. The entire time I was there, I never felt alone."

"Really?"

"Yeah, I spoke to him and I cried."

"You spoke to him? Angelina?"

"Don't start thinking I'm crazy! You know what I mean!"

I explained to Dante the closeness that I'd felt at the cemetery. I'd lived my life thinking about the man constantly and wishing with every inch of my soul for one moment in his arms. That day, I'd almost felt as though that wish had come true.

"I wish I could make it happen for you, Angelina. I've been thinking about you all the time and just hoping that you would hurry up and call."

"Really?"

"Yep!"

"You miss me?" I asked.

"Are you kidding? I'm going crazy out here!" he responded.

"Great!"

"What do you mean, great?"

"You know what I mean, Dante! So, have you spoken to my mother at all?"

"No way!"

"Why not?"

"I can't handle the lying part of all this so I've just stayed away. You have to hurry up and come home so that this can be over!"

"I will, Dante. I'm sorry you have to be a part of this, but I do need your help. I'll probably come home in a day or two because I don't feel like I can stay with Stephanie too long."

"Are you two not getting along?"

"We've had our moments but something's just not right and I know I'm making her uncomfortable. I think I remind her so much of my mother that it's bringing back memories of when my father was killed."

"Oh yeah? You never told me how that all happened. Have you found out more?"

"Yes, a little bit more, but I know it must go deeper than what I've been told so far."

I explained to Dante the whole story, as I knew it. I still didn't know much about Nicholas or the details of what made him so jealous, but I figured that he wanted to be with Mommy. Sometimes, when Stephanie spoke about the past, certain things didn't add up. Mommy had never told me any details about that day. She'd always concentrated on my father as a man and the way he'd tried to live his life.

"Maybe that's all you should know, Angelina. Maybe it's better to just go on knowing only the positive side of your father," Dante told me.

"What are you saying? Do you think that maybe he did something wrong?"

"No, I can't imagine that. I just wonder what the big secret is and usually secrets are for hiding the truth."

"Oh, Dante, I don't like the sound of that. My father had no secrets! He expressed every inch of his soul on paper!"

I was beginning to get very emotional with Dante. The direction of his comments had me thinking that my father had done something wrong. He was pointing the finger at the possibility of a negative influence in my father's life and that didn't sit too well with me inside.

"You're wrong, Dante!" I shouted.

"No, Angelina. I didn't mean it like that!"

I became silent for a while as Dante struggled to smooth things over. I could hear him becoming frustrated and, for a moment, I didn't mind. I was in pain because I was fighting the possible negative image of my father that Dante was creating. I knew in my heart that he'd died because of love and when I left here, that was the image that I wished to hold on to.

"Angelina, I'm sorry if I made you feel bad. I was just thinking out loud and trying to look at all sides. I know your father did nothing wrong because I've read his book, too. I know he was a good man."

"Its okay, Dante. I'm just really sensitive with everything going on right now. I'll call you tomorrow and let you know for sure when I'm coming back. I'm going to the cemetery again."

"Okay, call me as soon as you get in."

"Okay."

After hanging up with Dante, I could feel the tension behind the last words said. I guess when someone started to say something negative about what I held so dear in my heart, I'd get a serious attitude. I'd inherited that trait from my mother. Hearing any doubt about the goodness of my father was like putting a hundred-pound weight on me and I was gonna react strongly to get it off. I felt drained, but I wasn't beaten yet. I wished there were someone I could talk to that knew all the answers.

"I wish you could tell me, Daddy!"

I was really feeling homesick, because I had no one to lean on.

I couldn't run into Stephanie's room and talk to her because, if I got too deep, she would close up. I couldn't call Mommy because I would've had to reveal the lies that I'd told in order to find out more about my father. I was stuck with the realization that I might not ever know the whole story. That was frustrating to me but, after a good night's sleep, I knew I'd get over it.

Tossing and turning was all I did that night. If someone had been there with me, they would've been fighting me. I kept kicking the covers off and then, an hour later, I would get up and put it back on. Time would go by and then I'd just kick it off again. I was starting to really consider getting on the plane and going back home right that second. I was really feeling strange about being there. The best thing for me to do was visit my father one last time, say goodbye, and prepare for my flight back home. All the lying was just not worth it and dealing with the secrets from Stephanie was really a turn off. One day I'd just have to confront my mother about the truth on how Daddy died.

"Angelina, what time do you want to leave?" Stephanie shouted from the hallway.

"As soon as I get dressed!"

"Oh, you must be excited then!"

"No, I just need to go."

"What's wrong?" Stephanie said as she walked inside my room.

"I don't know. I just feel like no one is telling me the truth. I feel like something's missing but I don't know what. Maybe I'm just homesick and feeling kind of down about everything."

"I'm sorry, girl, but you have to understand that there are things I can't tell you. Your mother has to tell you."

"I understand, but it doesn't mean I have to like it!"

"I know, but just think positive. Christian was a good man and there's no reason for you to believe otherwise."

"I don't doubt that, Stephanie. I'll just get ready now, okay?"

"Okay."

I wasn't getting anywhere with Stephanie. I didn't really know what answers I was searching for, but I believed I'd know when it hit me.

During the drive to the cemetery, the conversation didn't get much better. After I told Stephanie that I would be leaving, possibly tomorrow or the next day, I could see that it hurt her feelings.

"So, you just came out here to do your thang without spending any time with me? I thought we would at least go out or do something."

"I know but I just don't feel right out here. I'm doing something behind my mother's back and that alone is giving me a constant guilt trip."

Stephanie remained silent as she drove on to the street where the cemetery was. Once again, I could see it in the distance and the beauty of the place brightened my spirits.

"Please don't be mad, Stephanie," I told her.

"Well, can you blame me? I've wanted you to come out with your mother and visit me for a long time now!"

"I know."

"Well, stay and let's have some fun!"

"I'll stay two more days. We can go out tonight or something."

"Alright, girl. Don't come home all tired and change your mind!"

"Stephanie, aren't you ever gonna grow old and want to stop chasing men or going out partying all the time?"

"I don't think so!"

Stephanie was my mother's age and still derived so much joy out of partying and chasing men. I felt like she was the young woman and I was the older sister. After she pulled inside the entrance to the cemetery, I felt a little more at ease.

"This is a sad place," Stephanie said.

"No, it's not. It's beautiful here and very peaceful. Why don't you come up with me and visit?"

"No thanks, girl!"

After Stephanie dropped me off, I retraced the steps that I'd taken the day before. I stopped at the grave of the little girl once again and removed some of the dead flowers that were on top. I imagined that she was a beautiful little girl. It kind of made me wonder what it would be like to have a little sister. The little girl died so young. Maybe she was in heaven talking to my dad. After spending a few moments with her, I continued on my way. I walked up the hill overlooking the area where my father rested. I began smiling immediately when I saw his name. I put aside all my feelings of doubt and worry. I felt relaxed and ready to speak to him again.

"Hi, Daddy!"

This time I didn't cry. I smiled and sat comfortably as I wiped the debris from his headstone. The day was beautiful and breezy; especially on top of the hill. I was much happier now that I was there, but I knew things would feel so different once I walked away. The whole experience would haunt me for a long time to come.

"Daddy, I sure wish you could talk to me right now. I've been going crazy trying to find out about the last days of your life. I guess I shouldn't focus on that but I just wonder what happened. I wonder why someone would take your life and ruin the chance of you ever meeting your daughter. I always think about the fun that we would've had if you were alive."

"Hello, young lady!" a voice said in the distance behind me.

"Hello," I responded.

A man walked by slowly as I was deep in my thoughts and conversation.

"I guess I look funny, huh?" I said to him.

"No, I see it all the time. Didn't mean to disturb you!" he said as he continued on his way.

I found myself slightly embarrassed but that soon gave way to the closeness that I was feeling. I wanted so badly to reach down and pull out the image of my father.

"I want you to be proud of me, Daddy. I read something last night in your book that spoke about finding yourself. Right now, I'm searching not only for myself, but also for more answers about you. I'm not so sure anymore that I'm gonna leave here better off than when I came. I guess you can say that I have a lot of self-doubt. I know you'd tell me that I shouldn't have this feeling."

As I continued speaking about the confusion that clouded my mind, I read a passage from my father's book:

Time seems to integrate the good with the bad. I'm often unsure of my direction but somehow I recognize and reflect the gift that I have. That which God blessed me with so that I may continue to speak even though I struggle to find words which bring recognition to my thoughts.

That one passage gave me hope in the simple fact that I would eventually outgrow any and all problems that I had then. My only trouble was that I was young and very impatient with anything that had to do with waiting. I was waiting on a greater sense of under-standing and it was driving me nuts.

"Excuse me," a female voice said to me from behind.

"Hi, how are you?" I asked.

"Fine. Did you know Christian?"

"Yeah, you can say that I guess."

"You seem very young. How could you have known him?"

I felt a strange vibe as I stood up to talk to this woman. She was really pretty and she carried a small arrangement of flowers in her hand.

Maybe she's the one whose been bringing the flowers to my father's grave, I thought to myself.

"Are you related to him somehow?" she continued to ask.

I was speechless and somewhat nervous because I couldn't imagine who this woman could be and how she might've known my dad.

"My name's Tanya. I didn't mean to disturb you, but I always figured I was the only one who visits Christian. I come up here at least twice a month because this man was so important in my life."

"Really?"

"Yes, and no one has ever come close to the way I felt about him."

"What do you mean?" I asked softly.

"I loved him very much and I hold onto those thoughts of what could've been if we had been able to get married."

My heart started beating really fast because of the way the lady was speaking about my father. Deep down, I was hoping that maybe she was talking about someone else. Maybe she was speaking about the headstone next to my father's.

"Are you okay? What's your name?" she asked.

"Angelina."

"Oh? That's a pretty name."

"Thank you."

"You really knew Christian?" Tanya asked.

"Sort of."

"Did you know how he died?"

"Yes, well, sort of," I responded with a big lump in my throat.

I was so nervous and almost afraid to swallow for fear of what she might say next. She was beginning to sound as though she had all the answers to the questions I'd been asking.

"I'm really intrigued as to how you knew Christian because you don't look old enough to have ever known him."

"I'm sixteen, almost seventeen years old."

"That's about how long he's been dead."

"Yes, he died before I was born but my mother always kept his memory alive and told me everything about him. My middle name is Christiana and, of course, I have his last name," I said excitedly.

"You do? Why?"

"I'm his daughter!" I said with a smile.

My smile soon disappeared slowly as Tanya seemed to object to what I'd said. I couldn't understand what was going on, but it did seem like she knew my father. Maybe this was truly the missing piece as to why my father was killed.

"Why don't you believe I'm his daughter?" I asked her.

"Because sixteen years ago I was his fiancée and Christian would've told me without hesitation if he had a daughter some-where. What's your mother's name?"

"Maiya," I said carefully.

"Maiya?"

"Yes. Why are you looking at me like that?"

"Because you seem so sweet, but your mother hasn't been very honest with you."

"I think I should go!"

"I'm not trying to upset you, Angelina."

"Well, you are!"

"I knew your mother and she was Christian's best friend, but never his lover. She and I stood over his body on the day of the funeral, sweetie."

My eyes began to fill up with tears and I couldn't focus on the woman standing before. I no longer wanted to hear what she was saying.

"My God, I don't want to make you cry, Angelina. Come here, sweetheart," Tanya said as she reached out to me.

I refused to let Tanya touch me. "That's okay. I don't know why you're saying all these things to me!"

"I can't believe you've been lied to all these years, Angelina."

"Can you please not say my name. We don't know each other!"

"Listen, I'm gonna give you my number so, if you want to talk about all this…"

"I don't need your number!" I shouted.

"Yes you do, honey. Here, you call me anytime and I can tell you everything. I believe you need to talk to someone and I have no intentions of hurting you, sweetie. I think everyone else has done a good job of that already."

Tanya stuck her phone number in my bag. I stared at her for a few seconds with so much anger in my heart. I was hurting deep inside as I stood before this stranger that walked in and destroyed all that I believed in. As I began to cry, I ran in the opposite direction as fast as I could. I didn't know where I was running to but I knew I couldn't bear hearing another word. I could hear Tanya shouting in my direction but the sound of my own breathing made it impossible to understand her.

So many things were going through my mind but mostly I was confused. I didn't know what to do. My first challenge was getting back to Stephanie's place and then, hopefully, I could go to sleep and wake up from my bad dream. That lady had me believing that my mother had lied to me about who my real father was. The things she'd said to me made sense, but there must've been a mistake somewhere. I didn't want to believe that the mistake was what I'd been told all my life. Other things seemed to click in my mind right then as well. Whenever I'd spoken to Stephanie about him, she'd never referred to him as my father. She'd always called him by name and I never thought much about that until then. I was so far away from home and my world was collapsing all around me. If my mother had lied to me, I didn't know how I'd be able to confront her about it.

As I made my way to the entrance of the cemetery, I was lucky enough to spot a cab. The drive home was such a lonely ride. I sat there staring out the window thinking about everything and what my life may be like from that moment on. I didn't imagine very many good things happening to me anytime soon. Before we reached Stephanie's apartment, we passed by this young family on the street. I could see the father holding his daughter and that made me sad. At least she would grow up knowing her real dad rather than just knowing the image of a man who could've been a great dad if he'd had children. I wanted to believe that none of it had happened but, as I reached down in my bag and pulled out the piece of paper that Tanya had given me, I knew the day was real.

Why would she say all those things if they weren't true?

I was gonna have to call her and speak to her again. I wasn't sure what Stephanie knew, but she'd better not deny me the truth at that point. I had a feeling that the lady knew everything about the day my father died.

"I guess I can't call him that anymore," I mumbled.

30.
I Lost My World

As soon as Stephanie walked through the door, I confronted her. I was waiting in the shadows of her living room, cold-blooded, and ready to strike.

"Why'd you lie to me, Stephanie?" I asked in a calculatingly calm voice.

She was startled and didn't answer me right away.

"Why'd you lie?" I repeated.

"Excuse me, but you don't talk to me like that. What's your problem now, girl?"

"Who's my real father, Stephanie?"

"I don't need to talk to you about shit, young lady. Plus, you're just out of high school and this is my house!"

"Yeah, but you owe me Stephanie! I found out today that everyone has lied to me my entire life. I met the woman that my so-called father was really in love with. Who am I, Stephanie? My name don't mean anything now!"

"Angelina, I'm so sorry."

"Who's my real father, Stephanie?"

"Nicholas."

When Stephanie told me that Nicholas was my father I put it all together and came up with the conclusion. At that point, it was pretty easy to see why he's been kept a secret from me.

I'd never felt a loss like that before in my life. It felt like everything that I'd believed in up until this moment had been a fantasy. I'd been living my life with a false sense of security and comfort. What guidance would I follow now and did that mean I had to change my name? I'd come so far only to find my world was never reality. My reality was negativity and maybe that explained why all the lying had come so naturally to me. After all, my real father was a murderer and I wondered just how much I took after him. I found myself hating my own memories because I no longer felt like I had a right to hold onto them. I could only fantasize about what it was like to have a good man as my father. I couldn't help but think over and over again: My father is a murderer!

"Where is he now?" I asked.

Stephanie couldn't say another word. She lost all expression in her face and walked out of the room. This has affected me in such a way that I now questioned what kind of man I deserved in my own life. My mother had told me in the past that she wanted me to find someone like Christian.

"Don't allow a negative soul to change your life baby," she'd once said.

Maybe it was my destiny to repeat her same mistakes. I know I wouldn't have much to say to her right then, after finally learning the truth. My thoughts begin to turn toward Dante. I'd found him to have the same beautiful spirit that my father had.

"My God! He's not my father!"

I had to keep reminding myself of that and simply call him Christian. I wondered how I could possibly hold onto Dante now that my life had changed completely. I didn't want to subject him to what I was feeling. I figured that I would have to hurt him after all, but he probably wouldn't be the last person I hurt. Hopefully, Dante would understand that it was important for me to find out the truth. Losing him was gonna be hard but, at that point, I felt like I had to walk away.

"I'm sorry! I had to call and tell you!" Stephanie said in the distance.

I could hear Stephanie shouting from inside her bedroom. I began to get images of her possibly talking to my mother. My heart started to race as I stood up not knowing what to do.

I think she's telling her what happened, I thought to myself.

"Maiya, what could I do? I had to help her, but I didn't want to lie!"

I heard Stephanie continue to plead and shout into the phone. She was definitely speaking to my mother and telling her everything. At that point, my mother knew that I was aware of who my real father was. As I walked closer to Stephanie's bedroom, I could hear her weeping. That alone let me know that I was in for the worse time of my life when it came to my mother and myself. I had no choice but to go inside, pick up the phone, and talk to her.

Stephanie was on her bed, crying and listening to whatever my mother was telling her. I could sense that what she'd said was very painful. I could see their friendship ending by the reactions on her face and in her body language.

"Let me talk to her," I told Stephanie.

"Angelina wants to talk to you," Stephanie said softly into the phone.

She handed me the phone and immediately walked out the

door. I could even hear the front door slamming soon after that. Stephanie was gone and now it was my turn to hear what Mommy had to say. The speaker part of the phone was a little wet from Stephanie's tears. I only hesitated for a second before I spoke without much emotion.

"Hello, Mommy."

For a long time, I got no response. The only way I could describe it was silent anger.

"I guess we're both angry right now, Mommy. I found out the truth about who I really am. Maybe this explains my behavior sometimes, don't you think?"

Mommy remained quiet, except for the time I heard her clearing her throat. Maybe I wasn't helping any, but I felt I had a right to be just as angry as she was.

"Do you know Tanya, Mommy?"

No answer was given.

"She told me the good news!" I said sarcastically.

"I guess this is gonna be a one sided conversation, but I just wanted to let you know that I plan on finding my real father. Stephanie wouldn't tell me where he is but maybe if I call Tanya, she'll help me find him."

It felt like my mother and I were on complete opposite sides of the world. After speaking with her, I could tell she was completely shattered. She hated me for being deceitful but, at the same time, she realized her own mistakes. I guess this was all inevitable, but now I had more than just a curiosity to satisfy. I had to meet my real father because he was still very much alive somewhere. Maybe, at that point, my mother didn't want me to return home. Even though she'd barely said a word over the phone, I could hear both our hearts closing when she finally did speak and I answered.

"I can't stop you from finding out the truth, Angelina, but why should you care when you've told so many lies?" she asked.

"I could say the same about you, Mommy!" I retaliated.

My own anger simply made matters worse and I continued to hurt her with everything that I said. I was at a point now where all consequences had caught up to me already and there was no going back. Mommy didn't want me to go further, but I felt like she'd lost all her say when it came to me finding out the truth. I was gonna find the man that was supposedly my real father and then figure out the next step in my life. My focus was so unclear because I no longer knew who I really was. I needed to find out so that I could know where I should go and perhaps where I belonged.

As I sat down, still feeling the pain of yesterday's conversation with Stephanie and my mother, I began to think about Tanya. I thought about how great her loss was since she was the one that Christian truly loved. I also thought about how much she could tell me about everything that had happened sixteen or so years ago. Despite her breaking the news to me about Christian not being my father, I could feel her concern for me. During that initial moment, I had nothing but anger and hurt inside of me and I wanted to get away from her. But now I felt like she was the one I must run to in order to find out who I was. A complete stranger would show me how to gain back my self-respect and that hurt because my mother was the one who should've been helping me. Maybe in the end Mommy would share her side of the truth with me, but right then I didn't think we would be talking for a while. I decided to call Dante that morning. Our conversation didn't last very long. Because I felt like a completely different person, I had no patience with any attempts at apology. I was feeling very cold-hearted and didn't need to hear Dante taking up for my mother. I realized he cared for her and had grown up knowing her, but he had no clue about the hurt-ful feelings that I was going through. I was glad that we didn't talk too long because I would've passed along a great deal of my pain to him. I would've taken out all my frustrations, even though I could tell that Dante was wounded from the little bit that I did say.

"Dante, I just wanted you to know what was going on," I told him calmly.

"Okay, and you're gonna call me later?"

"I don't know when I'm gonna call you, to be honest."

"You don't?" he asked in shock.

"No."

After a few seconds of silence, I told him goodbye and hung up the phone. I had no regret about my callous action and no reservations about the consequences. At that point, I wanted Dante to go about his own life and let fate work itself out.

When I called Tanya, she was happy to hear from me. She told me that she knew I'd call and that explained her very calm reaction when I told her who I was.

"Angelina, I'm glad you called. How are things? Did you tell your mother yet?"

"Things aren't good so I guess you can say that she knows all about it now," I told Tanya.

"Well, it's important that everything's out in the open. I'm sorry that all this has happened to you and your mom. When I saw you leaning over Christian, I could see so much love in your heart. I know you must be aching inside right now."

"Yes, I never expected all of this, Tanya. I thought I would come out here, share my life and my love with the man that I thought was my father, and then I could get on with my life knowing that I'd paid my last respects. With all that's happened, I'm not sure how my life will be from this moment on!"

"Don't let this change your life or the positive direction that you were headed in. I guess that's easy for me to say, huh?"

"It sure is!"

"Yeah, but I believe you can do it. I'm really sorry that I had to spoil everything for you, but I just didn't know how to react when you told me that you were Christian's daughter. That was a shock and made me wonder for a quick second if he'd held a secret from me all these years. But, I knew Christian and I know the circumstances of why and how he was taken away from all of us."

I remained silent as I listened to Tanya explain and tell the story of this beautiful man that I was named after. She spoke with so much love in her heart, as if he were still around. I guess if you leave this world after having touched people in a positive way, your spirit remains long after you've gone. Your memory can truly be celebrated and it felt as though Tanya was doing just that. I hated to bring up the details of that fateful day when he was killed, but I had to know.

"What about my real father?"

"Nicholas," she whispered softly.

"Yes."

"Well, I pray that everything that I tell you about him doesn't make you feel like it will be a reflection upon you. I know you'll take things hard and wonder if you carry the same traits as Nicholas."

"Yes, I think that all the time. I heard that he was a very jealous man and I've seen myself become jealous at times when I didn't have to."

"Everyone has jealous moments, Angelina, so please don't compare yourself to someone you've only recently discovered."

I thought about everything that Tanya was telling me but my mindset wasn't able to accept what she was saying. It seemed like I had more in common with my real father than ever before. The more she told me of his jealous ways, the more I thought I was destined to repeat the same weaknesses.

Tanya and I continued to talk about the day Christian was killed and the relationship between Nicholas and my mother.

"Did she love him at all?"

"Nicholas?"

"Yes, Nicholas."

"Not at all, sweetheart. Maiya was always looking for someone gentle, yet strong. She wanted someone that she could communicate with on every possible level. She found in Christian a very close friendship and I was thankful that she never tried to step beyond the boundaries of their friendship. She kept Christian focused on his pursuit of me and I thanked your mom when we stood over his casket. That day I felt very close to her but, after we let go of each other's hand, it was like we both completely disappeared."

"You never spoke to her again?"

"No, I was devastated because of Christian and I know that she was also. She left town and I went into my own world. I didn't come out of it until four years later when I met the man that I'm married to now."

"It seems like you still love Christian. I know my mother does."

"Yes, that's something that will be forever. I'm lucky that my husband understands and now I just find so much peace of mind when I go to the cemetery and visit Christian. I guess it's weird to most people, but I'm no longer sad when I go. I feel great."

"I wish I could say the same thing."

"I know but I believe you will get through all this. I think you need to repair the damage that's been done between you and your mom. What she did was wrong, but somehow I understand her motivation. I can even see the positive affect that it's had on you. You are so mature for a young woman your age."

"Can we not talk about her right now?"

"Okay."

I know I was sounding spoiled and troubled but my thoughts were not on reconciliation just yet. I never wanted to say that I hated Mommy but, at that point in time, I couldn't bear to talk to her.

"Do you know where he is now?" I asked quietly.

"Nicholas?"

"Yes, can you tell me?"

"Yes, he's in prison still."

I swallowed hard and became quiet for a moment. I was almost afraid to ask my next question.

"Are you okay, Angelina?" Tanya asked.

"Yes."

"Okay."

"Can you take me to him, Tanya?"

"Are you sure you want to do that?"

"Yes, I think I have to. I have to at least see him."

"Okay. I'll take you, but I can't go inside with you."

"I understand."

After I hung up the phone with Tanya, Stephanie passed through the living room. She kept her head down and didn't say a word. I could see so much in her that I'd never noticed before. Her spirit was completely broken and it was like everything had changed her life as well. I didn't like feeling responsible for bringing down someone else. I wasn't completely selfish unless I got angry. I made one attempt to speak with Stephanie but it seemed to fall on deaf ears.

"Stephanie, you want to talk? Are you okay?"

She made an attempt to smile but she failed. I could see there was nothing behind it as she rushed out the front door. I didn't want to hang around there and make her uncomfortable. I was waiting for Tanya to come pick me up and was very tempted to ask her if I could stay at her place for a couple days. I realized she was married so that may have been difficult for her to have me spend time in her house. All I could do was try and see what she said.

I was also missing my past at that moment. I missed Dante and I could've used a strong dose of Christian's love and wisdom. I packed his book in my bag. I no longer felt right about carrying it around like I did before. I thought about giving it to Tanya, but I wasn't ready to part with it just yet. I'd written things in it myself and a lot of it was very personal. I was beginning to miss Christian as if he were really alive.

Over and over I kept wanting to call Mommy. Talking to Tanya made me realize the closeness that I'd had with my mother. When I started to think about what had happened, it turned off any desire I had to repair the damage. I couldn't live that way for too long. All the negative thinking could only damage my own spirit. I was young and, most times, I just wanted to run and make a life for myself somewhere else. Then a voice would come on inside me and whisper the truth about what I was holding inside.

"No matter how crazy you get at times, sweetie, I believe that somehow you will stop for a moment and think about the things that Christian said during his lifetime and then, you will change your direction," my mother had once told me.

She was right about that and, sometimes, it drove me crazy to hear all those voices inside my head. The chilling thing was that the voices touched a deeper part of me than just my head. I could hear Mommy's voice all the time and I felt loved. I could think about Christian's words and how he'd lived his life and I felt inspired. Now that I was headed in the direction of meeting my real father, I only felt confusion and anger. I wondered constantly why I was putting myself through it all, but I just feel like I had to see this through. I was frightened to death about actually seeing the man face to face because I kept getting images of finding another side of myself. I hoped I was wrong. I didn't want to attach myself to someone who'd killed a beautiful and positive spirit. I didn't want to feel like I belonged in a negative environment like his and I didn't wish to ruin the lives of others. I'd hurt Mommy, I'd hurt Stephanie, and I could only imagine the disappointment that Dante was going through. Maybe it could all be repaired, but my confidence was pretty low whenever I thought about the outcome of it all.

Tanya finally showed up at the door. She had a look of concern and I could tell that she constantly wondered if I was making the right decision. Now that she' d gotten a chance to know me a little, I thought she was feeling guilty about exposing me to the truth of Christian not being my real father. She didn't say a word as we walked outside of Stephanie's apartment. Even when I thanked Tanya for opening her passenger car door for me, she remained quiet.

"Why are you so quiet, Tanya?"

"No reason, really."

"I hope you don't mind doing this for me."

"Taking you to see Nicholas?"

"Yes."

"Well, it does feel strange, but I feel responsible somehow and I don't think you should go through this alone."

"Do you miss Christian a lot?"

"How can you ask me that, Angelina?"

"I don't know. I just wanted to take your mind off of where we're going."

I could tell my question had kind of annoyed Tanya. That was a true sign of just how uncomfortable she was about the trip. I could feel the tension in the car. Her face was tight and without expression most of the time. To avoid any confrontation I simply turned my head and looked out the window. I let Tanya control any and all attempts at conversation once I realized her mood change. That may have been a mistake because it was taking forever for her to say something. I didn't know how many times I'd adjusted myself in my seat, but I was constantly moving.

"I'm gonna make a stop here, okay?" she said finally.

"Okay."

Just hearing her say that was a start, but I was hoping to hear more. I understood her change of mood, but I didn't think it would last so long.

"You want anything from inside?" I asked as she pulled into a gas station.

"No. Thanks anyway," she answered softly.

"Okay."

When I was inside buying a few snacks, I could see Tanya putting gas in her car and looking really uncomfortable. I felt bad about having her drive me to see my real father. Once we were back on the road, I was chewing my beef jerky with excitement. I had an orange soda and I was happy, but that feeling was temporary at best. The weather was getting hot and it didn't help that we were entering the California desert.

"You want some of my soda?"

"No, I brought some water with me."

"Tanya?" I shouted.

She looked at me as if I was crazy for yelling her name.

"Come on! Don't be mad at me now. I'm gonna need you."

"I know, Angelina. I just have this strange feeling about going anywhere close to Nicholas. I guess I shouldn't take it out on you, though!"

"Well, it feels like you are, Tanya!"

"Okay, your point is taken."

Things became less tense between us as we drove across the desert. It was getting hotter by the minute and the worse part was that Tanya had no cassette player in her car. We'd been listening to static for the last thirty minutes.

"I can't believe you don't have a cassette player, Tanya!"

"I've never really needed one and, besides, I don't buy that much music anyway."

"Uh-huh!" I responded sarcastically.

"I guess I'll have to entertain you somehow since you young people have short attention spans!"

"Who me?"

"Yeah, you, Angelina!"

"Oh, don't go there cause you ain't even old, Tanya!"

"Look at you with all that attitude! How old are you again?"

"I'm almost seventeen!"

"Uh-huh! See, I can move my head the same way!"

Tanya and I started laughing at the latest exchange between us. Finally we had moved past all the tension and really began to connect, sort of like sisters. I asked her about her current life and she wanted to know about mine.

"The most important thing is that I'm with a very caring man who understands my past and keeps me strong in the present and future. I'm very blessed to have had two very special men in my life, Angelina. Not very many women can say that."

"I guess not."

"Yeah, do you have a boyfriend? Is someone missing you back home?"

"Yeah, kind of."

"What do you mean kind of?"

"Well, because of all that has happened, I kind of brushed him off."

"Why?"

"I'm not sure anymore."

"Well, once this is over, I think we need to have a talk."

"A talk?"

"Yeah, mostly about your decision to suddenly change your life so drastically."

"Well, don't I have to?"

"No."

My attempts to ask why fell on deaf ears as Tanya returned to her silent mode. She just held up her hand and told me that we would talk about it later. I felt confused but that soon turned to fear. I was beginning to see warning signs about picking up hitchhikers and that could only mean that we were nearing a prison.

"Are we close?" I asked nervously.

"Yes, I think so," Tanya answered quietly.

This was worse than any plane ride. I was feeling ten times more nervous than when I first got on the plane to come out there.

"Oh my God! What was that?" I shouted.

"What was what?"

"That noise!"

"Are you nervous, Angelina? What's wrong?"

"It's too quiet out here!"

"Just relax, sweetie. I know you're getting scared because I am also. We are a long ways from home and I have no idea what we're gonna find out here. This is very scary!"

I could hear the road beneath us and the sound was deafening. I reacted to every noise so much that I had to cover my ears. Everything was going through my mind and it all had to do with fear. That was one of those moments where I wanted Mommy really badly. I needed her to be with me so that she could protect me from myself. I wanted her to tell me how dumb I was for going through with it. I wanted her to make me go to my room.

"I'd give anything to be at home in my bed right now!" I said out loud.

"Is that right?"

"Yes!"

"But you still want to go through with this, right?"

"Yes."

My answer didn't sound convincing, but I definitely didn't want to turn around after coming so far. I feared what I was about to do, but I had no thoughts of turning around.

"This is your last chance to say turn around because we're ten minutes away now," Tanya said with a forced smile on her face.

I could only shake my head no. I felt my whole body get tense as I saw the huge gates ahead of us. The sight of all the barbed wire fences sent chills through me. I could tell that Tanya was getting pretty nervous herself. If she felt half as bad as I did, then we definitely needed to stop the car right away. I could feel my stomach in my throat.

"I never imagined I would ever be coming to a place like this," I whispered.

Tanya said nothing. She continued driving as we reached the front gate. The guard motioned us through and we were finally inside. I could hear people on the other side of the walls and I was scared out of my mind. After we received our clearance and parked inside, Tanya and I walked to the entrance holding hands. I couldn't tell if it was her hand or mine that was doing the most shaking, but you could tell that we were very reluctant visitors.

"I thought you were gonna stay in the car?" I asked nervously.

"I'm too scared to stay in there by myself!"

"I'm glad you're coming with me"

"I'm not too crazy about it, Angelina, but I'm here for you."

As we walked through the entrance, it felt like all heads turned towards us. Maybe it was because we looked so frightened. I tried to straighten myself up but I had no courage to put up any kind of front. I asked Tanya to let them know why we were there and who we'd came to see. I just wasn't able to speak very clearly yet. When she came back to me, we sat down and waited.

"They said it would take anywhere from fifteen to thirty minutes for him to come to the visitors section," Tanya whispered.

"Oh my God! What am I gonna say?"

"I don't know, Angelina, but this is what you wanted."

"I know."

I had absolutely no idea what I would say to the man. I didn't feel at all like I was coming to visit my father. I was coming to visit a monster of some kind and I wondered what did that make me since I was his daughter.

"You okay?" Tanya asked.

I nodded yes as I held my hands together like I was praying. I closed my eyes and hoped that I could gain some kind of strength before I encountered him.

"Ms. Angelina Erickson?" a strong voice said.

When I looked up, it was a prison guard standing before me, smiling. I couldn't tell if his smile was real or not, but I could tell that he was ready to take me inside. Tanya and I slowly let go of each other's hand. It was time for me to meet my real father. As I walked with the guard, I continued to look back several times at Tanya. You'd think that I was going to prison myself by the look on my face. The guard checked all my belongings and made sure that I wasn't carrying anything. That alone gave me a really weird feeling. When we finally got inside the visitor's area, the guard sat me down in front of a window. I waited and waited until a man appeared with confused eyes and a tough exterior. I felt no connection at all with him as I glared into his eyes. I thought for sure that I would feel something. I thought it would all be clear to me if I saw him, but nothing felt right about that moment.

What am I doing here? is what went through my mind.

"Who are you?" he asked.

I shrugged my shoulders and remained silent.

"You remind me of someone I knew years ago, but you're too young to be her."

I remained quiet as I looked at him through the thick window. I looked at his rough hands and his dark, muscular arms. He had tattoos, but I couldn't make them out because of his complexion. I also couldn't focus too deeply on his eyes because they frightened me. I looked at him and thought about how he'd killed Christian years earlier. I thought about how he'd taken advantage of Mommy and ruined so many lives with his jealousy and hatred. I felt sick because I'd come there thinking of him as my father when he had nothing to do with me and who I was as a young woman.

Tears started to fall down my face as I thought about everyone that I was willing to give up in order to pledge myself to being his daughter. I was giving up love so that I could embrace a man filled with hate.

"Hey, I don't have much time. Are you gonna tell me who you are?"

"You don't recognize me at all?" I asked cautiously.

"No, you gonna tell me?"

"I'm Maiya's daughter"

"Maiya?"

"Yes."

His expression went blank for a moment as he scrutinized me closely. I couldn't tell what was going through his mind, but I could tell that he was in complete shock.

"You really Maiya's daughter? I haven't heard that name in years. Why you come out here to see me?"

I shrugged my shoulders because I had no idea what to say. This scary man before me was becoming agitated as he tried desperately to figure out what was going on. Even his angry stares were painfully intense.

"What kind of shit is this?" he asked.

I was very frightened at what he might say or do next so I got up without saying a word and left the room. I could still hear him trying to get my attention and the more he shouted, the faster I ran.

"Hey! What's going on in here!" he shouted. "Hey!"

His shouts sounded like echoes in the distance as I continued to run. I ran right passed Tanya and out into the parking lot. I was beginning to hyperventilate as I struggled to catch my breath.

"Angelina!" Tanya shouted.

I found myself doubled over near Tanya's car when I heard her running in my direction.

"Angelina what happened? Are you okay?"

"Oh my God, Tanya! Please tell me that's not my father! Why can't I go back to the way it was?"

Tanya didn't know what to say, but I was so thankful that she was with me. She didn't hesitate to hug me and wouldn't allow me to go through that alone. She put me in the car and we headed back. It took a while for me to calm down and catch my breath. Even when I was calm, I still found myself shaking from the experience.

"I wish I hadn't let you go through that, Angelina"

"There was nothing you could do, Tanya. I just didn't think it would be like that."

"I know, sweetie. We can talk about it when you feel more comfortable. I just don't want you to feel devastated by what you went through. It's tearing me up inside to see you crying and shaking like you are. You have to call your mother, Angelina."

I began crying even more than before. Tanya was right about it being a devastating experience. I felt like everything died inside of me and I was confused about what I should do next. Calling Mommy could only be the best thing for me to do, but I just couldn't bear it right then.

Tanya continued to talk to me and I just sat in a daze. I listened to every word she said and I was extremely thankful that she was with me. I wished I'd met her a long time ago because I felt very close to her already. I could understand why Christian fell in love with her.

"Hey, Angelina. I want you to really listen to what I'm about to say to you, okay?"

"Okay," I whispered.

I had no strength left to say anything, so I turned and focused on everything that Tanya had to say. I needed someone to show me that my life wasn't completely ruined.

"Listen, I took something away from you that has made you a very beautiful young woman. I just can't see myself taking it away from you any longer and preventing the positive affect that has touched your heart and become such a strong part of you."

"What do you mean?"

"I see so much of Christian in you. The way you talk and the way you think. It's as though he truly raised you into the woman that you are now. When I first saw you leaning over his grave, I felt threatened in a way."

"Threatened?"

"Yes, because not only are you beautiful, but you were in such a wonderful place emotionally speaking. It was like you were truly connected to him spiritually."

"You could see that, really?"

As Tanya spoke, my spirit began lifting. She was saying things that had me tingling all over as though I were falling in love. I wanted to hear more and she didn't disappoint me with that request.

"I could see it very much, Angelina," Tanya continued. "I watched you for a moment before I said anything. Of course, I was trying to figure out who you were. Then, when I saw your face and heard you speak, everything clicked. I remembered your mom and how beautiful she was. She loved Christian very much and was a very close friend to him. He adored her, too."

"You didn't feel jealous of her?"

"Well, at first I did, but then I put Christian through so much in our own relationship that I was impressed and convinced by the fact that he continued to pursue me. As I told you before, I found out later that your mom was the one who'd encouraged him to continue his pursuit."

"Thank you, Tanya, for telling me all this."

"You're welcome, sweetie. I don't agree with what your mother did as far as allowing you to believe that Christian was your real father. However, I do understand her reasons for the decision she made. I think in the end she probably did the best thing for you."

"I understand, too, I think."

"It's kind of strange because it's wrong what she did, but the result is that you grew up as a very loving and wise young woman. How can you fault a decision that led to such beautiful results?"

"What do I do now about Nicholas and everything else?"

"You leave him right where he is and just continue with your life. You saw him, but I think you now realize who your real father truly is."

"He's the man I just saw in jail!"

"No, he's in your heart and he's a part of your spirit."

"Christian?"

"Yes, and now you need to go and try to salvage everything with your mom! I know she's probably worried out of her mind right now!"

"I will."

"Don't forget your boyfriend either!"

"I haven't."

"Based on what you've told me about him, I believe you need to bring him back in your life. I'm sorry for taking you away from what has been willed to you through the power of someone's spirit. You've stopped crying now because I think you realize that Christian is definitely inside of you."

"Yes. I'm happy now, Tanya. I was miserable trying to find out the truth about Nicholas. Now I'm ready to go home, return to my life, and go to school for real this time."

"I hope so!"

Tanya and I smiled for the rest of the ride home. Talking the way we did made the long drive not seem so extensive. I was back to my old self and only separated by the night ahead of me before I would be back on that plane and headed home.

"Can we stop by the cemetery tomorrow before we go to the airport? I have to give my Daddy something."

I was smiling from ear to ear before Tanya could even answer my question.

"I knew you'd ask that. I was gonna take you anyway."

The night was only a little bit restless. The most important thing I had to do before going to sleep was call my mother. Every scenario in the world went through my head before calling her and I had absolutely no idea what I would say.

"Just say you're okay and that you'll be home soon!" Tanya had instructed me.

She said that once I broke the ice and let Mommy know I was okay, our conversation would flow naturally. She was almost right, but actually I did most of the talking at first. Once Mommy heard my voice, she became quiet and just listened to me speak.

"Mommy, it's me."

There was no response, but I could almost imagine the frown on her face that she was probably making. Right away, I let her know that I had seen Nicholas and what a traumatic experience it was. I explained the details of everything that had happened and I told her how grateful I was for having Tanya help me through all of it.

"Are you okay, baby?" Mommy whispered.

"What did you say?"

I was in shock because, after fifteen minutes of me talking and explaining, she'd finally said something.

"I'm okay, Mommy. Especially now!"

"Why is that?"

"Because you spoke to me!"

"I still don't appreciate the lies you told me in order to fly out to LA, but I've told my share of lies, too."

"Well, now that I've been through it all, I'm glad you did what you did, Mommy. Tanya made me realize so much on the drive home about my life up until now. I've been so lucky and she said that there was no doubt about my connection to Christian."

"I have no doubt either, Angelina. I know I was wrong in leading you to believe he was your real father, but I just wanted you to believe in a male figure. I wanted you to know that there are some really good men in this world and keeping you away from Nicholas is something that I was determined to do, wrong as it may seem."

"I know, Mommy."

"I just wanted you to understand that. Grandma was against it from the start and she always lets me know of her disappointment in my decision. However, she also knows that when my mind is made up, I stick to my decision."

"I know, Mommy!"

"You're the same way, sweetie, so watch your mouth!"

"Yes, ma'am."

Mommy and I talked until the wee hours of the morning. She told me what had been going on since I'd left and she let me have it about traveling alone so far away.

"It was the only way I could come to LA and visit with my father," I told her.

"That's true because I definitely wouldn't have allowed it."

"I know."

"Well, it's over now so please let's not go through this again!"

"We won't as long as you're not gonna tell me that I have a hidden brother or sister somewhere out there!"

"Ha, Ha, funny!"

"I'll be home soon, Mommy."

"How soon is soon?"

"Tomorrow!"

It was so great to hear Mommy laugh and smile over the phone.

I couldn't wait to see her. She also told me that Dante had been worried about me too.

"Dante never gave up, Angelina."

"What do you mean?"

"That young man loves you."

"I know."

"I think he'll wait for you, no matter how long it takes."

"He won't have to wait, Mommy."

"Well, I don't want no grand babies anytime soon!"

"What?"

"You heard me!"

"Umm, how's Grandma?"

"She's worried, she's angry with me, but at least her health is much better. I guess all this got her spirit so worked up that it made her get stronger."

"Great!"

"I think we all need to sit down at the table, talk, and just show that this is still a family."

"We will, Mommy."

I couldn't believe how many hours Mommy and I chatted over the phone. I was about six hours from getting on the plane and an hour from getting ready to go to the cemetery.

"This collect phone call is coming out of your allowance!" Mommy told me.

"Yes, ma'am."

Already, I could hear Tanya walking around and preparing breakfast for her family. When we'd gotten in the night before, everyone was asleep so I guess this would be my opportunity to meet her family. Maybe if I stayed in the room, I wouldn't have to meet anyone because I wasn't really feeling up to it.

"Angelina, are you getting up soon? I'm making breakfast!"

"I'll eat on the plane. I'm writing something to Christian right now."

"Okay, sweetie. Let me know when you're ready to go."

My lies never stopped sometimes, but that was just a little white lie. I really did need to write something down. I couldn't figure out what to say except to tell him how grateful I was to know that he existed. To hold him so deeply in my heart had given me life and given me a foundation that I based all my decisions on. I always considered how he would react if I did something that might be questionable. I no longer had doubt in who I was. I'd read every letter he'd ever written Mommy and I knew his book by heart. Every thought that he'd shared, I could remember as though I'd said them myself. If I'd said all this in a letter, the bottom line was that I wanted him to feel my sincerity. I wanted him to see how I'd come full circle to where I should've been. I wasn't finished with the process of learning from my mistakes, but I was definitely at home in my thoughts of him. I was reading a letter that Daddy wrote and placed in his book. Even though our experiences were different, I could relate to everything that he'd said. He wrote:

Can You Hear Sincerity?

I took steps with caution today. Memories kept tapping me on the shoulder and reminding me of where I've been. I don't ever want to go back physically but my imagination always returns me to moments that happened before. I constantly wish that I could right what's been wrong in my life. To give myself the strength and power to go back and say sorry to someone I left behind with anger.

I'm not sure who he wrote that to but I could definitely slip the letter under the door of my most recent experience. I was very happy, but nothing would be forgotten. The trip had opened my eyes, expanded my heart, and even deepened my soul. How could a sixteen-year-old young woman ever speak the way that I did unless there were some kind of special connection?

"I'm home, Daddy!" I said, leaning over his grave.

"I had to leave you for a moment and I was miserable. Now that Tanya woke me up and cleared the dust from my heart, I realized who I really am. I'm your daughter, Angelina Christiana Erickson and I feel really lucky to be able to say that!"

I said my name with so much pride that I couldn't stop myself from smiling. I felt as though he could hear me and was reaching out to welcome me back.

"I'm your daughter, your daughter by spirit, and no one can tell me differently. With you in my heart and soul, I have direction in life. Without you, I have no foundation. I might as well not be alive because I've seen that, without you in my heart, I have no spirit to share with the world. I'm gonna make you proud so watch over me because I will always keep you in focus."

I kissed his headstone and placed some flowers along with the letter that I had written. I found it was best to just write down exactly what I was thinking. My letter of sincerity was filled with a daughter's love for her father and that was more important to me than ever before.

On the drive to the airport, I was totally quiet. Everything that Tanya had said to me, I'd responded with a smile.

"I can tell you're okay, sweetie, so I won't get worried. You've found peace of mind and your heart is overflowing with love right now. I can understand your smile and the tears that fall occasionally. I almost envy you, but I know that what you share with Christian is yours exclusively."

I continued with my silence until it was time for that final goodbye with Tanya. Her words struck an intense cord with me and I cried when we hugged.

"This is not goodbye. Can I still call you, Tanya?"

"Of course! You better! I'll even come to your wedding!"

"Wedding?"

"You know what I mean! If you need me, I'm always here for you. I guess you can say that Christian has brought us together, too. We now have a common bond that will make us life long friends."

"My daddy was a beautiful man."

"Yes, and now he's a powerful spirit that's deep inside all of us."

I nodded my head in agreement as I continued to fight back my tears. I was unsuccessful in my attempts and Tanya couldn't resist joining me with her own tears.

"Call me when you get home!"

"I will, Tanya! Bye!"

"Bye, sweetie!"

As I wiped away my tears of joy, I almost ran to get on the plane. I was returning home with so much love in my heart. I didn't know if anyone would be able to recognize the difference in me, but as soon as I opened my mouth and talked, I knew they would see me as a woman. I didn't buy any souvenirs, but I was going back with something a lot more valuable.

Diana! I thought to myself as I walked down the aisle looking for my seat on the plane.

I could see someone further up that looked exactly like my friend that I'd met on the plane ride coming out there. That would be too good to be true if it really was her again.

"Diana?" I shouted.

The woman turned to look at me with the strangest expression. Either she couldn't speak English or she thought I was crazy. I'd been called crazy before so my ego was immune to that insult.

"Oops! I'm sorry. I thought you were someone I knew."

About the Author

Born and raised in Los Angeles with a very strong connection to east Texas where my family on my father's side originates, I'm blessed by the spirit of those that came before me. My life through recent years has been an interesting experience, especially as it relates to love, the pursuit of love, friendships lost and found, and family members no longer around. Through my recent experiences, or perhaps because of them, my creative expression has taken on a new direction and focus. It wasn't too long ago when my heart was crushed by a certain young lady that I began to write my thoughts down in a more intimate way. First starting off with inspirational quotes and poetry, I would share them with others and get requests to do calendars and mugs. I never pursued that avenue but enjoyed receiving such wonderful compliments.

Then one day a co-worker told me that it wouldn't be too long before I'd start writing novels. I just brushed her off and didn't take her seriously. I mean, once upon a time when I was in high school I wrote a short story about Billie Holiday (my romantic ode to that incredible lady called "Change Of Day") but never thought about becoming a writer. Well, I guess my co-worker could definitely recognize a blessing in the middle of this journey that I'm on. The gift of being able to write stories and create characters that live and breathe not only on page but also in the imaginations of those that read your work.

Anyway, that magical day came when I was sitting in the living room of a lady I was interested in. She seemed to think that I'd enjoy watching her study rather than actually talking and perhaps sharing a few hugs and other desires that evening. There I was bored to death and sitting on her couch. I glanced down at her coffee table and noticed a copy of a popular African-American novel, picked it up, and began reading it. As I was reading I started thinking to myself, I can do this! Ideas hit me left and right and I couldn't wait to get home. I said my goodbye to the young lady, went home, and started writing a novel that I called "Blame it on Desire," which is based on the experience I mentioned earlier. That time when my heart was crushed and my life impacted. It was a moment that I believe led me down the road to becoming who I am now: a sensitive yet mysterious romantic soul and yes, a writer as well.

I'm a graduate of Cal State Dominguez Hills and definitely single, though they tell me that wont last too long. I look forward to each second of life because the inspiration is endless. So many thoughts to explore and so many stories to be told. My television stays off now cause I'm having too much fun writing and reading... Life is incredible with an imagination to fall back on...

You can reach V. Anthony Rivers at RomeoDream@strebor-books.com.

V. Anthony Rivers
Everybody Got Issues

WELCOME TO THE WORLD we all come to know and dwell in so often today. I can remember how in the times of revolution and civil rights marches you might hear something like "masses of people are rioting in the streets." Well, in this world today, masses of people are confused about relationships and don't know where to turn. It affects their thought processes, their lives in the workplace and, most definitely, their relationships with the opposite sex. What's going on in the real world today brings credence to this story entitled *Everybody Got Issues*.

Centered around an advertising agency known as Montaqua Publications, *Everybody Got Issues* touches upon the lives of three people trying to climb the ladder of success yet always becoming sidetracked by personal issues. We always say we shouldn't mix business and pleasure or seek out office romances but most of the time that's easier said than done. Even friendships are subject to drama when taken beyond the workplace. When folks have *issues*, you can't even buy immunity from bruised egos, petty gossip, and jealousy.

Meet Avonte Douglas, a self-absorbed recent graduate of USC. Overconfidence is an understatement in his personality. His opinion of himself typically makes its way into every conversation he has. He'd probably carry around his own personal spotlight if he could.

When we first meet Avonte, he uses his charm to ride the shoulders of a young woman named Vanessa. She manages to obtain something that he wants very badly, a job at Montaqua Publications. Though Avonte is an attractive and sometimes very charming young man, one could assume that he uses his friendships as stepping-stones to reaching his next goal or opportunity. He's on the fast track to *Buppy Stardom*: a money-making lifestyle of beautiful women, sports bars, and nightclubs on the weekend. He believes that's his destiny, his calling.

Ina Sinclair is a thirty-something black woman, proud of her accomplishments and working hard toward her next opportunities. She's been at Montaqua for a few years already and is looking forward to one day being a part of management.

Ina's claim to fame is her level of intelligence combined with her sassy appeal. She loves her suburban lifestyle away from work. Takes trips to tropical locations where she can enjoy the fun and sun, relax her mind, and get her read on by listening to books on audio cassette. She's worked hard to obtain her comfortable lifestyle but ask her to go anywhere near the hood and you'll see Ina in a state of panic.

Nakia Davidson, a young woman from the hood, befriends Ina after seeing that different personalities can actually coexist. Sometimes it can require a great deal of patience and compromise but the friendship between the two is never dull. They always have something to talk about.

Nakia discovers Montaqua Publications through an advertisement seeking temporary help. She's in the process of finding a new life for herself and her daughter Tanisha after breaking up with her boyfriend Terence. She moves back home with her mother and begins her self-healing and rebuilding process. She is unaware that she will discover so much more about herself through the eyes of her new friend Ina Sinclair, a not always friendly Avonte Douglas, and a new man that enters her life by the name of Orlando Duncan. He's one of those very successful, very cultured, and educated African American men that could command the attention of any woman he desired. Influenced by her upbringing and where she comes from, Nakia is unable to accept that a man like Orlando could be interested in her. In her eyes, he is perfect.

Well, we may have gotten past the revolution, but running into folks with *issues* is a daily occurrence. How often have you reached the conclusion that *Everybody Got Issues?*

Chapter One

Introduction to Avonte'

A BROTHER IN THE NINETIES got plenty of options for advancement. I've learned that recently and especially because I'm due to graduate in about two weeks. I'll finally earn my master's degree in advertising and it's about time. I have to admit that my motivation for going to school in the past was a little suspect but I forced myself to finish this year. I used to be about the ladies and the opportunities in between classes but I guess I woke up a little bit.

Now in the year of nineteen hundred and ninety-eight, Avonte' Douglas is about to make his way in the world. I have some interviews lined up and I bought a couple of outfits so I'm definitely ready. I'm gonna be pissed off if the only thing I find is a job in the mailroom but I have to remain confident.

Friends of mine tell me to just think positively and my grandmother told me to go to church and pray. I've been doing my best to think positively. At times I'm probably overconfident. I've been sending out resumes like crazy.

When I put together my first draft, I described myself as a "Tall handsome man of color." After I finished, I had the best looking profile for a dating service that I've ever seen in my life. I put that in my desk drawer for later and made a second attempt at writing my resume. The women are gonna have to wait until after I start making some money.

The last two years have been hard on me because I believe I should be a lot farther along in my life. I'm living with my mother so I can save some money. That's been an okay situation but it cuts down on the amount of nights that I'm able to spend with the opposite sex. Whenever I want to spend the night with somebody, I have to get a hotel room. My budget has been tight so needless to say I haven't been getting any lately.

Avonte' can catch the ladies, but taking it beyond the initial attraction is something that doesn't happen too often. That dreaded word "Relationship" is something that I only know how to spell right now. But, then again, since I'm not where I want to be, why try to have somebody join me? I'm too young to be worrying about that right now anyway, especially since I just chase the ladies for sex and relationships? I haven't had a girlfriend since the eighties, back when I was sporting a high-top fade.

I took on a new journey when I got into college and discovered the pleasures of being immune to a deep commitment. Bells ring in my head when a lady just tells me she wants to have fun. I start smiling like the Grinch just about to steal Christmas. Of course I'm stealing more than just holiday time. But as I said earlier, that's no longer my focus. I'm about to graduate and as soon as I get a job then maybe I'll enter new arenas where the ladies are concerned. I can visualize myself already going to sports bars during the week and nightclubs on Saturdays and Sundays. I'm gonna live the lifestyle of a young "Buppy" to the hilt. I know I'm looking ahead but my friends said to think positively. I'm thinking positively and then some.

Celebrating too soon is always a habit of mine and today is no exception. I'm on my way to an interview and because I want this particular job so much, I know it's gonna be mine. I threw on my best suit and a funky fresh tie to go with it. I also brought a more conservative tie with me just in case I change my mind. I'll probably change it. This position I'm going for is entry level but they assured me that there's rapid growth potential. I had to catch myself when I talked to them over the phone.

"How rapid?" I wanted to ask.

I'm glad I didn't say half the shit that was on my mind. I played it cool and professional. I acted like a straight-A student with a respect for authority rather than the B+ egomaniac that I really am. Nobody needs to see my true colors until I've passed the probationary period. After that, I'm taking this bad boy over.

Daydreaming has always been one of my favorite pastimes. I can sometimes see my entire life before me. I usually visualize nothing but good times and opportunities. I guess that's why I get accused of having a devilish smile. That's my trademark and I haven't met a woman yet who wasn't attracted by it.

"You here for an interview?" a female sitting next to me asked.

"Excuse me?"

"I noticed there's only two other people here. I was expecting a lot more to show up for this job," she said softly.

"Probably so, but I just try to stay focused on me. Know what I'm saying?"

"So, you and I are gonna be competing for it then, huh?"

"Competing?" I asked.

I looked at homegirl like she was no competition at all.

"My name's Vanessa Jenkins."

"Sup? I'm Avonte'."

"Nice to meet you, Avonte'."

The girl had very lovely hands, a brown skin complexion, long silky black hair, and was beginning to take me out of my focus, which wasn't too cool.

"My pleasure, Vanessa."

I glanced at the rest of Ms. Jenkins when she turned her attention to someone walking into the office. She was wearing a champagne-colored, polyester crepe business suit with a long skirt. It looked like it came straight from the same JC Penny catalog that I ordered my size thirteen rugged leather boots from. I almost felt compelled to turn on the charm a little and see if I'd get a smile out of her. Maybe make her cross her legs in my direction.

"So, what's this I hear about me having competition? Who, pray tell, would give a brotha like me some competition?"

"This sista right next to you," she responded.

I like the way she sat up, crossed her arms, and gave me a cocky smile of her own. Avonte' was loving his surroundings. It's a shame that I may not see too much of her since I'm the one they're gonna hire for the job.

"Hey, Vanessa," I said softly.

"Yes?"

She still had her arms folded. Seemed like she was anticipating in a cute way what I might say next. She was shaking her head like she was gesturing for me to say what I had to say, but she still had that smile.

"Vanessa, since I'm all up in your area here."

"Huh?" she interrupted.

"Let me finish. Since we seem cool with each other already, how about we share a cappuccino or something and let bygones be bygones, so to speak."

"I hope you're not gonna talk like that in your interview."

"Nah, I'm gonna be professional."

"I hope so."

"What about my offer?" I asked her.

"Coffee sounds nice, but I'm not sure what you mean by letting bygones be bygones."

"Yeah, I don't want you coming after me when they hire me instead of you," I told her.

"Oh, is that right?"

"Yep. I wouldn't have bought this new suit if I thought I wouldn't get the job."

"I hope you saved your receipt and didn't remove the tag!"

Homegirl was flashing all her attitude, even though she tried to keep our conversation on the downlow. I was having fun talking to Vanessa. This kind of fun was borderline foggy for me, too. I wasn't supposed to be enjoying myself with the enemy, so to speak. I felt it was time to relax my efforts for the moment.

"Let me stop talking to you. We're still on for coffee right?" I asked.

"Uh-huh."

Vanessa went back to thumbing through magazines and I

returned to my usual active imagination. I was doing a mental balancing act. I was visualizing Vanessa in her panties on one side and celebrating cause I got the job on the other. Life feels good when you can imagine more than one way to have fun.

"Vanessa Jenkins?"

Some lady stepped out from inside the office and called the next interview. I thought I was the next person but that's cool. Vanessa looked good walking inside. Maybe she is my competition cause she walked in there like she already had the job. Trying to play the role by asking if that person had a good weekend. Now if I go in and ask the same thing I'll sound all fake and shit. I wish I could hear what else she's saying in there. I feel like I'm back in school cause I'm letting a female get the best of me again.

An hour went by before the door slowly opened. I was beginning to dose off from waiting so long. Plus they had it cold up in here like they think it's a hundred degrees outside. I should've got up and checked my eyes to see if I look tired but I didn't want to leave and miss my name being called.

I could see Vanessa slowly coming out of the door. Seemed like whomever she was talking to didn't want the conversation to end. I didn't like what I was feeling right now. Going in there could be a waste of my time and another opportunity to be embarrassed.

Finally Vanessa made it all the way through the door. She gave me a sweet smile and stood in front of me.

"I don't think I'll be able to have that coffee with you, Avonte', but give me a call sometime, okay? Here's my number," she said.

I looked up at Vanessa with my sleepy eyes not knowing what was going on. I couldn't match her enthusiasm but it was cool to get her phone number.

"Okay, I'll give you a call."

"Talk to you soon?"

"Okay, Vanessa."

She walked out the door and as soon as I turned around, the office door opened and the interviewer greeted me.

"I think you're next? Avonte' Douglas right?"

By the way this lady was looking at me I could tell this would just be a formality with her. I could play this interview in my mind already. I know the conclusion won't be in my favor. I'm just sleep walking through this experience.

"How are you today?" the lady asked.

"Good."

"That's excellent. Listen, I guess we should cut to the chase. We've found someone to fill the position but I'd like to hold on to your resume for a possible opening that may happen soon. Would that be okay with you?"

"Yes, ma'am, that would be fine."

Here I was, sitting like a young boy who just had his heart broken. Still, I tried to be professionally humble. Looks like Vanessa did her thing and got the job. My mind was going blank as I sat across from this lady. She was talking about the company and all I could see was her mouth moving in slow motion.

"I'm sure you're a little disappointed but we here at Montaqua Publications are always interested in young creative minds. Please don't be discouraged."

"Oh thanks, I won't. I guess it's a learning experience as they say, huh?"

"Exactly. Plus you never know because we could be calling you back very soon. You seem to be someone that will fit well inside of a creative environment such as this one."

"It would be a dream come true, ma'am."

"Well don't give up on that dream!"

"Thanks, I won't."

As I walked out the office, I took a look at the piece of paper with the phone number that Vanessa gave me. I started to crumble the page and toss it in the trash, but I didn't. I almost said a few curse words about my competition, but I passed on disrespecting her that way. I remembered how cool she seemed and maybe she has more going for herself on paper than I do.

My jealousy kicked in for a second and I returned to my thoughts of tossing the piece of paper. I didn't. Instead, I found a pay

phone in the lobby and tried calling Vanessa. I had a feeling this
was her beeper number. Even though I've been blessed to receive
phone numbers without trying really hard, I figured a woman like
this probably wouldn't give hers out so easily. I waited for the voicemail to kick in after I heard the dial tone for the fourth time.

"Hello?"

The sound of her voice was like drinking down one of those
smoothies on a hot day. She sounded so sweet.

"Hello, is someone there?" she answered a second time.

"Vanessa?"

"Yes, who's this?"

"Oh, wow!"

I guess she proved me wrong again. I'm batting a thousand with
my assumptions today.

"Do I know you?" she asked.

"Hey Vanessa, this is Avonte'."

"Hey, you, how did it go?"

"What you mean, how did it go? You got the job!"

"I thought maybe you could still talk your way into getting
something. You had me smiling even though I tried to hide it."

"Is that right?"

"Yes, you did, and I was thinking about you also."

"You were?"

"Yes"

"Damn, you got me in this lobby perspiring!"

"Doing what?"

"Sweatin', gurl!"

"Oh, you are funny, Avonte'."

Vanessa had me forgetting all about the fact that she stole my
job. Talking to her on the phone was just as cool as it was in person.
I felt like I was still sitting next to her. Still glancing down at her
smooth legs. I could even remember the scent of her perfume. I'm
not supposed to be feeling like this and thinking about another lady
in my life. My shield was having a hard time fighting this one off.

"Sweetheart, I'm gonna have to go but call me later, okay?"

Now she was fighting unfair because hearing a woman call me sweetheart was like touching my sensitive spot. She just pushed my button of vulnerability and it felt good.

"Where you headed to?" I asked.

"Well, if you noticed I'm on my cell phone sitting in traffic. I'm going to the mall to buy something new for my first day at work."

"Oh."

"Don't sound sad. I'm not trying to rub it in, Avonte'."

"Nah, it's cool."

"You're welcome to meet me at the mall if you want?"

"Nah, but I'll call you tonight, Vanessa. You gonna be home?"

"Yes, and don't feel bad."

"It's cool. Congratulations on the job."

"Thanks, sweetheart."

"Yep."

"Hey, listen!"

"Yeah, what's up, Vanessa?"

"I'm gonna put in a good word for you. I think it would be nice to work together. Hope it wouldn't present a problem, especially if we're seeing each other away from work."

"That would be cool. Thanks."

"Okay. Talk to you later, Avonte'."

"Bye, Vanessa."

I wasn't sure how to take her offer but I figured if I can get my foot in the door, then it would all be left up to me to prove my true value to the company. I could make the right connections and Avonte' would be on his way. Maybe that old saying about who you know could finally work for me.

Vanessa seems pretty sincere about helping me out. I'm glad she wasn't turned off by my earlier hints of conceit. But if she should discover the real me later on then that's okay. I'm determined to turn all my preparation from school into making my way up the ladder at this advertising agency. I'm excited that it's black owned too. Listen to me just talkin' shit.

A few days passed by and it took me the first two to realize that

I was celebrating way too soon. I needed to at least wait for Vanessa to give me a call and let me know I was in.

My other interview didn't work out at all. The interviewer just sat there sizing me up while reading my resume and application. That's a lonely feeling when I'm sitting there waiting for someone to decide my immediate fate before I gain a little control. I started to get up at one point but then the person ended my anxiety by letting me off in that familiar way.

"We're gonna review your resume and get back with you," I was told.

Uh-huh, how long is it gonna take you stupid? I thought to myself.

"Thank you so much," is what I actually said.

Now I'm sitting here doing more research and at the same time feeling sorry for myself cause preparation doesn't seem to be getting my foot in the door right now. Looks like it's gonna take some serious luck.

STREBOR BOOKS INTERNATIONAL ORDER FORM

Use this form to order additional copies of

STREBOR BOOKS INTERNATIONAL bestselling titles.

Name:_____

Company _____

Address: _____

_____

City: _____ State_____ Zip_____

Phone: (_____)_____ Fax: (_____)_____

E-mail: _____

Credit Card:☐*Visa* ☐ *MC* ☐ *Amex* ☐*Discover*

Number _____

Exp Date: _____Signature: _____

QTY	DESCRIPTION	PRICE	TOTAL
1.	*The Sex Chronicles by Zane*	$ 15.00	
2.	*Shame On It All by Zane*	$ 15.00	
3.	*God's Bastards Sons by D. V. Bernard*	$ 15.00	
4.	*Daughter by Spirit by V. Anthony Rivers*	$ 15.00	

		Subtotal
SHIPPING INFORMATION		*shipping*
Ground one book $ 3.00		
each additional book $ 1.00	*5% tax (MD)*	
		Total

Make checks or money orders payable to
Strebor Books International
Post Office Box 10127
Silver Spring, Maryland 20914

Books can be purchased at online booksellers

Printed in the United States
By Bookmasters